MW00571582

Dear Reader,

Welcome to *Butterfly Come Home, Caledonia Chronicles—Part 2*, another tale in the series of *Great Lakes Romances*®, historical fiction full of love and adventure set in bygone days in the region known as Great Lakes Country.

Like the other books in this series, *Butterfly Come Home* relays the excitement and thrills of a tale skillfully told, but contains no explicit sex, offensive language, or gratuitous violence.

We invite you to tell us what you would like most to read about in *Great Lakes Romances*®. For your convenience, we have included a survey form at the back of the book. Please fill it out and send it to us.

At the back, you will also find descriptions of other romances in this series, and a collection of reprints from long ago in the *Bigwater Classics* series, stories that will sweep you away to an era of gentility and enchantment, and places of unparalleled beauty and wonder!

Thank you for being a part of *Great Lakes Romances*®!

Sincerely,
The Publishers

P.S. Author Donna Winters loves to hear from her readers. You can write her at P.O. Box 177, Caledonia, MI 49316.

Used by permission:
Model on cover—Rachel Buist; photography by Kevin Owens

Bible quotes are from the King James Version.

Butterfly Come Home, Caledonia Chronicles Part 2
Copyright © 2000 by Donna Winters

Great Lakes Romances® is a registered trademark of
Bigwater Publishing, P.O. Box 177, Caledonia, MI 49316

Library of Congress Catalog Card Number: LC 99-94633
ISBN 0-923048-87-1

Edited by Pamela Quint Chambers and Joanne Olson
Cover design by Donna Winters

Printed in the United States of America

00 01 02 03 04 05 06 07 /   / 10 9 8 7 6 5 4 3 2 1

Butterfly Come Home

Caledonia Chronicles
Part 2

Donna Winters

Great Lakes Romances®

Bigwater Publishing
Caledonia, Michigan

Note

I would like to thank model Rachel Buist and photographer Kevin Owens for permission to use the lovely photo portraying the heroine on the front cover.

*To Joanne Olson
my Rockland friend and sister spirit
with thanks for your generous contributions
of time and energy to this project.
I look forward to the day when I will see
your name on the cover of a book!*

Psalm 32

1 Blessed is he whose transgression is forgiven, whose sin is covered.

2 Blessed is the man unto whom the Lord imputeth not iniquity, and in whose spirit there is no guile.

3 When I kept silence, my bones waxed old through my roaring all the day long.

4 For day and night thy hand was heavy upon me: my moisture is turning into the drought of summer. Selah.

5 I acknowledged my sin unto thee, and mine iniquity have I not hid. I said, I will confess my transgressions unto the Lord; and thou forgavest the iniquity of my sin. Selah.

6 For this shall every one that is godly pray unto thee in a time when thou mayest be found: surely in the floods of great waters they shall not come nigh unto him.

7 Thou art my hiding place; thou shalt preserve me from trouble; thou shalt compass me about with songs of deliverance. Selah.

8 I will instruct thee and teach thee in the way which thou shalt go: I will guide thee with mine eye.

9 Be ye not as the horse, or as the mule, which have no understanding: whose mouth must be held in with bit and bridle, lest they come near unto thee.

10 Many sorrows shall be to the wicked: but he that trusteth in the Lord, mercy shall compass him about.

11 Be glad in the Lord, and rejoice, ye righteous: and shout for joy, all ye that are upright in heart.

Chapter

1

Caledonia, Michigan
6 P.M. Saturday, September 2, 1905

Deborah Dapprich's hand grew moist, clasped tightly within Tommy Rockwell's as they stood outside the train depot of the small, agricultural community, anxiously awaiting the arrival of the Michigan Central. With them stood her closest kin, Aunt Ottilia and Uncle Charles Chappell, along with a hundred others eager to witness the return of their daughter, Caroline, who had been kidnapped before dawn that morning—the very day of her wedding—and miraculously rescued unharmed by her betrothed, Joshua Bolden, from the hands of the villainous Neal Taman.

Thoughts of that scoundrel, Taman, sent chills down Deborah's spine despite the heat of the afternoon. By that evil man's hand she had suffered humiliation beyond description for the past two months, held captive in his "resort" and forced to entertain men in ways . . .

With a shudder she pressed the dark memory from her mind, moving closer to lean against Tommy, the childhood friend who had become the white knight in her own rescue. The scent from the clove stud he was chewing drifted to her, intermingled with the fragrance of her uncle's lime cologne and the earthier smell of fresh-cut wood from the nearby lumberyard. Low voices full of expectation surrounded her—the murmurings of Mr. and Mrs. Bolden, and the quiet conversation of Charles and Ottilia with Tommy's father, Cy.

In mid-sentence the robust Mr. Rockwell fell silent, peered down the tracks with a hand to his ear, then shouted in his gruff, bass voice, "She's a-coming!"

Tommy squeezed Deborah's shoulder. "Carolina's almost home, Butterfly!" A smile tilted the right corner of his blond mustache.

Deborah smiled, too, hiding the despair that urged her to flit away to freedom like the creature of her nickname. The fact was, she felt more like a caterpillar ready to hide in a chrysalis than the beautiful butterflies that had been her obsession from childhood. But for now, she must forget her own problems and rejoice in the safe return of her pert, dark-haired cousin who looked none the worse for wear as she stepped triumphantly off the train, her fiancé, Joshua, beaming at her side.

Cheers filled the air, and spontaneously Joshua's brother and friends lifted the young couple to their shoulders, bearing them in the direction of the capacious Chappell residence a block east of the depot where they deposited the pair on the sweeping veranda.

Joshua, his arm tightly about Caroline, stood with her on the top step, joined by both sets of parents. When he tried unsuccessfully to make himself heard over the boisterousness of his friends, all eager to know the details of his heroic deed, Tommy let loose with a shrill whistle that quickly quieted the clamor.

Joshua addressed the gathering with a loud, clear voice. "Our wedding's been rescheduled. We'll be married at the church at nine o'clock. And you're all invited!"

Joshua's announcement spurred more cheers and

shouts, as well as arguments from Ottilia which were quickly put to rest by Charles. Caroline smiled and waved, blew a kiss to the crowd, then headed inside. A moment later, Tommy and Deborah joined her there, amidst a quartet of parents eager for hugs and reassurances of her wellbeing.

Elderly Aunt Luella, who'd come from way up north for the occasion, toddled in from the parlor to satisfy herself that her grandniece was indeed unharmed.

Caroline offered her favorite aunt a kiss and a hug, then broke away to draw both Deborah and Tommy into her embrace.

"Thank the Lord, the two of you are back!" she exclaimed, leaning away to give each of them a good looking-over. "Deborah, will you please sing at my wedding?"

Before she could answer, Caroline continued.

"Joshua will play a trumpet solo I wrote for him—I'll accompany him—then you could sing *Oh, Promise Me*. You could go over it with Mrs. Barber at the church beforehand—"

Ottilia interrupted. "Caroline, after all you and Joshua have been through this day, how can you possibly—"

Aunt Luella cut in. "Ottilia, hush. Certainly the girl knows what she wants at her own wedding."

Caroline nodded, explaining, "We discussed it on the train. We agreed that we want to perform the music just the way we originally planned."

Deborah spoke before her Aunt Ottilia could mount a new argument. "Cousin Caroline, I will most certainly sing at your wedding."

"Then it's all settled. Now, if you'll excuse me, I need to bathe and dress. I'll see you all at the church at nine o'clock." Brushing a kiss against Joshua's cheek, she headed up the stairs, a fretting Ottilia following in her wake.

9

With Tommy's help, Deborah swiftly arranged for a rehearsal with Mrs. Barber at the church a block away. The practice went smoothly, her voice being in top condition from the many musical entertainments—among other things—that she had performed for customers of the white slave house over the past two months. She had returned to her cousin's home, washed and changed into the almost new gown she had worn at her high school graduation two and a half months earlier, and still had half an hour to spare before she would need to leave for the church. When she descended the wide oak staircase of her aunt and uncle's Queen Anne home, she was not surprised to see Tommy, now formally attired in frock coat and cummerbund, waiting for her at the bottom.

Tommy admired Deborah openly, his heartbeat quickening as he took in the soft blush that came naturally to her cheeks, the pink lace collar trimmed with seed pearls just below, and the enamel butterfly pin she always wore on her bodice. Enfolding her hand in his, he leaned close, his whispery breath teasing the blond tendril that lay against her cheek. "You're beautiful enough to be the bride tonight!"

Without a moment's hesitation, she quietly replied, "And you're handsome enough to be the groom!"

Leading her toward the door, he said, "Come into the garden, Butterfly."

Deborah replied by intentionally misquoting Tennyson in her best theatrical voice, "Come into the garden, Tommy, I am here at the gate alone." Then, she began to giggle, a lilting sound that made Tommy's heart soar though he was certain she had no notion of what she was doing to him. Tommy laughed out of sheer delight as he escorted her off the veranda and into the garden east of the house.

He led her toward the white iron bench beneath the awning that had been pitched for Caroline's wedding reception. But seeing that Vida, the cook, was heading their way, her arms laden with a tray of confections for the guests that would arrive later, he continued down the path until he reached the end, where it overlooked Mr. Kinsey's cornfield. Taking both of Deborah's hands in his, he turned her toward him, gazed into the depths of her blue eyes—eyes that hid well the recent horrors she'd faced—and spoke the words that had been heavy on his mind since soon after his dramatic rescue.

"Marry me, Butterfly. Tonight, in this garden, when Caroline's reception is over, let me make you my wife."

Deborah tried to ignore the twinge in her heart. She'd feared—or perhaps hoped—Tommy was leading up to this. There'd been a magnetism between them since the night he'd freed her from Taman's "resort." Though a part of her wanted desperately to agree to his proposal—to partake of this fairytale-like ending to her troubling, shameful past— the voice of reason and a compulsion for freedom spoke deafeningly from within.

Framing her reply in lines from Cowper, she said, "Sir, 'the tale that I relate, this lesson seems to carry—choose not alone a proper mate, but proper time to marry.'"

Disappointed that Deborah was again hiding behind verse as she'd so often done since her escape from the house of ill repute, Tommy spoke in earnest.

"Butterfly, this is the best time I can think of for us to wed. The garden's decorated. The preacher will be all practiced up after marrying Caroline and Joshua, and my father's here to witness."

"What about your mother?" she asked, knowing Mrs. Rockwell had been a patient at the sanitarium in Battle

11

Creek for the last three weeks and that along with her health problems, she tended toward a fragile emotional nature.

"Papa says not to worry about Mother. He gives us his blessing, and he'll explain our circumstances to her when he visits her next week."

"But we have no marriage license," Deborah pointed out, confident that the lack of legal paperwork would postpone Tommy's plan.

He offered his lopsided smile. "It just so happens Judge Wolcott is a longtime friend of your uncle's. He's been invited to Carolina's wedding, and he's staying at the Caledonia Hotel. He can issue a license in no time!"

Deborah lowered her gaze. Tommy seemed to have all the answers. The problem was, she wasn't ready for an intimate relationship with any man—not even Tommy, who was the most trustworthy person in her world right now.

Tommy read the discomfort in Deborah's sorrowful expression, and silently berated himself. He should have been more sensitive to her situation. The last thing she probably needed was a man pressuring her for marital rights. He lifted her chin. Her blue eyes were brimming with tears.

Deborah struggled to repress the sharp sense of shame within. Unsure that she would ever want any man to do more than hold her hand, she told Tommy honestly, "I don't know that I'll ever be ready for the affections of a husband."

He enfolded her hand in his. "Butterfly, I won't force my affections on you. In my heart, I know you're the one I want for my wife, and I want to marry you tonight." He lifted her hand to press it to his lips.

His mustache brushed pleasantly against her skin, wearing down her defenses. At the same time, a new objection reared its head. "Tommy, you don't know what you'd be getting into, marrying me," she warned. "There are things about me—"

"I know enough," Tommy insisted, squeezing her hand and drawing her closer. "The rest doesn't mean a lick." He bent to kiss her on the forehead, but she turned away.

"Tommy, don't," she pleaded.

"Don't what?" he gently challenged. "Don't love you? Don't want you? Don't think you're the most beautiful woman I've ever known?"

She wrenched her hand from his. "Don't tell me those things! You sound just like all the men who came to visit me the last two months, all full of pretty words—and evil intentions!"

He reached out to her, an apology on his lips, but she spun around and fled, pausing halfway down the path to turn and approach him once more.

He didn't wait for her to speak. "I'm not like all those other men, Butterfly. I'm not handing out empty compliments. I'm sorry if the truth spoken from my heart offends you."

She drew a measured breath. "A lot of years have passed since you and I knew each other as kids, Tommy. A lot has happened. And it's changed me."

"It doesn't matter, Butterfly," he insisted. "Almost from the minute I found you there in Buffalo, it's as if we've never been apart."

Deborah longed to believe Tommy. She longed to trust that he knew his own heart. How simple life would be if they *could* marry and live happily ever after like a fairytale. But her life was a nightmare—an ongoing one that wouldn't be cast off with the exchanging of wedding vows. She reached up, caressing the strong line of his jaw with a butterfly's touch. "Are you sure you want to marry me?"

He clasped her shoulders, hope rising anew in his breast. "Of course, I'm sure."

"Even though there are things about me you don't know?"

"I said the rest didn't mean a lick and I meant it."

Her gaze fixed on him, she prepared to reveal the most important secret of her young life, the one fact that would overrule everything that had been said up until now.

"Tommy," she began slowly, her heart in turmoil over what she was about to reveal. "You ought to know that if we *did* marry, you'd become a father soon—of the child I'm already carrying." She watched him closely for his reaction. His cheeks lost color. His breathing halted momentarily. When it resumed, the rapid, shallow breaths spoke more than words.

Tommy's pulse quickened, his heart sinking at the news. He'd known all along there was a chance of his Butterfly being in the family way. He hated what her captivity had done to her—stripping her of all dignity, then leaving her in a delicate condition. It was a single girl's worst dilemma, and it sparked anger within him that he was barely able to control. But it wasn't enough to make him renege on his promise. In fact, it only made him more determined to right the wrongs that had been done to her by evil, godless men. With quiet confidence, he renewed his conviction.

"All the more reason to marry me, Butterfly. We'll raise the child as our own. Who's to know any different?"

"Everyone, once the poor babe is born. I'm just so certain it won't look like either one of us," she fretted, knowing in her heart that she didn't even want to have this child, let alone raise it. If she refused Tommy's proposal, she could put it up for adoption, or perhaps find some doctor or veterinarian who could rid her of the unwanted pregnancy.

14

But such procedures were risky. She'd heard talk from other girls at the white slave house. Some had suffered horribly—nearly died. And if they ever did escape the confines of the "resort" and marry, they would never bear children.

Tommy could almost read the troubled thoughts that were passing through Deborah's mind and wrinkling her delicate complexion. He offered the most logical argument he could think of. "If you give it a moment's thought, I'm sure you could name at least one or two people you've known who don't resemble their folks, or even their brothers or sisters."

Deborah remained silent, not because she couldn't think of anyone that fit Tommy's description, but because she was running short of arguments and resolve.

Tommy reached for her hand once more, lowering to bended knee as he did so. "Butterfly, will you please do me the great and distinguished honor of becoming my bride? I promise I will care for you, and *our* child, until my days on earth are ended."

Tommy's earnest bass voice resonated with a sincerity that went straight through her, piercing her heart with a persistence she could no longer press aside, and an ardor she couldn't ignore. Forcing words past the lump that was forming in her throat, she replied in a half whisper, "Yes, Tommy!"

He sprang to his feet, pulling her into an embrace that crushed her against the solid length of him. The impetuous move brought conflicted responses within Deborah—the warmth of his affection quelled somewhat the unwanted panic borne of her past abuse.

But as quickly as he had hugged her, he parted from her, words spilling out as he led her back toward the house. "We've got to get to the church and tell Pastor Phillips.

Besides, it's nearly time for the guests to arrive. You'll want a few minutes to collect yourself before your solo." Pausing in the middle of the path, he looked deep into her wide-set eyes—eyes that bore the unmistakable signs of doubt. "Butterfly, I promise you, I'll do everything in my power to make you happy. It will all turn out fine. You'll see!"

As he escorted her out of the garden, across the tracks, and toward the church, Deborah had no doubt that Tommy would live up to his promise, but she knew that their future happiness depended on far more than his actions, alone. She wondered if she was capable of matching his efforts.

Chapter

2

Seated in the left front pew, Deborah marveled at the majestic organ motifs and bright, spirited responses of the trumpet played by Joshua. The piece showed both her cousin's composing talents and Joshua's performing abilities to best advantage. And it told a story—the story of their friendship, their courtship, and their love.

The piece had begun with simple motifs adapted from school days songs. A transition into phrases from a trumpet duet they had performed in a recital this past June represented their earlier musical collaboration and the beginning of their courtship. Themes both lyrical and romantic hinted at the times that followed—a hot, summer day at a picnic, an evening conversation on the porch. The only thing missing from the piece was the dramatic rescue. It ended, instead, with a harmonious blend of organ and trumpet in a variation of *Love's Old Sweet Song*, testimony to the commitment they would soon make for a long future together.

The piece was so beautifully rendered it was all Deborah could do to keep from clapping her hands when they finished. While her cousin made her way to the vestibule where she would put off the choir robe that concealed her wedding dress and prepare for her trip down the aisle, Mrs. Barber began the introduction to *Oh, Promise Me.*

As Deborah took her place beside the organ, she noticed that every seat in the church was filled. In the interval between the originally scheduled ceremony at two that afternoon, and Caroline's rescue, some of the out-of-town wedding guests had reluctantly departed in order to return home by nightfall. In their stead sat townspeople whose invitation had been issued by Joshua from the porch steps less than three hours ago, and Deborah was pleased that the sanctuary was filled to capacity for her cousin's joyous occasion.

The organ introduction complete, Deborah opened her mouth and let her voice soar quietly over the tender phrases. As she did, the reality of the moment began to sink in—not that Caroline and Joshua were about to wed. Their coupling was not unexpected. But the fact that she herself was here at all was a true miracle—one she credited fully to Tommy.

In view of their own plans to be joined in matrimony, it seemed as though the words she was singing were meant for her soon-to-be husband.

Oh, promise me that you will take my hand, the most unworthy in this lonely land . . .

Indeed, she felt less than deserving of his eagerness to make her his bride. Yet somehow, she maintained control right through the *double forte* at the end. Waiting weak-kneed for Mrs. Barber to fade to *pianissimo* on the final organ phrase, she gratefully took a seat between Tommy and Mr. Rockwell in the third pew from the front, accepting their whispered compliments and cherishing the comfort of Tommy's hand about hers.

During the quiet organ passages that followed, Deborah was able to relax somewhat and for the first time, fully appreciate the flowers that tastefully decorated the church. The end of each pew along the main aisle was topped with ivory roses and day lilies tied together with satin ribbons in matching colors. Vases on the altar held showy bouquets of the same. The wires suspending the gas lit chandelier from the center of the ceiling had been wrapped with ropes of silk roses in the peach-and-ivory theme. Even the arch above the choir loft had been adorned with a bunting of filmy peach-colored silk caught up at intervals with bouquets of the ivory rosebuds.

Beneath this gossamer drape, doors on either side of the loft now opened. Pastor Phillips entered from the left to take his place behind the altar rail, while Joshua and the best man—his older brother, Zimri—entered from the right to stand in front of the rail.

Mrs. Barber lit heavily into the opening phrases of the wedding march and the congregation rose to face the rear door from which the ushers—Joshua's best friend, Solon, and Caroline's older brother, Parker—now proceeded. Behind them at a measured pace followed Roxana, Parker's wife, whom Caroline had chosen as her matron of honor. Her gown, of the palest mint green silk mull, flowed diaphanously about her.

With great expectation, Deborah awaited the appearance of her cousin, who now proceeded through the door on the arm of her father. Deborah had always attributed a certain look of distinction to her portly Uncle Charles. His frock coat and tails adorned with a peach rose boutonniere enhanced this impression even further. But Deborah doubted anyone really noticed, for on his arm was such a picture of loveliness that it audibly took away the breath of dozens of guests.

Hushed oohs and aahs and murmured comments of approval greeted Caroline, as she seemed to float down the aisle in a cloud of peach silk mull. A high, ruffled collar encircled her long, elegant neck. Translucent sleeves covered the length of her arms, ending in wide, satin-trimmed

19

cuffs. In her hands was a bouquet of two dozen ivory tea roses tied with a peach satin ribbon, partially hiding the pintucked bodice accenting her trim figure and tiny waist. From it flowed layer upon layer of skirting that was caught up at intervals by creamy rosebuds. On her head, nestled amidst a profusion of dark curls, was a brimless peach silk hat to which satin bows and more creamy rosebuds had been affixed. But the most poignant feature of all was Caroline's bright, triumphant smile—a fetching upward curve that expressed without words how truly thankful she was to be present at her own wedding.

Deborah struggled to hold back tears, so appreciative was she to be witnessing this stunning, happy occasion. There, at the altar, stood a perfectly matched couple. They'd known each other for years, held a common interest in music, and would begin their marriage with an unstained past.

When the guests were seated and Pastor Phillips began the ceremony, Deborah couldn't help thinking ahead to her own wedding. She and Tommy had barely had an opportunity to reacquaint themselves since her rescue. Even though they'd spent some time together in childhood, they hardly knew each other as adults. Aside from not knowing if they had anything in common, they would be going to the altar with the scar of scandal upon them—or more accurately upon her.

She listened to Pastor Phillips's words.

" . . . and therefore is not by any to be entered into unadvisedly, but reverently, discreetly, and in the fear of God. Into which holy estate these two persons present come now to be joined. Therefore if any can show just cause why they may not lawfully be joined together, let him now speak, or else hereafter forever hold his peace."

In the dead silence that followed, Deborah could sense an almost palpable relief of those present that the impediments thrown down by one evildoer had failed to prevent Caroline and Joshua's marriage. But could she say the same when she and Tommy stood before the minister?

Love could overcome many obstacles, she was certain, and she believed Tommy truly loved her as he'd said. She loved him too, but whether her feelings were simply a passing result of his heroic rescue, or of the lasting sort, she wasn't certain. She feared a marriage between them might serve only as a cover-up for her sordid past, a convenient way to solve the problem of her coming child. With such overwhelming obstacles at the start, she wondered whether their marriage stood any chance of success—whether Tommy would have a change of heart once her figure started to bulge with a child not his own.

She wondered, too, if she could push aside her desire for freedom—her yen to explore her own potential as an actress and singer. She had been attempting to do that very thing when she wound up in Taman's snare, expecting to be put on stage in musicals when instead his true plan was to put her in captivity for his own ill-gotten gain.

How she hated being manipulated by men. In a sense, she felt Tommy was manipulating her now—though supposedly for her own benefit and out of his love.

Chilly fingers of shame ran up her spine even on this warm night, realizing that she was doubting his sincerity—that she was ready to pass up the best offer that might ever come her way. In this day and age when a woman's moral character was the key to her success, what future would she have on her own, tarnished by a past she could not change? If she were waiting for a more exciting offer from a more appropriate suitor, surely she was fooling herself. Her only

21

hope in the future would be to lie about her past. Tommy *knew* of her past and *still* offered to marry her. She should simply accept his love with a heart of gratitude and go forward in faith that their marriage could work—*would* work—and that they *would* find happiness together.

She listened again to Pastor Phillips's words.

" . . . pour upon these persons the riches of thy grace, sanctify and bless them, that they may please thee both in body and soul, and live together in holy love unto their lives' end. Amen."

As he led the guests in the Lord's Prayer, Tommy's hand sought hers offering a reassuring squeeze which she returned, resigned to the necessity of pressing forward as the future Mrs. Rockwell.

Chapter
3

The hour was approaching midnight by the time all the friends and relatives—except for Parker, Roxana, and Great-aunt Luella—had gone home. Deborah stood with Tommy before the minister in the lantern-lit garden, the realization dawning on her that she was about to take on the most challenging role she had yet encountered—that of Mrs. Thomas Rockwell. With questions still nagging her about the wisdom of marrying, she began to see herself as a player on the stage of life, caught in a role she was neither convinced she wanted, nor able to refuse.

To her left, along with Great-aunt Luella, Parker, and Roxana, were Caroline and Joshua, who had insisted on postponing their wedding trip to be present at the hastily scheduled nuptials. Behind Caroline, who was serving as Deborah's witness, Aunt Ottilia looked on, undoubtedly thrilled with the prospect of marrying off her troublesome niece to an upstanding family friend. With Ottilia stood Uncle Charles, ready to give the bride's hand in marriage.

Tommy shifted his weight a tad nervously. Deborah glanced up at him, wondering—even hoping—he was having second thoughts—ready to call the wedding off. Instead, he offered an encouraging smile, as did his father who was the groom's witness to the occasion.

The scent of citronella mingled with the sweet essence of the roses in Deborah's bouquet—the same flowers Caroline had carried—now trimmed with a satin bow of pink to match Deborah's dress. When the minister asked who was giving her in marriage, Deborah transferred her borrowed roses to her cousin and allowed her Uncle Charles to place her hand in Tommy's.

His firm grip gave silent assurance. And when his gaze met hers, she found herself slipping into its blue depths to another time and place—one of a childhood fantasy she had acted out time and again on the stage of an empty theater where her mother was employed as an actress.

She was twelve years old and arrayed in a slightly soiled white lace gown that the wardrobe department no longer used. A frayed train of white satin trimmed with silk roses—some of them crushed from improper storage and others missing altogether to serve a new purpose on some other costume—flowed behind her. Such dreams, such fantasies had been her companions then.

How she identified with that worn-out gown. The smudges of dirt seemed to represent the stain on her reputation. The missing roses symbolized innocence lost—stolen by others. The crushed ones were her hopes and dreams of someday making a success of herself on stage. And the frayed edge of that once-perfect train reminded her of her nerves—now raw.

The words of the minister to Tommy, asking him if he would have this woman to be his wedded wife, momentarily brought her out of her reminiscences. But as she gazed upon her intended, more memories flooded in. She was on the stage in Detroit again with a boy she had bribed with candy pilfered from the nearby confectionery to play the groom in her childhood make-believe ceremony. He stood beside her in a royal blue military uniform complete with gold fringed epaulets and braid trim, but the costume was too large for him, its sleeves hanging down past his fingertips while the cuffs of his pants rested amidst folds of excess fabric on his oversized boots. Again, the symbolism seemed clear. Although Tommy's intentions were as pure as the gold in the fringe on her young friend's shoulders, the role Tommy was taking on was too large for any man to properly fill.

At least she hadn't bribed him to take the part. And his certainty when he spoke the words, "I will," renewed hope within Deborah's heart that this hastily planned coupling would work.

The minister was speaking to her now, asking if she would have this man to be her wedded husband. While he listed all the eventualities in which she would promise to remain true, she prepared herself to deliver the most important line ever required of her. Swallowing nervously, she reminded herself to speak neither too loudly as if a player in one of the skits at the "resort," nor too softly as if to appear unsure of her commitment. By some gift of grace, she managed to issue her two-word reply at the perfect volume.

While the minister prayed, her thoughts drifted again from the dimly lit garden where she now stood to a sun-brightened Eden of pure fantasy. There, she found herself beside a man who, though similar to Tommy, was but a transparent apparition of his tall, handsome form. She was attired in a multicolored gown of gauzy silk, each layer having a different hue. A flock of butterflies fluttered about her—not real ones, like monarchs or swallowtails, but fanciful ones of many colors—to match her dress. The longer she stood there, the paler the man became, until he seemed to fade into thin air. At the same time, the butterflies grew larger in number and size, lighting on her shoulders and on the train of her gauzy gown. When she glanced back at them, she realized she had sprouted a pair of silken butterfly wings of her own. Effortlessly, they flapped and lifted her from the garden, carrying her off with perfect freedom to follow her butterfly friends to some heavenly destination.

The fantasy left her as she joined in the Lord's Prayer led by Pastor Phillips. No sooner had the "Amen" been spoken, than she was showered with kisses—first from Tommy, who placed a swift and gentle clove-flavored kiss upon her lips. Then came the obligatory kisses and congratulations from Caroline and Joshua, Charles and Ottilia, and Parker and Roxana. When her new father-in-law bent to kiss her cheek, he took her hands in his, a smile more lopsided than Tommy's bending his mouth.

"Welcome to the family, Mrs. Rockwell. I can't think of a better guarantee for happiness than to have Tommy for your mate." He chuckled. "Of course, like any other man, he's got some habits you'll have to accustom yourself to, but I'll leave it to you to discover them over time."

His use of her new name, Mrs. Rockwell, sent a sharp current through Deborah. *Why did I let things go this far?* she silently fretted. *How can this marriage possibly succeed?*

Pasting on a smile, she spoke the lines of the part she was now playing with a confidence that defied reality. "I have habits of my own that will require some patience, but we'll manage to get along, I'm sure, Dad Rockwell."

"I like the sound of that—'Dad Rockwell'—coming from my new daughter. Now, if you ever need help keeping Tommy in line, you just let me know. I'll set him straight!"

Tommy spoke up, his arm about his Butterfly's waist. "Like my wife said, we'll get along." Smiling down at her, he inquired, "Where do you want to go on your wedding trip? I never did ask."

Great-aunt Luella stepped up. "You two are welcome to use my place in Calumet. I won't be arriving home till the 8:15 gets in on Saturday evening. My housekeeper will do the cooking for you and my hired man will drive you wherever you want to go."

Deborah wanted badly to accept the offer. For the last few years she'd heard much about the Calumet Theatre, and other theaters in Michigan's Upper Peninsula that had gained fame among acting troupes and theater-goers.

Before she could accept, her Aunt Ottilia told Luella, "Deborah and Tommy won't have time to go that far. Tommy's already been away from his position at Charles's office for several days seeing to her safe return from Buffalo." Turning to Charles, she said, "You expect him back on the job immediately following Labor Day, don't you, dear?"

Charles cleared his throat. "I don't think—"

A sharp poke in the ribs from his wife gave him a moment's pause before he spoke again.

"We have gotten a tad behind in his absence."

Ottilia continued. "Tommy, Deborah, I think you ought to take up immediate residence in Caroline's old room."

The suggestion aggravated Deborah. She'd run away from this home ten weeks ago because of differences with her aunt, and she surely didn't relish the thought of spending the first days of her marriage under the same roof with the woman. But in truth, if she'd listened to Ottilia in the first place, she never would have wound up in the white slave house. And no one could offer a more perfect example of success—in marriage and otherwise—than her Aunt Ottilia and Uncle Charles.

Tommy squeezed Deborah's waist. "It's up to you, Butterfly. We can move into Caroline's room, or you can

27

move into my apartment in Grand Rapids near Uncle Charles's office in the morning. But it *is* a bachelor apartment. It'd be pretty close quarters till we found something bigger, and you'd be alone all day long."

Caroline spoke up. "If you stay in Caledonia, you can use the music room here for teaching voice lessons the way we'd intended before you went away." She referred to the music academy they were to have run together following graduation. But then Deborah had taken off, winding up in the "resort."

Caroline continued. "Once Joshua and I come home from our wedding trip, I'll only be a couple of blocks away, in the apartment he built for us over his father's store. Think how much fun you and I can have, getting together any time we want!"

Pastor Phillips stepped out of the shadows. "If you folks don't mind, I'll excuse myself and get back to the parsonage. This has been a long, tiring day, and my presence is required in the pulpit tomorrow morning to deliver a sermon."

Tommy thanked him profusely for his service, then the reverend's gaze settled on Deborah.

"Mrs. Rockwell, I hope you'll seriously consider taking up residence in the village. Your voice would be a real asset to the choir, and an even greater blessing to us all if you'd be willing to sing a solo now and again the way you did in your cousin's recital last June."

Deborah could hardly have asked for a more perfect return to Caledonia despite her sordid past, than to have the complete acceptance of the local pastor. Feeling the burden of her new role as a respectable, married woman, she played the part, delivering her lines with perfection.

"Pastor Phillips, I realize now, there's no doubt but that

28

Tommy and I should accept Aunt Ottilia's generous offer and take up residence in my cousin's old room."

"Bless you, Mrs. Rockwell. Bless you all!" he pronounced, robe flowing behind him as he exited the garden.

Caroline spoke up, the strain of the day reflected in a yawn she struggled to suppress. "Now that I've given away my room, could I borrow it back for one last nap before Joshua and I board the 5:50 A.M. train for Grand Rapids?"

Tommy chuckled. "Of course, Carolina—or should I say, Mrs. Bolden?" To Joshua, he said, "I think these two new brides deserve a few hours of peace and quiet, don't you?"

Joshua nodded, along with Great-aunt Luella who leaned heavily on her cane as she spoke. "We're all in need of some rest. As for me, I'm going to my room before I expire of pure exhaustion right here on this very spot."

She'd taken one wobbly step toward the house when Tommy joined her—one hand clutching his Butterfly's, the other steadying the old woman. "It's time we turned in, too. We'll see you to your room, Aunt Luella."

Deborah couldn't help noticing Tommy's infinite patience with Aunt Luella—pausing with her on each step of the porch, then on each tread of the stairway leading to the second floor. She was occupying the room next to Aunt Ottilia and Uncle Charles's near the top of the stairs, and before she entered it, she turned to Tommy, finger wagging.

"Don't think just because you're married to this pretty young thing now, that the two of you are joined at the hip!"

"I . . . I . . ."

Ignoring Tommy's stammered response and the red blotches now flooding his cheeks, she added, "Your new wife is the sort that needs a little freedom now and again, and you're going to have to let her have it, or pay the price

29

for holding too tight a rein."

Turning to Deborah, she continued. "And you, my dear Mrs. Rockwell, must learn the value of obedience. It'll save you a wagon load of heartache if you'll just learn to stay put and heed the advice of your elders now and again."

Before Deborah could manage a reply, Aunt Luella had uttered her goodnights and closed her door.

Tommy pulled Deborah close, and as he walked her down the hall to the room she had once occupied with Caroline, she couldn't help sharing her opinion. "That woman sure has a way with words. But what does she really know about us?"

Pausing in front of Deborah's door, he offered a half smile, gazing down into her eyes and gently capturing her face in his hands. "My only concern is what *I* know about us. We're husband and wife now—legally wed—and I love you, Mrs. Thomas Rockwell!"

In the next silent moment, Deborah knew Tommy was waiting for her to declare reciprocal feelings for him, but her tongue remained frozen against the roof of her mouth, as if she'd forgotten her lines and the prompter had fallen asleep!

Tommy privately scolded himself for causing the discomfort he now read in his Butterfly's eyes. Even though she'd never said so, he was certain that she cared deeply for him. And he was fully confident that their feelings for one another would grow. But he must be patient. She'd need time to learn to trust again—to come out from the chrysalis she'd been hiding in for the past ten weeks.

He dropped a kiss on her forehead and released her. "See you in the morning, Butterfly. Sweet dreams!" He stepped down the hall to his own room. When he paused to glance back at his new wife, she blew him a kiss then disappeared behind her bedroom door.

The hours until daybreak offered little in the way of solid sleep for Tommy. His father shared his room, and was up by five to dress for the 5:40 A.M. train east. Half an hour later, Tommy helped Joshua load up Carolina's trunk for transfer to the depot, then saw the newlyweds off to Grand Rapids. But Deborah remained in bed, having sent a message via Caroline that she was tired as a tombstone.

Breakfast came and went without any sign of his new bride. He stayed behind when Charles, Ottilia, and Aunt Luella headed off to church, hoping his Butterfly would come down while they were away, but she didn't stir. He refrained from disturbing her until an hour before dinner when Ottilia insisted that her niece be awakened in plenty of time to ready herself for the main meal.

Tommy knocked softly on Deborah's door, hearing a sleepy, "Who is it?" in response.

"It's your husband. May I come in?"

Seconds later he heard a key turn in the lock. The door opened no more than two inches, and Tommy could see by the fatigued look on his Butterfly's face and the tangled web of golden hair resting upon her shoulders that she was barely awake.

She rubbed her eyes and yawned. "I'm not used to getting up this early."

The simple statement put a needle through Tommy's heart. Of course she wasn't used to being up and about in daylight hours. For the last ten weeks, she'd been forced to work through the nights and had slept through the days. But she could put all that behind her—live a new life on a new schedule.

"Your aunt asked me to tell you dinner will be served in

31

an hour," he explained.

"Thank you," was her only reply before closing and locking the door again.

Tommy listened from the hallway, his ear to the door, catching the disheartening twang of bedsprings as his wife evidently lay down to sleep some more. He was sorely tempted to rap on the door and urge her to make herself ready for the midday meal but he kept his silence, turning his steps toward the staircase. He wondered if he should tell Ottilia that her niece wouldn't be down for dinner, but decided against it knowing the friction that would cause. Feeling totally inadequate and ineffective on his first day as a husband, he slipped down the stairs past the parlor where Parker and Roxana were enjoying a lively discussion with Great-aunt Luella. Looking for quiet and solitude, he continued down the hall to the library where Charles was poring over some law books that lay open on his desk.

Tommy settled unnoticed into a corner chair and picked up the nearest newspaper—the most recent issue of the *Caledonia News*. He didn't really want to read it. He just needed a screen behind which to indulge in his own thoughts and the challenge that his new status as a husband had brought. What he hadn't intended was to get caught up in the news. He read a piece about the upcoming Labor Day celebration, a notice about a prominent actress, another notice about a literary and musical entertainment planned at the church for Tuesday evening, and a local business item that might be of interest to his Butterfly. He hadn't intended, either, to succumb to the drowsiness that took over when he'd finished reading the paper. He awoke to the sound of Ottilia's voice.

"Tommy, dinner will be served in five minutes. Perhaps you'd better go up and tell Deborah."

"I'll go get her," he promised, setting aside the paper. As he climbed the stairs, however, he harbored grave doubts as to his ability to live up to his word. They grew stronger when he saw that her door was still shut tight.

He knocked firmly. "Mrs. Rockwell, it's your husband. Are you dressed?" He leaned hopelessly against the door, hearing nothing but silence in response.

Chapter

4

The doorknob turned and the bedroom door swung open so quickly Tommy nearly fell into the room.

Deborah laughed as he scrambled to catch his balance, nearly trampling on her feet in the process.

Her eyes dancing with mischief, she told him, "I'd invite you in, but I can see it's already too late for that!"

He straightened to gaze down upon a playful smile bordered by rosy cheeks and framed by a carefully fashioned Gibson-girl pouf of golden hair. Encircling her neck was the lacy collar of a summer gown in ivory Swiss.

Deborah continued. "I suppose it would be needless for me to point out that I am dressed."   •

"And in a lovely costume," Tommy observed, taking her hand in his and placing it in the crook of his arm. "Shall we go down to dinner, Mrs. Rockwell?"

Her stomach growled. She laughed. "I guess I'm past due for my next meal."

"You and the future Master or Mistress Rockwell," Tommy replied.

She pressed a finger to his lips. "That's our secret—not a word to anyone until we've been married awhile."

He nodded.

When Vida's roast chicken, sage stuffing, and biscuits had been served, conversation at the dinner table was subdued. Ottilia expressed the hope that Caroline and Joshua's honeymoon trip was progressing as planned.

Great-aunt Luella replied that she was certain—both young people being of good judgement and sufficient means—that they could successfully solve any problems that might come their way.

Charles spoke of the Labor Day doings planned in the village for Monday, inquiring if Parker and Roxana would be staying on to participate, or returning to their apartment in Grand Rapids on the evening train.

Parker replied, "We'll be going home tonight. Roxana wants to . . ." he paused. Gazing affectionately at his wife, he added, "You tell them, darling."

The young dark-haired woman blushed, her brown eyes taking in Ottilia at one end of the table, then settling on Charles, seated cross-corner from her at the opposite end. "We have an appointment tomorrow morning to view a larger apartment. We'll be needing one with a nursery soon."

Ottilia gasped with delight. "You're in the family way again! Congratulations! And let's pray all goes well for you this time!" To Tommy and Deborah, she said, "Roxana had a problem at the beginning of the summer that delayed the start of her family, but now—I'm just so tickled to know they're going to be parents soon! Wouldn't it be simply divine if Caroline and Joshua . . . and Tommy and Deborah . . . Charles, just think of it! We could be grandparents twice over and Great-aunt and uncle by the middle of next year!"

Charles sighed. "Woman, you're making me old before my time!"

Tommy glanced at Deborah, seated across the table from him. Though she said all the right words and offered the appropriate happy smile to the expectant parents, he knew she must be dying a little inside, realizing that if her own circumstance were made known, it would not bring happiness and celebration but regrets and condolences.

When all around had offered congratulations to the expectant parents, Tommy deftly changed the topic, addressing Charles. "Sir, with your permission, I'd like to borrow your rig to take my wife on a buggy ride in the country this afternoon. I thought we could head out toward the river for a picnic supper." He sent Deborah a hopeful look, knowing he should have discussed it with her first. Her modest smile spoke of approval.

Charles set aside his drumstick. "I have no need of the rig today. You two enjoy yourselves."

When the main course had ended and Vida's chocolate layer cake had been served in generous helpings all around, Tommy went to the carriage house to hitch up the rig. Twenty minutes later he pulled up to the side porch where Deborah was ready and waiting, a straw boater shading her face from the bright sun, and a wicker basket covered by a blue checked tablecloth in her hand.

As Tommy drove toward Cherry Valley Road, he couldn't help noticing his wife's uncharacteristically subdued nature. Remembering the articles he'd read in the newspaper, he made an effort to generate conversation.

"The *Caledonia News* reports this week that Mary Mannering has canceled her theatrical engagements so she can take care of her baby."

"Mary Mannering has a baby?" Deborah asked with interest.

"Evidently," Tommy replied. "I don't suppose it will hurt her stage career, do you?"

When Deborah made no response, he tried a new topic. "There's a musical and literary entertainment at the church Tuesday night. Would you like to attend?"

"I suppose," she replied half-heartedly.

Determined to elicit more than a two-word response, he shared news about the Caledonia druggist. "Mr. Beeler was in Grand Rapids on Thursday buying holiday goods. I have a hard time thinking of Christmas on such a warm, September day as this. How about you?"

His Butterfly remained silent, withdrawn in a seemingly melancholy world of her own. Eager to break through, Tommy lit into a rousing verse of *Deck the Halls with Boughs of Holly.*

She turned to him with a disconcerted look. "Tommy, are you mad? It's the third day of September."

He ignored her, singing even louder as he traveled north along Cherry Valley Road.

She nudged him in the shoulder. "Stop it, Tommy! You're making me wonder if I'm married to a madman!" She grinned, despite her complaint.

"Fa la la la la, la la, la, la!" he concluded, leaning over to peck her cheek.

Her hand flew to her face, suddenly contorted in the dramatic frown of a wronged heroine.

He offered a villainous grin. "Yes, I'm mad. Mad about you, my Butterfly!" Shaking the reins, he picked up the mare's pace and continued on the holiday theme. "Christmas will be different this year—our first Christmas as Mr. and Mrs. Thomas Rockwell. What do you want from your husband for Christmas, Mrs. Rockwell?"

She laughed. "I don't have the slightest idea, but I'm sure I'll figure it out by December. What do *you* want for Christmas, Mr. Rockwell?"

"Contentment and health, merriment and—" he stopped short of adding the rhyming word, wealth.

"And what?"

Turning serious, he said, "All I really want is for the two of us to be happy."

She looked away. Again, she seemed to slip into her own world, taking flight from him in mind and spirit like a Monarch in search of a milkweed patch. He dropped his efforts at small talk, driving east on Eighty-fourth Street past the dam in the Thornapple River where power poles marched south delivering electricity to rural neighbors. A northward turn onto Alaska Avenue took them up a stretch of road that was thickly lined with maple trees on either side.

Deborah's quiet mood persisted as he proceeded toward Sixty-eighth Street, eventually reaching the little berg of Alaska. When he turned east, she broke her self-imposed silence.

"I hope you remember the route home. You've made so many turns, I'm sure I could never find my way back without you."

Tommy grinned. "Don't you worry, Butterfly, I'll get us home—by a different route than this, too."

"Where are we going, anyway?"

"You'll see. We're almost there."

True to his word, he soon pulled off the road at the place where he had attended a huge picnic less than two weeks earlier—Campau Lake. Then, he'd been one of over three thousand gathered at the annual pioneer picnic to hear tales of olden days in Kent County. Even though dozens of people had come to the lake today, the spacious grounds seemed relatively empty by comparison.

In the picturesque stand of maples stood a two-story frame pavilion graced by a long front porch overlooking the water. Above it, a sign bore the owner's name, which Deborah read with a note of surprise.

"Apsey! Isn't that where . . . "

Tommy nodded, explaining again the events that had led to his rescuing her from the white slave house where Neal Taman had held her captive. "That porch rail is where Taman left his jacket—the one bearing the card with your picture and the address of his so-called 'resort.'"

Her delicate complexion grew even paler. "I wish you hadn't brought me here."

"Nonsense! It's the best picnic spot for miles around! There are boats to rent for outings on the lake, and any number of shady picnic tables with a great view." Reaching for her hand, he gave a reassuring squeeze. "And we're the ones free to enjoy it while Taman sits behind bars and pays for his crime."

Gradually, a modest smile erased the apprehension on Deborah's face. "You're right. It *is* a lovely spot. Thank you for bringing me."

Tommy jumped down to secure the horse to a hitching post, then lifted his new wife out of the rig, setting her gently beside him. Tucking the picnic basket under one arm, he offered his wife the other. "Let's find ourselves a shady table with a view. Then I'll hire a boat and take you out on the lake."

They soon agreed on a table beneath a beautiful spreading maple tree where they parked their basket while taking a row around the lake. Tommy enjoyed watching Deborah relax completely against the bow of the boat, her straw hat tipped forward, covering her face and the fact that she was napping beneath it. Silently he thanked the Lord that he'd been able to restore her freedom, and that he now had the privilege of caring for her as his wife. He prayed for wisdom in the undertaking of his responsibilities. And he thanked God for the love that swelled in his heart for this delicate creature, and the child they would soon raise together.

When he had spent an hour or more rowing his sleepy passenger around the lake, he returned to shore, walking her back to the picnic table where their basket awaited them.

With a yawn, she peeked beneath the checkered cloth draped over the wicker, saying, "Vida has packed us the chicken legs, biscuits, and chocolate cake left over from dinner, but I'm not hungry yet. Are you?"

Tommy shook his head. "I sure could use an ice-cold lemonade, though. I'll fetch us a couple of glasses from the pavilion."

"No need," Deborah said, extracting a corked bottle of the beverage and two glasses from the basket.

Sitting side by side, they took in their view of the lake—the mowed pasture of a modest farm bordered by trees along the opposite shore and boats full of other picnickers making their way across the glassy surface. Their voices drifted to them—the sound of excited children and happy adults forgetting all but the fun of the moment.

Beside Tommy, his Butterfly remained quiet and intro-spective. How he wished she could leave her past behind and truly enjoy the afternoon. Soon enough they would return home to face the challenges life was pressing upon them. Just when he had resigned himself to her silent, sober mood, she rose from the table and shook out her skirt, a playful smile on her face and a twinkle in her blue eyes as she spoke.

"Since it's too early to eat, I've decided to entertain you with a story from long ago—of a Salem whaling captain who had retired from life at sea." She began to pace back and forth across the grassy stretch in front of the table. When she continued, her voice took on a theatrical quality, projecting loud and clear as if she were center stage at an opera house.

"This old captain lived in a big house where he proudly displayed his nautical treasures—curious corals from South Pacific seas, giant shells that played ocean rhythms when held to the ear," she pretended to pick one up and listen to the ocean waves, "and stuffed fish from the tropics that decorated the walls." With the sweeping gesture of her hand, Tommy could imagine a swordfish mounted above a large stone fireplace. From the corner of his eye, he saw that two young people had paused to listen. When Deborah continued, she played to them as much as to him.

"There was only one dilemma blowing cross winds in the captain's ocean side abode. His hired woman was a difficult old thing, and more tyrannical than even the toughest of whaling captains he'd known. Indeed, her domineering ways soured the sunniest of fair days at the good captain's 'castle.' But dependable hired help was hard to come by, and she *was* a good cook."

More people gathered—the parents of the boy and girl who had taken a seat on the grass nearby. Deborah's attention was on these newcomers as she proceeded.

"One evening, the captain was entertaining a half dozen brother skippers. Seafaring stories dominated the dinner table talk, and as often happened, the effects of the brandy they shared enhanced their tendencies toward exaggeration. Each taleteller made himself out to be bolder and braver than facts would have supported. When the others had finished their yarns, the captain spun one of his own, telling how he had once drunk a gallon of brandy at a sitting without any ill effects.

"At that very moment, the hired woman entered the dining room with a tray. Gazing at her master scornfully, she claimed, 'It's a lie. Ye never done it.'

"Her employer sputtered and stammered, finally putting his pique into words. 'Shiver me timbers, woman. If that ain't going too far.' He started to rise, stating resolutely, 'We must part at last!'

"The old woman pushed the captain back onto his seat. With the haughtiest of words, she replied, 'Hoity-toity. Where would ye be better off than in yer own home?'"

Tommy threw his head back and chortled. The family of onlookers laughed and applauded.

Deborah curtsied. Tommy could see that she was in her element, clearly enjoying herself, so it didn't surprise him when she launched into a song—a humorous rendition of *My Bonnie Lies Over the Ocean,* complete with a dance routine. She finished with a curtsy, then retreated to a place beside Tommy at the table, her face aglow.

"You're a born entertainer," he told her, kissing her cheek. "Where did you get that story?"

"From the newspaper," she replied. "I had lots of time to read the paper when I was—" With an abrupt change of subject, she stated, "I'm famished! Let's eat!"

Tommy helped her spread the tablecloth, set out the picnic plates, and divide up the chicken legs, biscuits, and chocolate cake. Half an hour later, having consumed all but one of the drumsticks Vida had provided, they climbed aboard the rig for the ride home.

As Tommy had promised, he followed a different route, driving west on Sixty-eight Street past the general store and a meadow of sheep in the village of Alaska, and continuing on until he turned south on Thornapple River Drive. Deborah remained quiet, but it was no longer the sullen silence that had plagued their earlier drive. Instead, her delicate mouth held a slight upward curve, and he assumed that she was reflecting on the little performance she'd given, and the enjoyment of her audience.

With plenty of daylight still available, Tommy took his time on the narrow country road that hugged the banks of the river, following bends and curves that offered scenic views, turning west onto Eighty-fourth Street. When they had traveled almost as far as Cherry Valley, Deborah suddenly clutched his arm, pointing excitedly.

"Look at that poor dog!"

Several yards ahead, a medium sized mongrel, white with large black spots, was limping along the side of the road on three legs, holding its right front paw a couple of inches off the ground.

"I wonder who it belongs to," Tommy said, slowly drawing close enough to notice that the dog was a female and that she was mighty thin.

"She looks like a stray," Deborah concluded. "Tommy, stop and let me out. That dog needs help."

"You stay put. She might not be friendly," Tommy warned, pulling to a halt and stepping down from the rig. With quiet words he slowly approached the mutt, who had stopped in her tracks to watch him suspiciously. Though still several feet away, Tommy could see that a layer of mud clung to her underside. Two scars—probably from deep cuts—marred her hind leg.

Softly he spoke to the dog, squatting down to extend a hand in her direction. "Hello, girl. Good girl. Can you come?"

She shied away, emitting a low growl as she edged toward the thick undergrowth in the woods.

"Don't frighten her," Deborah cautioned, "or she'll take to the woods and we'll never find her." Reaching for the picnic basket, she removed the drumstick that had been left over from their supper. Tearing off the meat, she discarded the bones in the basket and climbed down from the rig.

"Here, girl. I've got something special for you," she coaxed, advancing slowly.

Warily, the dog watched.

Deborah crouched down, extending a morsel of chicken toward the dog.

The mutt sniffed the air and took a tentative step closer.

"Good girl," Deborah encouraged. "Come on. I won't hurt you."

The mongrel continued to sniff the air, taking one tentative step at a time toward Deborah until she was close enough to fasten her teeth onto the piece of meat. Retreating a few steps, she set it on the ground, turned it over with her nose, picked it up, and set it down twice more before finally eating it.

With Deborah's constant coaxing, the routine was repeated.

"Good girl, pretty girl," Deborah cooed, reaching out ever so slowly to pet the dog.

Warily, the mutt allowed Deborah to stroke her head.

Having saved one last morsel of chicken, Deborah handed it to Tommy.

"Come and get it," he coaxed, pleased when the dog came forward. Tommy backed away, hoping to entice the dog to get into the rig. "Good girl! Come on, now. You can get it!"

With every step the dog took toward him, he continued to back up, Deborah with him adding her own words of encouragement.

"Come on, girl, you can trust us," Deborah assured the dog as step by step, they moved toward the buggy.

Within a couple of minutes, he and Deborah had

reached the carriage, the stray but two feet from them. Continuing their words of encouragement, first Deborah, then Tommy climbed into the rig. The dog stared up at them, then placed her good front paw on the running board.

Tommy held the meat just beyond her reach. "Good girl, come on, now. You can do it!"

She let out a quiet whimper and picked up her rear leg, preparing to step into the buggy. But the sound of an approaching vehicle distracted her. Instantly, she turned and limped off into the woods.

Tommy reacted without aforethought.

"Doggoned!"

"I'm afraid we'll never see her again," Deborah said, her disappointment obvious.

"I'm afraid you're right," Tommy concluded, setting the carriage rolling toward home. They'd gone but a few yards when the vehicle that had scared off the stray came up beside them—a rickety wagon driven by a rough-looking fellow.

"Say there! Ain't seen a white bitch with black spots wanderin' hereabouts, have ya? She ran off again, 'n the kids are heartbroke." Lifting a long whip from the seat beside him, he said, "I swear, if I ever catch up with that critter again, I'll fix her so she don't run off no more."

Tommy glanced at Deborah. Her lips were rolled into a thin line and he could tell she was struggling to control her tongue.

To the stranger, he said, "Sorry, sir. Can't help you."

With a crack of his whip, he set his wagon in motion, rattling down the road in a cloud of dust.

Tommy waited a few seconds for the dust to settle, then set a leisurely pace toward home. "I saw a couple of bad scars on that dog's hind leg and I think I know now how she got them."

Deborah made no reply, her mind in turmoil over the abuse the dog had suffered. At least she was free now to make her own way. But what future did she have, wandering alone in the woods, hungry and injured, and reluctant to trust?

Deborah considered her own circumstances. She, too, had escaped her cruel taskmaster. Her hurts weren't visible, but they were real. Would she ever learn to trust again?

With every mile that carried her closer to home, she silently fretted. Even though she had agreed to be Tommy's wife, she was desperate to postpone sharing a bedroom with him. Any such delay was sure to cause trouble with Aunt Ottilia, not to mention the affront to Tommy, who had been nothing short of heroic in his efforts to cancel out her shameful past and put a bright face on a questionable future.

Tommy couldn't help noticing the distant, sober expression that had darkened his Butterfly's fair countenance since their unsuccessful attempt to help the stray. All the way home, he tried to think of adequate words to console her. An idea finally came to him as he pulled to a stop at the side door of the house.

"Butterfly, I was just thinking. I haven't given you a wedding gift yet. Maybe you'd like a brand new puppy?"

Deborah lay her hand atop of his as it rested on his knee, attempting to smile despite her troubling doubts. "You needn't give me a puppy, or anything else for our wedding," she assured him. "You've already given me your name. That's quite enough." She jumped down from the buggy and hurried inside. In no mood for conversation, she offered a one-word reply to Vida when the hired woman inquired about her day. Thankful that Ottilia, Charles, and Aunt Luella were all on the front porch, she headed up the stairs and straight for her room, desperate to be alone. But the sight that met her when she arrived at her door only compounded her anguish and fears.

Chapter
5

Tommy wished his Butterfly had let him help her down from the buggy. He wished even more that he could think of a way to make her happy. Everything he tried seemed to upset her, and now she was nearly in tears and he had no idea why. He was about to pull ahead into the carriage house to unhitch the rig when he saw the picnic basket still sitting on the floor of the buggy. He carried it inside to Vida offering thanks for her help, then went to find Deborah. He was halfway up the stairs when she came running down, tears staining her face.

"Butterfly, what's the matter?" he asked, reaching out for her.

"The room . . . it's . . . never mind!" she cried, pushing him away to hurry down the stairs.

"Butterfly, wait!" He started to go after her.

"Don't follow me!" she warned.

He dared not defy her. Instead, he ascended the stairs, wondering what could have upset her. When he reached the room that his wife had slept in after their wedding—Carolina's former room that Ottilia had designated as his and Deborah's now that they were wed—he hardly recognized it. In their absence, Ottilia had been hard at work, moving in a double bed to replace the two single beds that the two brides had slept in; rearranging dressers and vanity; adding a dressing screen, easy chair, and rocker; and relocating his belongings from the guestroom. When he left, closing the door behind him, he saw that Ottilia had even posted a sign with a huge heart on it, lettered with her artistic calligraphy.

Tommy and Deborah's Place

He headed downstairs. Aunt Luella was just coming in from the porch, and must have read the concern on his face. Reaching for his hand with her old, wrinkled one, she offered a warm squeeze, and unsolicited advice.

"Things will smooth out with Deborah. Just be patient." She leaned close and lowered her voice, evidently so as not to be overheard through the screen door that separated them from Ottilia and Charles on the porch. "I told Ottilia not to go changing things upstairs till the two of you came back, but she's as headstrong as your wife."

Tommy nodded, then went out by the side door to see if his Butterfly was in the garden. He caught a glimpse of her in the lane that ran between the Kinsey's fields. Stepping into the rig, he drove it to the carriage house and began unhitching the mare, all the while racking his brain for some way to brighten his new wife's spirits. All he could think of was the Labor Day activities that were to take place tomorrow. Maybe the foot races and bicycle races, the horse race and a baseball game would take her mind off whatever was bothering her.

When he had finished his chores, he realized he was in no mood to return to the house where Ottilia was certain to remark on his wife's absence. Instead, he took a brisk walk toward the west end of town, sprinting past the Johnson farm that lay beyond the school, then turning back and slowing to a walk again as he reached the village. The exercise invigorated him, reminding him how much he had missed the athletics of his school days. Making a promise to himself to spend a few minutes each day in vigorous exercise, he returned to the carriage house. Full of ambition, he cleaned out the stalls, swept the floor, and reorganized the tack. Through the open door, he could see that daylight was now waning. He prayed that Deborah would have sense enough to come back before darkness fell, then he caught sight of her on the lane heading for home. Reluctant to force his company on her just yet, he decided to stay in the carriage house for a while longer. Stifling a yawn, he spread a horse blanket on the floor and lay down, resting his head against a bale of hay.

His next awareness was of a quiet whimpering sound. Struggling to come awake, he blinked his eyes open, but could see nothing in the total darkness that now enveloped the carriage house. Again, the whimpering came to him. Getting to his feet, he carefully felt his way to the light near the door. In the pale beam that spilled out onto the driveway, he discovered the spotted stray dog he'd seen earlier.

Crouching down, Tommy extended his hand. "Girl, what are you doing here?"

The dog let out a whine.

"You're hungry, aren't you, girl? Well, I can fix that," he quietly promised. Rising slowly, he began walking toward the side door of the house, coaxing the stray to follow him. By the time he had mounted the porch, she had limped to the bottom of the steps.

"You stay right there. I'll find you something to eat," he assured her. Checking his pocket watch in the lamplight at the side door, he learned that it was a few minutes before midnight, then he stepped inside. The house was dark and quiet. Turning on the kitchen light, he swung open the door to the icebox in search of leftover chicken, but could only find a bowl of hardboiled eggs. He took it outside where he found the dog waiting patiently at the bottom of the porch steps.

He descended partway, sat down, and took an egg from the bowl. "I've got a nice treat for you," he quietly promised. Peeling the egg, he split it into quarters with his pocketknife, then set the pieces on the bottom step and retreated to take a seat beside the bowl again.

The stray took her time sniffing his offering, testing one of the egg quarters with her tongue, then finally eating it. Within seconds she had downed the remaining three pieces. She looked up at him with unmistakable expectation.

Repeating the procedure, Tommy offered her another egg, then another until the bowl was empty. He carried the peelings to the trash can, then went inside, filled the bowl with water, and set it on the ground in front of the mutt. Thirstily, she lapped the water until the bowl was again empty, then she lay down on the ground beside it.

Concerned about the injury that made her limp, he cautiously reached for the dog's right front paw, discovering a burr lodged between her toes. Carefully, he pulled it out and discarded it.

"That ought to make you feel a whole lot better, girl. Now stay. I'll be back in a minute." He headed up the porch steps, glancing back to find that the mutt hadn't moved. Quickly, he went inside and upstairs. The hall was dark except for the light spilling from the open door of the room he was to share with his wife. When he reached the doorway, he saw that she was dressed in her robe, and had dozed off in the rocking chair.

Quietly, he approached her, bent and kissed her on the forehead, then spoke in a whisper. "Butterfly, wake up."

She let out a soft sigh, slowly coming awake. Then, all

at once, her eyes were wide-open. "Tommy! Where *were* you?"

Her obvious concern pleased him. "In the carriage house." Taking her by the hand, he said, "Come downstairs. There's someone waiting to see you."

"Who?" she asked skeptically.

"You'll see," he promised, pulling her to her feet.

"I can't go down like this. I'm not even dressed!" she protested.

"I guarantee your guest won't mind a lick. Now come!" His arm about her waist, he gave her no opportunity for further resistance, guiding her down the stairs and out through the side door.

The moment Deborah stepped onto the porch, the stray dog sat erect, wagged her tail, and let out a quiet squeal of delight.

"Spotsy!" Deborah cried. "How did you ever find us?"

The stray sat in place as Deborah approached, allowing her to stroke her head.

Deborah spoke quietly, continuing to offer affection. "Your dish is empty. Did you get enough to eat, girl?"

Tommy chuckled. "I'd say so. She polished off a dozen hard-boiled eggs and a bowl of water just before I came to get you."

Her focus still on the mutt, Deborah said, "That ought to hold you till morning, huh, Spotsy?"

The dog licked Deborah's hand.

"Spotsy . . . " Tommy echoed, trying out the name. "It suits her."

"We're going to keep her, aren't we?"

"That's up to you, Butterfly."

"I wonder what Aunt Ottilia will say."

"Let's wait until we've got Spotsy all cleaned up before

52

we introduce her to your aunt," Tommy suggested.

"What will we do with her until then?" Deborah wondered.

"I'll tie her up in the barn, and make her a bed of some straw and a blanket. Stay here with her while I go fetch some rope."

Tommy had soon found a length of suitable rope, and while his Butterfly went up to bed, he led Spotsy to the barn where he tied her to a rail and encouraged her to lie down on the blanket-covered straw he'd been occupying when the dog had awakened him. With quiet words of reassurance, Tommy turned to go, but the moment he got out of sight of the dog, she let loose with piercing objections that would surely awaken the entire household if allowed to continue.

Returning to Spotsy, he tried again and again to convince her to keep quiet, but unfailingly, when he headed for the house, she complained loudly. Giving up on the idea of spending the night indoors, he lay down on his side. Spotsy immediately nestled in the crook of his legs, and the two of them drifted to sleep with her head resting on his knee.

Tommy's next awareness was of Spotsy standing over him, pawing his arm and whimpering. The first light of morning had barely broken over the horizon and he was in no hurry to rise, but Spotsy was obviously in need of relief. When he had walked her behind the carriage house, he settled again on the straw bed and Spotsy curled up beside him.

Much to her surprise, Deborah was wide-awake by eight in the morning. Though she had spent the first several hours of the night dozing in her rocker, she had finally concluded that Tommy would not be coming inside, and she had allowed herself the comfort of the double bed. But toward morning, recurring visions of Spotsy had prevented further sleep, so she rose to dress.

Golden sunlight flooded the room, infusing her with a sense of hopefulness she hadn't known in months. Perhaps she could manage to keep dark doubts locked in a closet—if just for today.

Donning a dark skirt and blouse that would be suitable for the task of grooming Spotsy, she headed downstairs. The smell of Vida's coffee greeted her before she reached the dining room where breakfast had been laid out on the sideboard. Ottilia and Charles were already seated, and her aunt spoke first.

"Good morning, Deborah. I'm surprised you're down ahead of Tommy."

Unwilling to reveal that Tommy hadn't spent the night in their room, or to lie, she said, "Actually, Tommy's out in the carriage house. He has a little project out there that requires attention. I'd like to take him a bite to eat, if you don't mind."

"Suit yourself," Ottilia replied.

Lowering his paper, Charles asked, "What kind of project could keep Tommy from the table at mealtime?"

"You'll have to ask him," Deborah replied, piling scrambled eggs and bacon onto a plate and hurrying for the door.

Her aunt's words gave her pause. "You might take that new husband of yours a fork, and some coffee."

"Of course," Deborah agreed, quickly complying with the suggestion. She was about to exit the side door of the house when Vida came dashing out of the kitchen, an empty dish in her hand—the same dish that Spotsy had eaten from last night.

"Mrs. Rockvell, my boiled eggs have vanished. Vould

you know what became of them?"

"Have you asked Mr. Rockwell?" she replied, slipping out the side door.

The brightness of the morning and the sweet smell of freshly mown hay gave her a new appreciation for the freedom that she now enjoyed. And when she reached the carriage house, the sight of Spotsy snuggled up beside Tommy touched her in a way she hadn't expected.

Spotsy was the first to see her, rising to her feet, shaking herself awake, and greeting her with a soft whine.

"Good morning, girl. I brought you something," Deborah said, setting the plate down in front of her.

Spotsy dug in without hesitation.

Tommy stirred and stretched. "'Morning, Butterfly."

"Good morning. Here's your coffee."

When he took hold of the cup, his hand overlapped hers with a warmth that was both soothing and disturbing. "Thanks, Butterfly, but I'd prefer my morning cup with—"

"Cream and sugar. I'm sorry. I wish I'd have known," Deborah apologized, troubled by her vast lack of knowledge about her new husband—and the fact that she had a husband at all.

"That wasn't what I was going to say," Tommy told her, a grin spreading wide. "I drink it black. But you could sweeten it with a kiss."

Reluctant to engage in an affectionate exchange, Deborah nevertheless obliged him, brushing a quick kiss against his lips, then pulling her hand free from beneath his. Eager to focus his attention elsewhere, she pointed to Spotsy.

"Would you look at that dog eat!"

"She's a hungry one, all right."

No sooner had Tommy spoken, than his stomach

growled, causing both he and Deborah to laugh.

She patted him on the midriff. "I'm sorry I couldn't bring you a plate of eggs, but I couldn't explain two breakfasts—not even for an eater as big as you! And another thing—Vida wants to know what became of the boiled eggs you fed to Spotsy last night. I told her to ask you."

Tommy sipped his coffee, his expression thoughtful. "Sounds like we'd better get busy and make Spotsy presentable so we can show Vida that her hard-boiled eggs and that plate of breakfast went for a good cause." Finishing off the last of his coffee, he handed his cup to his Butterfly. "You'd better take this—and Spotsy's empty plate—back to the kitchen and bring out a bar of soap and some towels. I'll fill a tub with water for Spotsy's bath."

When Deborah bent down to reach for the plate, Spotsy licked her hand and nudged it with her wet nose, begging for attention.

Deborah obliged, even setting down the cup to leave both hands free for petting the dog and scratching her ears.

The generous exchange of affection between the two raised conflicting responses within Tommy—pleasure in Deborah's enjoyment of the dog, and jealousy that his wife's affections were not so freely given to him as to the stray. Silently, he thanked God that at least the stray was bringing pleasure to his wife.

After she had gone inside, Tommy set about pumping water into a large tub. Regrettably, it would be a cold bath for Spotsy, but heating the water would take more time and cause more suspicion than it was worth. A few minutes later, Tommy was pleased to see that his Butterfly had returned with not only the towels, and soap he'd requested, but also a brush to untangle the knots in Spotsy's medium-length hair, and a sweet roll to make up for the breakfast he had missed.

They soon had lowered a reluctant Spotsy into the chilly tub and set about lathering her up—getting as much of the soapy water on themselves as on the dog in their efforts to keep her from jumping out. But it didn't bother Deborah, whose happy chatter punctuated by occasional laughter kept Tommy issuing silent thanks to God.

As they scrubbed Spotsy's underside to loosen the caked-on mud, Deborah said, "When I went back in the house, Uncle Charles asked if we were going to the Labor Day doings later on. I told him he'd have to ask you."

Tommy remembered his concern last night when his Butterfly had become upset over changes to their room, and his idea to invite her to the celebration. But Spotsy's arrival had changed circumstances considerably.

Leaving the decision to his wife, he asked, "Do you want to go?"

"Only if we can take Spotsy," she replied.

Her swift bonding with the pet pleased him immensely. "I don't see why Spotsy can't go, too. She'd probably enjoy it."

Awhile later, when Spotsy was squeaky clean, towel-dried, and free of knots, Tommy stepped back to admire her. "Except for the scars on Spotsy's leg, she's really quite attractive, now that she's washed up."

"I think she could look even nicer," Deborah stated. Reaching inside her skirt pocket, she pulled out the length of wide pink ribbon from her wedding bouquet and knelt beside Spotsy to tie it around her neck in a huge bow. "There! The finishing touch! You could take first place at a dog show—for mutts, that is!"

Tommy said, "I think she's ready to meet the rest of the family. I'll gather Vida, your Aunt Ottilia and Uncle

Charles, and Great-aunt Luella on the front porch. When they're all there, I'll give a whistle and you can bring Spotsy to meet them."

While Tommy was gone, Deborah slipped the rope around Spotsy's neck as a temporary collar and leash, then led the dog in a large circle. With an abundance of coaxing, Spotsy was capable of walking nicely beside her. When Tommy's whistle pierced the air—so loud it nearly caused Spotsy to bolt—Deborah calmed her with soothing words and led her up the front porch steps.

Ottilia stared at the mutt, her gaze as disapproving as her words. "Married not even two days, and you've already added to your family."

Deborah ignored the comment. Drawing a deep breath and putting on her best theatrical smile, she introduced the dog.

"Aunt Ottilia, Uncle Charles, Great-aunt Luella, Vida, this is our new dog, Spotsy."

Tommy focused on Vida. "I'm sorry about your boiled eggs. They were all I could find to feed Spotsy when she showed up late last night."

With a forgiving smile, the housekeeper reached down to pet the mutt. "No deviled eggs for us today, Fräulein Spotsy."

Luella said, "I think Spotsy will make a very fine pet. Dogs are such a comfort."

Ottilia scowled. "If they're such a comfort, then why don't *you* have one?"

The old woman replied sweetly, "My decrepit legs couldn't do justice to a dog. They need regular, brisk walks, and goodness knows I'm in no condition for that. I'll leave it to the youngsters to enjoy the blessings of dog owner-ship."

"Blessings? Ha!" replied Ottilia. "I suppose the muddy paw prints on the floor and carpet, the malodorous atmosphere that permeates every room of the house, and the constant need to go out or come in are all blessings, not to mention dog hair everywhere you turn."

"It all depends on how you view it, my dear," Luella replied.

Charles took a step toward the dog, but Spotsy backed away, emitting a low growl. Despite encouragement from both Deborah and Tommy, she would not let Charles near. He backed away, speaking soothingly to her. "Welcome to the family, Spotsy. I'm sure once you've grown accustomed to me we'll be good friends."

Ottilia addressed the dog. "And I'm sure we *won't* be good friends. But you may stay, as long as you don't set foot in the house."

Almost as if she understood, Spotsy eased up to Ottilia until she was brushing against her skirt.

With a flick of her wrist, Ottilia shrunk back. "Shoo! Go away before you have me covered with dog hair."

Spotsy ignored the complaint, lying down at her feet, and bringing a round of chuckles from all but the object of her affection.

To Tommy, Ottilia said, "You'd better get busy and build her a dog house."

Charles said, "No need for that. There's plenty of room in the carriage house for Spotsy."

Turning toward the door, Vida said, "I fetch an old cushion for her."

Tommy thanked her, then focused on Charles. "About the Labor Day activities, my wife and I have decided to go and take Spotsy."

Charles consulted his watch. "The competitions start in

twenty minutes. I suppose we should head over to Center Street soon."

"We'll be ready as soon as we make Spotsy's bed."

A few minutes later, he set the cushion Vida had given him on the floor of the carriage house and covered it with the blanket while Deborah and Spotsy looked on.

When he had finished, Deborah asked, "Do you think Spotsy will be happy sleeping out here with the horse?"

Tommy shook his head. "Not if last night is any indication. Every time I tried to come inside, she protested."

"What are we going to do if she's uncooperative tonight?" Deborah wondered.

Tommy's mouth slid into a crooked smile. "We'll figure something out." Taking his wife by the hand, he said, "Come on, Butterfly, let's walk Spotsy over to Center Street. I aim to get in on the running competition and win you the $15 prize I read about in the newspaper!"

Chapter
6

Spotsy trotted along nicely beside her new master and mistress as they followed Charles and Ottilia down Lake Street. How pleased Deborah was by the way the mutt carried herself, with pomp and dignity as if she were strutting out on stage before an audience. It made Deborah hold her own head a little higher, proud to be the owner of this attractive pet.

But when they turned the corner onto Center Street where throngs of people were beginning to gather, Spotsy grew timid, hesitating and growling when strangers came near.

Deborah stroked her head. "It's okay, Spotsy. There's nothing to be afraid of."

No sooner had the words left her mouth, than the mutt lunged forward, barking fiercely at a loose dog on the opposite side of the street. The rope burned Deborah's hand. She was about to lose her grip when Tommy took hold.

"Spotsy, heel!" he commanded, but the dog paid him no heed until the stray had taken flight, disappearing from sight in the alley on the north side of the street.

Deborah rubbed her hand where the rope had left a red mark.

Ottilia clucked her tongue. "Shame on that dog. She's more trouble than she's worth."

Deborah wanted to argue, but Charles spoke first.

"Spotsy was only doing what comes natural."

Tommy said, "I'd better keep a tight hold on her. I'm sure that's not the last time today something will set her off." Inspecting his Butterfly's hand, he said, "At least she didn't break the skin. We'll get a leather collar and leash tomorrow. She'll be easier to control."

Charles said, "She might choke herself straining against a collar. There's a place in Grand Rapids not far from my law office where you can buy a dog harness."

Just then, an announcement came over a megaphone.

"Attention! Will all contenders in the free-for-all race please meet in front of the Caledonia Hotel."

Charles told Tommy, "You'd better put me in charge of that feisty mutt if you want to run."

Handing Spotsy's rope to Charles, he told Deborah, "Just you wait. I'm going to get you that $15!" Pointing to his cheek, he said, "Give me a kiss for good luck!"

Deborah obliged, the scent coming to her of the clove Tommy was chewing.

Ottilia told Charles, "If you'll keep that beast under control, we can head down to the other end of the block for a good view of the finish line."

Charles offered his arm. "My dear, after all these years with you, I'm sure I've had sufficient practice with attractive, albeit headstrong females to keep Spotsy in check."

"Charles!" she scolded, a smile belying her displeasure.

As Deborah followed her aunt and uncle down Center Street, she realized that some of the old familiar sights had undergone changes while she'd been away. On the north side, the Caledonia Hotel now sported a large wooden cutout of a Scottish bagpiper in a red plaid kilt on the balcony above the front entrance. Deborah wondered if H.B. Cavanaugh, the proprietor, was simply paying tribute to the town's Scottish heritage, or engaging in some form of self-aggrandizement with the image that bore such close resemblance to himself.

Farther along, the VanAmburg sisters had set up a lemonade stand in front of their grocery store. Judging from the warmth of the sun and the size of the crowd, Deborah expected they would do a brisk business. Their neighbor, C.F. Beeler, hadn't wasted an opportunity for advertising to the Labor Day throng. A large sign posted in his window proclaimed "Pure Rye Whiskey, an excellent alcoholic stimulant preferable to brandy as a medical agent. Price—75 cents to $1.25 per quart."

His neighbor to the west, Charles Kinsey, was ready to make the most of the day's opportunities at his general store, filling his windows with school outfits and supplies that spilled out onto tables set up beneath his bright red awning. Boys' knickers, girl's wide-collared dresses, along with tablets of ruled paper, lunch buckets, pens, and more catered to every need of those who would head back to school tomorrow. Even Bolden & Sons Furniture and Hardware had prepared for the occasion, displaying a child-sized roll top desk in the front window for the seriously studious to covet.

Reaching the other end of the block, Deborah squeezed in beside Spotsy and her uncle for a good view of the finish line. Looking back, she could pick out Tommy crouching down amidst a horde of contenders at the starting line. When the center of the wide dirt street had been cleared of stragglers, the sound of gunfire rent the air. Spotsy dropped to the ground with a whine. The contestants shot forward.

"Go, Tommy! Go!" Deborah shouted, her voice barely distinguishable in the din.

Spotsy began to bark, uncertain what to make of the

sudden fracas.

For an instant, Deborah lost track of Tommy. Then she caught sight of him pressing ahead of Solon Winter, who'd graduated with her this past June in the Class of "Naughty Five."

Tommy fought for the lead that alternated back and forth between him and Solon until Tommy finished first by half a stride.

The second heat began like the first, Zimri Bolden—Joshua's older brother—claiming victory by a stride.

The third heat opened with two false starts by Dell Wood, a sure winner from the neighboring town of Alto, according to Charles and Ottilia. Deborah hoped he would make a false start a third time and be disqualified, but he made good on the third try and won the heat easily.

Now the winners of the three heats lined up for the feature race—Tommy, Dell, and Zimri. In an instant, they were off. Dell shot ahead. Tommy ran two strides behind him, with Zimri a close third.

"Go, Tommy! You can do it!" Deborah shouted, knowing others were drowning her voice out. By the midway point, Dell's victory seemed assured. Then he faltered. A turned ankle forced him to the sidelines. Tommy charged ahead, Zimri at his heels. Just when it seemed Zimri was pulling out front, Tommy pressed forward with one last burst of speed to cross the finish line first.

"Hooray, Tommy!" Deborah cried.

Winded, he sought her out, raising her hand with his in victory.

His gesture, along with the applause, made her heart soar.

Elmer Hale, the village president, spoke through his megaphone from the opposite end of the block. "Will the winner of the race please return to the starting line and claim his prize."

Tommy took Deborah with him.

Mr. Hale counted three five-dollar bills into Tommy's hand. "Congratulations, son! Don't spend it all in one place—unless, of course, it's at Hale's Dry Goods and Grocers!" He referred to an establishment owned by his relative, Eugene Hale, on the south side of the street.

"Thank you very much, sir. I'll be sure and heed your advice." Tucking the cash into his money clip, he shoved it deep in his pocket and slipped his arm about Deborah. "Just think of it, Butterfly, fifteen dollars!"

When he had escorted her back to where Ottilia and Charles were waiting with Spotsy, he reclaimed the dog's leash, bending down to scratch her ears. "What do you think of that, Spotsy? A whole fifteen dollars for running half as fast as you can!" Turning to his Butterfly, he pulled her close and whispered in her ear, "The money I won is all yours to spend as you please. I'll give it to you when we get home so you can hide it away in some secret place for safe-keeping."

Deborah was about to thank him for his generosity when gruff words came from behind them.

"Hey! You two with the spotted dog!"

Deborah recognized the voice before she turned to face the man she and Tommy had encountered on their way home from yesterday's picnic.

Spotsy crouched, letting out a low growl.

The crowd grew quiet. The man's hard glare was fixed on Tommy. "That's my dog and I want her back!"

Tommy forced a crooked smile. "Sorry, sir, you must be mistaken. This dog belongs to my wife and me."

"No it don't. It ran away from my kids last week 'n you

65

know it. Now give her here." He reached for the leash.

Spotsy growled again.

Deborah pressed the man's outstretched hand aside. "You've got no right to this dog. You abused her, and when she ran away, you threatened to whip her if you ever got your hands on her again. You ought to be ashamed of yourself!"

His face grew red. "You're one to talk, with *your* past, missy!"

Instant dread coursed through Deborah.

The man went on. "I heard all about you—runnin' off to that sin palace, offerin' yourself up to any man who came a-callin'. *You're* the one who ought to be ashamed."

Tommy handed Spotsy's leash to Charles and stepped chest to chest with the fellow. "That's my wife you're talking to, mister. You'd better watch your words or I'll rearrange your mouth."

The man laughed derisively. "You ain't much of a man, if ya cain't find better for a wife than that piece of pretty trash."

Before Tommy could stop himself, his right fist connected with the man's jaw.

He faltered, his hand to his face as he regained equilibrium. A wild look flashed in his eyes. He came at Tommy, both arms swinging.

Tommy ducked, arms raised to fend off blows. Three hefty farmers subdued the man. As they forced him to move on, the fellow cast a foul look back. "You ain't seen the last of me. That's my dog, and I aim to git her back!"

Deborah's stomach churned. If only she and Spotsy could turn invisible! As if her humiliation were not complete, Ottilia addressed her accusingly.

"How in heaven's name did you ever get mixed up with

that fellow and his dog?"

Tommy replied for his wife, his arm encircling her waist reassuringly as he explained their separate encounters with the stray and its owner on their way home from yesterday's picnic, and the subsequent appearance of Spotsy in the carriage house last night.

Ottilia sighed. "I told you that mutt was more trouble than she's worth." Turning to Charles, she said, "Don't you think I'm right?"

He took her hand in his, placing it affectionately in the crook of his arm. "My dear, I know you'll think I'm an old softy, but if Tommy and Deborah want to give the dog a good home, then I'm surely not going to criticize. Now let's get ourselves some lemonade. You young folks care to join us? My treat."

Try as she might to put the incident behind her, the remainder of the day was ruined for Deborah. During the three-legged race, the potato race on horseback, and the slow bicycle race, she couldn't think of anything except the words that horrible man had said about her. She wondered how he'd known about her past, and dreaded the inevitable—that in a small village such as Caledonia, it wouldn't be long before everyone else knew about it, too.

In the humid warmth of the afternoon, when Tommy walked her down the railroad track to the baseball game just outside of the village, her fear was confirmed by the looks she received. One woman—whose round face and soft blue eyes spoke of a gentle heart—offered her a look laden with sympathy while the ramrod-stiff lady next to her refused to look at Deborah at all. One thing she knew for certain. She had no desire to endure such reactions every time she showed herself in public in the Village of Caledonia. Like the clouds creeping over the baseball diamond, a gray veil was descending over her heart, and the darkness would only increase once her pregnancy became evident.

How in heaven's name would she find any measure of happiness in her future? Would she be forced to live the life of a recluse, tucked away in the big white house on Railroad Street in order to avoid the painful responses of others?

Chapter
7

That evening, after a light supper of Vida's German potato salad, sliced cold ham, and peach muffins, Tommy invited his Butterfly to accompany him on a walk with Spotsy down Kinsey's lane before the thickening clouds sent down their rains. In the time since he'd rescued her from the white slave house, he'd developed a sort of sixth sense about her. She'd been too quiet. She'd tried to appear interested in the ball game that had lasted the better part of the afternoon, but he could tell her mind had been else-where, and her enthusiasm for the overwhelming victory of the home team a response born of an actress's skill. He remarked about her subdued nature as they strolled hand-in-hand along the two-rut path that ran between the cornfields.

"You seem mighty distracted—like a Monarch in search of milkweed. What's on your mind, Butterfly?"

Deborah didn't want to speak of the possibility that she would be forced into seclusion in order to avoid incidences similar to their encounter with Spotsy's former owner. Nor did she want to talk about the looks she had received from the ladies watching the ballgame. Keeping these troubling thoughts to herself, she took another angle with her reply, her words both truthful and appropriate.

"I'm thinking of how I'll miss you tomorrow when you go to work in Uncle Charles's law office. It's going to be a long day without you."

Tommy squeezed her hand, unconvinced that his new wife was being completely honest, but reluctant to question her further. "I'll miss you, too, Butterfly. But I'll feel better knowing you've got Spotsy to keep you company. You could take her for a walk tomorrow, but remember—she can pull mighty hard if something sets her off."

"I'll be careful," Deborah assured him, planning to go early in the day when streets were quiet.

Reaching deep into his pocket, Tommy retrieved his winnings from the race, pausing to hand the three five-dollar bills to her. "And treat yourself to something nice from Mr. Kinsey's place—or Mr. Hale's. A little shopping trip should lift your spirits."

Deborah accepted the gift and pressed a kiss against Tommy's cheek, the clean smell of clove coming to her. "Thank you, Mr. Rockwell. You didn't have to be so generous with me." She knew the amount was nearly equivalent to what he'd make in three weeks of clerking at her uncle's law office. She pushed two of the bills back at him. "Are you sure you don't want to keep some of this to spend for yourself?"

He pressed her hand away. "Most certainly not. It's all yours—and my pleasure to give it to you—especially since I didn't even have a wedding gift for you."

Shoving the bills into her skirt pocket, she said, "Nor I for you, but I'm certain I'll find something when I go shopping tomorrow."

Tommy was about to protest when Spotsy jerked forward, straining and barking excitedly as a rabbit hopped across the lane a few yards ahead of them.

"Heel, Spotsy! Heel!" he commanded, bringing her under control.

Deborah said, "I'm wondering if she'll sleep quietly in

the carriage house tonight."

Tommy shifted the clove he'd been chewing from one side of his mouth to the other, glancing up at the dark clouds before his gaze again met hers. "I don't know. But I don't intend to spend the night out there."

Suddenly an old, familiar dread revisited Deborah—the reminder that she was not ready to share her bed with Tommy despite their status as husband and wife. Just as quickly, a thought came to mind. "You'll need a good night's sleep if you're going to catch the 5:50 train with Uncle Charles tomorrow morning. You take the double bed tonight. I'll keep Spotsy company in the carriage house."

"No, ma'am!"

Tommy's swift objection preceded a more leisurely, somewhat mischievous grin and suggestion. "You take the double bed and leave the problem of Spotsy to me. I told you I'd figure something out, and I have."

"What's that?"

"Never you mind right now, Butterfly."

"But Aunt Ottilia said Spotsy wasn't to set foot in the house."

"I know. Don't you worry."

When sprinkles of rain began to fall, Tommy suggested they take Spotsy with them to the veranda to sit with Aunt Luella, Ottilia, and Charles. The approaching hour of nine o'clock and the onset of rain soon sent the others inside to prepare for bed. When the door closed behind them, Tommy told Deborah, "You go on up and get ready for bed. I'm going to settle Spotsy in the carriage house."

"But what if—"

"Go on, now," he insisted, leading Spotsy away from the veranda at a trot.

Deborah took her time climbing the stairs, still reluctant to share her room with Tommy yet guilty over her unwillingness. As she approached Aunt Luella's room, she heard the old woman talking and wondered if Ottilia was with her. When Deborah reached the open door, she realized Aunt Luella was alone, her eyes shut as she rested against the back of her rocker. Hands folded on the open Bible in her lap, her conversation was obviously with God and was clearly audible. Deborah paused in the hallway to listen.

"Holy Father, I believe You have brought me here at this time for a purpose beyond the witnessing of the union between Caroline and Joshua. I ask You, Lord, to work a miracle in Caroline's cousin, Deborah, who has fallen victim to the iniquity of this world. Use me to tell her of Your love, heavenly Father. Make me eloquent in Your service. And if it be Your will, Father God, make these old bones of mine last long enough to see genuine happiness in Deborah's countenance."

As Aunt Luella's prayer continued for good health and safekeeping of other family members, Deborah stood frozen in the hallway. Never had she heard anyone pray for her, and never had she heard anyone—except trained clergymen—pray as eloquently and earnestly as Aunt Luella. Surely she had a powerful link to the Almighty and a confidence that she was being both heard and answered.

By comparison Deborah's own prayers were few and faltering. Yes, she had prayed for a way out of the white slave house and had been rescued, but not until she had suffered indescribable indignation for ten long weeks. Why had God ignored her pleas for so long? Why had He left her there to suffer?

A loud crack of thunder interrupted her thoughts and she continued down the hall to the room she now shared with Tommy. Behind the dressing screen she slipped into her nightgown and wrapper, then turned back the covers on the bed. But she would not sleep in the double bed tonight. Tommy needed a good night's sleep before boarding the 5:50 train to Grand Rapids.

Settling in her rocker, she leaned back and closed her eyes, listening to the rumbling and cracking of thunder outside. Within minutes, Tommy entered the room, his shirt and pants showing large blotches of dampness. He bent and kissed her forehead, leaving it moist from the rain that had spattered his face. Pulling his handkerchief from his pocket, he blotted her dry, then went behind the screen, talking as he draped damp shirt and pants over the top.

"Spotsy wasn't one bit happy when I tied her up. And as soon as I headed for the door, she raised such a fuss, I half-expect we could hear her all the way up here if it weren't for the thunder."

"She's probably frightened to death," Deborah concluded, resenting Ottilia for barring the dog from the house.

"She'll adjust over time." Tommy emerged in his robe and grabbed a pillow from the bed. Reclining in his easy chair, he propped the pillow beneath his head and stretched his long legs out in front of him.

"You're not spending the night there," Deborah stated.

"Why not?" Tommy asked, eyes already closed.

"Because you have to get up early and go to work tomorrow," Deborah reasoned.

"Good night, Mrs. Rockwell," he murmured.

With no small amount of guilt, Deborah removed her robe, lay it at the foot of the bed, and slipped beneath the sheet. Thanks to Tommy, the awkwardness she'd dreaded between them had never materialized. She didn't deserve such consideration and kindness. As she pondered what she could do in return, drowsiness crept over her, and despite the occasional rumble of thunder from the passing storm, she fell asleep.

Her next awareness was of a dog's mournful cry. The sound repeated several times too close to be coming from Spotsy in the carriage house. Gradually waking up, Deborah wondered if anyone else was hearing it. Tommy's breathing pattern remained heavy and even. Someone stirred down the hall and Deborah prayed Aunt Luella hadn't been disturbed by the noise. Softly, a knock sounded at the door, then Ottilia's hushed voice from the other side.

"Deborah? Tommy? Are you awake?"

Tommy stirred in his sleep.

Deborah scrambled to open the door, stepping into the hall that was dimly lit by the spill of light from her aunt and uncle's room at the far end. "Tommy's asleep. What is it?"

"Can't you hear it?" Ottilia asked, pausing until the dog wailed again. "Spotsy's at the side door. Go down and bring her up the back stairs to your room."

"Pardon?"

"You heard me. Go down and bring that noisy dog of yours up the back stairs to your room. Your Uncle Charles hasn't had a wink of sleep since Spotsy got out of the carriage house and commenced that pathetic wailing. Now go!"

"Yes, ma'am!"

Deborah turned to leave, but Ottilia caught her by the arm. "And one more thing."

"Yes, Aunt Ottilia?"

"Make sure you take that bothersome creature out of the house first thing in the morning. Understand?"

"I understand, Aunt Ottilia."

Within two minutes, Deborah led Spotsy into the bedroom. Tail wagging, she went to Tommy, licking the hand that dangled down from the arm of his easy chair.

"Spotsy, come," Deborah whispered, attempting to lure her atop the bed before Tommy awoke, but it was too late.

His eyes blinked open as he patted the dog's head. "I hope I'm dreaming, Spotsy, because you're not supposed to be in here."

Spotsy sat beside his chair, basking in his affection.

"It's all right," Deborah assured him. "Aunt Ottilia told me to bring her up here. She'd gotten out of the carriage house and was crying up a storm at the side door."

"And I slept through it?"

Deborah nodded. "Now you'd better get back to sleep. In a couple of hours you'll have to get on the train."

He scratched Spotsy's ear. "Did you hear that, girl? The boss says we've got to get our sleep. Now, lie down."

Obediently, she lay her head on her paws and let out a contented sigh. Sometime later, Deborah felt the bed jiggle, then Spotsy's cold, wet nose gentle as a butterfly kiss against her eyelashes. "Lie down, girl," she whispered, patting the mattress beside her. Again, Spotsy obeyed, settling into the crook of Deborah's legs.

At half-past five, Charles tapped on the door and called Tommy's name. The sound so startled Spotsy, she leaped off the bed, barking and growling at the bedroom door, refusing to quiet down. When Tommy was dressed and gone, Spotsy still would not sleep, pacing and whimpering over the absence of her master despite Deborah's quiet monologue of reassurances.

At six o'clock, Deborah gave up hope of getting more sleep and got dressed. With a wish and a prayer that Spotsy wouldn't encounter any rabbits or other distractions, Deborah leashed her and took her a short distance down

Kinsey Lane to relieve herself. Rain had left the road dotted with puddles, and despite Deborah's best efforts to prevent it, Spotsy managed to drink the murky water and collect a respectable amount of mud on her hairy paws.

When they arrived home, she wiped Spotsy's feet with an old towel, tied her to the side porch, then served her a bowl of leftover meat and some not-so-leftover eggs Vida mixed up. With pangs of hunger prompting Deborah to eat her own breakfast, she went inside to the dining room.

Aunt Luella had already settled herself at the table with a cup of tea and a peach muffin. "How's your new charge behaving this morning?" she asked with a smile.

Deborah rolled her eyes heavenward with dramatic exaggeration. "I didn't realize how demanding a new dog would be."

"How's that?"

Serving herself a glass of milk and a muffin, Deborah sat across from Aunt Luella to describe Spotsy's wailing at the side door, her unwillingness to sleep after Tommy had left, and her appetite for muddy water.

"Give her time. She's smart. She'll soon learn the routine here," Aunt Luella predicted.

"You're a lot more sure of that than I am," Deborah admitted, wondering how Aunt Luella could be so confident about everything—dogs, prayers, even the advice she had given her and Tommy on their wedding night. But it wasn't the old woman's confidence that piqued Deborah's interest in her the most. It was another aspect of the woman's life that prompted a question. "Aunt Luella, what's it like living in Calumet? It must be a lot different from Caledonia."

Aunt Luella laughed. "The two towns have only three things in common, far as I can tell." She paused, eyes twinkling as she took a bite of muffin.

"What are they?" Deborah asked.

"The first three letters of their names!" Aunt Luella replied, laughing again.

Deborah laughed, too. After a sip of milk and a bite of Vida's luscious peach muffin, she said wistfully, "If only Caledonia had a theater like Calumet's."

"It's quite the place," Aunt Luella agreed, proceeding to tell of the opera house that, unlike all others in Michigan, had been erected with public funds. She described its unique electric sign, its grand proscenium arch, and its unusual chandelier. "And I remember well the very first performance ever staged there—on the twentieth of March in 1900. My husband was still alive then, and he took me to see it," she continued. "It was *The Highwayman*, and absolutely everyone of importance in the Copper Country was in attendance. Tickets were reasonably priced except for the box seats. And how much do you suppose they charged for those?"

Deborah shrugged. "Five dollars?"

Aunt Luella shook her head. "Five times that amount."

"Twenty-five dollars for a box seat?" Deborah asked in awe. "Did anyone actually buy them?"

Aunt Luella nodded. "Nearly every one of the twelve hundred seats were filled—all except a few vacant seats on the wooden benches in the top gallery. My husband had received two box seat tickets from Mr. Agassiz—he's the president of the mine where my husband worked for over thirty years—so we had exceptional seating for the performance."

"Was it good?"

Aunt Luella nodded, a contemplative look overspreading her countenance. "The curtain went up a little late, as

77

I recall. The train bringing in the Portage Lake people was running behind schedule. But soon enough, the orchestra struck up the overture." She paused for a sip of tea. "The actors were quite accomplished—Reginald somebody-or-other—"

"De Koven?" Deborah asked.

"Yes, that's it. And the other fellow's name was Smith, I think."

"Harry B. Smith," Deborah supplied.

Aunt Luella nodded. "They were both fine thespians. But they were completely upstaged by none other than—"

"Let me guess. A horse?"

"You've seen the play?"

Deborah shook her head. "I only heard about it when I was living in Detroit with my mother."

Ottilia's voice preceded her into the dining room. "What was it you heard about when you were in Detroit with your mother, dear?"

"The horse Aunt Luella was just describing." Eager to abandon the topic of the theater, Deborah quickly asked, "Aunt Ottilia, I was wondering if you'd like to go over to Center Street with me after breakfast? Tommy gave me the prize money from his race yesterday with instructions to spend some of it on a wedding gift from him."

Ottilia took her place at the end of the table, stirring her coffee. "In *my* day, a husband gave his bride a very carefully chosen gift, an heirloom from his own family or a special item he had worked hard to purchase from his earnings." She sipped her coffee. "But I would have much preferred Tommy's method. At least that way, the bride ends up with something she will enjoy."

Aunt Luella smiled. "Why don't you tell Deborah just what it was that Charles gave you for a wedding gift?"

Ottilia started to laugh, nearly choking on her coffee. And when she tried to return her cup to its saucer, Deborah was certain it would spill on the fine white linen tablecloth before her aunt's shaking hands set it down.

Chapter
8

Deborah had never seen her aunt laugh uncontrollably. It was so unexpected and so contagious—a mature version of Caroline's woodpecker-like staccato laugh—that both she and Luella were laughing with Ottilia before she had calmed herself sufficiently to discuss the wedding gift Charles had given her.

"Aunt Luella, I assume you remember that silver piece."

She nodded. "I don't believe I've seen it since your wedding day."

"Nor have I!" Ottilia admitted, lapsing into laughter again.

Her curiosity high, Deborah said, "I can't imagine what Uncle Charles could have given you to cause all this laughter."

Luella answered. "It was a very fine serving piece of silver plate. It had a silver base about so long and so wide." Luella indicated a rectangle of about three inches by eight inches. "On the very front of this base stood the likeness of a proud silver peacock. The peacock was attached to a miniature silver cart about so square." She formed the size of a small box with her fingers. "It was lidded, and a u-shaped handle curved above it. The cart had engravings of fish and seaweed along the sides."

"What was supposed to be served in it?" Deborah asked.

"Sardines," Luella replied. "The cart was the same size as a sardine tin."

Her laughter under control, Ottilia explained, "Charles loves sardines—a real delicacy when we were married—so naturally he thought this was the perfect gift. The subject of sardines had never come up during our courtship, so he didn't know that I absolutely *abhor* even the smell of them! I was horribly disappointed. I had my heart set on a different gift entirely that I was certain Charles would give me."

"What was that?" Deborah asked.

"A cameo. His mother always wore a beautiful cameo—a full-figure one dressed in a flowing gown. I commented on it several times to Charles, but instead I received the sardine server. I was so let down that I never so much as lifted the lid on the thing. I simply packed it away. It's sitting in the attic of this house somewhere."

Luella said, "Since then, a most unusual tradition has developed between them concerning anniversary gifts."

Deborah waited eagerly for Ottilia's explanation.

"Every year I ask Charles what he wants for his anniversary, and he replies, 'a tin of sardines served in that silver sardine server I gave you on our wedding day.' Then he asks me what I want, and I tell him a cameo like his mother used to wear. Every year on the fifteenth of July, I give him a tin of sardines, but I make him go out on the porch and eat them from the tin so I won't have to smell them."

"And what does he give you?" Deborah asked.

"A rose bush for my garden. He even plants it for me!" Ottilia grew pensive. "Maybe next year he'll give me a cameo. We'll celebrate our twenty-fifth anniversary next July."

Deborah vaguely recalled something about a rose bush and sardines during one of her childhood summer visits with her cousins, but she hadn't understood it at the time. Her thoughts returning to the present, she said, "Since I'm

81

picking out my own wedding gift, I don't expect I'll have to wait twenty-five years for Tommy to give me exactly what I want."

Luella said, "I'm sure Ottilia will help you find the perfect gift. Charles still uses the one she gave him on their wedding day."

Ottilia smiled smugly. "A gold pen with his name engraved on the barrel. Until then, Charles was always losing his pen."

Deborah said, "I don't think Tommy is a gold pen type of husband."

Much to her surprise, Ottilia agreed. "Perhaps not, but we'll find something, and I can guarantee it will be a lot more useful than that sardine server was to me!"

After breakfast, Deborah and Ottilia headed down Lake Street, careful to skirt the puddles. The sun shone brightly, but the rain had cleared the moisture out of the air, and a pleasant breeze was keeping the heat to a comfortable level. The atmosphere was ripe with the smell of horse droppings, sweetened by an occasional hint of fresh-mown hay from the Kinseys' nearby field. Passing the grain elevator, Deborah saw that feed sacks lined the loading dock, ready for pick-up by rigs and farm wagons that were creaking and rattling as they bustled to and fro.

At Center Street the town was somewhat quieter. The bell on the door of Hale's Dry Goods and Grocers announced Deborah and her aunt's arrival, and Deborah was glad to see that they were the only customers in the shop at this early hour. Eugene Hale greeted them heartily, tugging on the points of the gray striped vest that fell shy of covering his belly as he came out from behind the cheese case.

"Good morning, ladies! Come to spend some of those

Labor Day winnings, have you, Mrs. Rockwell?"

Deborah smiled. "Yes, sir, if I find something to strike my fancy."

Ottilia said, "Deborah's in search of a wedding gift for her new husband. What have you along those lines?"

"So glad you asked! Right this way, ladies. I have any number of items that should suit."

Without hesitation, he showed them watches, watch chains, fobs, stick pins, cuff links, match safes, and fountain pens. Leaving them to wait on a woman in need of pillow ticking, he returned a few minutes later. "See anything to your liking, Mrs. Rockwell?"

When Deborah made no immediate reply, he said, "Come take a look at my catalog. There are hundreds—no, *thousands* of items you could order—with delivery in two weeks or less!"

"I . . . uh . . ."

Ottilia gave her a nudge. "It won't hurt to look, Deborah."

They followed Mr. Hale to the counter where he opened a catalog two inches thick. "Here's the table of contents, and there's an index, too. Peruse at your leisure, ladies!"

Ottilia ran her finger down the list, then turned to a page filled with fancy storage cases. "Look here, Deborah. There are collar and cuff boxes, glove boxes, handkerchief boxes, necktie cases—and look at these fancy shaving cases! One of these would make an excellent gift for Tommy."

Deborah studied the advertisements closely. The fanciest shaving case—with a scalloped edge—caught her eye. She read its description aloud. "'Open gilt trimming around outside, heavy embossed top, all made of silk plush lined with satin; contains detachable plush-covered mirror, fancy mug, comb, lather brush and scissors. Each . . . $4.50.'

Seems awfully expensive."

"But Tommy would love it," Ottilia assured her. "Should we have Mr. Hale order it for you?"

Deborah leafed through the next few pages showing hairpieces, brushes, combs, and mirrors. "Not yet. I want to browse some more."

"While you're browsing, I'm going to speak with Mr. Hale about something Aunt Luella asked me to buy."

Deborah turned to the front of the catalog and began thumbing through. Tommy certainly didn't need a Heidelberg electric belt to cure nervous disorders, nor did he need a new watch, a secret society emblem, silverware, clocks, or spectacles. The photographic equipment, stereopticons, and talking machines were intriguing, but intended for professional use in studios. She skipped the organ and piano department, violins advertised as "Genuine Stradivarius Model" for $7.85, and the guitars, mandolins, banjos, and autoharps. He needed no rifles, pistols, boxing gloves, or hammock. She also passed the fishing rods, tackle, and bicycles. Men's apparel came next. She thumbed past men's suits, overcoats of natural black Russian dogskin—shuddering at the very thought of wearing the skin of a dog—and paused on the page showing men's hats. There, a "men's Scotch Cheviot Golf Yacht Cap" caught her eye. Silently, she read the description.

Handsome broken plaids and nobby checks in brown and gray. Finest Russian leather sweat band, lined with soft, rich satin lining. Each . . . 50¢.

The cap looked perfect for Tommy, and would make a fine accompaniment to some other, more formal gift—the shaving case, perhaps—so she left the catalog open to that page and went to join her aunt and Mr. Hale at the other end of the counter.

The shopkeeper addressed her as he tied string around a medium-sized package. "Find something in the catalog to strike your fancy, Mrs. Rockwell?"

"As a matter of fact, I did. A Scotch Golf Yacht cap."

Mr. Hale knotted the string and broke it off. "A Scotch Golf Yacht cap? Right this way," he said, heading to the opposite side of the shop.

Deborah followed him, with Ottilia at her heels.

From a hat rack, he snatched a cap that looked like the one in the catalog. "Is this what you had in mind, Mrs. Rockwell?"

Deborah studied the cap, running her fingers over the various fabrics that had been sewn together, two of each pattern in six wedge-shaped sections to make the whole— brown and green check with black nubs; gray and black tweed; taupe and navy blue plaid with tiny red flecks. Handing it back to Mr. Hale, she said, "Wrap it up. It's perfect!"

"Will there be anything else?" he asked, heading for the other side of the counter.

"Not today, thank you."

Ottilia said, "Nothing from the catalog?"

"I'd like some time to think it over." She paid Mr. Hale with one of the five-dollar bills Tommy had given her, tucking four dollars and fifty cents change into her pocket.

Ottilia asked, "Have you given any thought as to what you'd like for a wedding gift from your Uncle Charles and me?"

Deborah shook her head.

Ottilia reached for a silver creamer displayed on a shelf near the counter. "I was thinking of something like this. Mr. Hale could have it engraved with your monogram."

Deborah ran her finger over the shiny, smooth surface of

the creamer, noting its unique, oversized spout and graceful handle. On the bottom was the stamp of a Cleveland silversmith, Horace Potter. "This is very nice, Aunt Ottilia, but—"

"Perhaps you'd prefer this," Ottilia suggested, indicating a small clock in a china case that had been hand-painted with delicate pansies and edged with gilt trim. Deborah didn't want to point out that the dainty piece was more in keeping with her aunt's taste than her own.

"Or maybe your Uncle Charles and I should give you a nice piece of cut glass. That's been the rage in wedding gifts for the past few years, hasn't it Mr. Hale?"

The shopkeeper nodded, coming out from behind the counter with just such a pitcher in hand. "I've sold several of these. Everyone seems to like them."

When he offered it to Deborah, she put palm out. "Not for the likes of me, Mr. Hale."

Ottilia said, "Maybe you and Tommy would like a lamp instead." Taking Deborah by the elbow, she led her to an enameled silver lamp with a pierced silver shade and lace ruffles. "This would look lovely in your room, don't you think? I've been admiring it for quite some time, thinking it would make a lovely gift from Parker and Caroline for our silver anniversary next summer, but I'd be more than willing to give it to you and Tommy, if you'd like."

While Deborah was looking it over, Mr. Hale returned with a silver basket in hand. "Here's a suggestion, Mrs. Rockwell, to hold your cakes for afternoon tea."

The basket had a fancy, fluted handle and a lacy pattern pierced into the sides. Deborah was wondering how to tell Mr. Hale that she would have no need of such a piece. Then something unusual on a shelf behind him caught her eye.

"I think I might have found the perfect thing!" Stepping

past him, she reached for a brown dish the shade of choco-late that had been made in the shape of a dolphin. On the top of its turned-up mouth was a cover with a handle shaped like a small fish. "This is it, Aunt Ottilia! You may give Tommy and me this dolphin dish."

"Are you sure?" she asked, inspecting the whimsical creation with notable skepticism.

To Mr. Hale, Deborah said, "Wrap it carefully. I'd hate for anything to happen to it."

Ottilia reluctantly turned it over to the shopkeeper for packaging, asking him to deliver it to her home along with the parcel for Aunt Luella and the cap for Tommy.

"You'll have your purchases by half-past five today," Mr. Hale promised, "sooner, if my hired boy doesn't daw-dle on his way from school. But you know how kids are the first day back, catching up with all that's new with their friends."

"Half-past five is fine," Ottilia assured him. Bidding him good-day, she and Deborah headed for the door. Ottilia paused on the sidewalk out front. "We should go directly to Mr. Kinsey's," she told Deborah. "Perhaps you'll find something there to give Tommy along with that cap you've picked out."

They crossed the near-empty street to Kinsey's General Store where the door was propped wide open by a flat iron. Again, Deborah was relieved to find no customers in the store—not even the shopkeeper, although she was certain he couldn't be far away. In the front were displays of school supplies Deborah had seen during the Labor Day festivities. A sign hanging in the center aisle touted pumps, rope, bas-kets, wood, and willow ware. Beyond the school parapher-nalia, practical household goods jammed shelves on both sides of the aisle—sprinkling cans, rural mailboxes, coal scuttles, copper and iron kettles, oil cloth, and tins of coffee, coconut, crackers, peanut butter, and chocolate. Deborah was wondering where gift merchandise might be displayed when Mr. Kinsey emerged from a back room to greet them.

"Good morning! How may I help you ladies on this fine day?"

Ottilia said, "We've come to see your selection of gift items. Are they still in the alcove at the back?"

Mr. Kinsey's thick mustache rose with a grin that spread wide above his narrow chin. "Indeed, they are. Anything in particular I can show you?"

"We'll just browse, if you don't mind," Ottilia replied, stepping past him into the small alcove that had been reserved for the fragile, more expensive goods. Lifting the lid of an ornate sugar bowl, she told Deborah, "I've admired this piece several times. Isn't it charming?"

Deborah ran her finger over the raised decorations on the pale yellow glass. "Charming enough to sit on your table, Aunt Ottilia."

"Or yours some day. Would you like it?"

Deborah hesitated, saying, "No, thank you, but I think you should have it."

"Then I just might treat myself to it."

Finding a porcelain owl on the next shelf, Deborah said, "This is different—a night light. I believe I'll take Mr. Owl home with me."

When Mr. Kinsey had wrapped the owl and the sugar bowl, they headed for the door, pausing to browse a display case of brooches near the front of the store. A woman of about Ottilia's age entered and Deborah's aunt greeted her cordially.

"Good morning, Grace."

With a frigid glance from eyes of blue ice, the woman

silently brushed past them, her narrow chin held high. She proceeded to the counter where she recited her list of needs to Mr. Kinsey.

Ottilia whispered in Deborah's ear, "I wonder what's bothering Grace Nixon today?"

Her stomach sinking, Deborah whispered in reply, "She's probably heard something bad about me."

"Just you never mind," Ottilia whispered. They browsed for a few minutes longer and were moving toward the door when the Nixon woman caught up with them.

Pausing beside Deborah, she said disparagingly, "And to think I was considering sending my daughter to the likes of you for vocal lessons!"

Ottilia stiffened. "Grace Nixon, that's no way to speak to my niece!"

The woman's brow arched. "It's not? Well, let me tell you, if *my* niece were a piece of soiled calico—"

Ottilia cut in. "Deborah is a married woman and her husband—"

"Her husband is a fool!" Chin high, the Nixon woman made her exit.

Chapter

9

Deborah's face grew hot with shame.

Ottilia started for the door. "Grace Nixon should talk! It's time I remind her that her own daughter was born but a short six months after she and Harry were wed!"

Deborah caught her aunt by the elbow. "Please, Aunt Ottilia, let's just go home. I'm not feeling well." She held her stomach, which suddenly felt like a butterfly riot.

"You are looking a tad peaked," Ottilia said. "Should I hire a buggy from Daklin's Livery to take us home?"

"I can walk," Deborah assured her, quickly heading out the door. The streets were busier now and Deborah focused on the sidewalk, hoping desperately that no one would issue an insult before she reached the safe haven of the big white house on Railroad Street.

Ottilia entered through the front door while Deborah went around to the side porch to find Spotsy. Panic set in when the dog was not to be found on her rope.

"Spotsy!" she cried, setting down her parcel to gaze across the backyard and field beyond.

A sharp bark sounded from the opposite side of the screen door. Deborah quickly let Spotsy out, stooping down to hug the dog and receive wet and sloppy welcome-home kisses. Inside, she could hear Ottilia lecturing Vida about the proper place for a dog, and Luella insisting that she alone was to blame for Spotsy being allowed in the house.

Leaving the domestic dispute behind, Deborah untied the rope from the porch rail. Using it as a leash, she took Spotsy on a short walk down the lane before tying her up again and taking her parcel inside. As soon as Deborah disappeared from the dog's sight, Spotsy whined. Deborah turned back, only to become the target of Ottilia's disapproval.

"She'll never learn to be content by herself if you cater to her every whimper. Just ignore her. She'll quiet down."

When Deborah hesitated, Ottilia shooed her away. "Go on! Let her be!"

Deborah headed up the stairs feeling guiltier with every step. In her room, she quickly unwrapped the owl nightlight and plugged it into an outlet near the door, then pulled the shades. Its eyes glowed amber, bathing the rest of its body in a soft, golden sheen.

Raising the shades again, she gazed down the street at the train depot wishing this day were over and Tommy was stepping off the 7:25 on his way home for dinner. The clock on the dresser read a quarter past ten. How would she ever pass the remaining nine hours until his return?

She rummaged in her bottom dresser drawer for the embroidery supplies she'd kept there before her ill-fated sojourn at the "resort" and found them undisturbed. Centering her hoop on a twelve-inch square of white linen, she gathered together needle, floss, and scissors and headed down to the front porch, leaving them on one of the wicker chairs while she brought a loudly complaining Spotsy around and tied her to the front rail. In less than a minute, the dog had settled down at her feet. With a sigh of contentment, she rested her chin on her paws, let out a sigh, and closed her eyes.

Deborah yearned for the tranquility that came so easily

to Spotsy. Instead, she felt edgy over the encounter with the Nixon woman. Deborah couldn't accept the fact that each time she ventured out, she might become the target of insults and slights, even in the company of someone as respected in the community as her Aunt Ottilia.

Deborah threaded her needle with black floss to outline the wings of a butterfly and began to stitch, trying her best to put the Nixon woman from her mind. But hurtful words echoed in her head . . . *piece of soiled calico . . . her husband is a fool . . . And to think I was considering sending my daughter to the likes of you for vocal lessons.* It was clear to Deborah that, if she pursued her cousin Caroline's idea of the music academy, Grace Nixon would see to it that no students enrolled for singing lessons.

When Deborah paused to assess her needlework, she discovered that all these thoughts about Grace Nixon had made her more tense than she'd realized. Her black stitches were way too tight, causing the linen to distort. Picking them out with her needle, she started over again. As she worked the stitches more carefully, she began to dream about a place where she could start over. It would be a place where no one knew of her past. A place where she and Tommy could raise a family and no one would know that this first child wasn't his. And it would be a place where she could stand on a stage, deliver a song, and curtsey to the applause of an appreciative audience. And though she'd never been there, she imagined that she was on the stage of the Calumet Theatre, singing her heart out to a packed audience that responded with thunderous applause and whistles of praise.

Minutes later, her thoughts still hundreds of miles away, she heard the telephone ringing and Ottilia answering, although she couldn't make out her aunt's words. Shortly after, Ottilia came out the front door.

"Mrs. Barber is on the telephone. She'd like to speak to you about singing at the literary and musical entertainment at the church tonight."

How she wanted to help Mrs. Barber, the music teacher who had spent hours and hours transforming her untrained, ordinary voice into a finely tuned instrument with an impressive range and volume. But the very thought of going out in public again, let alone performing, set her stomach off anew. "Please tell her I'm sorry to decline, but I am feeling unwell."

"You'll probably be over it by this afternoon. Are you sure you won't reconsider? Mrs. Barber says that Leona and Russell Beeler were each scheduled to sing solos, but they're both so congested with hay fever, they can't sing a note between them."

Deborah shook her head. "Sorry, I can't. Besides, I'd like to spend the evening with Tommy."

"Whatever you say," Ottilia replied with obvious skepticism.

A few moments later, she returned to stand directly in front of Deborah. "I'm terribly disappointed that you won't help Mrs. Barber."

Deborah remained silent, knots tightening within as her gaze slowly rose to meet Ottilia's.

Her aunt continued. "This indisposition of yours is only temporary—a little perturbation over Grace Nixon's bad manners. As for Tommy, the two of you have your entire lives to spend together."

When Deborah's silence continued, Ottilia went on.

"It's bad enough that you repaid Mrs. Barber for all her hours of voice lessons by running off with that Taman fellow and singing in a 'resort.' I can't believe that you won't

93

do her even this one little favor!"

Deborah stood, anger rising. "I'm sorry, I can't. Please, let's not discuss this any further." Tossing needlework on her chair, she pressed past Ottilia and untied Spotsy. "Come on, girl, we're going for a walk."

Nearing the rose arbor, she realized she had not heard the last from Ottilia.

"Don't take that mutt near my garden! I'll have her hide if she ruins my prize roses!"

Cutting across the back yard to the lane, she and Spotsy wandered between the rows of ripe corn. All Deborah could think about was how badly she wished Tommy were home—Tommy, who got along with everyone so well. How desperately she needed him as a buffer between her and her aunt right now.

Nearing the end of the field, she saw that the Kinsey's were beginning to harvest their corn. Large shocks stood as sentinels where the laborers had finished their work. Spotsy barked at a wagon bumping toward them on the lane. Deborah pulled the leash in tight, using all her strength to restrain the dog when she was determined to give chase.

Returning home, Deborah spent the balance of the morning on the front porch, keeping her distance from Ottilia. At the midday meal, she sat silently munching oyster crackers and sipping the chicken broth that Vida had prepared to soothe her touchy stomach. She was wondering how to pass the long afternoon hours when Ottilia addressed her.

"While you were walking Spotsy, Mr. Bechtel delivered three bushels of apples. I expect your help in the kitchen after lunch, peeling them while Vida and I can applesauce."

"Yes, Aunt Ottilia," Deborah replied, hoping the hours would pass with a minimum of conflict. To her surprise, the time passed more quickly than she had expected. Spotsy, though noisy at first, soon quieted down for an afternoon nap on the side porch. Aunt Luella, hampered in her apple-peeling efforts by arthritic fingers, contributed to the efforts with entertaining recollections of her youth in Lower Michigan, of her move north and adjustment to life in the Keweenaw, and of her courtship and marriage in Calumet.

Deborah found her thoughts drifting to Tommy when Aunt Luella described her wedding—a small one held in her parents' home—and the early days of her marriage to a miner. She had missed her husband during his long hours at work—worrying and praying that he would come to no harm in the mine.

When the telephone rang at a quarter past five, Ottilia went immediately to the parlor to answer it. Returning to the kitchen, she told Deborah, "You and I have just become 'widows of the firm' for the balance of the week."

When Deborah offered a puzzled look in response, Ottilia explained her meaning.

"That was Mr. Beeler, the only man in town with a telephone connection to Grand Rapids. Charles rang him up and asked him to pass along a message. He's so busy at the law firm that he and Tommy won't be home until Friday, at the earliest." To Luella, she said, "Charles sends his apologies and his love to you. I know he's terribly disappointed not to spend more time with you before you take your leave on Friday."

Luella nodded in understanding. "He's an ambitious one, that Charles—the most successful nephew I have."

Ottilia laughed, explaining to Deborah, "Charles is the *only* nephew she has."

Moments later, the delivery boy from Hale's arrived

with the brown dolphin dish, the cap for Tommy, and the parcel for Luella. Deborah carried the items upstairs, leaving Luella's brown paper package on her bed, then she returned to the kitchen.

The telephone rang again, and once more, Ottilia answered. This time, she immediately summoned Deborah to the parlor. Hand over the mouthpiece, she told Deborah, "It's Mrs. Barber. She still hasn't found anyone to fill in for the Beelers. Since Tommy won't be home until Friday, I think you owe it to her to sing at the church tonight."

Deborah took the receiver from Ottilia, reluctantly agreeing against her better judgement to meet Mrs. Barber at the church in an hour to go over two solos she'd sung many times in the past.

When she'd hung up, Ottilia said, "Thank you for agreeing to help Mrs. Barber. Go on upstairs and change. Vida will have your supper ready by the time you come down."

Stomach souring at the thought of going out in public again, Deborah said, "Just a cup of chicken broth and a few crackers. You know I can't sing on a full stomach."

Alone in her room, Deborah changed from her simple white blouse and dark skirt to the pink gown she'd worn on her wedding day. Carefully transferring her butterfly pin to the delicate fabric of the bodice, she recalled the vision she'd had of herself taking flight with a flock of those elegant winged creatures, ascending to a height where worldly cares could no longer trouble her. Eyes drifting shut, she continued to finger the pin while thoughts soared. Somehow she *must* escape the butterfly net of Caledonia, freeing herself of the condemnation that shrouded her with unhappiness. But even as the net magically dissolved in thin air, tethers appeared on either wing, held fast by Tommy who grounded her flight like the string on a kite.

Ottilia's voice cut through her daydream, coming from the opposite side of her door. "Deborah, your soup is hot. Are you dressed?"

Too swiftly, her feet touched ground and she hastened to the door. "I'm ready, Aunt Ottilia." She'd no sooner spoken the words than she wanted to take them back. She *wasn't* ready. She'd *never* be ready to expose herself again to the shunning that was fast becoming her lot in this town. But she stepped out with false confidence, following her aunt downstairs to the dining room without complaint, playing the part that was expected of her, and was now testing her acting skills to the limit.

The organ strains of Mrs. Barber's accompaniment greeted Deborah as she entered the sanctuary an hour before the program was to begin. Picking up a copy of the program from a stack near the door, she saw that one of the Beelers had been listed as the second performer of the evening, and the other as the ninth. The schedule would give her plenty of recovery time between solos.

Within minutes she had gone over her vocal warm-up and the two pieces she would perform. Others on the program began to trickle in—Edna Bowman, Alice Wilson, and Chester Allen who would each present readings; the Misses Maud and Mildred Phillips who would perform a vocal duet; and the members of the Clemens orchestra who would open and close the program. While the orchestra members warmed up and tuned their instruments, Deborah retreated to Pastor Phillips's study with the others that waited anxiously for their moment on the platform. She could hear the hushed voices of the audience as people from the village and township began to fill the seats. Mildred Phillips opened the door a crack to peek out.

"Mary and Jane Wenger are here. So are Pearl Colby and Sada McCullough. And here come Carrie Diefenbaker and Ellen Kreidler." Mildred named former classmates of Deborah's from high school. "The way it looks, we'll have nearly every seat filled." To Deborah, she said, "Your Aunt Ottilia and Great-aunt Luella are already sitting in the right front pew with my mother."

Deborah nodded acknowledgment, deciding to focus on Aunt Luella when the time came for her solo. She silently reviewed the words and melody until Mrs. Barber came in to say the orchestra was about to begin.

"When they're finished, I'll announce the change in the program and introduce you, Deborah." Pressing fingers together in the shape of a heart—the sign of encouragement Mrs. Barber traditionally offered her students before a performance—she turned to the door, waiting and listening while the musicians struck up a lively rendition of *The Yankee Doodle Boy*. When the last strains of the orchestra faded away, she motioned for Deborah to come stand by the door. As soon as the applause died down, she stepped out to make her announcement.

"Ladies and gentlemen, thank you for coming. I'm sure you're going to enjoy your evening. I regret to inform you that there has been a slight change in the program. Leona and Russell Beeler are ill and will not be performing. Instead, Mrs. Thomas Rockwell has graciously agreed to fill in. She will now sing one of the most beloved airs from Handel's *Messiah*, *I Know That My Redeemer Liveth*.

As Mrs. Barber took her place at the organ Deborah stepped out to the center of the platform, gaze downcast while she drew a deep breath. The sanctuary fell silent. Not a program rattled. Deborah was certain she could have heard the fluttering of a butterfly's wings, the place was so quiet. Folding her hands at her waist in the tradition of the classic vocal soloist, she prepared to give Mrs. Barber a nod to begin. But as she lifted her gaze, a sudden movement in the front row caught her eye.

There stood Grace Nixon!

With a flick of her wrist, she tossed her program down on the pew. "Well, I never!" she said loudly, turning to the young girl beside her. "Come along, Julianna. We're not going to listen to the likes of *her.*" With great indignation, she strode, heels clacking, toward the back of the sanctuary, her daughter following in perfect imitation.

Not waiting for Deborah's signal, Mrs. Barber sounded the first notes of her introduction.

Deborah's heart pounded. Her face grew hot. She was certain that the pink in her dress paled in comparison to the rosy color flooding her cheeks. She wished she were invisible. She wished she could spread butterfly wings and take flight!

Chapter

10

The first several bars of introduction had already passed. Only a few more remained before Deborah must sing. But she felt frozen, unable to move her jaw and open her mouth. In the haze of her humiliation, the audience had become a blur.

She blinked. Her eyes focused. There was Aunt Luella with a determined smile. She mouthed the words, "You can do it!"

Mrs. Barber paused on the note prior to Deborah's entrance into the piece.

Deborah drew a breath.

Her lips parted.

The melody flowed from deep within like an angel's voice on high.

I know that my redeemer liveth, and that he shall stand at the latter day upon the earth.

Upon her return home with Ottilia and Luella, Deborah didn't wait to change out of her gown before walking Spotsy. She immediately untied her from the side porch and headed down the lane despite the encroaching darkness. While Spotsy sniffed and relieved herself and indulged her natural instinct to investigate every scent in her path, Deborah reflected on the evening's performance. Despite the Nixon woman's snubbing, she had sung as well as she ever had—maybe better. Even so, the audience's reaction to her was subdued, the applause sparse by comparison to others on the program whose songs or readings were delivered with no greater skill than Deborah's and in most cases much more amateurishly. Deborah knew the difference between polite applause and enthusiastic applause. There was no doubt in her mind that she had been the recipient of the former.

Returning to the side porch with Spotsy, she tied her there and went inside, following the voices of Ottilia and Luella to the parlor where they were taking tea. It was Ottilia's opinion that filled the air when Deborah reached the door.

"I tell you that Grace Nixon had no business walking out the way she did. Who is she to make a display of righteous indignation when her own past is blotted with sin?"

Reluctant to lend audience to Ottilia's venting, Deborah turned away, only to change her mind at Aunt Luella's prompting.

"Please join us, child. I have something I want to say to you."

While Ottilia poured her a cup of tea and passed the plate of butter cookies—which suddenly looked tempting now that the strain of the performance had passed—Luella continued.

"Your voice is a great gift from God. I pray you'll continue to use it to His glory, despite what others may think."

Before she could reply, Ottilia chimed in. "And pay no heed whatever to those Nixons. I've half a mind to inform Julianna that she's really three months older than she thinks, and that her mother changed the date of her birthday celebration just so she wouldn't know that her folks got too familiar with one another before their wedding."

101

Luella promptly responded. "I trust that's only a threat, Ottilia. Two wrongs don't make a right."

"Try telling that to Grace Nixon. She's perfected the art of turning two wrongs into a right!"

"I don't intend saying a word to Mrs. Nixon. According to the Good Book, vengeance belongs to the Lord. And as for the righteous indignation that bothers you so in the Nixon woman, you've got to admit you've been practicing hard at it all night, yourself."

Ottilia drew a sharp breath but refrained from arguing, taking a long sip of tea instead. In that silent moment, Deborah could hear Spotsy beginning to whine, unwilling to remain alone on the porch when she could hear voices inside. She was about to go get the dog when Luella set aside her teacup and rose.

"If the two of you will excuse me, I think I'll retire. The outing to the church was good for heart and soul, but these old bones are worn out and in need of a night's rest."

Deborah stood. "I'll see you up the stairs. It's time I turned in, myself." To Ottilia she said, "Should I take Spotsy upstairs for the night?"

"Absolutely! I won't have her ruining our sleep. Good night."

Quickly, Deborah untied Spotsy from the side porch. With her rope leash in one hand, and the other on Luella's elbow to steady her, the three made their way up the stairs. When they reached Luella's door, the old woman invited them in.

"Come, sit a minute. I have something I want to give you."

Deborah took the straight chair beside Luella's rocker while Spotsy settled on the floor so that her chin rested on her mistress's feet.

From the bedside stand, Luella retrieved a present wrapped in a length of beautiful white lace and tied up with white satin ribbon. "This is my wedding gift to you and Mr. Rockwell. I wish he were here, but since he won't be home for three more days, I'd just as soon give it to you now."

Deborah could tell from the feel of it that the lacy fabric hid a book. When she untied the ribbon she saw that the lace wasn't just a length of fabric, but a dresser scarf, and that the book wasn't just any book, but a Family Bible bound in black leather that was lettered in fancy gold type. Opening carefully to the first page, she read Luella's inscription.

To Deborah and Thomas

May God bless you with
Joyful days
Happy songs
Heavenly praise
And a marriage long

"Aunt" Luella Dunston

Below the inscription, lines had been filled in with her name and Tommy's and the date of their marriage. Blank lines followed for the birth dates of their children. Conflicting emotions battled within as Deborah's imagination took divergent paths into the distant future. One path was a butterfly-filled lane. Along it, she met children, grandchildren, and great-grandchildren whose names would be written on the next several lines. The other path was dark and foreboding, ending abruptly on the verge of a bottomless black pit. She shuddered at the thought.

Luella pressed her hand against Deborah's cheek. "You're not taking a chill, are you? You don't feel feverish, but with that stomach of yours being off—"

Deborah squeezed Luella's hand with her own warm one. "I'm fine, just moved by your gift."

Luella laughed. "I've given away a good number of Bibles in my lifetime—to the students in Sabbath school— and this is the first time anyone has shivered at receiving the Good Book!"

Deborah chuckled, but the sound was mirthless even to her own ears.

Luella turned solemn. "What is it, child? What's troubling you tonight? It's more than that Nixon woman, I fear."

A short silence later, Luella continued, her voice full of quiet compassion.

"I can't imagine the hurt you must feel at all you suffered this past summer, but there's Someone who can. His name is Jesus. Do you know Jesus, Deborah? Have you given your heart to him?"

She thought a moment before answering. "Years and years ago, during one of the summers when I was staying with Aunt Ottilia and Uncle Charles, Caroline and I both went forward during a tent meeting and gave our hearts to Jesus. But most of the time since then, it seemed like He just wasn't there."

"But He was, and He knows your heartache," Luella assured her. "He's suffered as much as you have, and worse, *far* worse. Open your heart to Him again, child, and trust Him to help you." Sliding the Bible onto her own lap, she opened it and read, "'Many sorrows shall be to the wicked: but he that trusteth in the Lord, mercy shall compass him about.' It says so right here in Psalm 32, verse 10." Bowing her head, she placed her hand over Deborah's and prayed, "Heavenly Father, I ask you right now to grant mercy to Deborah according to your promise. Let her see Your face, hear Your voice, and claim Your promises for her own, in the precious name of Jesus, Amen." With a squeeze of her hand, she returned the open Bible to Deborah.

Deeply touched by the prayer, Deborah focused on the page, reading the words of the Psalmist to herself. *Many sorrows shall be to the wicked: but he that trusteth in the Lord, mercy shall compass him about.* How wonderful was the promise, but Deborah was unable to trust completely in God when He had seemingly abandoned her in her greatest hour of need.

Luella must have sensed her discomfort, for she asked, "What is it, Deborah? What's on your mind?"

"I'm wondering how I can believe in a God who ignores me?"

Luella's brow arched.

Deborah explained. "When I was at the 'resort,' I prayed every day for God to rescue me, but for ten long weeks, He ignored me."

"Then He sent Tommy to rescue you."

"But He ignored me for ten whole weeks! I suffered such humiliation. . . " Deborah broke off, realizing she could never put the nightmare into words.

Moisture welled in the old woman's kind blue eyes. "I'm sorry, child, I don't know why God waited ten weeks to send your rescuer—we may never know the answer to that question until Judgement Day—but this I do know. He's given you a new chance, a fine husband, and an opportunity to make your life count for good. Now, you can make something wonderful of it with His help!"

Deborah thought, *Easier said than done.*

Again, head bowed, Luella's hand covered hers. "Almighty God, Deborah is searching now—searching for answers to difficult questions, searching for the direction You want her to go. Lead her, Father God, fulfill Your promise to be a lamp unto her feet and a light unto her path, in Jesus' precious name, we pray, Amen."

"Amen," Deborah echoed with meaning. She closed the Bible, folded the dresser scarf, and coiled the ribbon. Leaning to kiss Luella's cheek, she said, "Thank you for your gifts and your prayers. I want to make something good of my life, but . . . " Again, she broke off, all too aware of the life growing within her, and her own doubts as to how this unplanned child could lead to something good.

"'Trust in the Lord with all thine heart; and lean not unto thine own understanding. In all thy ways acknowledge Him, and He shall direct thy paths.' Proverbs 3, verses five and six."

"I'll try to remember them. Good night, Aunt Luella."

"Good night, and God bless."

In her room, Deborah spread the new dresser scarf out on her dresser and lay the Bible in the center. When she had changed into her nightgown, she knelt beside her bed. Spotsy lay at her side while she prayed. "God, I want to make my life count for good. And I need to find a place where I'm not the constant object of scorn. Help me, please. In Jesus' name, Amen." She slid beneath the sheet and Spotsy hopped up, settling down with a sigh. Rather than falling asleep, ideas started flowing through Deborah's mind—ideas of how to rid herself of the shunning that had turned her life miserable. Details came to her, flowing with a strong current she couldn't ignore. Certainly they were God's plan for her future. She would take action starting

106

early tomorrow morning.

In his small apartment in Grand Rapids, Tommy lay back on his bed unable to sleep. Even after a work session that had lasted well into the evening at Charles's office, and a brisk run along the bank of the Grand River, he felt wide-awake, images of his bride filling his mind. How he wished Deborah had been here to greet him at the door. He could see her now, the fairness of her face, her dawn-tinted cheeks, and melon-pink lips. Her shining blond hair would be caught loosely in a topknot with fragile tendrils caressing her cheeks. How he wished he were close enough to brush a fingertip against her silken skin.

He wondered if she was thinking of him now, this very moment, and imagined that she was, and wanted to share her day. He wondered how Spotsy was getting along, and felt guilty that he hadn't even had time to buy the leather leash and harness as he'd promised. He'd do it tomorrow.

He thought about tomorrow and the next day and the next. How could he last without Deborah until Friday evening, now that he had rescued her from the jaws of iniquity and taken her for his wife?

He couldn't spend weekdays apart from her the way Charles often did with Ottilia. Distance might be fine for a marriage that was long, and strong, and accustomed to regular absences, but it wouldn't do for his marriage to Deborah. Ottilia's offer to put them up in Caledonia had seemed to be the best arrangement when suggested. He could see now that it was no good when Charles expected him to remain in Grand Rapids for days at a time. But he couldn't expect Deborah to be happy in this tiny place, where they wouldn't even have enough room to keep from bumping elbows, and wouldn't be allowed to keep Spotsy.

Then an idea came to him, a remedy so obvious he should have thought of it from the start. He would act on it first thing tomorrow!

Chapter

11

Spotsy nudged Deborah awake at the crack of dawn the following morning, obviously in need of relieving herself. Pulling wrapper on, she took the dog downstairs and tied her to the rope at the side porch. Vida was already busy in the kitchen and offered to feed the dog while Deborah went upstairs to dress. Twenty minutes later, she came down to take Spotsy for a morning walk.

A golden sun had cleared the horizon and now lent the promise of a perfect September day. Spotsy pulled in the direction of the lane and Deborah half ran to keep up with her. A few minutes later, they turned back, but instead of going home, Deborah took Spotsy across the railroad tracks to the depot.

Having concluded a piece of business with the railroad agent, she led Spotsy to the lumberyard where one of the young fellows stacking boards on a wagon asked if he could pet the dog. Deborah paused, finding it the perfect opportunity to inquire as to the whereabouts of the manager.

The young man pointed toward the other end of the loading dock. "That'd be Mr. Wilson, the tall fellow down yonder."

Deborah quickly located him and after a brief conversation that involved the taking of measurements and payment for services, Deborah turned toward home. For the first time in months, she felt lighthearted, buoyant, as if her butterfly friends had returned to lift her by the shoulders so she could walk on air.

During the mid-morning break at the Chappell law firm, Tommy quietly carried a cup of hot tea into Charles's office so as not to disturb his boss who was poring over the document Tommy had finished preparing for him earlier that morning. Setting the beverage near the telephone on the wide mahogany desk, he discreetly consulted the list of important numbers lying there, memorizing the number for Parker and Roxana's apartment. Back at his own desk in the anteroom, he rang them up. Roxana answered.

"Hello, Roxana. This is Tommy Rockwell. I was wondering if you and Parker had located a larger apartment yet."

"Yes, we have, and it's just been vacated. We're moving this weekend!"

Tommy could hear the excitement in Roxana's voice, then disappointment as she continued.

"The only bad thing is, we've already paid for the entire month here and our landlord won't refund any of our money."

"Then you're in luck!" Tommy exclaimed, knowing it wasn't luck at all but God's guidance that had prompted him to solve both the Chappells' problems and his own. "I'll gladly pay you for the remainder of the month if your landlord will accept Deborah and me as tenants. My place is too small for the two of us, but yours would be just right."

"I thought you and Deborah were staying with Mother and Dad Chappell in Caledonia."

"We are, but . . ." Tommy explained his long work hours and how he missed Deborah.

"I'm sure our landlord will be more than happy to rent to you. We'll be out by noon, Saturday. You're welcome to move in then. The place is fully furnished. All you need is your personal effects. And Tommy, if you want to bring Deborah over to see the place before Saturday, just ring me up."

"Thanks, Roxana, but that won't be necessary. It's kind of a surprise." Before Tommy hung up, he asked, "By the way. How does your landlord feel about dogs?"

"He doesn't allow them, he says, but he's got two of his own living with him downstairs."

"Thanks, Roxana. Good bye." Tommy hung up, ecstatic that he had solved both the problem of his separation from Deborah and the young Chappells' double rent dilemma. Like Parker and Roxana, he and Deborah would want more rooms for raising a baby later on, but he needn't worry about that now. He went into Charles's office, thankful that his boss had finished reading the document and was sipping his tea before it turned cold as so often happened.

Charles greeted him with a smile and a compliment on the speed and accuracy of his work, then listened with interest as Tommy explained his plans for new living arrangements.

He concluded by saying, "It's not that I don't appreciate all you and Mrs. Chappell are doing to make us feel at home in Caledonia. It's just that Deborah is there and I'm here, and by the looks of the work coming into your office, I'll be spending lots of weeks like this one working every night."

Charles confirmed his conclusion with a nod, his expression empathetic. "I remember what it was like to be a newlywed." He paused, eyes twinkling. "I could hardly wait to get home to Ottilia, and when my boss kept me after hours, I could barely keep my mind on my work for missing her so." He gazed out the window thoughtfully, then abruptly refocused on Tommy. "I'll tell you what I want

111

you to do. On lunch hour today, go over to Herkner Jewelers and pick out a nice present for Deborah." He reached into his pocket, then pressed several golden eagle coins into Tommy's hand. "These ought to help you out— a wedding gift from Ottilia and me." Picking up a page of legal notes from his desk, he shoved it at Tommy. "Now promise me you'll keep your mind on your work until lunch. I need you to look these up and have them on my desk before noon."

"Yes, sir! And thank you, sir!"

Deborah thought Wednesday in Caledonia would never end. With every train whistle that blew, she wished desperately that she were on the rails riding out of town. The morning passed much as had Tuesday afternoon, pealing apples for Ottilia's canned applesauce. By midday they had finished putting by the apples Mr. Bechtel had delivered, all except enough for Vida to bake a pie, and had started canning tomatoes that had come from Mr. Kinsey's farm. The chore reminded Deborah of a time many years earlier when she had visited her aunt and uncle in the town of Marshall. Her naughty ways had earned her the punishment of helping her aunt to can tomatoes. She hadn't liked the chore then, and liked it less now. When the evening meal was served, including sliced tomatoes and fresh apple pie, Deborah could find no appetite, but managed to eat some of everything so as not to hurt Vida's feelings or invite Ottilia's criticism.

Thursday brought little change. Morning and afternoon were spent canning the last of the tomatoes. By evening Deborah could almost believe her marriage to Tommy had never existed. In her room alone with Spotsy, she picked up the Bible Aunt Luella had given her and opened it near the

112

center. It opened to the same Psalm Luella had read from earlier, Psalm 32. Certain words jumped out at her.

I will instruct thee and teach thee in the way which thou shalt go: I will guide thee with mine eye.

The passage seemed to speak to her specifically of the persecution she had felt in Caledonia and confirm the plan God had revealed to her on Tuesday night for remedying the situation. Feeling encouraged and emboldened by the text, she closed the Bible and re-wrapped it in the dresser scarf, tying it up with the same satin ribbon Luella had used. Then she made preparation to act on God's direction, setting out the hat she had bought for Tommy and writing a note to go with it.

Climbing into bed half an hour later, Spotsy settled alongside, she closed her eyes without any expectation that sleep would come. Her mind raced ahead like a locomotive on a straight stretch of track. Aunt Luella would be taking the one o'clock train tomorrow afternoon, heading for Chicago. Tommy would arrive with Uncle Charles on the evening train at 7:25. Again and again she reviewed her plans for an early start to her day, falling into a light sleep that was interrupted by the whistle and rumble of the early morning train going east at 1:15. After four more hours of restless waiting, she arose in darkness and dressed, then tied on Spotsy's rope leash. With the small valise she had packed for herself in one hand and Spotsy's leash in the other, she led the dog downstairs and out the side door.

Tommy could hardly wait for the train to pull into Caledonia on Friday night. All the way from Grand Rapids, he thought of nothing but Deborah and how much better the

113

depot would look if she were standing outside it waiting to greet him when the train rolled into town. But he knew in his heart that it was very likely she would wait for him at the house, so he also imagined her sitting on the veranda in a white wicker chair, smiling and waving as he approached.

He would brush a kiss against her delicate, silken cheek denying his heart's desire to kiss her full on the mouth. They would join Ottilia and Charles at the dinner table for one of Vida's home-cooked dinners. He could taste it now—her delicious roast beef, mashed potatoes smothered in thick gravy, homemade cinnamon rolls, and fresh-baked apple pie for dessert.

After dinner, he would put Spotsy's new harness and leash on her and he and his Butterfly would take her for a walk down the lane. He would ask his wife about her week and he would hear all about her shopping and how she had spent the money he had won in the race. She would laugh and tell him she hoped he didn't mind, but she had gone shopping every day and spent every last penny of the fifteen dollars on whatnots, clothes, millinery, and other fine pretties that had taken her fancy at Mr. Hale's and Mr. Kinsey's stores.

Then she would tell him how she had missed him, and how she hoped he wouldn't have to spend any more weeks like this one, working at the office until well past the dinner hour every night. He would take her by the shoulders, look straight into her cornflower blue eyes, and tell her that they needn't spend another week apart, ever again.

"We're moving to our own place in Grand Rapids, to the apartment Roxana and Parker had! I'll take you to the city tomorrow so you can see it."

"But, what about Spotsy?" she would ask. "I won't move unless Spotsy can come, too."

"Spotsy can come," he would assure her, thrilled that the two had developed a loyalty to one another in his absence.

Then he would describe the apartment to her in detail—the large room that doubled as a parlor and dining area; one end furnished with two forest green velvet chairs. He would describe the lacy ivory curtains hanging at the tall windows that overlooked the quiet street, and he would tell her of a modest but pleasant eating area at the other end of the room with its bay window overlooking a small, fenced backyard. He would not speak of the bedroom unless she asked. Neither the tiny sleeping chamber nor the closet-sized bathroom was worth mentioning. But he would describe the kitchen with its modern gas range, efficient little ice box, and porcelain sink. He would tell her of the glass-door cupboards that held china plates, cups, and saucers, and the little kitchen table and two chairs where they would eat breakfast together each morning. She would hug his neck and tell him she couldn't wait to see it all. Then he would present her with the wedding ring he had purchased at Herkner Jewelers and she would be thrilled with the custom design he'd had made especially for her.

He prayed to God for self-control and restraint when she pressed against him. He must uphold his promise that he would wait until she was ready before showing her how deeply his affections ran for her.

Abruptly, his reverie ended. The conductor was passing through the car, his announcement loud and clear.

"Next stop, Caledonia!"

Beside him, Charles stirred from the nap he'd been taking almost since they'd pulled out of the Grand Rapids terminal. He folded the newspaper that lay unread in his lap as the train entered the village. When they pulled alongside

115

the depot it was evident that Deborah had not come to greet him. And when he stepped off the train, a glance in the direction of the big white house a block away told him she was not waiting on the veranda, either, though Ottilia was. It seemed strange that Deborah was not on the porch on such a perfect September evening as this. Not a cloud blemished the sky and the temperature was warm and inviting. Then again, her relationship with Ottilia was not always smooth and perhaps she had chosen to spend her time elsewhere with Spotsy. No matter. His heartbeat quickened as he and Charles walked toward the house. He had to force himself to shorten his strides and temper his pace so as not to leave the shorter, stockier Charles behind. When they turned on the sidewalk that led up to the veranda, Ottilia rose and moved toward the front steps, an envelope in her hand.

Tommy's gaze met hers. A strained look dominated her features. Unbidden fear sent an electric current straight to his heart. Even before she spoke, he knew what she would say.

"Deborah's gone. She left a note for you. I hope you'll forgive me for reading it first."

Chapter

12

Tommy hadn't planned to be on the 5:50 morning train to Grand Rapids alone. He'd planned to be on it with Deborah. But all that existed of her on this train was the cheviot golf yacht cap she'd bought for him, and the note she'd left him. He lay the cap on the empty seat beside him and slid the note from his inside jacket pocket where it rested over his aching heart.

He didn't really need to read the words. He'd already committed them to memory. Still numb with disappointment, he gazed down at them.

> *Dear Tommy,*
> *Hope you like this cap I bought for you.*
> *Life in Caledonia is too painful for me. I simply had to leave.*
> *Your wife, Deborah.*
> *P.S. I took Spotsy. Hope you don't mind.*

She said nothing of love; neither did she speak of regrets nor sorrow for the action she had felt compelled to take. Despite her failure to reveal her destination, she issued no warning against following her or any statement that she intended to end the marriage. The entire situation was most puzzling, even though a lengthy discussion with Ottilia led Tommy to conclude that the public slights Deborah had suffered on Tuesday had sent her packing.

He was thankful that Ottilia's legwork had uncovered Deborah's destination. An inquiry of Joseph Carey, the railroad agent, revealed that Deborah had bought a ticket for herself to Chicago. If that bustling metropolis were her final destination, it would be next to impossible to find her. But before she had left Caledonia, she had hired a crate built for Spotsy at the lumberyard. And at the depot, she had paid the dog's freight as livestock clear to Calumet, expressing great concern that Spotsy be delivered there as quickly as possible. Carey had sent the dog on a route through Chicago then up through Wisconsin, explaining that it was more expedient for livestock, with the great number of animals shipped to the meat-packing city, than going north in Michigan through the sparsely populated Upper Peninsula.

By the grace of God, Ottilia had learned all of this before Luella's departure Friday afternoon. Since the older woman had no knowledge of Spotsy's impending arrival in her city, and had not been asked to receive the dog on the other end, the conclusion was drawn that Deborah herself planned to continue to Calumet after purchasing the remainder of her fare in Chicago. Any other plans Deborah may have made for Calumet were left to conjecture, but knowing her passion for drama, the obvious conclusion was that Calumet's renowned opera house had drawn her to the copper mining town.

Tommy prayed that his assumption was correct and that with the Lord's guidance he would be reunited with his wife soon after his own arrival in Calumet. Reaching into his trouser pocket, he retrieved the slip of paper upon which he'd written Luella's address: 1025 Mine Street. At least he would have accommodations with a relative of the Chappell family once he arrived. Above it was the address of the new apartment he'd rented in Grand Rapids. If only Deborah had waited for him to come home last night.

At least he needn't worry about his position at the Chappell law firm. Charles had readily given him leave to go after Deborah despite the work that awaited him at the office. And even though Tommy had sufficient savings to pay for several days on the road, his boss had forced him to accept a traveling allowance generous enough to pay for a cross-country adventure. Silently, he thanked God for the blessings he could claim even on this difficult day.

The sound of Spotsy's pitiful whimper when she was boarded up in her crate and shoved into the livestock car haunted Deborah as she tossed and turned in her narrow Pullman berth. She prayed that the dog had been transferred properly and with due care in Chicago, and that she was, even now, part of this train heading north through Wisconsin to the Upper Peninsula.

As worries of Spotsy faded, her concern resurfaced for Tommy. She couldn't deny strong feelings for him. How could anyone fail to love a man willing to rescue a woman from the jaws of iniquity and take her for his wife despite the impending birth of a child not his own? Such a man was too noble to be tarnished for life by her stained reputation. Yet she hadn't discouraged him from following her. She hadn't penned false words warning him not to come after her, claiming untruthfully that she didn't love him. Such sentiments were the fodder of melodramas she'd seen played out hundreds of times on stage in Detroit when her mother had been alive.

But Deborah had to admit that her own life held frightening similarities to those tearfully sentimental plays. Her marriage bore the mark of convenience. But unlike those theatrical performances with a happily-ever-after ending,

Deborah's romance was headed for disaster. Once Tommy had gone back to work in Grand Rapids, it seemed to her as if they weren't married at all. He wasn't there to ease the pain of her shunning on Tuesday or to offer reassurances that together they could build a bright future. She couldn't fit into the role of wife to an absent husband the way her Aunt Ottilia did. It was better for Deborah to accept her shortcoming in that regard and do what she felt she had to do—put the pain of Caledonia in the past.

Nevertheless, her heart ached, knowing the grief she must have caused Tommy. A sense of guilt sliced straight to her soul, gnawing at her all through the night. It diminished only slightly with the onset of sunrise. She only nibbled at the cheese Danish pastry served at breakfast as the train made its way out of Wisconsin and into Michigan's Upper Peninsula. The morning passed as the landscape of the North Country unfolded with its flatlands merging into rolling hills, its forests alternating with clear-cut, bald stretches. A young redheaded woman who was also traveling alone got on at Champion and asked to sit next to her, wasting no time initiating a conversation.

"'Tis sure a bother with the bridge out, don't ya know?"

"What bridge is that?" Deborah asked.

"Why, at Houghton, of course!"

"I've never been this far north before. I didn't know there was a bridge there," Deborah admitted.

The young woman explained that the bridge across Portage Lake connecting Hancock and Houghton had been knocked out last April when the steamer *Northern Wave* had struck it. Still under reconstruction, they would have to wait for a ferry to transport them across the watery gap.

"It takes a good three hours longer, or more, than before the bridge went out. A patient lass, I'm not!" she exclaimed, tucking a stray strand of hair beneath her boater. "Where ya headed?" she asked, blue eyes dancing. "I'm puttin' off at Calumet."

"I'm going to Calumet, too," Deborah replied, "to visit Luella Dunston."

The girl drew a sharp breath. "Luella Dunston, ya say?"

"Do you know her?"

"Not personally. But I know *of* her. There's hardly a soul in all of Laurium or Calumet who ain't heard of Luella Dunston!"

"How's that?" Deborah asked.

"She's only the widow of the Calumet and Hecla's best loved mining captain, may he rest in peace. He worked for them more than thirty years. Was boss to my papa. And when Captain John Dunston was put in the ground the mine even closed the shops and the surface operations for a day so their men could attend his funeral!"

"I didn't know," Deborah replied, mulling over all that the girl had said.

During her silence, the girl eyed her with suspicion, finally asking, "How is it y've come to visit the Widow Dunston, even though ya don't seem to know much of anything about her?"

"I know her from her visits downstate," Deborah explained. "She's my great aunt. Actually, she's the great aunt of my first cousin, but I think of her as my aunt, too."

When the girl looked unconvinced, Deborah reached into her valise and pulled out the Bible Luella had given her, opening to the inscription on the first page.

"Well, I wish ya a pleasant sojourn with Mrs. Dunston. I'm sure she'll be anxious to greet ya when ya reach the depot."

"Actually, she doesn't know I'm coming. This is a surprise visit." Deborah turned to the back inside cover of the Bible as if in search of something, then began thumbing through the pages, muttering, "It's got to be here somewhere."

"Lost something?" the girl asked, lifting her skirts a tad when Deborah began to look on the floor.

"Aunt Luella's address," she fibbed, wishing she had thought to make note of it before she'd left Caledonia. "You wouldn't know it, would you?"

"Most everyone knows her home on Mine Street. It's one of the finest company houses ever built for a surface manager. Go down past the roundhouse and y'll find it easy enough," Molly assured her a tad resentfully.

"Mine Street," Deborah repeated, ignoring Molly's pique. "Thank you kindly, Miss . . . "

"Mulligan. Molly Mulligan."

Deborah extended her hand. "My name is Deborah."

The conductor entered the car, voice loud and clear.

"Houghton Station. Everybody off. All passengers for points north transfer to the Hancock ferry."

During the long wait in the ferry terminal, Deborah and Molly fell into a lengthy conversation. Deborah learned that Molly was a year younger than herself and was on her way home from a trip to her older sister's in Champion where she had helped care for her niece while her sister gave birth to her second baby. She was planning to accept a position that had been offered her as a domestic in Superior, Wisconsin. But first, she must return to her widowed mother's tiny apartment in Laurium, a few blocks from the Calumet Depot. It was the only housing they could afford on her mother's earnings as a seamstress for Haas Clothiers on Fifth Street. She spoke ruefully of their cramped living quarters.

122

"Up until last month, we lived in a nice company house on Caledonia Street."

"Caledonia Street? Caledonia is the name of the town I came from down near Grand Rapids!" Deborah exclaimed.

"Ya don't say!" Molly went on. "There's a whole row of fine company houses for the men who work down in the mines, but Mr. Agassiz—he's the president of the Calumet and Hecla Mine—won't let ya stay long once y'r widowed. He gave Mama some money and a year to find a new place. His men even came and moved us to the apartment. So that's our home now, like it or not. I suppose it's best I'll be moving to Superior." Molly turned away, her eyes watery.

Deborah pondered the girl's circumstances, a question coming to mind. "Aunt Luella's been a widow for two years now, and you said she's still living in the company house."

"It's different for a mine superintendent's widow," Molly said, her explanation accounting for her earlier pique. "Besides, if they ever dared put out the Widow Dunston, the whole community would rise up in arms. It'd be a cold day at the bottom of the C&H—the Calumet and Hecla—before that'd happen." Molly explained that deep down in the mine the temperature is eighty degrees—even hotter once a miner turns on his drill. "Some fellas say goin' to work at the C&H in wintertime is like workin' in the A&H—the Arctic and that hot place mentioned in the Good Book!"

She said temperatures in February could be twenty below zero or colder when men like her father got up for the morning shift. They'd bundle up against frigid winds that always seemed to blow in off Lake Superior during the winter months and trudge through four-foot snowdrifts to get to the dryhouse, a building near the mineshaft. There, they'd put on hob-nailed boots, work pants, work shirt, and a lighter jacket. Out they'd go, dashing to the shafthouse.

There, they'd get on a man-car, a staircase-like elevator, and crowd in with the other fellas on a narrow bench seat to ride down into the mine. At first, the warmth would be welcome. But once they started drilling, they'd have to shuck off jacket and shirt.

Then the dust would start to fly. Molly explained that when a miner drilled overhead, it showered down on him, caking sweaty face, arms, and chest with grime. It got into his nose, and when he coughed, he hacked up spit black as pine tar. The work was loud, dirty, and dangerous.

"Some miners die in cave-ins and some die in fires," Molly explained. Her voice turned grave. "My daddy died when the rope that was tied to a skip—that's a cart for hauling rock out of the mine—anyhow, the rope broke and the skip fell down and crushed my daddy and another man." She turned away, pulling a wrinkled handkerchief from the cuff of her worn, but clean blouse to dab away a tear.

"I'm sorry," Deborah said, awed by all she'd learned about mining. How different it was from the business of farming that dominated Caledonia. Eager to brighten Molly's spirits she asked, "Have you ever been to the Calumet Theatre?"

The girl shook her head. "Been past its huge clock-and-bell tower and big electric-lit sign enough times."

"Then you know where it is."

"Anybody who's lived in Calumet more than a day knows where it is—the corner of Sixth and Elm!"

"Is that far from my aunt's house on Mine Street?"

"An easy walk."

Deborah's heart danced. The first thing she'd do after claiming Spotsy and taking her to Aunt Luella's place would be to find the theater.

Molly asked, "You like the theater?"

124

"I was practically born in one!" Deborah replied, launching into a description of her days in Detroit when her mother was a regular on the stage. She told of the bit parts she sometimes played when a child was called for in the script, and the hours she'd spent backstage learning the art of stage makeup and costuming. She spoke, too, of her days of watching rehearsals, learning the fine art of diction, projection, inflection, gestures.

In no time, it seemed, their turn to board the ferry arrived and they were across narrow Portage Lake and headed by train for Calumet. The hills north of Hancock were peppered with mine buildings and smokestacks. Deborah's excitement grew as they rolled past one mine after another—the Quincy, the Franklin, and farther on, the Osceola. Molly described the different buildings and their uses as they passed.

The shafthouses towered high over the landscape. Hoisthouses contained huge stationary engines to power the hoists. The rockhouses alongside contained the crushing equipment for breaking up the rock that was extracted from the mines. Not far away from each shafthouse stood the small dryhouse where miners changed into work clothes as Molly had previously explained.

Other structures included mills, carpenter shops and blacksmith shops. Huge logs, the largest Deborah had ever seen, lay outside the mills. These timbers, Molly told her, would be sawn for use as supports in the mines.

"See that carpenter shop, yonder?" She indicated a sizable one-story building. "In there's the latest woodworking appliances. And that blacksmith shop ain't any ordinary smithy. It's got forges, all right, but it's got steam hammers, too. And over there," she pointed to another shop, "is where they make and sharpen the drill steels."

Her description continued—of a machine shop containing planers, lathes, and drills, and smaller buildings that served for pattern making, company offices, and bathhouses. The trails of black smoke that rose above the land seemed the perfect parallel to the dirty, dusty work that was being carried on below.

When the train neared Calumet, Molly told Deborah, "The depot is on Fourth Street. It's only a few blocks from Mine Street, so ya won't have far to go to the Dunston place. How long ya stayin'?"

"I . . . uh . . . a week, maybe more," Deborah replied, covering the fact that she had no plan for her future beyond Calumet.

"Well, you have a nice time. And thanks for lettin' me keep ya company. It's been a pure pleasure, makin' y'r acquaintance," Molly said, offering her hand.

"The pleasure was mine," Deborah assured her, thankful for all she'd learned from Molly.

Minutes later, they stepped off the train onto the platform in Calumet and parted company. The Calumet Depot was much like dozens of other small town depots Deborah had passed. On one end, a two-story structure with two chimneys provided a first-floor waiting room and office, with the agent's living quarters located above. An overhang ran all along the platform to protect passengers from the elements, and a lower one-story extension housed freight.

The Calumet and Hecla mining buildings dominated the view to the east, and the smoke they sent forth caused a stench that made her nose sting. The earth seemed to tremble slightly beneath her feet, and above, the sky had taken on a dull gray cast, not so much from clouds, she concluded, but from the smoke spewing forth from huge stacks and other mine buildings.

A dull pounding played background to the more immediate sounds of people's voices. The strange thing was, she could barely understand what was being said. At least half of the people around her were speaking in foreign tongues. There was the occasional French or Italian accent she recognized from her days at the theater in Detroit, but a good share of the conversation was taking place in a mystery language. It had a pleasant, musical sound, and made her think she should be able to understand it, but it was completely unintelligible to her ears.

Concern for Spotsy overriding her curiosity about these foreigners, Deborah went in search of her dog, wending her way through the crowd toward the sign with an arrow pointing in the direction of the freight office. Calumet was busy and congested, she concluded, from the number of people arriving and departing, and the numerous wagons coming and going from the loading dock around the backside. Freight handlers were offloading dry goods by the barrel and crate. Down the line, she could see a livestock car with cattle on board. Certainly Spotsy wouldn't be in with the large animals. She went up to a young man who was rolling a barrel to the edge of the dock for pickup by a merchant.

"Excuse me, sir. I'm looking for my dog. She was supposed to come in on this train. Have you seen her?"

The young fellow shook his head. "No Engliss." Then he spoke a few words in that mysterious language and seemed to be waiting for her reply.

Deborah shrugged. "Sorry. I don't understand." Remembering the claim check that bore the number on Spotsy's crate, she pulled it from her valise and showed it to the man.

He nodded and took the ticket to another fellow, a hefty young man who approached her with a smile, his gaze traveling from her head to her toe before he spoke.

"What kind of livestock was this, miss? Chickens?"

"It's ma'am, and it was a crate containing the dog belonging to my husband and me."

At that moment, she heard an anxious bark through the closed door of the freight office behind her. The fellow opened it wide. There was Spotsy scrambling at the end of a rope that had been tied to the desk inside. She hurried to greet the dog, bending down to hug her and receive wet kisses that washed her face.

The oversized fellow freed the rope from the desk. "There ya go, ma'am. Nice dog," he ruffled Spotsy's head. "I gave her some water. She swallowed near a quart all at one time!"

"Thanks for your kindness." Deborah headed for the door, pausing to ask, "What country is that fellow from who gave you my ticket? I couldn't understand a word he said."

"Him?" The big fellow laughed. "He's a Finn. There's a good many of his countrymen here to work the mines, or any other job that can be had."

Again, Deborah headed out the door, then paused. "One more thing. Which direction is Mine Street?"

He pointed. "Up that road one block. Who ya lookin' for there?"

"My aunt, the Widow Dunston."

"That'd be a right turn. She's a block and a half past the library."

"Thank you kindly!"

Deborah stepped off the loading dock, Spotsy's leash in one hand, valise in the other. They'd not gone far when a dog on the loose came toward them. Spotsy barked loudly, straining so hard at the end of her leash that Deborah had to set down her valise in order to restrain her. The other dog, smaller but sturdier with its deep chest and muscular hindquarters, ambled in another direction. Taking grip in hand, they proceeded again down a street called Red Jacket Road. Deborah soon wished she had hired a cab. This road was lined with stacks of timber and mining buildings. The timber lay in gigantic piles on her left. A small pattern shop, and farther on, a large warehouse loomed on her right. Their sturdy stone construction looked as if it would last well into the next century. Beyond the timber rose the steeply pitched roof of some other mine building, its arched windows checkered with dozens of small panes of glass. Nearby, a shafthouse and hoisthouse jutted into the sky.

Interspersed amongst the larger buildings were several smaller ones built long and low to the ground. Deborah felt like a fish out of water, walking her dog through this industrial district, dodging wagons and drays that were constantly on the move, but no one bothered her. A couple of minutes later she reached the corner of Mine Street where the library stood, and turned right. She couldn't help thinking that the library would be the envy of Caledonia and just about any other town in Lower Michigan. It was built handsomely of alternating dark and light stone, with a sturdy chimney at one end, and plenty of windows across the front trimmed in creamy white paint. Beside it was an armory, another impressive stone structure distinguished by a large arched door at center front.

Deborah continued, passing a long, narrow shop from which emanated the smell of paint, and the roundhouse that marked the intersection with Depot Street. Another small shop stood across the road. Then, just as she'd been told, she arrived at a substantial two-story home. Beside it stood a spacious carriage house.

Aunt Luella's home was not as impressive as the big white house Uncle Charles had built, but it was roomy enough. It was an irregular L shape with steeply pitched roofs, an expansive front porch, two chimneys, and a small log storage building to one side. The lower half was clapboard, the upper story, shingled. She led Spotsy up the cement steps that rose from the street level to the front walk, and headed straight to the porch. She couldn't help noticing that the cement was unlike any she'd seen in Lower Michigan, a pinkish hue. She'd ask Aunt Luella about it later.

For now, Deborah's concern was in explaining herself convincingly enough to the housekeeper to gain entrance until Aunt Luella's arrival later in the evening. The Bible should be evidence enough. Up the front porch steps she marched, setting her valise down beside her to turn the key on the front doorbell with a firm twist of her wrist. During the silence of the moment, her stomach growled. She hadn't noticed how hungry she was, in the confusion of arriving at the depot and claiming Spotsy. She realized now that her appetite was ferocious, and she longed for a good home-cooked meal.

Deborah twisted the key on the doorbell several times, but to no avail. Going around to the back, she rang the bell at the service entrance, but no one answered. Her stomach growled. Spotsy sat down at her side with a whimper. Deborah stooped to pet her. "This is no good, is it, girl? What are we going to do?"

As if she understood, Spotsy stood up and barked at the closed door, then began to paw at it.

Deborah pulled her away. "Scratching the paint off Aunt Luella's door will only get you in trouble when she comes home, Spotsy. Now, sit."

The dog obeyed, letting out a soulful whine. Then she lay down, resting her head on her paws with a sigh.

"I know you're mighty hungry, girl. Hungrier than I am, I'd guess, but we're not having any success getting our noon meal here. I suppose we'll have to go over to town and see what we can find. Come on." She tugged on Spotsy's leash. The dog rose, albeit reluctantly.

Chapter

13

As Deborah and Spotsy started to walk away from Luella's home, a fellow in dirt-smudged clothes came out of the carriage house pushing a wheelbarrow that held a rake, trowel, and pair of gardening gloves. He was singing merrily, and if Deborah guessed correctly, his song was in the Finnish language.

"Excuse me, sir," she interrupted, "would you be Mrs. Dunston's hired man?"

"Yeah," he replied. "Her gardener and driver. What needs doing, I do. Today, I pull veeds outa dat garden." He bobbed his head in the direction of the backyard. There bloomed a beautiful garden of bright yellow chrysanthemums, purple cone flowers, and daisies that Deborah had been too preoccupied to notice until now.

"A fine gardener, you are! Maybe you could help me." She introduced herself and explained her circumstances, showing him the Bible from Luella.

He listened carefully, then checked his timepiece. "Lempi—hired girl—go market, but come home any minute, make you dinner. Come inside, Mrs. Rockwell." Picking up her valise, he led her and Spotsy through the back entry, kitchen, and dining room, to the front parlor, leaving her valise by the front stairs.

Deborah crossed the flowered Oriental rug and made herself comfortable on one of a pair of burgundy plush chairs that were separated by a table near the front window. Spotsy lay at her feet.

From the view out the window, Deborah saw several stone buildings that belonged to the mining company. She could understand why a superintendent's home had been built here, so close by.

Turning her attention to the table beside her, she noticed a small framed portrait next to the telephone—a likeness of Captain Dunston, she presumed. How handsome he looked, even as an older gentleman with thick white hair that formed a wave over the right side of his forehead. Beside it was the August issue of *The Delineator*. She thumbed through pages of the latest dress and skirt fashions taking note of the dip-front waists in skirts, suits, and gowns. There was even a blouse with a necktie very like a man's, held in place by three narrow fabric strips spaced evenly down the front of the bodice.

She turned past the fashion section to articles that described athletics for women, fancy stitches and embroideries, and near the back of the publication, an article on raising butterflies. The last sentence of the article stated that, "You will learn much of the wonderful ways of butterflies and can find delight in watching your curious caterpillar pets which come forth at last in such beauty."

Deborah fingered the butterfly pin on her bodice. Despite her nickname, "Butterfly," she felt anything but beautiful. She pushed back the haunting memories of summer and tried not to think of the fact that she had left her husband after less than a week of marriage. Reaching down to pet Spotsy, she redirected her thoughts to the future. After she and Spotsy had eaten their midday meal, she would go in search of the theater. There would be some small job she could do there, some way she could earn her keep until her singing and acting abilities paid off.

She closed the magazine and set it aside, looking again out the window. An apron-clad girl of about sixteen was coming up the walk. Moments later, Oskari introduced the slender, dark-haired girl, saying, "Lempi speaks Engliss very little." After a few words with her in her native tongue, Oskari said, "I feed Spotsy and take her outside while Lempi makes dinner. Okay?"

Deborah nodded, thankful that the old Finn had tucked some bits of sausage in his pocket that immediately gained Spotsy's cooperation. When the others had left, Deborah sat again to read the magazine. Awhile later, Lempi returned to say the meal was ready. In the dining room, the table had been set beautifully with lace-edged linen, fresh chrysanthemums, and delicate gold-rim china. A silver cover kept Deborah's meal warm. The aroma of herbs piqued her appetite.

Her dinner consisted of some sort of poached fish that had been sprinkled with herbs, a fluffy roll, sliced fresh tomato, cinnamon applesauce, and a pastry dessert unlike any she had seen before. It had a flaky crust topped with vanilla glaze and crushed walnuts. On the inside was a raisin filling. When she had eaten the last delectable bite and finished her tea, her hunger was perfectly satisfied. She had barely set aside her napkin when Lempi returned.

The hired girl led Deborah to the front stairs, picked up her valise, and started up the steps. Deborah followed her past a dressing room with a fireplace at the top of the stairs to the end of the hall at the front of the house. There, she opened the door to a spacious bedroom furnished with two single canopy beds, a large oak dresser, a matching vanity, and two small wing chairs. Taking a luggage rack from a closet for Deborah's valise, Lempi left the bag there and showed Deborah to the bathroom where she hung a fresh set of thick towels on a brass bar.

Deborah thanked her, and when Lempi left, she freshened up. In her room, she unpacked the extra blouse she had brought and put it on, then headed downstairs to find Spotsy. She discovered Spotsy and Oskari in the shade of the carriage house. Oskari was sitting on a wooden stool and Spotsy sat attentively in front of him. Deborah approached them, quietly observing as the old man repeated the word, "Shake," taking Spotsy's right paw in hand to demonstrate each time.

As soon as Spotsy saw Deborah, her concentration was broken, and she ran to greet her mistress, dragging her leash behind. Deborah caught hold of the rope, gave Spotsy a hug, and led her back to Oskari. "Thanks for watching my dog. You're very good with her."

The old man smiled and ruffled the dog's ears. "I try to teach her 'shake.' She not understand."

"She will. Would you like to continue your training session while I walk over to Sixth Street? I have some business to see to."

Oskari nodded and reached for the leash. "Back in old country, I have goot dog. Not like Spotsy, but goot. Then I come America. Miss dog. Been here fifteen years. Still miss dog!" He laughed.

"You and Spotsy enjoy yourselves, and I'll see you later."

Before Deborah was even out of the dog's sight, Spotsy started barking and whining at being left behind. Though tempted to turn back and reassure her pet that she would be all right, Deborah kept going. Her mind was set on finding the theater and some way of supporting herself, and with most of her money already spent, she couldn't afford to delay.

The air smelled faintly of coal smoke that rose from the many tall mining stacks that jutted into the sky. A dull pounding played background to the rattle of street traffic, and in the block and a half to Red Jacket Road, Deborah often stepped off to the side to leave more room for the Calumet and Hecla conveyances that were constantly coming and going. Even though the drivers looked rough and rugged, not a derogatory word was spoken to her. Rather, they often nodded courteously and smiled politely.

Nevertheless, she hurried past the warehouse in her eagerness to hunt down the theater. At the intersection with Fourth Street, she continued straight, passing a substantial bank built of sandstone on her right. A sign identified it as the Union Bank. In no time, she had reached Fifth Street. The twin steeples of St. Anne's Church loomed in front of her. Other, less imposing church steeples rose on her left. She quickly concluded that Calumet must be a town full of church-going people.

Continuing past the church, she cut down Scott Street past the S. Olson Company with its furniture for sale and paused on the corner of Sixth Street. She stood for a moment simply taking in the sight, wondering where on this busy thoroughfare the theater could be found. In front of her was what appeared to be a manmade valley with cobblestone floor, streetcar tracks, and sandstone walls. The street took a slight dip, then made a gentle rise along the course of its three-or-so blocks. Across the street on her left, a shingled tower protruded from the corner of one building giving it a distinguishing mark from its strictly rectangular neighbors. The large sign read "Esther House Hotel," but

smaller signs indicated that clothing and grocery businesses occupied its first floor. She continued past the Gardner
and Ecker Grocers. Crossing Portland Street, she soon
found herself in front of the Vertin Brothers Department
Store.

This four-story structure was more imposing than its
neighbors by virtue of its size. Deborah found it curious that
the lower two floors were of sandstone and upper two were
made of brick. The windows were varied in shape, too.
The third floor had simple rectangular ones while above and
below the more pleasing arched design had been used. She
lingered to gaze at the merchandise shown in the large, first
floor display windows. Every conceivable type of dry good
was shown: fashions for men, women, and children offering
the latest in fall suits and warm outerwear; toys and games
to keep little ones happy at play; and linens for bedroom,
bathroom, and dining room. She asked a woman coming
out of the store where she would find the theater, and
learned that she needed only to proceed to the end of the
next block where a stone canopy could be seen arching over
the walk. Off she went, across Oak Street and past the
Michigan House Hotel that prominently occupied the corner.

On the opposite side of the street rose an attractive
three-story red sandstone building occupied by a harness
maker and an insurance agent. Of more interest to Deborah
was the store immediately beside it, one with a large electric sign that read "Gately-Wiggins Co." Even from across
the street Deborah could see that it carried the latest in fashions. She waited for a streetcar to pass then crossed to the
opposite side for a better look. Dip-front waist walking suits
of broadcloth, venetians, and coverts; hats with stylishly
curved brims that were festooned with ostrich feathers and

wide satin bows; and stylish men's coats in plaids and camelhair covered the mannequins on display. But the most stylish mannequin of all wore a long-skirted coat. A mirror had been positioned behind it so all could see its Prince Albert back. She was tempted to go inside and try one on just for fun, but reminded herself that she must make haste to the theater.

Turning to continue on her way, she caught a better glimpse of the Calumet Theatre on the opposite side of the street. There it stood in all its glory, a magnificent sandstone and brick three-story building with a tall, stately tower rising from the center. The arched windows on the second story were mimicked by arched recessions in the façade at the third floor level. Even the tower played out the arched theme with curved openings in its support structure. Copper cornices added a classy contrast to the sandstone and buff brick exterior. Dodging traffic, Deborah swiftly crossed the street to the double arched canopy. She paused to contemplate the twin oak doors. Here, one could gain admittance to the only municipally owned theater in the state—perhaps even the nation. In the five-and-a-half short years since its opening, it had gained renown among the most professional acting troupes as the best opera house in the country. Madame Helena Modjeska, the Polish woman who had distinguished herself as the most skilled tragic actress alive, had named the Calumet Theatre as her favorite place to perform because of the heat and running water in her dressing room there. Despite the warmth of the day, a shiver traveled up Deborah's spine. She was about to realize the dream of many an aspiring actor and actress. She was about to enter the hallowed halls where the best theatrical entertainers in the country had come to perform.

Pulling on the brass handle, she stepped across the

threshold and onto the tile floor of the lobby. At once, the hustle and bustle of street traffic ceased. Instead, she heard the faint sounds of an orchestra in rehearsal. A few feet in front of her, a double set of oak doors topped by a transom invited her into the theater itself. She would pass through them in a moment, but first, she wanted to soak in the atmosphere of this remarkable place. On either side of her rose marble staircases with polished brass rails inviting her to visit the balcony. Deborah was tempted to go up there, but resisted, preferring instead to catch her first glimpse of the theater from the first floor.

Drawing a deep breath, she passed through the door. Her foot sank into the deep green velvet carpet. In front of her, hundreds of green Waldorf tapestry seats were set on curved, tiered rows, contrasting nicely with the crimson walls. Stunning also was the intricate plaster molding with its highly decorative accents covered in gold leaf. It gave striking contrast to the ivory background. Even Detroit could not boast a theater with décor the likes of this. Below the impressive stage, the orchestra had set up in the pit, the conductor doing his best to sing the part of a solo while directing the instrumental accompaniment.

With a sense of someone watching her, Deborah cast a backward glance, and noticed three portraits hanging on the wall. She didn't have to read the caption beneath the only male portrait to know that the handsome fellow with the arrogant arched brows, the ruffled shirtfront, and silk jacket was none other than Richard Mansfield. The caption noted his roles as Prince Karl, Cyrano De Bergerac, and Beau Brummel. Deborah had seen him as Beau Brummel in Detroit, and a very talented actor he was.

Beside Richard Mansfield hung a portrait of Helena Modjeska. Deborah would never forget the night she saw her performance in the roll of Lady Macbeth. None could match her.

A portrait of Mildred Holland hung beside her, another actress Deborah had seen on stage in Detroit. The portrait flattered the Holland woman whose eyes held a dramatic expression achieved only by those who had taken many a curtain call in the best of theaters. When Deborah turned away to look down at the stage, she could almost see Miss Holland coming out from behind the empire green drapery to take a curtain call. With a little imagination, she saw herself on the same stage these great theatrical figures had trod, delivering her lines or a song in a musical.

The sound of the orchestra rehearsing in the pit intruded on her daydream. The director's voice was coarse and untrained as he sang the solo that the musicians were to accompany in some future performance. Deborah wanted to put her hands over her ears! But she refrained from doing so.

As she advanced down the aisle to get a closer look at the stage, a more majestic sight came into view. From the back, she had been completely unaware of the wide proscenium arch that curved high above the stage. Now, as it came completely into view, she reveled in the astonishing paintings that decorated this grand curve. Taking a seat in the center section to study them, she realized that five individual paintings separated by depictions of metallic gold lattices portrayed the five muses of the arts: drama, music, poetry, sculpture, and painting. The cherubs that surrounded the muses, and the lush greenery of the backgrounds, gave them a Garden of Eden appearance.

The orchestra's music seemed to fade away the moment she noticed the chandelier, a huge, copper sphere that hung in the center of the theater. Most impressive were its electric lights reflecting off the copper. The effect was stunning. Her focus moving upward past the chandelier, she saw now the peak of the impressively high vaulted ceiling from which it hung. She paused to admire it, and turned to gaze up at two balconies, each of them fronted by ivory molded plaster that was highlighted with gold leaf.

Shifting her gaze to the front once again, she noticed the two box seat sections below the proscenium arch on either side of the stage. Each section held two white wicker chairs with plush velvet cushions. Deborah recalled Aunt Luella's mention of them, and her privilege to sit in one of those seats on the night the theater opened. From their position so close to the ends of the stage, Deborah knew that these seats were not so much for seeing the action onstage, but to be seen by others who sat in the audience.

Again, the gruff voice of the orchestra director began to grate on Deborah's ears. While the violinists bowed a lilting accompaniment, he sang roughshod over their delicate phrases with a decidedly unromantic sound. She listened to the simple words and tune that were uncluttered by trills or grace notes.

Only forty-five minutes from Broadway . . .

The challenge lay in its subtle modulations, yet all the notes were within the range of an ordinary soprano. But the director was a bass, and giving voice to the tune two octaves below its intended range was anything but musical. Suddenly, an idea came to Deborah. Before she could stop herself, she was on her feet marching down the aisle toward the orchestra pit. With perfect timing, she arrived at the very moment the director stopped to make a correction. She spoke up loudly from behind.

141

"Sir! Sir!"

The paunchy fellow wheeled around, gaze boring into her.

His cold, gray gaze could have frozen a polar bear in its tracks, but she boldly continued. "Sir, I couldn't help noticing your need for a rehearsal soloist. If I may." She sang the first phrase of the chorus loud and clear. Her voice rang throughout the theater, sounding better than it had ever sounded before—far better than in the little Methodist Episcopal Church in Caledonia.

The violinists tapped their bows against their stands.

The percussionist played a drum roll and clashed his cymbal.

The director pointed to the music on his stand with his baton. "You know this new Cohan song, *Forty-five Minutes from Broadway?*"

"Only that one phrase, but if you lend me the soloist's part, I'm sure I could sight read it."

He shuffled through the thick stack of music on his stand. Pulling out several sheets, he thrust them into her hands. "Get up on stage. If you can sight read those songs, I'll pay you fifty cents an hour to be the official rehearsal soloist for the Calumet and Hecla Orchestra."

"Yes, sir! Thank you, sir!" Deborah's heart raced as her feet carried her up the narrow steps and onto the stage. Taking a position at the center near the footlights, she nodded to the director, signaling her readiness, then followed the notes on the page while the orchestra played eight bars of introduction. Taking a deep breath, she began to sing the verse, her confidence increasing with each successive phrase. The director never had to stop to correct her, and stopped only once to correct the violinists for their bowing.

They went on to the other songs the director had given

142

her: *Retiring from the Stage, Mary's a Grand Old Name, So Long Mary, If I Were on the Stage, Wait 'till the Sun Shines, Nellie,* and *Will You Love Me in December As You Do in May?* Even though the songs were completely new to Deborah—and to most musicians, she concluded, by the 1905 copyright date for each—they were uncomplicated by comparison to the Handel solos she'd sung in Caledonia.

The orchestra needed little rehearsal now that she was singing the solo parts. After two times through with stops, the third time went flawlessly. Before Deborah knew it, the director was dismissing the orchestra.

"That's all for today. Those of you who are in the band, remember the concert behind the library tomorrow. Warm-up at half past one, concert begins at two o'clock sharp!"

The percussionist let loose with a roll and a rim shot, joking, "Better than flat!"

Deborah chuckled. Reluctantly, she descended the steps to return her music to the director, sorry her opportunity on stage had come to an end so soon.

The percussionist who had made the wise crack was now busy covering up his drums, but he paused to compliment her singing when she passed by. The principal violinist offered laudatory words, too. But her biggest compliment came from the director when she handed him her scores.

"You've got a real future on stage, miss! Now, you'd better give me your name and address for the payroll clerk. You can pick up your pay next Friday at the mine office."

"My name is Mrs. Thomas Rockwell—Deborah, that is. I'm staying with Mrs. Luella Dunston on Mine Street." She waited for him to write it down, then asked, "When will you be needing me again, Professor—?"

"Professor Broadman. Don't know when I'll need you

next. I'll ring you up. What's your number?"

"Sorry, I haven't any idea. I just arrived at Mrs. Dunston's place. The operator should be able to put you through."

He made a note, then began packing up his scores as if she weren't there.

Reluctantly, she ascended the aisle, then slipped into a seat in the last row of the center section to take one last look at the stage. In her mind, she saw herself in flowing costume at center stage performing before a packed theater. Her voice rang out clear and strong, her face was full of expression. Her gestures were choreographed to reach out to the audience and draw them in. At the conclusion of her program, they rose to their feet. The applause seemed to never end. After three encores and ten curtain calls, the manager brought up the house lights and the orchestra began packing away their instruments despite calls for more music.

Deborah sighed, her thoughts returning to the present. Someday her dream would come true. But for now, she must face reality, and the fact that soon she would be required to explain her presence at Aunt Luella's. She was about to get up from her seat when her world turned pitch black. Every light in the theater had been shut off!

"Hello!" she cried. "I'm still here! Please turn on a light!"

Still, the theater remained black. In the distance, she heard the sound of a door shutting with a thud. She rose to her feet and felt her way to the aisle, then to the back of the main floor. Hand against the wall, she proceeded slowly toward the double doors that exited to the lobby. With both hands outstretched, she walked forward toward the outside doors, but somehow missed them, coming in contact with the wall instead. Feeling her way along the wall, she found the door, then the handle, and pressed against it, but it wouldn't budge. Her heart raced. She was locked inside, and no one would even miss her!

Chapter
14

Determined not to remain prisoner in a dark, abandoned theater over night, Deborah pounded against the door and shouted.

"Let me out! Somebody, please!"

Suddenly, daylight sliced through the darkness. A door immediately to the right of where she was standing had swung open. She had forgotten that there were *two* doors leading to the street.

A gentleman in a twill coat and derby hat greeted her in a deep, smooth voice. "Trouble with the door, miss?"

"I . . . it was dark inside. Somebody turned out all the lights, and . . . " Seeing the wry smile on his face, she gave up her futile explanation. "Thank you, sir."

He dipped his head and went on his way.

Deborah paused, letting her eyes adjust to the brightness. Something about the man's voice, his dress, and his tall, stately build seemed familiar, but she couldn't quite place him. She pushed him from her mind and tried to decide which way to turn. Across the street, almost opposite the theater, stood the firehouse with its large arched doors. She hadn't noticed its grand façade and tall bell tower earlier. They carried out the stately theme of Calumet's business district to perfection. A store beside it offered furniture and general merchandise for sale.

To Deborah's left were the three blocks of Sixth Street

she had passed on her way to the theater. To her right was the intersection with Elm Street. She headed in that direction, planning to go around the block and return to Red Jacket Road by way of Fifth Street.

When she had passed the village offices that were contained in the north end of the theater building, the sign "R.J. Loughead, Jewelry" above the store on the northwest corner of Elm and Fifth caught her eye. She crossed the street to peer in the window, but was caught short by a sign on the next establishment.

Bijou Theater

A smaller sign was posted on the door. She hurried to read it.

Tonight's Program
Adams & White
Novelty Musical Artists
John Hall
Popular Singer
Dear Old Hills of California
Dilla & Templeton
World's Greatest Contortionists
M. Samuel
Recently from Europe
A Great Character Impersonator
The DeGrees
Spinners and Balancers
A Feature Act
Moving Pictures
Always Interesting
Amateur Night Friday

Amateur Night Friday. The words nearly jumped out at her. She tried the door, eager to know more, but it was locked. Behind her, the clock tower above the Calumet Theatre rang five. The afternoon was almost over. She would have to come back later. For now, she must get back to Aunt Luella's to check on Spotsy.

Crossing Elm Street again, she noticed Chynoweth Groceries on the opposite side of Fifth Street. A tempting, aromatic essence, a blend of sugar and cream and vanilla beans emanated from it, almost masking the less appealing odors of coal smoke and horse droppings. She crossed the brick-paved street to gaze into the window of the modest, two-story building.

There, she found a display of candy like none she had ever seen: chocolate bars in the most novel of shapes. Some resembled the firehouse; still others looked like mine shafthouses; but her favorite of all was a chocolate replica of the Calumet Theatre. She hastened inside to purchase a theater-shaped chocolate bar.

Continuing down the street, she paused to gaze into the window of the Russian Furriers. Ladies' coats of otter, mink, seal, and Persian lamb filled one window, while men's coats and cloaks with red squirrel linings and fox collars filled the other. On a day as pleasant as this, Deborah couldn't begin to think of the cold and snow that would require such heavy outerwear.

The next store she encountered carried a large sign that read, "The Fashion. The Style Store for Women and Girls. Leo Gartner, Prop." Its windows displayed tailored suits, woolen coats, rubberized raincoats, and cotton and woolen waists for all ages. Clothiers were so plentiful in Calumet, Deborah wondered if there were enough customers to keep them all in business.

Continuing across Oak Street, she paused to look in the windows of Herman Jewelers. A display of wedding rings pricked her conscience, stirring a strong sense of guilt over the way she had left Tommy. She stepped away briskly, biting off a large chunk of the chocolate theater and pressing from her mind any conjecture over the time and place of her next encounter with the man she had so hastily married one week ago today.

Her path took her past the Merchant and Miner's Bank with its rounded tower extending from the corner of the second floor. Across Portland Street from the bank stood Ed. Haas & Co., Clothiers. *So this is where Molly Mulligan's mother works*, Deborah thought, looking in the display window at the beautifully dressed mannequins.

Deborah continued to the end of the next block taking Red Jacket Road to Mine Street. Within minutes she was on Aunt Luella's front walk. She continued around to the back of the house to find Spotsy, and discovered the dog stretched out on her side, fast asleep in the shade of the carriage house, her rope tied to an iron stake Oskari had planted there to confine her while he weeded the garden.

When the old Finn saw Deborah near the back door, he leaned his hoe against the wheelbarrow and came to greet her, his gruff voice just above a whisper. "Vhile you vere gone, Spotsy learned tricks!" A smile carved grooves in his weathered cheeks.

Deborah smiled, speaking quietly in return. "You'll have to show me when she wakes up."

Even though Spotsy was a good fifty feet away, she jumped to her feet at the sound of her mistress's voice, and began straining at the end of her leash, barking with excitement.

Deborah hurried to greet her, ruffling her ears and hugging her neck. When Spotsy began sniffing at the bag of candy, Deborah held it out of reach. "That's not for you,

149

girl. Now, settle down and show me the tricks Oskari has taught you."

The moment the old man untied the rope from the stake, Spotsy's attention was riveted on him. With one word, she sat attentively before him, anticipating his next command.

"Spotsy, shake!" he ordered, hand extended.

Without hesitation, the dog raised her right paw, receiving lavish praise.

"Spotsy, down!" Oskari ordered, his crooked finger pointing to the ground.

The dog lay down on her belly.

"Spotsy, roll over!" He made a circular motion with his hand.

She executed the command to perfection.

"Goot girl!" Oskari exclaimed, offering her a tiny morsel of beef jerky and a pat on the head as reward.

Deborah added her praise to Oskari's, telling him, "You've done wonders with Spotsy. Thank you!"

He dipped his head. "I teach her more tomorrow." Tying Spotsy to the stake again, he pulled out his pocket watch. "Nearly supper time. I go clean up." He headed for his wheelbarrow, humming a tune as he pushed it toward the carriage house.

When Deborah entered the back door with Spotsy, she found Lempi in the kitchen arranging slices of bread, cold meat, and cheese on a plate. Beside it were a dish of scraps and a bowl of water. Lempi immediately offered the two bowls to Spotsy, and while the dog was busy eating, tied her leash to the leg of the heavy kitchen table. Seeing that her dog was in good hands, Deborah went upstairs to wash.

When she came downstairs, her supper had been neatly laid out on the dining table: an open-face sandwich on one plate, smoked herring on another, and slices of sharp cheese with a fresh apple and a knife for paring it on a dessert plate. A small teapot held hot tea ready to be poured into a delicate china teacup of a forget-me-not pattern.

Deborah sat down and pushed the herring far enough away so the smell wouldn't interfere with her enjoyment of the sandwich, cheese, and apple. When she had finished eating, she sipped the last of her tea, gazing at the forget-me-nots that encircled the cup. Thoughts of Tommy came to mind causing an unsettled feeling in the pit of her stomach.

How did I ever let things go this far? How could I have married him and left him in less than a week's time?

As her sense of guilt increased, so did her self-loathing, turning the unsettled feelings to pure nausea. Nearly dropping the teacup, she set it down with a clank and hurried out the front door, desperate for fresh air. The best Calumet had to offer was the smoke-riddled breeze that stirred the tiny pine tree in the front yard. She drew a few deep breaths, telling herself that she couldn't change the past.

"What's done is done," she said out loud. "I'm here now, and I'll make the best of it."

Nausea abating, she channeled her thoughts to the future. Someday, she would stand at center stage in the Calumet Theatre—not as a rehearsal fill-in but as the featured soloist—and deliver songs to a packed audience. This was the dream she would cling to.

In the distance, a train whistle blew. She could hear the rumble growing louder. It was too early for Aunt Luella's arrival, so Deborah went inside to get Spotsy, then took her for a walk past the library. When she returned, the sound of music drew her to the back of the house. On the porch step sat Oskari playing an accordion and singing a sentimental melody of his homeland in a deep, bass voice. Beside him

151

sat Lempi, singing along with him in her high, soprano voice. Deborah made herself comfortable in a lawn chair while Spotsy lay at her feet, adding her low, soft howl to the impromptu performance. Deborah lost all track of time until Oskari rose and announced, "I go now, hitch up buggy to fetch Mrs. Dunston. You come?"

Deborah shuddered. She knew she must go. But she dreaded the tongue-lashing she would almost certainly receive when the elderly woman saw her.

When Oskari pulled up in front of the depot, Deborah stepped out to wait for Luella on the platform. In no time, it seemed, her train arrived, and she emerged from a passenger car, cane in one hand, small valise in the other. Deborah pasted on a broad smile and hurried to greet her, taking the valise from her.

"Welcome home, Aunt Luella! I hope you don't mind that I've come to visit. I needed a change of scene, and—"

"Have you told your husband where you are? Or Ottilia and Charles?" she asked sharply.

Deborah made no reply.

"Come. We'll send a wire." Luella headed for the Western Union desk inside the depot. When news of Deborah's safe arrival at Luella's had been sent, she escorted the elderly woman to the carriage where Oskari was waiting.

They settled themselves for the short ride home, and Deborah braced herself for a scolding. But Luella had something different on her mind. "What became of Spotsy?"

"She's at your place. I hope you don't mind. Oskari took to her right away, and so did Lempi," Deborah quickly explained.

Luella smiled. "I'm not surprised. Oskari has affection

152

for all animals. And Lempi—her name means 'love' in English—did you know?"

Deborah shook her head.

"Lempi truly lives up to her name."

When nothing further was said about Deborah's abrupt departure from Caledonia, she began telling of her day, words rolling off her tongue faster than she could stop them. "I went to the Calumet Theatre this afternoon, and the most amazing thing happened! I got myself hired as a rehearsal soloist at fifty cents an hour! I've already earned a whole seventy-five cents!"

"And what will you do with this newfound wealth?" Luella wanted to know.

"Pay you for my room and board, of course!" Deborah replied. "I'm probably going to have to supplement my income with some other type of employment, perhaps as a sales clerk in one of the shops. I'm under the impression that the theatre doesn't have many musicals on the schedule. You wouldn't have a list of this season's performances, would you?"

Luella nodded. "It's in the drawer of my table. I'll find it for you when we get home."

A few minutes later, Deborah helped Luella up the steps and into the front door. After greeting Spotsy and Lempi and requesting tea, she went directly to the table between the two burgundy chairs in the front parlor, sat down, and opened the drawer. She was still looking for the theater schedule when the telephone rang. She immediately answered.

"Dunston residence . . . Yes, this is she . . . Go ahead . . . . I understand, on the twelve thirty-five tomorrow. Thank you." She hung up the receiver, her focus on Deborah, who was sitting on the other burgundy chair, Spotsy at her feet.

"That was a wire from your aunt and uncle. Your husband is arriving on the twelve thirty-five tomorrow."

Deborah's stomach churned. She wasn't ready to face Tommy. How did he catch up with her so soon?

Luella continued matter-of-factly. "The two of us will attend church services at eleven, and proceed from there to the station to meet him. Understood?"

Deborah nodded.

Luella located the theater schedule and a few minutes later Lempi rolled in the tea tray. Luella requested a box of stationery and a pen, then commenced pouring a cup of tea for Deborah, and one for herself. Lempi returned with the stationery and pen, setting it on the table beside Luella.

The old woman sipped her tea, then fixed her piercing gaze on Deborah. "You will write to your aunt and uncle before you leave this parlor. As for your living arrangements, we'll hold off further discussion until your husband arrives. Now tell me again. How was it that you so cleverly got yourself hired as a singer when you went to the theater this afternoon?"

It was nearly midnight when Deborah helped Aunt Luella up the stairs to bed. Deborah had penned a note of profound apology to her aunt and uncle for any worry she had caused them. Then they had discussed Calumet and the upcoming performances at the theater. Aunt Luella had explained that the pink color in the sidewalks was due to red rock crushed as gravel for the cement, and she had reminisced about earlier performances she had attended at the theater. She had spoken highly of Helena Modjeska, Richard Mansfield, and Mildred Holland, whose pictures Deborah had seen on the back wall of the theater.

Alone in her room with Spotsy, Deborah changed into

154

her nightgown and sat in the middle of her bed, Spotsy sprawled across the foot of it while she studied the theater schedule one more time. "The Marriage of Kitty," a comedy about life in Continental Europe was coming on September 21. There wouldn't be any call for a rehearsal soloist for that performance, but the one that followed two days later, "Hans 'An Nix," was a musical comedy. She looked forward to sight reading the parts.

"The Mummy and the Hummingbird," a comedy play would occupy the stage on September 26. Then "San Toy," a musical, was scheduled for October 5 featuring a Michigan girl, Miss Mabel Strickland. Deborah wasn't familiar with the Strickland girl but she couldn't help feeling jealous. She looked forward to rehearsing the musical score and meeting the Michigan girl who had made good on the stage.

Deborah read through the descriptions of the other comedies, dramas, and musicals scheduled for the last three months of the year, losing all track of time. It was nearly one in the morning before she lay her head on the pillow and fell asleep, visions of herself on stage at the Calumet Theatre filling her dreams.

Too soon, a persistent knocking and the sound of Aunt Luella's voice riled Spotsy to a barking frenzy and forced Deborah out of bed. When she answered, Luella stood wrapped in her robe, leaning on her cane, her tone curt.

"It's your turn in the bathroom. The curtain rises on breakfast in half an hour. Don't be late." Pointing to Spotsy, she added, "You'd better take her outside right now, before she messes in the house."

"Yes, ma'am," Deborah replied, yawning widely as she pulled on her robe and headed downstairs with the dog. Lempi was already in the kitchen where the aroma of some delectable pastry still baking in the oven had permeated the air. When Spotsy had done her duty, the Finnish girl offered her a bowl of scraps for breakfast.

Deborah returned upstairs and was sorely tempted to go back to bed, but resisted the urge, gathering together the few toiletries she'd brought and heading down the hall to the bathroom. Somehow she managed to arrive downstairs exactly on time.

When Luella had been seated at the head of the table, and Deborah at her right, the old woman said, "I'll ask a blessing. Heavenly Father, we thank You for the food that we are about to receive, and I thank You for Deborah's safe arrival here in Calumet. We ask Your protection over Tommy, and Your help in the activities this day. In Jesus' name, Amen."

"Amen," Deborah echoed.

"The Sheldons will be by to drive us to church. Have you a Bible to take to services?"

"I have the Family Bible you gave me."

"That's a bit cumbersome. I'll loan you my husband's. It's filled with his margin notes but it will do." She passed Deborah a tray of pastries still warm from the oven, then filled her cup with tea.

Lempi's pastry, a delightful combination of a multi-layered flaky crust, an apricot filling, and vanilla glaze, slid down easily with the tea. After breakfast, Luella took Deborah into the back parlor. It was a smaller, less formal room than the front parlor. Against one wall stood an upright piano. An Autoharp leaned against it. Across from the piano were two chairs with a table between. On it set the Bible that had belonged to Aunt Luella's husband, old ribbon bookmarks still tucked between the pages as if he'd been there reading it the day before.

"You may sit and read until the Sheldons arrive," she told Deborah, pointing to his chair and handing her the Good Book. "I've found that it's good to spend a little quiet time before Sunday services preparing your mind for worship." She sat down in her own chair, closed her eyes, and folded her hands on her Bible.

Deborah could see her lips moving in silent prayer, and closed her eyes to offer a prayer of her own.

God, as you know, I'm not much good at prayer. Tommy is coming today and I don't know what to say to him. Please help me. Thank you, God. Amen.

She opened the Bible to Psalm 32 and read again God's promise in the eighth verse.

I will instruct thee and teach thee in the way which thou shalt go: I will guide thee with mine eye.

She pondered the words anew. Perhaps God would guide her in what to say to Tommy. Thoughts came to her. Words flowed through her mind—words she needed to say to Tommy when he came off the train and other words for when they were alone together.

Aunt Luella's voice interrupted her thoughts. "The Sheldons will be here any moment. We'd best go into the front parlor and watch for them."

Within a couple of minutes a carriage drawn by a pair of chestnut horses pulled up and Deborah helped Luella down the porch steps. The hired driver hopped down from his bench to open the carriage door. The second Deborah saw the man sitting inside, her heart raced and her cheeks burned.

Chapter

15

Before Luella had even made introductions, the man in the derby hat said in a deep, mellow voice, "I know you! You're the young lady who couldn't find her way out of the theater yesterday afternoon!"

"I'm embarrassed to admit to it," Deborah replied.

When Deborah had explained how her unfamiliarity with the place had led to the predicament, Luella formally introduced her to Mr. and Mrs. Sheldon and Penelope, their daughter of fifteen. "This is my honorary grandniece, Mrs. Thomas Rockwell. She's come to stay a spell. Her husband is arriving on the twelve thirty-five train. Would you be so kind as to drop us at the station after church? Oskari will take us home from there."

"Be glad to," Mr. Sheldon replied. To Deborah, he said, "What line of work is your husband in, Mrs. Rockwell?"

Deborah explained his position at her uncle's law office.

"If your husband is looking for work here in Calumet, I have need of an assistant."

"I'll keep your offer in mind," Deborah promised.

While Luella made pleasant conversation with Mrs. Sheldon and Penelope, Deborah again sensed that Mr. Sheldon seemed somehow familiar. She wouldn't be so impolite as to stare at him, but glanced his way, embarrassed to discover that he had been looking at her.

He offered a casual smile and turned to look out the

window. Her cheeks burned, still feeling warm when they reached the Calumet Methodist Episcopal Church and he helped her out of the carriage. Even the scent of his cologne was one she had smelled before. Then she recognized it as the same lime fragrance her Uncle Charles used. Her mind somewhat at ease, she steadied Aunt Luella as they followed the Sheldons to the door of the church.

This house of worship with its corner tower and multi-peaked roof was much grander than the little Methodist Episcopal Church in Caledonia. The arched, stained-glass windows were of the same style as Caledonia's but much larger. In the foyer, the polished maple floor and curving oak staircases leading to the balcony welcomed worshippers with a warmth only native woods could offer.

Deborah accompanied Luella halfway down the aisle to a pew with enough room for five. The usual hymns, announcements, and offering opened the service, followed by the choir's anthem, *Trust and Obey*. When they had finished, Luella leaned close, whispering in Deborah's ear, "They could use you in their soprano section."

Deborah smiled but kept her silence.

Stepping into his pulpit, the Reverend Coombe began to deliver his message on the penalties of disobedience and the rewards of obedience. He opened with a reference to the Israelites when they came out of Egypt.

"Had the children of Israel but obeyed the Lord, they could have arrived in the land of milk and honey forty years earlier. Rather, their complaints, murmurings, idol worship, and iniquity kept them in the desert wilderness. How many of us remain in a spiritual wilderness for as long, or longer, because of our unwillingness to obey God?" he asked, pausing to take in the whole congregation with his piercing gaze. "The Good Book tells us, too, the rewards for obedience.

'Honor thy father and thy mother that thy days may be long upon the land.'"

The verse caused Deborah a prick of guilt. Too late she had learned the consequences of disobedience when she had defied her Aunt Ottilia, who had tried to be a mother to her, and followed her own heart and that evil Taman fellow, certain she would be rewarded with opportunities to sing and act in his theater. Little had she suspected that his theater consisted of the parlor in his house of shame. She listened while Reverend Coombe recounted other acts of disobedience in the Old Testament, then sang as he led the closing hymn, *Walk in the Light!*

On the way out of the church, it seemed as though Aunt Luella was greeted by just about everyone who'd sat in the congregation. Deborah tried to remember their names as the old woman introduced them to her, but it was impossible—except for Professor Broadman, whom she'd met at the rehearsal yesterday afternoon.

He greeted her warmly. "Mrs. Rockwell, a pleasure to see you again. I'll be in touch. We have another musical coming up in a couple of weeks."

"I look forward to hearing from you," she said, asking Luella to tell him the telephone number where she could be reached.

Minutes later the Sheldons' driver turned down Fourth Street where carriages and wagons were beginning to congregate in anticipation of the twelve thirty-five train. Deborah helped Luella up the steps to the platform where they waited amidst a cluster of relatives eager to greet returning travelers.

Though the day was not hot, Deborah's palms grew moist. Her stomach churned. She hated to think how disappointed Tommy must be with her. He had every right to admonish her soundly for what she'd done. She struggled to remember the words she'd planned to say to him, but they were like a flock of butterflies released from a net, taking flight from her mind in a dozen different directions all at once. Suddenly, she felt like an actress on stage ready to deliver a soliloquy, but she had forgotten her lines, and no prompter waited in the wings to feed them to her.

The rumble of the train drew near, its whistle piercing the air. Huge puffs of steam shot out from the brakes as it rolled to a stop beside the depot. Within seconds the passenger car doors opened and weary travelers stepped down.

Then she saw him. He was wearing the golf yacht cap she'd bought for him. He paused at the top of the steps looking for her, his brows furrowed even more deeply than when he'd whisked her away from the house of shame.

Luella waved and called his name. Deborah added her voice to the old woman's, lifting her own gloved hand high.

He looked their way, his expression transforming to a broad, slanted smile.

"Butterfly!"

There was no mistaking the relief in his voice. With swift, long strides, he slipped through the crowd. An instant later, he stood face to face with Deborah.

His hands firmly gripping her shoulders, he pinned her with a solemn gaze. "Mrs. Rockwell, I don't know whether to hug you or take you over my knee."

She made a lame attempt to smile. "I'd much prefer a hug."

He wasted no time pulling her to him, crushing the butterfly pin on her bodice against her shoulder and breathing the sweet scent of clove into her hair.

Tommy knew he shouldn't hug his Butterfly so tightly. He'd promised not to force affection on her until she was ready. But he couldn't help himself. He'd ached with missing her since Tuesday morning when the train had rolled out of Caledonia. He'd been in torture since Friday night when the train had rolled back in. He thanked God that he was here with her now, and he asked for His help in their troubled marriage. Then he released his wife and searched her beautiful blue eyes.

"How are you, Butterfly? Are you feeling all right?"

"Never better," she replied. "So much has happened since I got here. I've already sung on the stage in the Calumet Theatre!"

He should have known that the theater was first on her mind. It angered him that she loved the stage more than she loved him. It was her first husband, and he was her second, in a bigamous marriage. But he'd known that before he'd proposed. He couldn't expect her to change over night or in a week's time. He was a patient man, but her flighty ways were testing him to the limit. He prayed silently for help, hiding his frustration with forced enthusiasm when he replied, "You'll have to tell me about it on the way to Aunt Luella's!"

He kissed the old woman on the cheek. "Thanks for coming to meet me."

"I wouldn't have missed it!" Her eyes twinkled. "Now let's get home. Lempi will have dinner on soon."

On the way home, Tommy listened to Deborah's detailed description of how she was hired on the spot to be the rehearsal soloist for the Calumet and Hecla Orchestra. From the enthusiasm in her voice, he knew there was no way he could expect her to give up this opportunity to live with him in Grand Rapids while he labored day and night for her Uncle Charles. Their lives were taking turns he'd never expected when they'd said their wedding vows.

Thankfully, Charles had seen things more clearly and had helped prepare him for this turn of direction before he'd headed north.

When they arrived at Luella's, Deborah was pleased to see that Spotsy hadn't forgotten Tommy. She yipped with delight when she recognized him, the wag of her tail moving her entire body back and forth with glee. When he stooped down to pet her, she gave him a thorough face-washing. And when he followed Deborah upstairs to put his valise in their room and wash for dinner, Spotsy shadowed his every step, even lying in the hall outside the bathroom door until he came out again.

Deborah waited in the bedroom for Tommy to finish. Sitting on her vanity stool, she studied the Calumet Theatre's program again, dreaming of the performances to come. When he returned, Spotsy at his heels, she rose to go and wash her hands, but he closed the bedroom door, his gaze solemn as he stood before her.

"Butterfly, there's something I'd like to say to you."

Deborah could see the hurt in his eyes and wished that she could magically take flight and disappear out the window. But that could happen only in her imagination. In reality, she would not try to escape from Tommy's gentle trap as his hands rested lightly on her shoulders.

"First of all, I want to say that I love you, Mrs. Rockwell, but—"

"You're sorry you married me and you want an annulment. I can't blame you. I've been a horrible wife—"

"Mrs. Rockwell, hush!" he commanded with a gentle squeeze of her shoulders. Then he bent to kiss her forehead, the scent of clove adding warmth to the atmosphere. "You're never far from the stage, are you, Butterfly? You write my lines and deliver them. It's second nature for you to just steal the scene. Well, I've got news for you, Butterfly. That's not what I was going to say."

"It's not?" she asked meekly.

He chuckled. "No, it's not. Now, I'm going to start over and I want you to listen until I'm finished."

Deborah nodded.

"I'll say it again—I love you, Mrs. Rockwell, but one thing I've learned this past week is that it's no good when we're apart. So we've got some decisions to make about where we're going to live." When he paused for the slightest instant, his hands dropping from her shoulders, Deborah jumped in.

"I was miserable in Caledonia, Tommy." She turned and paced toward the window with a dramatic flair. "A horrible woman, Mrs. Nixon, humiliated me beyond words. I was afraid to go out in public for fear I would run into her!" She stood at the window, gazing down on Mine Street, but not really seeing it.

Tommy came up behind her, his hands encircling her waist as he spoke softly into her ear. "Your Aunt Ottilia told me, and I don't blame you for wanting to leave." He turned her toward him. "Now, like I said, we've got to decide where we're going to live. Would you be happy here, with Aunt Luella?"

"Oh, yes!"

"Then, when dinner is done, we'll have a talk with her, and we'll ask her if she'll take us on as boarders."

"Oh, Tommy, you're so wonderful!" She kissed him impetuously on the cheek.

He caught her face in his hands and started to lower his mouth toward hers. But he stopped short of her lips when a look of terror flashed in her eyes, dousing the sparkle of happiness that had been there a split second earlier. He released her and backed away, wanting to kick himself for having pushed too far.

Deborah hated the current of terror that coursed through her. She hated herself for not being able to let Tommy kiss her. For it wasn't the kiss that frightened her, but what might come after. At the "resort," what had always begun as an innocent kiss had ended each time in a nightmarish experience of shame. She simply couldn't risk it, even with Tommy.

Grasping for some way to ease the tension, he said, "We'd better take Spotsy outside before dinner. Coming?"

"As soon as I wash my hands. You two go down without me."

Tommy opened the door, telling Spotsy, "Come on, girl, we're going outside!"

She leaped down from Deborah's bed and raced for the stairs.

Tears formed unbidden in Deborah's eyes. She hated herself for the way she'd reacted to Tommy's affection. She hated herself for the way she had left him, with barely an explanation. She didn't deserve the kindness he'd shown. She deserved less his love. And she deserved least of all the privilege of being his wife. As she washed her hands in the upstairs bathroom she made sure to lather them thoroughly, but there wasn't enough soap on earth to wash away the guilt she felt over her treatment of Tommy, or the dark stain that blotted her deep within her soul.

Drying her hands on the fluffy white towel, she dabbed away her tears and put on a happy face. She would not let her glum mood spoil Aunt Luella's dinner. If there was a shred of acting talent residing within her bones, she should be able to put aside her troubled thoughts for the next few hours.

Tommy went to the base of the stairs when he heard Deborah coming down, and was relieved to see the smile with which she greeted him. She was beautiful no matter what the mood, but one smile from her could make him melt. He took her hand and placed it in the crook of his arm to escort her to the dining room, whispering, "You look lovely, Mrs. Rockwell."

Deborah was tempted to contradict him. She didn't *feel* lovely. She felt ugly and defiled. But the wounds were her private scars—secrets easily hidden behind sweet smiles and soft words, which she offered in return. "Thank you kindly, Mr. Rockwell. You're looking more than handsome, yourself."

He winked, sensing that Deborah was overplaying her part, but he'd let it go for now, thankful for the compliment even if it did sound like a line from a play.

At the dinner table, conversation flowed from Aunt Luella's reminiscences of early days in Calumet to Tommy and Deborah's recollections of childhood days when she would stay with her Aunt Ottilia, Uncle Charles, and cousins, Parker and Caroline, for the summer. Lempi's pork roast dinner with sweet potatoes and herbed, buttered peas ended with wedges of peach pie, their crumbly tops drizzled all over by warm vanilla glaze.

When all had finished the tasty dessert, Tommy said to Luella, "My wife and I have something we'd like to discuss with you."

The old woman smiled. "Then let us adjourn to the parlor."

In the parlor, Tommy escorted Deborah to the burgundy balloon-back sofa where he sat close beside her, holding her

166

hand in both of his. Luella took one of the matching velvet chairs across from them. She wasted no time in getting to the point.

"Now what was it you two love birds wanted to say to me?"

Tommy squeezed Deborah's hand nervously. "My wife and I had a little talk before we came down to dinner, and we both agree that we'd like very much to settle in Calumet. In fact, we'd like to live right here, with you—that is—if you'd be willing to take us on as boarders."

No sooner had he posed the question than Spotsy came dashing into the room, jumping onto the sofa with Tommy and Deborah.

Luella laughed. "I suppose that includes Spotsy, too."

Tommy commanded Spotsy to get down, saying, "Yes, ma'am, it does."

As if pleading her own case, Spotsy eased up to Luella, nudging her hand for affection.

Luella scratched her ears and told her to sit. Instead, the dog lay down, resting her chin on Luella's foot.

Luella let her be, focusing again on Tommy. "So, you've decided to stay on in this mining town?"

"Yes, ma'am," Tommy replied.

"You're giving up your position at my nephew's law firm?"

"Yes, ma'am. I'll start looking for a new one here, in Calumet, first thing tomorrow."

Deborah squeezed Tommy's hand excitedly. "Mr. Sheldon, from Aunt Luella's church, says he's looking to hire. You could apply to him!"

Luella said, "Tommy will need good references. Mr. Sheldon won't hire just anyone."

"Not even on your say-so?"

"Not even on my say-so."

Tommy released Deborah's hand to pull a long envelope from his inside jacket pocket. "Your nephew wrote me a letter of reference before I left—just in case I should need it. It will stand me in good stead."

Luella smiled. "Charles is the wisest nephew I have."

Deborah laughed. "Uncle Charles is the *only* nephew you have."

"That, too," Luella admitted.

Seeing the pensive look that stole over the old woman's features made Deborah anxious to settle the question that had started the conversation. She made an appeal, her words earnest and sincere, "We'd be much obliged if you'd allow us to stay with you, Aunt Luella."

Luella spoke as if thinking out loud. "It's no secret homes are hard to come by here in Calumet, what with all the miners and their families needing places to stay, and the company houses in such high demand."

Tommy slid the letter of reference back in his pocket. "We'll pay whatever you think is fair for our room and meals."

Luella pondered his words before continuing. "I never have had any boarders here. But if I did, they would have to abide by some rules."

Deborah asked, "What are those?"

"The first rule is that you would be expected to attend church services every Sunday."

Tommy reached for Deborah's hand again. "We should be able to follow that rule, don't you think, Butterfly?"

Deborah nodded, asking Luella, "What are the other rules?"

"You would be expected to keep your room tidy so as not to burden Lempi unnecessarily."

Deborah said, "I promise to keep our room tidy. Is that all?"

"Not quite. The rest of my rules are a private matter between you and me." To Tommy, she said, "Would you please take Spotsy for a walk around the block?"

Reluctantly, he rose and turned his attention to the dog. "Spotsy, do you want to go for a walk?"

Instantly, the mutt was on her feet, tail wagging.

When they had left the room, Luella grinned at Deborah, saying, "That man is so smitten with you that for a minute, I didn't think he was going to leave!" Smile fading, she gazed solemnly into the younger woman's eyes. "The problem is, you've been so hurt by the bad men of this world, that you can't even trust someone as devoted to you as Tommy, can you?"

Deborah turned away. Her feelings for Tommy were so confusing, she didn't want to think about them, much less discuss them.

"Deborah, please look at me when I'm talking to you," the old woman said, her tone more sympathetic than chiding. Deborah's focus was instantly on her, and she continued.

"My dear, what you need is time enough with that husband of yours to see how wonderful life can be when you have a good man by your side. I'm just afraid that you won't light long enough in any one place to give Tommy a chance."

"I'm sure I'll like it here," Deborah countered.

"Why? Because of the theater?" Luella challenged. "Well, let me tell you something. Life is more than a chance to sing on the stage of the Calumet Theatre."

"What is your point, Aunt Luella?" Deborah asked impatiently. "I thought you were going to tell me about

169

some rule I'm to follow if I'm to live here."

"The point is this. It's time that you face reality. It's time that you stop running from your past. There are people who love you and have done everything possible to help you, and how have you shown your gratitude? By running away and causing all kinds of hurt.

"Well, I simply won't be a party to it. You may stay here for as long as you like, but living with me is a privilege. Privileges carry responsibilities. If you don't like the responsibilities I require, then you may run off somewhere else. But if you *do* run off, don't you ever dare to darken my door again. Understood?"

"Is that your rule?"

"One of them," Luella replied.

"What are the others?" Deborah asked, feeling the burden of Aunt Luella's requirements closing about her like a butterfly net.

"While you are under my roof, you will spend time with me each day reading and studying the Bible. God knows best how we should lead our lives, but we can't discover His will if we aren't reading His word."

When Aunt Luella paused, Deborah said, "Let me see if I understand the rules." She counted them on her fingers. "Keep the room tidy, attend Sunday services, don't run off, and study the Bible with you each day. That's four. Is that all?"

Luella shook her head, a smile erasing the lines that had creased her brow. "That's all the rules, but that's not all I have to say to you. I'm about to tell you something far more important than rules." Pushing herself up from the chair, she came to sit on the sofa beside Deborah.

"My dear, I pray that you'll not only listen to the words I'm about to say, but that you will hear them and believe them with all your heart."

She paused, enclosing the young girl's hand in her bony, wrinkled one. "Deborah, you are a very talented young woman. I have no doubt that the gifts God has given you for singing and acting could make you a star in the theater one day. But did you know, you're already a star?"

Deborah shook her head. She was no star. And her talent for singing and acting had come from her mother.

Luella went on. "You're a star in Tommy's eyes, and there's Someone who considers you to be even more precious than your adoring husband. His name is Jesus."

Deborah looked down. She didn't want to hear about Jesus.

Luella gently lifted her chin until their eyes met again. "Jesus loves you, Deborah. He loves you, and He wants to be a part of your life. He was once, wasn't He?"

Deborah gave a reluctant nod. Yes, she'd accepted Jesus years ago when she stayed with her cousin, Caroline, but when she'd gone back to Detroit at the end of the summer to live with her mother again, Jesus seemed too far away to matter.

Luella continued. "Do you remember what it was like, watching your mother and the other actors and actresses in rehearsals?"

The sudden change of topic took Deborah by surprise. She waited eagerly for Luella to continue.

"There was one person who was in control. He was down in front, watching everything that happened on stage, making suggestions for improving the performance."

"You're talking about the director," Deborah said.

"Yes," Luella agreed. "And there was another person up on the stage whom no one could see. He stood off in the wings with a script in his hands and if someone forgot their lines, he was there to remind them."

"The prompter."

Luella nodded. "Did you know that God, our heavenly Father, has given us a director, and a prompter, to guide us, and remind us, not just when we're on stage acting in a play, but for everything in life?"

Deborah waited for Luella to continue.

"God gave His son, Jesus, to be an example and a director, and the Holy Spirit to prompt us by speaking softly to our hearts."

The comparison was a new one to Deborah. She had never thought of Jesus or the Holy Spirit in quite this way. A vision came to mind of a bearded man dressed in robe and sandals down in front of a stage, directing with kindness and gentleness all that was happening, and the Holy Spirit, a ghost-like apparition hanging in the wings, whispering the right words whenever a player needed them.

Luella continued. "The nice thing is, the powers of Jesus and the Holy Spirit aren't confined by the four walls of the theater. They are always with us, and they are far more loving and dependable than is any human director or prompter. No matter how badly we act in this life, no matter how many times we forget our lines, our Father in Heaven is ready to forgive us and supply all our needs if only we will ask."

The truth of Aunt Luella's words wasn't new to Deborah. She'd heard it as a child, but she hadn't understood it. She still didn't fully comprehend it, but the concept was beginning to take on deeper meaning, and offer comfort.

Luella squeezed her hand. "I've known a lot of people who have made a lot of bad mistakes in their lives, and every one of them who repented was forgiven by God. But some of them were still miserable, and do you know why?"

Deborah shook her head.

"Some of them were miserable because they hadn't for-given themselves. They continued to chastise themselves because they didn't feel worthy, even when God, the Father had washed away their sins by the blood of the Lamb, His son, Jesus.

"Other people I know were miserable because they were angry with those who had done them wrong. I know that some very evil, vile men stole your innocence, Deborah, and that you are very angry and hurt over what they did to you, but over time, you must learn to forgive them."

Deborah pulled her hand from Luella's and jumped up. "Never! I'll never forgive them! Not if I live to be a hun-dred!" she cried, running from the parlor and up the stairs.

Chapter 16

Deborah slammed the bedroom door, nightmarish memories of Taman and other men she'd known at the house of shame flooding her mind. "I *hate* you, Taman! And you, and you, and you!" she cried as images of their faces flashed unbidden before her eyes. She paced the floor, shame and self-loathing overwhelming her. Tears stained her cheeks and her body shook with sobbing. Collapsing face down on her bed, she cried so hard, she had to gasp for breath.

She didn't know how long she'd been there when she felt the gentle touch of Aunt Luella's hand on her shoulder, and realized that the old woman was sitting on the bed beside her. She hadn't heard footsteps in the hallway, or the clunk of Luella's cane as she'd crossed the bedroom floor, but as Deborah's sobs quieted, she heard Luella's soft words.

"Father God, comfort your child, Deborah. Send your healing balm into her troubled heart to calm her and mend her. And forgive me if I've spoken too soon of certain truths, Father God. Help me to help her in Your time. Thank you, Jesus, Amen."

Deborah sat up, accepting the handkerchief Luella offered and drying her cheeks. Luella put her arm lightly about her shoulders.

"Deborah, I'm sorry for your hurts, and I'm sorry if I've

added to them by speaking out of turn. I love you, Deborah. And I only want to help."

"I know you meant well," Deborah replied. "I just feel such anger sometimes."

"Then let's pray about it, shall we?"

Deborah bowed her head while Luella prayed.

"Almighty God, help Deborah to let go of her anger, knowing that she must start to give it over to You before Your healing can come into her heart. Thank you, Jesus. Amen."

"Amen," she said timidly, not at all sure that Luella's prayer would work, but promising herself to give it a try.

Luella hugged her, then rose to go, turning at the door to say, "There's a band concert behind the library this afternoon. It would do you good to get out. You might ask Tommy to take you there when he and Spotsy—"

The unmistakable patter of Spotsy's feet dashing down the hall and the sound of Tommy's voice stopped her mid-sentence.

"Go find your mistress, Spotsy! Ask her if she wants to go to the concert!"

Spotsy dashed into the room, leaped onto the bed, and licked Deborah's face. Then she went down on her front paws, barking excitedly.

"Okay, girl! Okay!" Deborah said, rising as Tommy came in the door.

"There you are, Butterfly. Spotsy and I just discovered there's a concert being given about a block from here. Want to go?"

Deborah laughed. "Aunt Luella was just suggesting that very thing, and I don't think Spotsy will take no for an answer."

"Neither will I!" Tommy claimed, offering his arm.

Extending the other to Luella, he asked, "Care to join us?"

She shook her head. "You young people enjoy your-selves. I'm going to my room to put my feet up and rest. I'm still tired from the trip home."

"We'll see you later, then." Tommy escorted Deborah out of the room behind an excited Spotsy who barked all the way to the front door.

When they had stepped off the porch, Deborah sudden-ly noticed something new and different about Spotsy. "You bought her a new leash and harness!"

Tommy nodded. "From the harness shop in Grand Rapids near your uncle's law office, like I promised."

"But how did you know you'd need them? How did you know you'd find Spotsy here? Or me, for that matter?"

"Your Aunt Ottilia checked with the railroad agent. He knew for sure that Spotsy was headed for Calumet. We assumed you were, too." He pulled her close, the scent of clove coming to her. "I'm sure glad we're all together again. Now let's enjoy the concert."

They continued down Mine Street past the armory to the library, turning down Red Jacket Road. The band was play-ing a peppy rendition of *In My Merry Oldsmobile* when they reached the backyard of the library, a big open space where families were gathered, some standing, some sitting on blankets. They stood at the back of the crowd, Spotsy snuggling in between them to sit quietly while the band played *Everybody Works but Father* and *Heart of My Heart*. Then, much to Deborah's delight, they played selections from "Mlle. Modiste," a comic opera: *Love Me, Love My Dog*, *Hats Make the Woman*, *I Want What I Want When I Want It*, and *I'm Always Misunderstood*. They finished with *If I Were On the Stage*, a song she had learned weeks ago. She couldn't resist singing the words that were sung by a young woman in the story who dreams of acting different roles, and it didn't bother her in the least when the people in front of her turned to stare.

> *But best of all the parts I'd play*
> *If I could only have my way*
> *Would be a strong romantic role,*
> *Emotional and full of soul*
> *And I believe for such a thing*
> *A dreamy, melodious waltz I'd sing*
> *Sweet summer breeze, whispering trees,*
> *Stars shining softly above*
> *Roses in bloom, wafted perfume*
> *Sleepy birds dreaming of love*

Tommy listened with pride to Deborah's rendition of the song, and he watched in amazement as her every gesture played to him and those around her. Her countenance, beautiful in the solemn moments, grew even more becoming as the words of the song turned romantic. He couldn't help smiling when she sang the closing lines.

> *Safe in your arms, far from alarms*
> *Daylight shall come but in vain*
> *Willingly caught up by your charms*
> *Kiss me, kiss me again.*

He was sorely tempted to take her up on the invitation to kiss her, especially when those around them began teasing for him to do so. But he reminded himself that this was only a role she was playing.

Then the unexpected happened. There, in front of everyone, Deborah pressed her mouth against his.

The feel of her soft lips shot warmth through him like steam through a radiator. His arms went automatically around her. Total strangers erupted in applause. Somebody let loose with a shrill whistle.

Before Tommy could prevent it, Spotsy bolted, yanking her leash free of his grip to run full speed through the crowd.

"Spotsy, come back!" he shouted, taking off after her.

She ignored him, zigzagging through the audience toward the band.

"Spotsy!" he cried again, but the dog kept going, circling around the band director and tripping him with her leash. Before Tommy could reach her, she ran off again, disappearing between the armory and the library.

Tommy followed in hot pursuit, hardly noticing when his cap flew off his head. But he couldn't stop now. Running between the two buildings, he caught sight of Spotsy, now chasing a stray cat. They were headed down Red Jacket Road toward the warehouse.

Deborah pressed through the crowd, reaching Professor Broadman in time to help him to his feet.

"I'm sorry, sir! We didn't mean for our dog to—"

"So it was *your* mutt, was it?" His gray eyes frosted over. "A doggoned nuisance. Plum ruined my jacket!" He brushed futilely at the dirt and grass stains conspicuous on the gold braid trim of his sleeve.

"I'm sorry about your uniform. We'll pay the damages. I promise!"

"I'll have it deducted from your wages!" he threatened as she hurried off.

178

Worried that she'd lose track of Tommy and Spotsy, she lifted her skirt and opened her stride in an effort to trace their route. Finding Tommy's cap, she pulled it on her head and hurried across Mine Street. In the distance, she saw Spotsy running along the railroad track near the Calumet and Hecla Warehouse. Tommy was running after her, but far from catching her.

Deborah hurried after them. Then she heard a sound that made her blood run cold. A train whistle blew. A rumble grew louder. She couldn't tell which direction the train was coming from. "Dear God, don't let Tommy or Spotsy get hurt," she prayed.

They were hidden from view by the warehouse now. Deborah headed toward Red Jacket Road. Her heart raced. She lifted her skirt higher and started to run.

The train came precisely down the track where she'd seen Tommy and Spotsy. With a mighty blast from its brakes, it slowed to a stop, blocking Red Jacket Road. Stalled in her path and cut off from her view of Tommy and Spotsy, she looked for a way around the train. Doubling back and cutting behind the warehouse, she had one foot on the track and was about to cross in front of the engine when the train's whistle blew. She jumped back. The train crept forward. She heard a dog cry—a bone-chilling yelp that cut straight to her heart. A vision played before her eyes of Spotsy crawling beneath the train when it had stopped, then getting caught by her leash when it started up again, and dragged beneath the wheels.

"Spotsy!" she cried.

The train stopped again, about a hundred yards to her left.

Again, she hurried to go around it, this time crossing the tracks successfully. About two hundred yards away, where

179

the train blocked Red Jacket Road, lay Spotsy. Tommy was kneeling over her.

Deborah ran to join them.

Spotsy was whimpering in pain, licking blood from her left hindquarters.

"Spotsy! You poor thing!" Deborah cried, eyes blurring with tears as she knelt at the dog's side.

"I think it's just an abrasion," Tommy said.

"But she's badly cut. She could have a broken leg!" Deborah argued.

"I don't think it's that serious. I saw a horse kick at her, but he only nicked her. It happened when a fellow turned his rig around to go back the other way."

Deborah stroked Spotsy's head, speaking soothingly to her. "Let me see, girl." She gently probed the area of the wound, parting Spotsy's medium-length hair to inspect the gash.

Spotsy seemed to understand, making no complaint while Deborah examined her. The cut was about two inches long, but the bleeding had almost stopped. Pulling gently on her leash, she asked, "Can you get up, girl?"

Spotsy made it to her feet, standing gingerly on her left rear paw.

"Good girl. Now, can you walk?" Deborah asked, intending to lead her to the side of the road.

Spotsy took one step, whimpered, and collapsed to the ground again, licking her wound.

The train began to roll, starting out of town.

Deborah knelt again by Spotsy's side, stroking her head. "Poor thing. I know it hurts, but you can't stay here, in the middle of the road."

"Maybe she'll let me carry her." Tommy waited until the caboose had cleared the tracks, then he bent down, lifting Spotsy ever so carefully into his arms.

They hadn't gone far when a rig pulled alongside them. "Mrs. Rockwell, is that you, under that cap?"

Deborah instantly recognized the voice of Mr. Sheldon. Her face burning with embarrassment, she quickly removed the cap from her head and placed it on Tommy's. "Hello, Mr. Sheldon!" To Tommy, she said, "It's the gentleman I met at Aunt Luella's church."

Sheldon said, "Looks like you all could use a lift. Hop in." He opened the carriage door for them.

When they had settled inside the rig, Deborah made introductions and explained about Spotsy's accident.

Mr. Sheldon instructed his driver to take them to Luella's, then focused on Tommy. "This is certainly Divine timing. Your wife told me earlier that you were joining her at Mrs. Dunston's today. I have an immediate opening for an assistant at my store if you have good references and are planning to stay on in Calumet."

"As a matter of fact, the answer to both is yes," Tommy replied, pulling the letter of reference from his pocket.

Sheldon read the letter and returned it to Tommy with a nod of approval. "Come see me tomorrow at nine. I'm at the corner of Sixth and Elm, directly across from the Calumet Theatre."

"Across from the theater?" Deborah asked excitedly, remembering the furniture and general merchandise store she'd seen there. "Oh, Tommy, it's perfect! We'll be right across the street from each other when I'm at rehearsals."

Mr. Sheldon smiled. "When I see you tomorrow, I'll explain the duties you'd be expected to perform."

"Much obliged. I'll be there at nine, sharp."

When they reached Luella's, Deborah couldn't help the strange feeling of familiarity that came over her when Mr.

Sheldon took her arm to help her down from the carriage. Again, she attributed it to his lime cologne and pushed the matter from her mind.

Tommy carried Spotsy inside, laying her on the kitchen floor while Deborah fetched a clean washcloth. With Tommy's help to keep Spotsy still, she knelt beside the dog, humming quietly as she washed the dirt from the wound.

Tommy hardly needed to hold Spotsy down. She seemed to trust Deborah not to inflict pain. As she carefully cleansed the dirt from the cut, Tommy couldn't help wishing his Butterfly would show as much tenderness and affection toward him as she was for their dog. He had no doubt that she would be a good mother to her baby when the time came. He need only be patient and pray that gradually she would warm toward him even when there was no audience to encourage her.

The moment Deborah finished with her nursing chore, Spotsy commenced licking her injury.

"Spotsy, don't do that!" Deborah chided, trying to lift the dog's chin to make her stop.

Tommy took Deborah's hand away, enclosing it in his own. "Let her be, Butterfly. There's a healing balm in a dog's saliva. She'll be fine."

"Perhaps so, but that licking sound is driving me crazy."

Tommy rose, pulling his wife up with him. "Then come out on the porch and sit a spell. Do you suppose Aunt Luella has a newspaper I could read?"

"I saw one in the back parlor," she said, leading him to the room where she'd sat with Aunt Luella before church that morning. She gave Tommy the newspaper from beneath the Bible and he immediately opened it to the front page.

"It's Friday's paper, but it's news to me," he said, continuing to browse.

On a whim, Deborah lifted the piano cover and with one finger, plunked out the first phrase of *Polly Wolly Doodle.*

Tommy set aside the newspaper and joined her, striking the bass chords.

"You remember!" Deborah said with surprise. "I didn't think you'd remember that old ditty you used to play with Cousin Caroline."

"Of course I remember," Tommy said defensively. "I played it with her not too long ago. Do you know it?"

"I'm afraid not," Deborah lamented, "but I know the words."

"Then sing!" Tommy said, sitting on the bench to play accompaniment while Deborah put words to the piece.

On the chorus, he began singing with her. But when Deborah switched to the harmony part, Tommy had difficulty staying on the melody. He sang and played louder, but his finger went off on the wrong keys making sour notes. Nevertheless, he kept on, his voice and his piano-playing growing louder and louder until he had drowned Deborah out.

In the kitchen, Spotsy began to howl.

The two carried on, Tommy with his missed notes and Spotsy with her shrill howls, making Deborah laugh so hard that tears ran down her cheeks and she had to sit.

When Tommy had finished his off-key rendition of *Polly Wolly Doodle*, he closed the keyboard cover with a flourish.

Deborah applauded.

"Thank you very much," Tommy said, rising from the piano bench to bow deeply at the waist.

"Thank *you*—for stopping that horrible caterwauling."

Tommy scowled. Taking newspaper in hand again, he

said, "I know when it's time to make my exit. I'll be out on the porch reading the paper if you care to join me."

"Maybe later."

When Tommy had gone, Deborah lifted the piano bench cover to look through Aunt Luella's music. She discovered dozens of pieces of sheet music, all more than five years old, leading her to conclude that arthritis had prevented the elderly woman from playing in recent years. But the songs were ones Deborah knew and loved, and even though her own piano skills were too limited to play the accompaniments, she could find the starting notes easily enough, and began singing through the collection *a cappella.*

On the porch, Tommy could hear his Butterfly's voice soaring through favorite melodies of past years: *Hello! Ma Baby, Hearts and Flowers, Rock-a-Bye Baby.* The sound of her music filled his heart with joy. He wished that she could always be as happy and contented as she seemed right now, making music for the shear pleasure of it, but such was a temporary delight. Well he knew that she was a flighty young woman as full of ups and downs as a Monarch's path from one milkweed plant to another, and he prayed to God for the strength and wisdom to guide her along the way.

The house had grown dark and quiet, the hour late when Deborah, the only one still up, wandered again into the back parlor where she had spent a pleasant afternoon singing through Luella's collection of sheet music. She sat in Luella's chair, her mind drifting over the events of the day. She saw Tommy stepping off the train, and even now, her heart fluttered remembering the apprehension of the moment. She didn't know why he hadn't been angrier with her for running off, or reluctant to live in this far-north town, but she was grateful beyond words for his willingness to settle here with Aunt Luella.

Immediate employment in Mr. Sheldon's store would ease the transition to Calumet considerably. The situation couldn't be more perfect—except for one small, vexing matter. Deborah still couldn't decide why Mr. Sheldon seemed familiar to her. She'd thought at first that it must be the scent of his cologne. The lime fragrance evoked fond memories of her Uncle Charles, but that didn't explain the uneasiness that set in whenever she was in Mr. Sheldon's presence.

She mulled it over, his face clear in her mind. Perhaps she'd known someone in the theater in Detroit who had been similar in features and height—an actor, a director, or even a prop man who had worn a derby—but she couldn't remember. Then a horrifying thought struck her.

What if she had met him at the white slave house?

Chapter

17

A wave of panic swept over Deborah. Her head spun at the horrifying possibility that she had met Mr. Sheldon while in Buffalo. She tried to remember the men she'd known there, but one thought paralyzed her mind. She had traveled all this distance to escape her past, and now, it was haunting her again like a shadow that would never go away.

She stood up and paced the floor, reasoning with herself out loud. "He's probably never been to State of New York, let alone the city of Buffalo. He probably only *looks* like someone I met there. When the opportunity comes up, I'll ask him. I'm sure he'll say he's never been east of Michigan."

Taking a deep breath, she wandered into the kitchen, drank a sip of water, and went upstairs to bed.

Tommy had been asleep for some time when Deborah's stirrings awakened him.

Spotsy, who was lying on the floor between the two beds, let out a soft whine.

Deborah's mumbled words, though muffled by the pillow, grew louder and clearer until they were understandable.

"No! Leave me alone!"

Even in the darkness, Tommy saw her shoulder jerking beneath the sheet. Realizing she was having a nightmare about her "resort" nights, Tommy turned on the light and went to her. Sitting on the edge of her bed, he spoke soothingly. "Butterfly, wake up."

"Go away!" she warned, her hand flying up to hit him in the face.

When he captured her wrist with a solid grip to prevent further assault, the fight went out of her and her pleas became a heart-wrenching wail.

"Let me go! I beg you, *please!*"

"Wake up, Butterfly! It's me, Tommy!"

Deborah's tearstained eyes fluttered open. Suddenly she stopped struggling against him, her sobs nearly choking off her words.

"Tommy . . . I thought . . . oh, Tommy!" She clung to his neck and pressed her face against his shoulder, her tears dampening his nightshirt.

He enfolded her in the shelter of his arms, stroking her hair. "It's all right, Butterfly. You're safe with me."

Spotsy jumped up on the bed and snuggled against her.

A moment later, a knock sounded at their door followed by Aunt Luella's voice. "Is everything all right?"

"We're fine," Tommy assured her. "Deborah was having a nightmare, but it's over now."

"Good night, then," Luella said, the sound of her cane retreating down the hall to her room.

As Tommy held his sobbing wife, he couldn't help hating the evildoers who had upset her so. He prayed to God that they would meet their just reward, and that Jesus would cleanse him of the anger he felt against those vile men. He prayed, too, that Jesus would cleanse his beloved Butterfly of the ugly memories that were troubling her sleep and their new marriage.

Deborah grew calm. Leaning back, she reached for the handkerchief on her bedside table and dried her eyes and blew her nose. Noticing the damp place on his shoulder, she said, "I'm sorry, Tommy. I've spoiled your sleep and gotten you all wet."

"That's all right, Butterfly. I'm glad I'm here to comfort you."

Spotsy nudged Deborah's hand, begging for affection.

Deborah stroked the dog's head. "I'm sorry, Spotsy. I woke you up, too didn't I?"

Spotsy lay her head on Deborah's lap, let out a sigh, and closed her eyes.

Deborah chuckled. "If only I could fall asleep as quickly and easily as Spotsy."

"Someday you will," Tommy told her. "Until then, you can count on me to see you through the bad nights." Kissing Deborah's forehead, he asked, "Are you all right now?"

She nodded and kissed his cheek. "Thanks, Tommy. Good night."

"Good night, Butterfly." When he had tucked her beneath the covers and switch off the light, he paused to gaze at his wife, all snuggled in with Spotsy in the crook of her legs. He prayed that the night would soon come when the three of them would sleep soundly all the way through, undisturbed by past problems. Then he climbed into his own bed and prayed some more—that he would be everything his Butterfly needed in a husband.

Deborah wasn't ready to get out of bed when Tommy rose before eight the following morning to prepare for his interview with Mr. Sheldon. Nevertheless, she dragged herself down the hall to the bathroom, splashed cold water on her face, and managed to get washed and dressed in time to breakfast with Tommy and Aunt Luella. Afterward, with Spotsy at her side, she saw Tommy to the door and kissed his cheek. "Good luck! I'm sure Mr. Sheldon will hire you," she said brightly, though privately she wished she'd never met the man.

Tommy kissed her forehead. "Thanks. I certainly hope so." He bent to pet Spotsy's head. "You behave yourself, now, girl. I'll see you later."

Spotsy kissed his hand. When the front door had closed behind him, she bounded off to the front parlor, jumping up on a chair to watch him through the window.

"Spotsy, down!" Deborah commanded, pointing to the floor.

Head low, she stepped off the chair and sat at her feet.

Deborah couldn't suppress a smile at the dog's obvious desire to please. "Good girl. Now, come. I don't want you climbing up there when no one's around to see." She headed for the back parlor, Spotsy at her heels.

Deborah's intention was to start the day with song and clear away the remaining remnants of last night's bad dream. She had opened the piano bench to take out the sheet music when Luella walked in.

"I thought this would be a good time for our Bible study." In the silent moment that followed, she added, "We could start with a song, if you like. How about *What a Friend We Have in Jesus?*" She sat in her chair and began to sing. Spotsy lay at her feet.

Deborah sat in Captain Dunston's chair, joining in on the first verse, which was the only one she knew by heart, and listening to the two verses that followed. The words couldn't have been better suited, reminding her that trials and troubles shouldn't discourage her and that when she felt despised or forsaken by others, the Lord would take her in his arms and shield her.

She remembered the shelter of Tommy's arms last night

and realized that God had provided His comfort through them. She silently thanked Him for her tender, caring husband, and asked Him to help her become a better, more deserving wife. But a cloud of unworthiness hung over her, and the long, dark shadow it cast made her wonder whether the light of lasting happiness would ever come to clear it away.

Luella interrupted her thoughts. "Deborah, do you have anything you'd like to talk about this morning?" When she made no reply, Luella prompted, "About your nightmare?"

Deborah shook her head vigorously. "I . . . " She was about to claim she couldn't remember, but stopped herself from telling an outright lie, saying instead, "I want to talk about the Bible—or rather, hear you talk about it and I'll listen."

Luella opened to a page near the center of her Bible, a smile wrinkling her mouth. "Would you turn, please, to Psalm 32 and read aloud, verse seven."

Deborah read, "'Thou art my hiding place; thou shalt preserve me from trouble; thou shalt compass me about with songs of deliverance.'"

"What do you think that means?" Luella asked.

Deborah replied thoughtfully. "That God will protect you, and put His music round about you to keep you from trouble."

Luella nodded. "Now let's see how we can prepare ourselves to receive what you just described."

Starting at the beginning of Psalm 32, Luella taught Deborah that the first step to receiving God's protection was to confess and receive forgiveness for sin. She explained how King David, who had written the psalm, had let his sin go unconfessed, and during that time, he had suffered great anguish. When he acknowledged his sin, he was forgiven, and assured that overwhelming sorrows would not come near him. He was then given the promise of verse seven, that God would protect him.

The verses that followed promised instruction and guidance for the faithful; many sorrows for the wicked; and mercy for those who trust in the Lord. The eleventh and final verse reminded the righteous to be glad in the Lord and rejoice.

Closing her Bible, Luella bowed her head. "Let us pray. Heavenly Father, thank You for Your Holy Word, for Your forgiveness, for Your instruction, for Your guidance, for Your mercy, and for giving us the opportunity to learn together and to rejoice in all these things, in Jesus' precious name, Amen."

"Amen," Deborah echoed, her mind swimming with all she had just learned about God's truth.

"Do you have any questions?" Luella asked.

Deborah shook her head.

"If you'll excuse me, I'll go and see if Lempi is ready for her English lesson."

Alone in the parlor, Deborah bowed her head and prayed in silence.

Heavenly Father, I've made a lot of mistakes and I need your forgiveness. I'm sorry I ran away from Aunt Ottilia last summer. And I'm sorry I ran away from Caledonia without talking to Tommy first. I still think you meant me to leave that place, but I can see now that Tommy would have understood. Now that we're here, help me to honor and obey my husband, and help me to do Your will. Amen.

Putting the Bible aside, she went to the piano, got out the sheet music, and began to sing, chasing nightmarish memories from mind.

*   *   *

Late that evening, after Luella and Deborah had gone upstairs, Tommy sat down at Captain Dunston's corner desk in the back parlor to pen three letters and a telegram. The telegram was to Charles explaining in brief his new circumstances and thanking him for his help. Tommy would drop it by the Western Union office first thing tomorrow.

As for the three letters—the first one was to the landlord of his bachelor apartment in Grand Rapids notifying him that he would be vacating the apartment by the end of the month. The second letter went to the landlord of the apartment he'd planned to occupy with Deborah, telling him that he and his wife had changed their minds and would not need the place after all. The third letter went to his father.

Monday, September 11, 1905
Dear Father,

 I am writing to tell you that Deborah and I have removed to Calumet, to Mrs. Dunston's where we have taken a room. Circumstances were not working out for Deborah in Caledonia and this seems the perfect solution, what with the big theater here. She has already found herself a position as a rehearsal soloist with the Calumet and Hecla Orchestra and seems well pleased with the opportunities that will be coming her way in that regard.

 As for me, I have obtained employment with a Mr. Sheldon, a shop owner who sells furniture and general merchandise. He is a good Christian man and I expect my tenure with him will be an amicable and profitable one. He has no lack of customers, and with the copper mines booming, folks have plenty of money to spend. I have sold two living room suites already, and

192

this was only my first day on the job! Best of all, in addition to my hourly wage, Mr. Sheldon is paying me a commission on each piece of furniture sold!

In light of all these changes, I must prevail upon you for your help in wrapping up my affairs in Grand Rapids. My removal to the North Country came so unexpectedly and abruptly, that a few loose ends need attending to. I would be most appreciative if, when you next pass through Grand Rapids, you would call on my landlord and remove the few belongings I left in my bachelor apartment. I have already told him to expect you. Don't bother sending the clothing to me here, as I will soon be purchasing new attire to meet the needs of my new position and the colder climate.

Now, I have said enough about my affairs. Please write and tell me how it goes with you, and especially with Mother. Is she improving? Will she be able to come home from the sanitarium soon? My thoughts and prayers are with you both.

Affectionately, Tommy

"Lost the Ring."

The article on the fourth page of the *Copper Country Evening News* for Friday, September 15 caught Tommy's eye as he perused the paper. He could hardly believe that his first five days in Mr. Sheldon's employ had passed so quickly, and that his first week's pay lay tucked in his trouser pocket.

His Butterfly seemed happy, and had already developed a routine of walking to Mr. Sheldon's store at midday to eat the lunch she brought for the two of them to share. At day's end, he often sprinted the last couple of blocks to the house, and when he arrived, they walked Spotsy together.

Tommy yawned. Soon, he would go up to bed. The work at Mr. Sheldon's store was more physically demanding than at Charles's office, but the hours were shorter, allowing him to have most evenings free. But tonight he had worked until nine and now he needed time to let his nerves calm down from the demands of the many customers who had come to patronize Mr. Sheldon's store on payday.

Tommy was tired, too, from Deborah's nightmares interrupting his sleep. Last night was the first time she had slept straight through, and he hoped the bad dreams were gone for good, but he wasn't counting on it. He thanked God that he could be of comfort to his wife, and prayed that she would sleep soundly tonight.

Again, he read the headline of the story at the top of the page, and the subheadings that followed. "Lost the Ring. Groomsman Causes a Commotion at a Calumet Wedding. Went Through Pockets Twice. Blames Groom for Causing of Whole Trouble—Was Repeatedly Nudged and Questioned as to the Resting Place of the Circle of Gold." The paragraphs that followed described with humor how the temporary misplacement of the wedding ring led to a few troubling moments, and how it was finally found deep in the groomsman's vest pocket to the relief of all.

A sudden thought struck Tommy. He put the paper aside and doused the downstairs lights, hurrying up the stairs, two at a time. He expected to find Deborah asleep, but was pleased to see that she was still wide-awake. She was sitting up in bed, leaning on pillows she'd propped against the headboard, studying the theater schedule while Spotsy lay at her feet.

"Don't you have that memorized by now?" Tommy

teased.

"Just about," Deborah replied. "I was double-checking the date for the next musical, 'Hans 'An Nix.' It's scheduled for a week from tomorrow. I should be hearing from Professor Broadman about a rehearsal soon. If he doesn't contact me by Tuesday, I'm going to go and look him up." She closed the program and set it on her bedside stand.

Tommy removed his tie and loosened the celluloid collar that had been chafing at his neck all day. Then he opened the top drawer of his dresser, tucked a tiny box into his shirt pocket, and went to his wife, sitting on the edge of her bed.

No sooner had he taken Deborah's hand in his own, than Spotsy nudged in between them. He stroked the dog's head, then focused again on his wife. They had only been in Calumet a short while, but his Butterfly was growing more beautiful and precious with each passing day. He loved her midday visits at the store, and the evenings they spent together walking Spotsy and performing impromptu musicales in the back parlor. She loved life here, too, he was certain, by the smile he often saw on her face, and the tunes he heard her humming when she thought no one was listening.

He squeezed her hand. "Butterfly, ever since we got married, there's been something missing from—"

The intensity in Tommy's eyes and the solemn tone of his voice put a skip in Deborah's heartbeat. Fearing what he was about to ask of her, she pulled her hand from his and jumped out of bed.

"I have a sudden need to visit Uncle John," she claimed, hurrying from the room as fast as her bare feet would carry her.

Chapter

18

Crestfallen over his wife's sudden exit, Tommy reached for Spotsy, intending to scratch her ear, but the mutt pulled away, leaping off the bed to follow her mistress out of the room. Soon after, Tommy recognized the unmistakable sound of Spotsy plunking down in the hallway with a sigh to await Deborah's exit from the bathroom.

Suddenly, it dawned on him why she had left so abruptly. It wasn't because of some urgent call of nature. She had misunderstood what he was about to say, assuming he was pressing her for affections she was not ready to share. Silently, he berated himself for his poor choice of words. Returning the tiny box to his dresser drawer, he began to change into his nightshirt.

Deborah stared into the bathroom mirror, wondering if the woman she saw reflected there would ever be worthy of the man who waited in their room. Would she ever be ready to share herself completely with him? She hated herself for all that she was not, and even more for all that she *was*. She lowered the lid on the commode and sat down, chin in hands. No matter how much she disliked herself for running off, she was not ready to return to the bedroom—not yet.

She recalled the days since Tommy's arrival on Sunday. Time and again he had proven his love and kindness, comforting her after nightmares each night, thanking her profusely each noon when she had come with their lunch. He had even insisted that she attend amateur night at the Bijou tonight while he was working, and he had bought an extra ticket for Aunt Luella to go with her. And now she was repaying him for all his love, patience, and kindness by hiding in the bathroom.

She bowed her head, remembering the Bible lesson Aunt Luella had taught her this morning, to take everything to God in prayer. "Heavenly Father, help me to be a better wife. I know how patient and considerate Tommy has been, and I thank you for such a good husband. But could you please make him patient for a while longer? Thank you, Lord. Amen."

With determination, she stepped out of the bathroom, her foot nearly landing on Spotsy in the process. Then she marched down the hall, her canine pal at her heels.

Tommy had just pulled on his nightshirt when Deborah burst into the room.

"Tommy, I'm sorry about the way I—"

He was so surprised by her sudden return that he couldn't wait to make an apology of his own. "No, Butterfly, *I'm* sorry."

"You have nothing to be sorry about," she claimed.

"I should have been more careful in my choice—"

She cut in. "I can understand why you think you made a bad choice in marrying me."

"I've never thought I made a bad choice in marrying you, Butterfly."

"Good. I'm glad. Then you'll understand when I say

that I need you to be patient—"

"I'm plenty patient."

"Then why do you keep interrupting me?"

"You interrupted me first," he reminded her.

"Did not."

"Did so."

"Did not."

"Did so."

"Did not, did not, did *not!*" Deborah insisted.

Spotsy began to bark, adding her voice to the argument. Tommy threw his head back and chortled.

Deborah laughed, too, returning to her bed and inviting Spotsy to join her there.

When quiet reigned, Tommy retrieved the tiny box from his dresser drawer and stood at his wife's bedside. "Let's start over."

"Please do." She patted the bed, inviting him to sit.

"What I was trying to say when you interrupted to go visit Uncle John—"

"Fun and folly! You were right! I *did* interrupt you first! I'm sorry, Tommy. This time, I assure you, I do not need to go and visit Uncle John. Now—what's that?" She reached for the jeweler's box.

Tommy hid it behind his back. "Patience, Mrs. Rockwell. Close your eyes and don't open them until I say so."

Deborah squeezed her eyes shut.

"Now, hold out your hand."

She extended her right hand.

"No, the other hand."

When Deborah held out her left hand, palm up, Tommy took it in his, turned it over, and began slipping the wedding ring he'd had custom made in Grand Rapids onto her finger.

Deborah didn't wait for Tommy to tell her she could look. The moment she felt him pressing a ring over her knuckle, her eyelids popped open. There, on her left fourth finger, rested the most unusual yellow gold wedding band she had ever seen. The top flared out, forming butterfly wings, each encrusted with a sparkling diamond.

"Tommy, it's beautiful," she said, her voice awe-hushed, "and so unique."

"Like the woman who wears it," he said, leaning close to kiss her forehead.

She kissed his cheek and stared at the ring again, unable to take her eyes off it. Then she slid it off her finger.

"Why are you taking it off?" Tommy asked. "I thought you liked the ring."

Deborah smiled up at him. "I love it. I just wanted to see if you had it inscribed."

She turned the ring slowly, reading aloud the sentiment written inside the circle of gold. "From T.R. to D.D. With all my love." Sliding it back onto her finger, she paused to study it a moment, moisture enhancing the blue of her eyes. Then she reached up, hugging his neck and kissing his cheek, her words muffled by his nightshirt. "You are the most amazing husband in all the world."

Tommy wrapped his arms about her, reluctant to speak, knowing that if he did, his voice would surely crack. Within him, desire grew making him want to cling forever to his precious, fragile Butterfly. But reason demanded that he release her, and that he do it now. Pulling away, he said, "I'm glad you think I'm amazing, but right now, I'd say I'm amazingly *tired*. Good night, Butterfly. Sweet dreams."

"Good night," she said, gazing at her ring until he turned out the light. As she snuggled beneath the covers, she knew that for once, her dreams truly would be sweet.

Deborah took her customary seat in Captain Dunston's chair for Bible study, realizing that in no time at all, six days had passed and another Friday morning had arrived.

Aunt Luella offered a prayer for God's help with their study, then asked her to turn to Psalm 32. "I'd like to talk about a difficult problem that God will help us to conquer, if we let Him." She looked up from her Bible, fixing her gaze on Deborah. "It's a problem you and I touched on several days ago—one you weren't ready to discuss then. But I pray you'll hear me out on it now."

Deborah waited for Luella to continue.

"I expect you're still mighty angry at the men who did you wrong, and I don't blame you. But if you're going to be angry, why not put that anger to good use?" She paused, her voice softening. "Wouldn't it be better to let God help you transform your anger into a determination not to allow ungodly fellows to steal away your future happiness?"

The concept sounded reasonable to Deborah, but her anger surpassed reason. "I don't know if I can," she admitted. "I don't know how."

"I do," Luella said confidently. "Ask God to help you, and rely on his promise in verse ten. 'Many sorrows shall be to the wicked: but he that trusteth in the Lord, mercy shall compass him about.' Let God bring justice to those who hurt you. Put your trust in Him for His mercy."

Deborah silently read the words to herself. Aunt Luella was right. Her anger would burn and get in the way of happiness for a very long time unless she turned it over to God. She looked up, reaching for the old woman's hand. "Aunt Luella, would you pray for me now, and ask God to help me claim the promise of verse ten for myself?"

The old woman smiled. "Of course I will, child." She

bowed her head, praying with great eloquence that Deborah's anger would be transformed by faith.

When she had finished the prayer and gone to teach Lempi her English lesson, Deborah continued to meditate on God's promise for sorrows to the wicked and mercy to those who trust in Him. She would need time for this concept to yield results in her own life, but the seed had been planted in her heart, and she was sure that it would bear fruit if she would only nurture it properly.

She closed the Bible, gazing down at the gold-and-diamond butterfly ring on her finger. She could hardly believe all that had transpired in the week since Tommy had presented it to her. The next morning, before he had gone off to work, he had given her a generous allowance for new clothing. At Luella's insistence, Lempi had accompanied her to the best clothiers in town—The Fashion, Ed Haas and Company, Vertin Brothers, and Gately-Wiggins. In the last store, she had settled on a new woolen shirtwaist of the directoire style. The lapels offered the perfect place for her butterfly pin, and the black braid trim set off the pale pink fabric to perfection. For her walks to Mr. Sheldon's store on days when declining temperatures put a Lake Superior chill in the air, she had chosen a woolen coat with a Prince Albert back, the height of current fashion.

Laying her Bible on the small table beside her, she noticed the program from last Saturday's performance of "Her Only Sin" starring Julia Gray. Tommy had come home from work that day with tickets to the play. The performance had been well executed, but as Deborah looked back on the experience, it was the performance that had taken place beforehand outside of the theater that remained foremost in her mind. She had never seen such an assemblage of uncouth, impolite young men—at least fifty of them—

congregating outside the theater doors in such a manner that they nearly blocked the entrance. They milled about, some tossing insults to theatergoers, others engaging in wrestling contests, and nearly all of them expectorating to the annoyance and disgust of those forced to walk through it.

She pushed the revolting memory from mind, recalling instead the rewarding experience two days ago when she had been requested to rehearse with the Calumet and Hecla Orchestra for tomorrow night's production of "Hans 'N Nix." How she loved standing on the stage, projecting in song until her voice filled the theater. It didn't matter that all the seats were empty and her only audience was the orchestra. It was still a tremendous thrill.

And so was last night's production of the play, "The Marriage of Kitty." She hunted for the program, hiding beneath her Bible, and gazed at the five characters gathered around a perfectly set table as she recalled the evening's events. Tommy had surprised her by coming home a little early and inviting her out to dinner at the Michigan House. When they had eaten their fill of beefsteaks and bread pudding, he had produced two tickets to the comedy starring Alice Johnson. The set evoked the flavor of life in continental Europe, especially in the last two acts, which took place at Kitty's Lake Geneva villa. Deborah chuckled to herself at the humorous performance containing characters who were sometimes bumbling, sometimes erudite, sometimes both.

The only discomforting part of the evening had been when they had encountered the Sheldons on their way out of the theater. Since the nightmares about him had begun, she had been avoiding face-to-face encounters with the man, entering by the back door when she took Tommy's lunch to the store each noon, turning away from him if he came into the back room for inventory to restock shelves. She lived in fear of the moment that he would gaze into her eyes with a lurid look of recognition.

Pressing the horrifying thought from mind, she lay the program aside. The morning was slipping by. Tonight, she would be singing at amateur night at the Bijou. She needed to warm up her voice now and put in a good practice session before she left to meet Tommy for lunch. Stepping over Spotsy, who lay contentedly at her feet, she reached for the Autoharp she would be using to accompany herself in tonight's performance, strummed a chord, and began to sing.

Deborah took Fifth Street toward The Fashion after her lunch with Tommy, her gait brisk. Her confidence in this evening's performance at the Bijou had just been elevated by the news that he had been given the night off so that he could come to hear her. And her already buoyant mood had been lifted higher by the instructions he had given her, along with a portion of his pay for this week, to go and buy herself a hat to wear tonight.

She was humming the song she would perform as she hurried along. Then, a sign on the sidewalk in front of the Central Hotel stopped her silent in her tracks.

Now In Our Parlors
for a short time only
Palmist and Clairvoyant
PROF. CARLE

The eminent medium is now in residence. So strange and mysterious are his powers that you will be amazed at the marvelous things he will reveal about your **Past, Present and Future.** He will give you reliable advice about business, travel, courtship, marriage, separation, telling you names, dates, facts and figures. Mr. Carle never fails to remove evil spells, reunite lovers or cause speedy and happy marriages. If in doubt as to anything, perhaps from him you may learn a secret power whereby your life will be made happy and successful.

Special Low Prices This Week
Hours: 9 to 9
Prof. Carle is positively here for a short time only.

Deborah reached into her pocket, fingering the gold coin meant for a hat. Curiosity burned within to know whether she would ever be successful in the theater. Certainly a palm reading wouldn't cost more than a hat. With great expectation, she stepped into the hotel, following the sign to the parlor where Professor Carle could be found.

Chapter

19

Deborah took a seat beside an elderly woman waiting to hear Professor Carle's words of wisdom. A gentleman stepped out, and the other woman went in. Deborah waited several minutes, and was on the verge of leaving when the door opened again.

She expected to enter a dimly lit room where she would encounter a turbaned gentleman of short stature and dusky complexion. She found instead a parlor brightened by several fringed lamps, and occupied by a tall gentleman whose gray suit, white shirt, and black bow tie gave him the appearance of an ordinary businessman.

"Welcome, Miss . . . "

"Mrs. Rockwell," Deborah supplied, extending her hand.

Indicating the straight chair in front of a table in the center of the room, he invited her to sit, taking his place across the table from her in a cordovan leather chair. "Mrs. Rockwell, today's reading will cost three dollars in advance. Is that agreeable?"

"Yes, sir," Deborah replied, reaching into her pocket for the five dollar gold piece Tommy had given her. When he had placed two silver dollars' change on the table, she lay both of her hands face up. "Which palm do you read, Professor Carle? The right or the left?"

"The one with the most distinct lines," he replied, studying each of hers for a moment. "With you, it is the left. Did you know, Mrs. Rockwell, that palmistry existed three thousand years before Christ?"

"It did?" Deborah asked in awe.

"Oh, yes! Aristotle and Hypocrites have both written about it. The ancients widely believed in the meaning of the marks on the 'organ of organs.' Now, this line here," he ran his finger along a crease at the ball of her thumb, "this is the line of life. Yours is a very long and distinct one, indicating that you will live a long and distinguished life."

"I will?" Deborah asked in surprise. "What else do you see?"

Tracing a line in the middle of her hand, he explained, "This line indicates that you have above average intelligence. And this one," he traced another line below it, "is the line of the heart. Yours suggests strength uncommon to most women. And this line," he touched a crease between the middle of the wrist and the middle finger, "is the line of fortune—oh, oh, oh!"

"What is it? What do you see?"

"There is a large fortune in your future, Mrs. Rockwell. Of this, I am certain."

"From the theater? Will I become a rich and famous actress?"

He gazed into her eyes. She felt as though he was looking straight into her soul to discern the answer. "I cannot tell the source of your future wealth. It may come from the theater, or from . . . I cannot say." He let go of her hand, asking, "Have you anything else in mind that you are wondering about today, Mrs. Rockwell? Perhaps concerning a family member—your husband?"

"Actually, I'm only wondering whether I'll ever be successful on the stage. Are you sure you can't tell whether I'll make my fortune there?"

His gaze went above and beyond her. He pressed his fingers to his temples, as if to concentrate harder, then shook his head. "I'm afraid no message is coming to me. But wait. I'm getting something . . . " He pressed his fingers to his temples again. After a moment's pause, he said gravely, "A cloud hovers."

"What does it mean?"

He continued to gaze beyond her, his eyes unfocused. "I can't quite make it out. But perhaps . . . " He gestured toward her two silver dollars still on the table. "Perhaps with a little encouragement, the message will come through."

Deborah slid the coins toward him. "Try again, will you please?"

He pocketed the coins and placed his fingers against his temples, the faraway look again overtaking him. "The cloud is dark . . . it hovers near . . . it is too dark to see through . . . ah, but wait! An opening appears . . . and beneath it lies a loved one . . . a dearly departed loved one in a casket."

"Is it a woman, or a man?" Deborah asked.

"I can't quite tell," the professor replied. "I can only see that this person was dearly loved by the sadness of those left behind. Above the casket is a silver lining to the cloud. The lining is in the shape of some particular object important to your future. I can't quite tell what it is. It may be a st—"

"Is it a stage? Will I make my fortune on the stage after this person's death?"

With a small shake of his head, he said, "I'm sorry, Mrs. Rockwell, it's gone. That's all for today." He rose.

"But I want to know who died, and what the silver lining was in the cloud," Deborah insisted.

"Have you some encouragement for me?" he asked,

clearly implying the need for more money.

"No, I'm sorry."

He began to usher her out. "Come again when you have some encouragement for me, Mrs. Rockwell. I'm sure the images will be clear to me then. But don't wait too long. I'm only here for the week."

"Thank you, professor! I'll be back!"

Deborah hurried home as fast as her feet would carry her. She could hardly wait to tell Aunt Luella about Professor Carle. After a brief reunion with a boisterously happy Spotsy at the front door, she sought out her aunt, who was resting in her favorite chair in the back parlor, Bible open on her lap.

"Aunt Luella, I've just had my palm read, and you won't believe what I've learned!" Deborah announced excitedly.

"You *what?*" Luella's look of surprise bordered on shock.

"I've just had my palm read by Professor Carle," Deborah repeated.

"Heavens to hickory nuts! What ever possessed you to do such a thing?"

"I saw his sign in front of the Central Hotel on my way home from lunch with Tommy," Deborah explained. "You won't believe what Professor Carle saw in my palm!"

"Let me guess," Luella replied with the tone of a skeptic. "A long life, a strong heart, a high degree of intelligence, and a large fortune."

"But . . . how did you know?" Deborah asked, lighting on Captain Dunston's chair to hear more.

Luella's mouth wrinkled with a cynical smile. "The palmistry swindle has been around for a long, long time," Luella replied.

"How could palmistry be a swindle?" Deborah challenged. "It goes all the way back to three thousand years before Christ."

"Maybe so, but there's nothing to it. And those so-called professors who go around claiming to read palms are really taking unfair advantage of folks who don't know the truth. Why don't you fetch the 'P' encyclopedia from the bookcase, and look under 'Palmistry?'"

Deborah did as Luella suggested, learning that palm reading did have its start thousands of years before Christ, but that, like Aunt Luella had said, the characteristics of a person's palm were in no way related to their future. She closed the book, deeply disappointed that she had wasted Tommy's hard-earned money. Another thought troubled her as well.

"Aunt Luella, when I asked Professor Carle if I would be successful on the stage, he took on a sort of distant look, and claimed that he was seeing things in my future."

"What did he see?" she asked with concern.

Deborah told of the vision the professor had described, including the nebulous image of something in a silver lined cloud. "He said it would come clear if I came back with some 'encouragement.'"

"I'm sure he was clearly seeing a chance to part you from more of your money," Luella warned.

"He says he's a clairvoyant. He says he sees the future," Deborah explained.

The wrinkles deepened in Luella's forehead. "You must keep your distance from that man and have nothing more to do with him, do you understand?"

"But—"

"Hear what the Bible says about such individuals." Luella turned to the Old Testament. "Leviticus 19:31.

'Regard not them that have familiar spirits, neither seek after wizards, to be defiled by them: I am the Lord your God.' And Leviticus 20:6 warns, 'And the soul that turneth after such as have familiar spirits, and after wizards, to go a whoring after them, I will even set my face against that soul.'"

"Familiar spirits? What does that mean?"

Luella explained. "Demon spirits that possess people who give their will over to them to make predictions."

"Professor Carle is demon possessed?" Deborah asked.

"He certainly is in league with the devil, claiming to read palms and tell the future, whether or not his information is coming straight from the evil one. Like I said, you must keep your distance and have nothing more to do with him. Now let us pray about this." She took Deborah's hand in her own. "Father God, forgive your child, Deborah, for going unawares into the company of one who claims the power of familiar spirits. Protect her by the blood of the cross from any attacks of the evil one. Thank you, Lord. And Father, I ask Your blessing on Deborah when she performs at the Bijou tonight. Let the beauty of her music be a blessing to all that hear her. In Jesus' name, Amen."

"Amen." Deborah rose. "I'd better practice one last time."

Luella set aside her Bible and reached for her cane. "I'm going up to my room for a nap. I don't want to be too tuckered out to enjoy the evening."

Deborah's practice had been flawless, but she was worried over Tommy's reaction when she descended the stairs in the same hat she had always worn. Lingering in front of her dresser mirror, she told herself, "Performance time is fast arriving. You've got to go downstairs, and you've got to do it *now!*"

Tommy set aside the newspaper, his gaze on her as she stepped into the front parlor. "You look wonderful, Butterfly, but I thought you were going to buy a new hat for tonight."

She nibbled her lip. "Oh, Tommy, I've made a terrible mistake!" Perching on the edge of the chair nearest his, she told him of Professor Carle, his predictions, and the scolding she had received from Aunt Luella. "I'm sorry I wasted your money, Tommy. I didn't mean to."

He chuckled. "We all make mistakes, Butterfly. Now put it straight out of your mind and think about your performance!"

Chapter

20

"Bravo! Bravo!"

Tommy's boisterous words, shrill whistle, and wild applause had led the audience's enthusiastic response to Deborah's performance at the Bijou.   But two weeks and five days later, she sat uneasily in the front parlor watching through the rain-spattered window for Mr. Sheldon's rig to pull up.

She could not believe the fix she was in on this cold, wet evening. She hadn't wanted to accept his offer of escort to the Palestra, the sports arena in the neighboring village of Laurium. But she had no choice if she were to honor her commitment to sing a solo with the Calumet and Hecla Band at the concert they were performing there tonight. They had taken up a schedule of playing on Monday, Wednesday, and Saturday nights for roller skaters at the arena.   This night, they had planned a special perform-ance—a band concert in which she would be featured as a soloist—followed by more music for skating and dancing. October weather what it was in the Keweenaw, the clouds had already rolled in off Lake Superior, pushed by cold winds and filled with moisture that sometimes poured out by the bucketful. The elements had thoroughly eliminated the possibility of walking to the arena.

Deborah recalled the circumstances that had led to her present dilemma.   The night before last Aunt Luella had come down with a mild case of the grippe. Afraid it would spread, she had given strict orders for all but Lempi, who was nursing her, to keep their distance. Ironically, it was not Lempi, or even Deborah who had become infected, but Tommy who had come home from work today suffering from a fever and upset stomach.

Before Tommy had left the store, he had arranged for Mr. Sheldon to accompany Deborah to the concert. Deborah dreaded sitting face to face with the man. After carefully avoiding encounters with him each lunch hour at the store, and having insisted that she and Tommy walk to church for Sunday services rather than accepting Mr. Sheldon's week-ly offers of rides, she could no longer escape the inevitable. The prospect of being in near proximity to him unnerved her far more than the prospect of singing a solo. At least she had found a double layer of black netting to attach as a veil to the hat she was wearing. When she saw the man's rig drive up, she pulled the translucent silk down over her face.

He emerged from his carriage, popped open his umbrel-la, and headed briskly up to the porch to ring the doorbell. Deborah answered with all the graciousness she could muster.

"Hello, Mr. Sheldon! I'm so sorry you've been put to the trouble of escorting me to the Palestra tonight."

He offered his arm, the scent of his lime cologne drift-ing to her when he held his umbrella over her and led her down the steps. "No trouble, Mrs. Rockwell. I've been looking forward to this concert all afternoon!"

His mellow voice and smooth way with words made Deborah apprehensive. She wanted desperately to turn back rather than get into the carriage alone with this man. Then he opened the door and the sight of Mrs. Sheldon and Penelope in the back seat put her somewhat at ease.

When they arrived at the arena, Deborah was thankful to

213

part company with the Sheldons to join the band as they warmed up before the start of the concert. Even though the Palestra was a much less prestigious location for a musical event than the Calumet Theatre, Deborah appreciated the fact that it was practically brand new, and capable of seating almost three times as many in the audience. Of course, the arena would be nowhere near capacity tonight, but Deborah would have happily performed for an audience of one just for the chance to sing her solo, *Battle Hymn of the Republic* with the Calumet and Hecla Band.

She sat behind the percussion section and folded back the veil as the band opened the performance with three rousing Sousa marches. The audience, though perhaps not as refined as a theater audience, was highly enthusiastic with applause and whistles at the conclusion of each piece. Then Deborah stepped to the front for her solo, nodded in readiness to Professor Broadman, and drew a deep breath as he led the band through a few measures of introduction.

Like butterflies floating on an updraft, the notes of the song flowed from deep within her, projecting to the uppermost rafters of the curved ceiling to fill the arena with her heartfelt rendition of the cherished hymn. For the first time, she seemed to hear her singing as if she were outside herself. And for the first time, she began to understand that the voice she was hearing was not simply a result of her inheritance from her mother or her long and hard hours of dedicated practice. But as Aunt Luella had told her a month ago, it was a gift from God.

When the last note of her song had died away, the audience erupted in loud applause. Mr. Sheldon, his wife, and his daughter who were sitting in the front row several yards away, stood up, then others stood until everyone in the place had come off their seats to applaud her performance.

Deborah curtsied again and again while the audience shouted for more.

Professor Broadman tapped his stand with his baton, asked her to sing the first and last verses again, then raised his arms and began the introduction for a second time.

When she had finished, the audience again favored her with enthusiastic applause, and she returned to her chair behind the percussionists to listen to the rest of the performance. She was secretly pleased to see that, while the cornet soloist, John Williams, and the trombone soloist, Harry King, each received heavy applause, neither of them was honored with a standing ovation or a request for an encore.

When the concert ended, Deborah pulled her veil down over her face again and headed for the Sheldons, receiving many words of praise and congratulations from members of the audience as they dispersed for dancing and skating. Penelope had already joined the skaters when Deborah joined her parents.

Mr. Sheldon got quickly to his feet, the first to offer a compliment. "What a shame Tommy and Luella couldn't come to hear you tonight. You're the best woman singer we've ever heard in Calumet, isn't she, dear?" He gazed down at his wife, who was still seated.

Mrs. Sheldon nodded vigorously. "I'm sure we'll be hearing a lot more of you after this, Mrs. Rockwell."

"I certainly hope so," Deborah replied, taking a seat beside Mrs. Sheldon.

Reaching for his wife's elbow, Mr. Sheldon said, "Shall we dance, dear? They're playing a waltz."

"No, thank you, George."

"But we haven't danced in months," he insisted.

"I'm too tired. Remember, I filled in for Tommy all

afternoon at the store, and I'll be there all day tomorrow and until he recovers. Mrs. Rockwell will do the honors."

He turned to Deborah. "Mrs. Rockwell, shall we dance?"

"No, I—"

Mrs. Sheldon nudged her firmly. "Oh, go on. I took your husband's place at the store. The least you can do is take my place on the dance floor."

Dread surged within as Deborah rose.

On the dance floor, Mr. Sheldon proved to be a skilled and graceful partner, making for immediate synchronization of their steps. Deborah had begun to feel somewhat at ease when he initiated conversation on a topic she had hoped to avoid. "Mrs. Rockwell, is it my imagination, or have you purposely been keeping your distance from me for the last three weeks?"

"Avoiding you?" she asked innocently.

"You keep your distance at the store, and you've declined offers of rides to church, even in questionable weather. If I've been guilty of some offense, I surely wish you'd tell me what it was."

"You have quite an imagination," Deborah replied, purposely looking past his shoulder to the skaters who occupied the other portion of the rink. From the corner of her eye, she could tell that Mr. Sheldon was looking right at her, trying to see through her veil. After a few more steps, he spoke again.

"Mrs. Rockwell, I sometimes wonder if we've met before, but it's hard to tell with the black netting covering your face."

Fear shot through Deborah. She miss-stepped, nearly landing on his foot as she tried to think of a reply. Summoning her fortitude, she spoke with a lightness she didn't feel. "That's quite a coincidence, Mr. Sheldon, because I've sometimes wondered, too, if we've ever crossed paths before. Have you ever been to Buffalo?"

"Buffalo?" he asked thoughtfully.

A silent moment lapsed—a moment that seemed to stretch to eternity. Deborah's heart stopped, her hands turned clammy, and her breathing halted.

Reluctantly, he replied, "I'm not a well-traveled man, Mrs. Rockwell. The truth is, I've never been east of Detroit."

"You're sure you've never been to Buffalo?" she asked, eager to believe the good news.

He chuckled. "I think I would know if I'd ever been to Buffalo."

"Yes, I suppose you would," Deborah quietly agreed.

As the good news began to sink in, relief flooded over Deborah, making her chuckle.

Mr. Sheldon smiled down at her. "I don't know what I've said that's so funny, but I'm glad you're enjoying yourself."

"I'm sorry," Deborah apologized, regaining control. "I'm laughing at myself for having ever thought we'd met in Buffalo. But I'm still wondering why you look familiar."

"Have you ever seen the moving picture, 'The Great Train Robbery?'" Mr. Sheldon asked.

"I saw it in Detroit," Deborah replied, remembering how the film, which had debuted two years earlier, had earned popularity as the first moving picture with a plot.

"People tell me I look like the fellow in that story," Mr. Sheldon explained.

"Max Aaronson! Of course!" Deborah agreed, pulling back the veil of her hat.

Mr. Sheldon's gaze locked with hers. "Now I know

217

who you remind me of—my wife's second cousin. She's from a fine, fair-haired family in Wisconsin. We met only once a few years back, but you do resemble her."

"Thank goodness we've settled that question," Deborah said as the waltz came to an end. Mr. Sheldon was escorting her off the dance floor when she heard a young woman's voice calling her name. She turned to find a familiar face.

"Mrs. Rockwell, remember me? Molly Mulligan, from the train."

"Of course!" Deborah exclaimed, recalling their long chat en route to Calumet almost five weeks earlier.

When she had introduced Molly to Mr. Sheldon, the girl continued.

"Ya sure do have a beautiful singing voice, Mrs. Rockwell. Better watch out. The angels 'll be downright jealous!"

"Thank you for the compliment, Molly but I don't think the angels have anything to fear." Remembering their earlier conversation, Deborah said, "I'm surprised to see you here. I thought you'd be in Superior, working as a domestic."

"Postponed my plans," she replied with obvious disappointment. "Mama broke her ankle the day I come back from my sister's. I've been washing dishes at the Michigan House and taking care of her till she gets back on her feet. Won't be long now, though. The family in Superior said the job's mine soon as I can get there."

"I wish you the best!" Deborah offered her hand.

"Thanks, and the same to you, Mrs. Rockwell. I'm sure y'll be a star, with that voice of yours!"

Molly's compliment was still ringing in Deborah's ears on the ride home. How thankful she was that her performance had gone well, and that the evening had turned into a truly delightful experience rather than the dreaded one she had feared. Catching a glimpse of Mr. Sheldon on the seat across from her, she thanked God that his familiar look was due to his resemblance to a movie actor. She drew a deep breath, silently thanking God for putting this nightmare to rest, and wishing she had trusted Him sooner, rather than giving in to her own unfounded fears.

On the following Sunday evening, Deborah sat at the piano practicing the songs from the musical, "Floradora" in preparation for her upcoming rehearsal with the Calumet and Hecla Orchestra. A newly recovered Tommy was sitting nearby, reading the newspaper and enjoying the sound of his wife's clear soprano voice when Luella entered the room, her first time downstairs since the onset of the grippe. Deborah and Tommy were instantly at her side.

Tommy eyed her critically. "You're looking better. How do you feel?"

"A tad weak in the legs," she admitted.

Deborah held her hand to Luella's forehead. "Thank goodness, your fever is gone, but you still look tired."

Slowly, Luella made her way to her chair. "I'm weary, I'll admit, but thankful to be over the worst of it." To Tommy, she said, "You're looking well."

"Fit as a fiddle! I've already rung up Mr. Sheldon and told him I'll be in to work tomorrow."

Deborah chuckled. "Mrs. Sheldon will be grateful, I'm sure." She sat at the piano again, resuming her practice. She had sung only a few notes when Luella interrupted.

"What in heaven's name is all this clutter?" She was rummaging through a stack of papers on the table beside her chair—Deborah's collection of theater programs and the newspaper articles about them that Tommy had saved for her.

Deborah scrambled off the piano bench. "Those are mine. I'll find another place for them." Opening the piano bench, she lay them beneath Luella's hymnal and again sat down to practice. But again, her singing was interrupted when Lempi came into the room, Spotsy at her heels.

"Spotsy sick!" the Finnish girl announced with obvious distress. "She beg and beg, eat, and eat. Now, look!" Lempi placed her hand against the dog's belly, which was beginning to expand.

Luella said, "Spotsy, come!" The dog obeyed, allowing the elderly woman to examine her.

Deborah knelt to do the same. "Why is she getting so fat all of a sudden? I've been walking her twice every day, even this week when Tommy's been sick."

The old woman's eyes twinkled. "I'll tell you why she's so hungry. She's going to be a mother soon!" She explained the situation in words Lempi could understand. The young girl laughed and returned to her kitchen duties.

Tommy knelt beside Spotsy, stroking her head. "So she's going to be a mother, but when?"

Luella said, "In a week and a half, or so, things should get mighty interesting around here."

Chapter
21

Ten days later

Deborah was in the back parlor practicing when she heard Tommy come through the front door after work whistling *Hello! Ma Baby*. She hurried to greet him, taking his golf yacht cap and coat, and hanging them on the hall tree as he sang made-up words to the tune he'd been whistling.

"Hello, ma Butterfly, hello, ma Butterfly, hello, ma Butterfly gal!" He slipped his arm about her waist and headed for the back parlor, pausing after a few steps to glance about. "Where's Spotsy? She's usually at the front door before you are."

Deborah shrugged. "I think she's upstairs. She's been keeping to herself all day. Aunt Luella says her pups could be born anytime now."

"I'll go up and see her in a minute. First, I have a surprise for you." He led Deborah to Captain Dunston's chair, greeting Aunt Luella as he entered the back parlor.

Shaking a finger at his wife, he warned, "Now stay put, Butterfly. I'll be right back."

Deborah did as he requested. He returned a moment later, presenting her with a medium-sized box wrapped in tissue and decorated with a large silk butterfly.

"How beautiful! But it isn't my birthday," she reminded him.

Luella said, "I wouldn't complain if I were you." To Tommy, she said, "You're spoiling her rotten, you know."

"I know," he said with a grin. Perching on the piano bench, he told Deborah, "Open it!"

Deborah carefully removed the butterfly, then tore off the tissue and lifted the lid. "Roller skates! I haven't had a pair of these in years," she exclaimed, holding them up. "Remember how you and Cousin Caroline and Cousin Parker and I used to race up and down the street on our skates?"

Tommy nodded. "Butterfly, would you do me the honor of accompanying me to the Palestra this evening for roller skating? The band will be playing."

"But—" She thought of the production of "The Show Girl" taking place only this one night at the theater and had harbored hopes that he'd come home with tickets to it. He'd taken her to nearly all the performances there in the last six weeks, including "Trilby" four nights ago.

Luella spoke up. "Of course, she'll go. It'll do the two of you good to get a little exercise. Goodness knows, Spotsy won't be going on any walks for a while."

Deborah offered Tommy a bright smile. "Of course, I'll go skating with you tonight."

"Good! I've been looking forward to it ever since I hit upon the idea earlier this afternoon. Mr. Sheldon thought it was such a good plan, he's taking Penelope and her friend. They're picking us up at twenty minutes past eight. Afterward, they'll drop the two of us off at the Michigan House for hot chocolate. I'll even treat you to your favorite dessert—pecan pie!"

Luella smiled wistfully. "If only I were young again."

222

Two hours later, when Mr. Sheldon came by to drive them to the Palestra, Deborah couldn't help wishing that their destination was the Calumet Theatre. But she concealed her disappointment with the skill of an actress, keeping a smile on her face and sweet words in her mouth as she and Tommy made small talk with Penelope and her young friend, Arthur, on the way to the arena.

Mr. Sheldon dropped them off at the door with the promise to pick them up at ten. Inside, Penelope and Arthur donned their skates in no time, and were rolling around the rink the moment Professor Broadman struck up the band. When Tommy had put on his own skates, he helped Deborah with hers. Then, with his arm about her waist, he carefully led her into the flow of skaters. She enjoyed the secure feeling of Tommy at her side, and soon wrapped her arm about his waist, as well. The band played one waltz after another, and the ninety minutes that Deborah had thought would drag by were over too soon.

She was taking off her skates when Molly Mulligan rolled to a stop in front of her.

"Hello, Mrs. Rockwell! Nice to see ya again!"

"Well, hello, Molly!" To Tommy, she said, "Tommy, this is Molly Mulligan. We met on the train back in September. Molly, this is my husband, Tommy."

"Glad to meet ya," she said, shaking Tommy's hand. To Deborah, she said, "Just wanted to tell ya my Ma's back on her feet, so I'm off to Superior tomorrow."

"I wish you success in your new position!"

"I'll do fine. You just keep on singin' like an angel, ya hear?"

Deborah nodded, smiling as she waved good bye to the young woman.

Mr. Sheldon arrived promptly at ten, driving her and

Tommy to the Michigan House as planned, suffering complaints from Penelope because she and Arthur were not allowed to indulge in the outing there due to school the following morning.

In the restaurant, Tommy requested a table looking out on Oak Street. By the time the waiter had delivered two orders of hot chocolate and pecan pie, huge flakes of white had begun drifting down outside their window. Soon the air was filled with their beauty, transforming the sandstone storefronts and brick pavement into an enchanting winter scene.

Tommy lay down his fork and reached for Deborah's hand, his voice warm with affection. "Butterfly, have I told you lately how beautiful you are?"

Deborah could see the love in his blue eyes, and feel it flowing through the warmth of his hand, straight into her heart. He had told her daily that she was beautiful, but she had privately brushed off his compliments, feeling unworthy. For some unknown reason, she yearned desperately to hear him say it now. Setting down her fork to lay her hand atop his, she replied softly, "I need to hear you tell me again, Tommy."

Casting a glance at the snowflakes as they fell, he gazed straight into her eyes, saying quietly, "To me, you're like that veil of white. My life is much more beautiful because you're in it." Then, he whispered, "I love you, Butterfly."

A knot formed in her throat. She didn't understand the mystery of love, or how Tommy could care so deeply for her after all she'd put him through, but she was thankful that he hadn't given up. Over the last several weeks, she had gradually grown accustomed to being Tommy's wife. She still wasn't ready to give herself completely to him, and she often wondered when this and other situations that had resulted from the trouble in her past would be resolved. Whispering around the lump in her throat, she told him truthfully, "And I love you, Tommy."

He squeezed her hand so hard, she could feel her wedding ring pressing painfully into her fingers, but it was a good kind of pain. Soon enough, they were finishing their pie and hot chocolate and walking home through the gently falling snow. When they reached Aunt Luella's, Lempi came rushing down the stairs, her face flush with excitement.

"Come! See puppies!"

Swiftly shedding hats and coats, they rushed up the stairs. Deborah had expected to find Spotsy in the whelping box they had prepared for her in Tommy's closet, but instead, they found her in Lempi's room at the back of the house, curled up on an old rag rug in the corner.

Luella sat a few feet away, observing the new mother. She spoke words of caution to Deborah and Tommy the moment they stepped through the door. "Don't try to get too close. Spotsy's mighty protective right now."

They approached slowly. Deborah had never seen newborn puppies, and she was surprised at the looks of the three nursing at Spotsy's side. "They're so tiny, and so bald!"

Luella said, "That's perfectly normal. Puppies tend to look like pink mice at first, but they'll grow fast. You'll see."

Tommy asked, "Have you gotten close enough to see if they're girls or boys?"

Luella shook her head. "Some of each, I'd guess." Rising from the chair, she said, "I'm turning in. Lempi will be staying in the guestroom until we can relocate Spotsy and her brood. It's a sure thing no one will get much sleep in here for awhile. Good night."

Deborah and Tommy bid her good night, then Deborah sat in the chair Luella had vacated to watch the new mother and her little ones. "I suppose mothering just comes natural to a dog."

"I suppose," Tommy said. Stepping behind her to rest his hands on her shoulders, he gave a gentle squeeze. "It will come naturally to you, too, Butterfly."

Deborah wanted to argue, but instead, kept her reservations to herself—thoughts that cast a dark veil over the future. How she wished her outlook could be magically transformed into the beautiful white veil Tommy had seen in the gently falling snow, but she doubted that even God could cause such a miraculous transformation.

Saturday morning, December 9

Deborah sat at the dining table, theater programs and newspaper clippings about the performances spread out before her. After breakfast and Bible study, Aunt Luella had handed Deborah an empty stationery box and insisted that her collection of theater memorabilia, haphazardly stashed in the piano bench, be put into some semblance of order. She sorted through the various pieces now, arranging them by date and recalling the events that had delighted her so since her arrival in Calumet.

The newspaper article on the musical, "Hans An' Nix," performed on September 23, showed a photograph of the star, Katherine Roberts, her hat overburdened with dainty flowers, her eyes soulful. The picture brought to mind the sweet melodies Deborah had rehearsed and later heard the actress perform in perfect blend with the silvery tones of her co-star, Kerker Morton.

The next performance, a comedy called "The Mummy

and the Humming Bird," had truly brought many laughs with its eccentric scientist hero and his overlooked wife who managed to entangle herself in questionable circumstances. Deborah thought of Tommy, at work in Mr. Sheldon's store today. As busy as he was, putting in long hours during the holiday season, she needn't worry that she would ever go wanting for his attention.

Her focus again on the array of articles that lay before her, she searched for the next in order of occurrence, the amateur production, "Karnival Kermes." With less than a week of rehearsals, Mr. Luke, a professional director from Chicago, had masterfully pulled the show together from local talent. Deborah hadn't performed in it since it had been sponsored by a guild from another church, but she had enjoyed seeing women and children from Calumet and Laurium on the big stage, especially "Babes in the Wood," involving a hundred people in one act.

The performance that followed on the very next night was "Heart of Chicago," a play about the Windy City from the fire of 1871 to the World's Columbian Exposition of 1893. Deborah would never forget the heart-stopping experience of watching a locomotive complete with sound effects and steam, moving from the rear of the stage, right down to the footlights.

The next production that came to the theater, "San Toy," was Deborah's favorite. As she sorted through the many stories that had appeared in the newspapers before its October fifth arrival, she remembered the joy of rehearsing the twenty-six songs from the musical with the Calumet and Hecla Orchestra.

She loved the romantic plot of the story, about the mandarin father, who, in order to save his daughter from the emperor's harem, dressed her as a boy. All was well until

San Toy fell in love with an English officer and the secret leaked out. What Deborah loved most about the story was that San Toy so captivated the emperor that she saved her father's life, and gained permission to marry the English soldier.

She read again about the costumes in the play imported from China at a cost of $35,000, and about two of the actresses, Miss Viola Kellogg and Miss Mabel Strickland. She remembered, too, going backstage with Tommy after the performance and introducing herself to Miss Strickland, who was from Michigan. Until their meeting, Deborah had envied the actress, traveling the country with a production company. How surprised she was to hear Miss Strickland say, "I'm jealous of you Calumetites, or whatever it is you residents of this fine town call yourselves. You have the best theater I've ever seen, and you get to wake up at the same address every morning." Glancing at Tommy, she again focused on Deborah, adding, "And I'm especially jealous of you, Mrs. Rockwell, with a fine looking husband who obviously adores you, and is willing to take you to the theater."

Deborah chuckled to herself at Tommy's embarrassment over the compliment, and his quick recovery, quipping, "I pray my wife will put great store in your opinion, Miss Strickland." She wondered if Tommy realized his prayer had been answered. As she placed the "San Toy" articles in order behind the others, she realized that she had come to a much greater appreciation of both Calumet and Tommy since meeting the actress.

Having organized the "San Toy" articles, she methodically put the remaining clippings from October and November in order. One piece contained glowing compliments on her solo at the Palestra on October 11. Another article reviewed the October 18 production, "Floradora," a musical she had rehearsed with the Calumet and Hecla Orchestra. After that came the articles about "The Show Girl," "The School Girl," "Ole Olson," "His Highness the Boy," "Down by the Sea," "The Woman in the Case," "Mary Stuart," "The Triumph of an Empress," and "Tenderfoot."

Only the most recent clippings still lay on the table before her. She paused to read again about this week's productions of the Lilliputian Opera Company, a most unusual cast of fifty children from Australia, all under the age of fourteen. They had been playing at the theater all week, beginning on Monday with "The Belle of New York." The same musical had repeated on Tuesday, the night Deborah and Luella had gone to the theater. With Tommy working every weeknight until Christmas, she had asked Penelope and Arthur to go with her to the performances of "A Runaway Girl," "The Geisha," and "The Gaiety Girl" on Wednesday, Thursday, and Friday. This afternoon, they would attend the matinee of "Pinafore."

But tonight would be different. Tommy would be home from work in plenty of time to take her to "An American Millionaire," and he had promised to make it a very special evening with dinner out before the performance. She ran her hand over her waistline and wondered how much longer she could continue to squeeze her expanding tummy into her costumes. Twice she had loosened the laces on her corset and let out the waistlines of her skirts. She'd had such cravings for Lempi's specially preserved and pickled mushrooms and her rye bread slathered with thimbleberry jam, that at times she couldn't stop eating them. Chocolate candies had held a special appeal on a few occasions, too, but she pushed thoughts of food aside.

Gathering up her tidy stack of programs and clippings, she placed them in the box Luella had given her and headed for the back parlor, eager to sing her way into forgetfulness about the problem of her waistline and the reason for its increasing size.

Later that morning, she filled a basket with lunch provisions for her and Tommy. Bundling up in a long scarf, heavy coat, and tall boots, she trekked through the crunchy snow that had been accumulating for the last several weeks, bowing her head to the frigid breeze that bit her cheeks. In spite of the inhospitable weather, Fifth and Sixth Streets bustled with shoppers, and Mr. Sheldon's store was no exception. Mrs. Sheldon had been pressed into service, helping Mr. Sheldon wait on customers while Tommy took his lunch break in the back room.

Biting off a larger than usual portion of his ham-on-rye sandwich, he chewed rapidly. When he had swallowed it down with a long sip of milk, he spoke hurriedly. "I'm sorry I can't take the usual hour for lunch today, Butterfly. We're so busy, I've got to get back out front as quickly as possible. But I'll be home soon after six, and I'll take you out for dinner before we go to the theater, just like we planned." He applied himself diligently to the task of finishing his lunch. Then he rose from the table and kissed her cheek, promising, "I'll have a surprise for you when I get home tonight!"

He was gone before Deborah could ask any questions. All the way home, she wondered what he meant. After his gift of roller skates back in October, there was no predicting what he might bring her.

When she arrived home, she put away the lunch basket and spent some time playing with Topsy, the only pup of Spotsy's litter to survive. The young female was white with a black patch on her head, and the two dogs had been confined to the kitchen until Topsy was housebroken. Deborah missed Spotsy's companionship around the house and on walks, and she wasn't looking forward to the day when Topsy would go to a new home, but Aunt Luella insisted that she would not keep two dogs, and was already looking for a home for the pup.

The balance of the afternoon seemed to drag by, and Tommy's late arrival made his return all the more anticipated. Deborah watched for him from the front parlor, surprised to see him laden with not one, but three parcels as he came up the walk.

She hurried to the front door to greet him with a kiss on the cheek, removing his scarf and cap as she asked eagerly, "Are all these packages for me?"

"Every one of them!" His mustache slanted into a wide smile. "But you must wait until we're upstairs before you open them." He set them aside to take off his coat and boots, then tucked them under one arm and wrapped the other one about her waist to escort her to their room. Setting the three parcels on her bed, he picked one of the two smaller ones to hand to her.

Deborah quickly slipped off the string and brown paper wrapper. Beneath the lid, white tissue paper encased a pair of long lace gloves in forest green. She rolled back the sleeve of her shirtwaist and tried one of them on, noticing a unique design crocheted into the lace. "Butterfly lace gloves! I've never seen such a thing!" She stretched out her arm for Tommy to see.

Even as she admired the gloves, Tommy detected a wrinkle marring her brow, and wasn't at all surprised at her next words.

"It's a shame I haven't a thing of this color to wear them

with."

Reaching for the large box, he said, "I think I can remedy that."

Deborah rushed to open it, finding a velvet gown to match the gloves. She removed it from the box and held it up to herself in front of the mirror, thankful that the costume had been designed with an expandable waistline free of the usual boning to accommodate her changing size. Laying the gown out on her bed, she wrapped her arms about Tommy's neck and kissed him on each cheek. "It's gorgeous, Tommy! Thank you! I wish I had something special to give you in return."

He pulled her close to kiss her forehead, then leaned back to look straight into her eyes, saying, "There is something you could do."

"What's that?" Suddenly uneasy at what he might ask, she stepped out of his embrace.

Aware of her discomfort, Tommy gently explained. "It's time to tell Aunt Luella that you're in the family way—"

"Don't you think she's guessed by now?" Deborah replied sharply. "I mean, it's no secret that my waist keeps getting larger."

"Perhaps she knows," Tommy said quietly. "Nevertheless, you should discuss it with her and see a doctor. She'll know a good one for you to go to."

Deborah turned away, idly running her hand over the soft velvet of the gown that lay on her bed. Suddenly, this moment so filled with excitement and happiness had turned sour. How she wished she were not carrying this unwanted child. She wasn't ready to be a mother. She had only begun learning to be a wife.

Tommy approached her, his hands resting gently on her

shoulders. "I love you, Butterfly. My only concern is for you, and our baby."

She twisted away, freeing herself from his touch. "I don't care about the baby! I wish to God—"

"Deborah Rockwell, don't you dare say it, or even think it! Don't you dare wish that God would take our child away!"

Tommy's loud voice and quick temper surprised even himself. He hadn't meant to speak in anger. He was tired. The week had been long, the customers difficult. Still, he shouldn't have lost his patience.

Deborah silently stared at him, her mouth open. He hadn't called her "Deborah" in all the time they'd been married.

"Butterfly, I'm sorry—"

"No, *I'm* sorry."

"I was wrong to speak—"

"I was wrong. Please forgive me."

Tommy pulled her close, whispering, "Of course, I forgive you."

"I'll tell Aunt Luella tomorrow," Deborah promised.

Tommy leaned back, his blue eyes soft with love. *"We'll* tell her, after dinner."

Deborah nodded.

Tommy retrieved the last of the three parcels from his bed and offered it to her. "Open this. Maybe it will make you feel a little better."

She untied the string and pulled off the lid to discover a large chocolate butterfly, its dark brown wings inset with gumdrop jewels, and its antennae fashioned of licorice. "Where in Calumet did you ever find this?"

His mouth slanted into a proud smile. "I had a special mold made just for you."

"It's too beautiful to eat," Deborah said, adding, "at least not until after dinner."

Tommy checked his watch. "Speaking of dinner, we'd better get dressed. Oskari will take us to the restaurant in twenty minutes. Should I get Lempi to help you into your gown?"

Deborah saw that the criss-cross bodice closed with front hooks, and that the skirt had only a few hooks in back. "Don't trouble her. I can dress myself with a little help from you."

Tommy gladly assisted his Butterfly with the hooks she couldn't reach, standing back to admire her when she had finished pinning on her enamel butterfly brooch and pulling on her new lace gloves. "I can honestly say that you've never looked more beautiful, Mrs. Rockwell!"

Deborah studied herself in the mirror, surprised at how nicely the dress masked her thicker waistline, accentuating instead the lace-trimmed neckline and paneled skirt. Moments later, they stepped into the buggy that carried them through the cold and windy night to the Michigan House Restaurant, where they dined on creamy potato soup, veal cutlets, orange baskets, and spice cake for dessert.

When they walked to the theater, Deborah noticed that the golf yacht cap she had given Tommy after their wedding, and of which he was so fond, was insufficient to keep him warm now that the Upper Peninsula weather had turned harsh. By the time they had walked the one short block, his ears were bright red. But when she suggested he buy himself a warmer hat, he grew indignant, insisting that that cap she had given him was just fine.

Letting the subject rest, Deborah spoke instead of the child actors they were about to see, extolling the virtues of the Lilliputian Opera Company of Australia until the curtain opened on "An American Millionaire," their final performance. Again, Deborah was not disappointed in the young actors and actresses who had been presenting their musical comedies at the theater all week long. Daphne Pollard, Fred Pollard, Teddy McNamera, and Olive Moore all acquitted themselves admirably, with strong voices and comedic timing that Deborah envied. Even the sets and stage managing were of impressive quality, and Deborah marveled at the fact that Alfi Goulding, the stage manager, was no more than a boy in his teens.

When the performance ended, Tommy walked her back to the Michigan House where they ordered hot chocolate and chatted about the impressive youth they had just seen on stage. At midnight, Oskari drove them home, and when Deborah had changed into her nightgown and robe, she sampled a piece of the chocolate butterfly Tommy had given her. The dark chocolate was smooth and rich, mixing lusciously on her tongue with the chewy spearmint gumdrop that decorated the wing. When she had finished sampling the special treat, she went down to the back parlor where Tommy was reading the newspaper. He offered her a few pages to browse, and she read about the special Christmas services to be held at the various churches in Calumet and Laurium on both Sunday, December 24, and on Christmas Day. She had already been requested to sing solos—*O, How a Rose Ere Blooming* on Sunday, and *O, Holy Night* on Christmas Day, and weeks ago Charles Briggs, the choirmaster, had begun rehearsing the *Alleluia Chorus.*

The thought of Christmas reminded her of something she'd been meaning to discuss, and now was the perfect time.

"Tommy, what do you want for Christmas?"

"Hmm?" He turned the page of the paper, almost as if he didn't hear.

"I was thinking of buying you the Taj Mahal, but then, I thought maybe you'd like the Eiffel Tower better."

"Either one would be fine," he mumbled, nose still buried in the paper.

"Tommy, have you heard anything I've said?"

Suddenly, he lowered the paper, breaking into the refrain from *Deck the Halls*.

"Fa la la la la, la la, la, la!" Grinning broadly, he said, "You asked what I wanted for Christmas."

"And?"

He reached for her hand, encasing it in his own. "Contentment and health, merriment and . . . "

"And what?"

He folded the newspaper, then focused on her once more. "Butterfly, I love you. You believe that, don't you?"

She nodded.

"Good." He paused, evidently giving careful thought to his next words before he continued. "It's just that in some ways, I feel like you belong to me, and in other ways, I don't." He brushed a kiss against the back of her hand. "I'm going to turn in now. How about you?"

When she shook her head, he released her hand and headed upstairs.

She sat alone, contemplating what he had said. It was true that she had held a part of herself in reserve since becoming Tommy's wife. Aunt Luella's Bible lessons had helped her overcome the fears from her past in many ways, but she still needed time. Reaching for Captain Dunston's Bible on the table beside her, she opened to her favorite passage, Psalm 32. Though she had it memorized by now, she read through the words on the page, finishing with a prayer that the Lord would abide with her in conquering the last of her fears and facing the challenges that still lay ahead of her and Tommy.

Closing the Good Book, a thought came into her mind. As if by Divine inspiration, she hit upon a plan to make Christmas Day very special for Tommy. Heading for Captain Dunston's corner desk, she pulled out paper and pen, and began to write a letter.

Chapter
22

Midnight, Sunday
Christmas Eve

Tommy sat by the window in the front parlor, catching up on the latest edition of the *Copper Country Evening News,* and occasionally pausing for a sip of hot chocolate and a glimpse of his wife. She was all wrapped up in her pink chenille robe and nestled beneath an afghan on the sofa across from him. Softly, she hummed Christmas carols while adding stitches to her new embroidery of a holiday butterfly, but occasionally, she simply stared at the Christmas tree they had put up earlier that evening. Her wide-eyed, childlike fascination with it made him smile, and enhanced a love that had grown ever deeper, ever wider, ever stronger for his precious mate.

He marveled at the transformation she had undergone since living in Calumet. Her singing, beautiful before, had risen to a more professional level with the many opportunities to rehearse, and to watch the stars of the musical productions in performance at the Calumet Theatre. She had studied, analyzed, and practiced diligently, and the results were truly beautiful to the ear.

But the greatest change in his beloved Butterfly was not in the quality of her voice, but in the hidden beauty beginning to unfold deep inside. With the help of Aunt Luella, she had come to terms with her delicate condition. Under the influence of the Word, her very soul was breaking out of the dark chrysalis of her troubled past, and unfolding radiant wings designed by the hands of Christ. Her face beamed with this new, inner glow. Now, more than ever, he wanted to hold her and press his lips to hers, and more.

He folded his paper and lay it aside. He must remain patient and refrain from entertaining false hope where her affections were concerned. And he must go upstairs to prepare for bed, first taking the dogs outside where the frigid winter air would help to cool the burning desires of his heart. He rose and headed for the door, knowing what his Butterfly would ask him before she even spoke.

"Going up to bed now?"

"I'll let Spotsy and Topsy out first."

She nodded, and resumed her humming and stitching.

In the kitchen, Spotsy and her puppy were curled up as usual on the rug by the warm stove. As soon as Tommy unlatched the back door, Spotsy stood, shook herself awake, then stepped tentatively outside, breaking a path through the newly drifted snow. While she saw to her business, Tommy shoveled off the back porch and hollowed out a spot in the three-foot drift for tiny little Topsy.

Cooled to a shiver by the biting wind and frigid air, Tommy returned to the front parlor to kiss his Butterfly good night. But first, he couldn't resist presenting her with the special gift he had placed under the tree a few hours ago. He sat beside her on the sofa, package in hand.

"This is for you, Butterfly. Open it now."

Deborah looked up from her embroidery to find a twinkle in Tommy's eyes and a wide smile slanting his blond mustache when he offered her the parcel, all covered in red paper and tied with a huge gold bow.

"It's too pretty to unwrap, Tommy. Besides, we're supposed to wait until Christmas Day to open our gifts."

He knew from the glimmer in her eyes that she desperately wanted to know what was inside the wrapping. He pulled out his watch and popped open the cover, showing her the time. "It's well past midnight, Butterfly. Go ahead, open it."

She ran her hands over the rectangular item, concluding, "It must be a book."

Tommy only smiled.

Deborah wondered what type of book Tommy could have chosen for her, knowing she wasn't in the habit of reading, except for the Bible. Carefully, she slid off the wide gold ribbon and folded back the red paper, discovering a scrapbook with a fancy cover stamped in butterflies of burgundy, blue, and cream. Inside the front cover, she read the words he had neatly written.

> *Thou art my hiding place; thou shalt preserve me from trouble; thou shalt compass me about with songs of deliverance. Psalm 32:7*

> *To my Butterfly for memories past and those to come. All my love, Tommy, Christmas 1905.*

The Bible verse was the one she had been claiming as her own in these last several weeks. His inscription set her heart a-flutter.

"Oh, Tommy, it's beautiful! Thank you! Now I have a special place for all those theater programs and the newspaper articles you saved for me. Aunt Luella can stop complaining that they're taking up space in her piano bench!" She leaned over and kissed his cheek.

How tempted he was to pull her into his arms and kiss her full on the mouth. Instead, he kissed her forehead and her nose. "Good night, Butterfly. Don't stay up too late. Remember, you're singing at the Christmas service at half past ten."

"I'll come to bed soon," she promised. When he had gone upstairs, she put her embroidery away in her sewing bag, folded the afghan that had been keeping her warm, and reached for the plug to douse the Christmas tree lights, but she simply couldn't bare to pull it—not yet. One last time, she needed to admire the tall, stately Christmas tree at close range.

How she loved the strands of electric lights that illuminated every bough to reflect off the dozens of ornaments that she and Tommy had hung a few hours ago. There were German mold-blown ornaments of apples, pears, and bunches of grapes all painted gold. Even more impressive were the Dresdens, the three-dimensional paper ornaments covered in silver or gold in every shape imaginable. Deborah still couldn't get over the details etched into these fascinating decorations—the fish with hundreds of scales, the swan with dozens of feathers, the peacock with an array of plumes, and the dog and the cat showing the very hair on their backs. Her favorite of all the Dresdens was the one Tommy had brought home from Mr. Sheldon's store after work last night: the golden butterfly with filigree wings. She smiled at the way Tommy had insisted that she hang it in the most prominent location at the very front, center of the tree. Tucked into the branch beside it was an envelope with the word "Butterfly" neatly penned on its face. She reached for it, curious to know what treasure lay inside, then left it where it lay.

Outside, she heard the frozen breath of Lake Superior

blow in a loud gust against the leaky windowpane. The parlor air stirred, then the register struck up its patter of pings and pangs while the steam piped in from the Calumet and Hecla industrial line heated the room, enhancing the essence of pine. As the warm air rose, Deborah's attention was drawn to her most favorite ornament of all, the Nuremberg angel slowly spinning on the thin wire that suspended her above the very top of the tree. Her spun-glass wings, crinkled gold skirt, and innocent face of bisque reflected perfectly the message lettered in silver on the scroll in her hand, "Peace on Earth."

Peace had come to reign in Deborah's heart as well, a peace she hadn't known since she was a child. But how different this holiday season was from those of her youth! She recalled wintertime in Detroit, where only a few inches of snow fell with each storm and the temperature rarely dipped below twenty. Calumet already lay blanketed in three feet of snow, with snow banks along the sides of the streets at shoulder height, and the temperature was hovering near zero.

In those long-ago Detroit years, Deborah's mother had never put up more than a tabletop tree for the holidays. Often they had no tree at all. Gifts were limited to the two modest presents she and her mother exchanged with each other. Tonight, dozens of packages clad in all patterns of red, green, and gold lay piled beneath Aunt Luella's eight-foot evergreen.

On the table beside it, Aunt Luella had arranged a nativity, an intricately carved set of wooden figures depicting the night of the Savior's birth. Deborah's mother had never owned a nativity, and the miniature scene fascinated her. She reached for the Baby Jesus, feeling the rich details of its form while recalling some words from Tommy's reading of the second chapter of Luke a few hours ago. *For unto you is born this day in the City of David a Savior, which is Christ the Lord.* The Christmases of Deborah's youth had never included a Bible reading. How thankful she was for the holy story of the miracle birth of her Lord and for the ever-greater comfort Jesus gave her as Luella continued teaching her about His ways.

How thankful she was, too, for Tommy. He continued to treat her with a patience and kindness that could only come from his close walk with Jesus. Again, she reached for the envelope he had tucked into the tree, this time taking it to the sofa where she sat to open it. Sliding the card from the envelope, she saw that on its face was a young couple in their Christmas best, the gentleman's hand raised toward a spray of green leaves with white berries. Across the bottom, the sentiment, "Come under the mistletoe" captured the moment. Opening the card, she read the words Tommy had penned.

> *To my beautiful Butterfly,*
>
> *On this, the first of many happy Christmases we will spend together as husband and wife, words cannot express all that you have come to mean to me, but I shall try to tell you anyhow.*
>
> *I hope that you believe by now that you truly are my precious gift from God, my crown. My heart soars with thoughts of the happiness we will share in the years to come!*
>
> *I am so proud of all that you are, and all that you will yet become as you continue to grow in the Lord. Forgive my paraphrase of one of my favorite Bible passages, but I earnestly believe that it is most appropriate for the two of us, and I claim it for all the days and years ahead.*
>
> *We can do all things through Christ who strength-*

ens us.

And so, my precious Butterfly, on this day in which we celebrate the birth of our Savior and Lord, I celebrate also the love He has given us for each other, a love that grows with each passing day.
Your loving husband, Tommy

Moisture welled in her eyes. She dabbed them with her handkerchief and gazed at the packages piled under the tree, her focus centering on the one she had wrapped in gold paper for Tommy. It would surely please him, but it couldn't compare with the gift of love Tommy had given her since he'd rescued her in Buffalo. Despite her early doubts over the wisdom of their union, God had surely blessed their marriage once she had been willing to put Him at the center of it.

As she read the card again, a desire grew within to share with Tommy something as precious and meaningful as the steadfast love he showed her every day—something that would bring them closer as husband and wife than they had ever been before. Because of him, nightmares of the past had faded to mere unpleasant memories while his unfailing devotion had won her trust. Making certain to turn out all the lights including those on the tree, she climbed the stairs, entered the bedroom, and quietly closed the door, ensuring complete privacy for the most intimate gift of all.

As Tommy listened to his Butterfly sing her solo, *O, Holy Night,* in church the following morning, his heart soared with the notes of her song. His Butterfly had finally become his wife in every sense of the word, and he thanked God for the precious gift she had given him! His only prob-

lem was that now, more than ever before, he simply could-
n't take his eyes or his mind off of his beautiful, precious
Butterfly.

When the service ended and Mr. Sheldon had driven
them home, Tommy helped Luella and Deborah down from
the carriage and escorted them up the front walk. Though
Oskari had shoveled it only two hours ago, the dry, white
powder was already beginning to drift, and in it were fresh
footprints leading straight to the front door.

"Someone's been up this path within the last few minutes," he observed as he steadied Luella on the front steps.

"Perhaps Mr. MacNaughton," Luella speculated.

"You don't mean James MacNaughton, Superintendent
of the Calumet and Hecla?" Tommy asked, incredulous that
such a high-ranking official from the mine would be stopping by on Christmas Day.

"He's come every Christmas with a fruit basket since
I've been a widow," Luella explained.

Deborah said, "Then he must be waiting for you inside.
I don't see any tracks leading away from the house."

Tommy caught an exchange of smiles between the
women as he opened the front door and helped Luella over
the threshold. Hanging up the ladies' coats on the hall tree,
he shucked off his own and unbuckled his goulashes. When
he entered the front parlor, a slimmer version of a most
familiar form emerged from the far side of the Christmas
tree.

"Papa! What are you doing all the way up here?"

"Merry Christmas!" Cy Rockwell embraced his son
firmly, then stood back, a deep slant of a smile slicing the
width of his too-thin face. "Your wife invited me. Said it
was the best gift she could give you. Between you and me,
she must be a little touched in the head if she can't do bet-

ter than this." He winked at Deborah.

Tommy pulled his Butterfly close and kissed her on the lips. "Thank you, Butterfly. Papa's right. You *are* touched in the head, in the very best of ways."

He released her, his attention again on his father, who appeared to have lost considerable weight. "Tell me, Papa, how are you, and how is mother?"

Before Cy could answer, Luella said, "Why don't you gentlemen have a seat here in the parlor and catch up while we ladies see to the Christmas victuals." To Deborah, she said, "Come along, dear. Lempi needs our help if we're to get everything on the table in half an hour as we'd planned."

Tommy expressed concern for his father's health. "Papa, I've never seen you this thin." Though he didn't say so, it was obvious that his color had grown pale, too.

Cy waved Tommy's concern aside with a bony hand. "I've been worried about your mother. She took a bad turn at the start of the month, and I ran myself ragged, visiting her every day at the sanitarium. But she's been on the mend for the last couple of weeks, and insisted that I come up here and spend Christmas with you and Deborah." He smiled again. "So tell me, did you have a prosperous Christmas season at Mr. Sheldon's store?"

"Indeed, we did!" Tommy described the long hours and large number of customers he had served since Thanksgiving Day. Keeping his voice low, he confided, "I've saved a considerable sum from my commissions. Butterfly doesn't know it yet, but come spring, I expect I'll have enough put aside to start looking for a place of our own."

"So the two of you are really happy living way up here in this icebox?" Cy asked.

Tommy ignored the hint of doubtfulness in his father's

246

voice, repeating what he had written home in his letters over the past three months—that Deborah loved rehearsing with the orchestra, attending theatrical performances, and occasionally performing when the opportunities arose. He asked his father about his own work, learning how his business travels had been curtailed sharply during the month of December due to his mother's condition. In no time, thirty minutes had passed and Aunt Luella reappeared in the parlor.

"Come to the dining room, gentlemen. Cy, would you do me the honor of sitting at the head of the table?"

"I'd be delighted, Mrs. Dunston!" When all had been seated at the table, he bowed his head to ask a blessing, his deep, mellow voice filled with quiet reverence. "Heavenly Father, we give thanks for this opportunity to fellowship together in celebration of our Savior's birth. We ask Thy blessing on those who could not be with us, and on this food which we are about to receive, in Jesus' name, Amen."

Tommy watched closely as his father carved the turkey, promising himself that one year from now, he would be sitting at the head of his own table doing the same for family and guests. While Luella added the dressing, mashed potatoes, squash, and gravy to the plates, he noticed an unusually large pretzel in the middle of the table, its cavities filled up with gingerbread men and other holiday confections. "I've never seen a centerpiece such as yours, Aunt Luella. Did you bake it?"

She shook her head. "Lempi made the bread according to her Finnish custom. It's called Viipuri Twist. She baked the gingerbread cookies, too. Then Deborah and I helped her decorate them. You're welcome to try them."

When Tommy reached for a cookie, Luella intercepted, handing him a plate mounded with food. "I mean when you've finished your dinner."

Once all had been served and Luella lifted her fork, Tommy wasted no time trying the turkey, tender and tasty, and the dressing laced with onion, celery, and sage. Conversation flowed with his stories of customers at Mr. Sheldon's store, and Deborah's musical experiences, attending rehearsals and performances at the Calumet Theatre and singing with the band at the Palestra.

Cy told of a visit he'd made to Grand Rapids just prior to heading north. "I stopped by Charles's law office and he gave me some delightful news. He said he's keeping mum about it in Caledonia, but that I'm perfectly free to tell you folks up north that Caroline and Joshua are expecting in June!"

Tommy grinned. "So Carolina's going to be a mother! Isn't that wonderful, Butterfly?"

Deborah nodded. "We have news, too, don't we?" To Cy, she said, "Even though you've been too polite to mention it, I'm sure you've noticed that I've gotten larger in the middle. A few months from now, you'll be a grandfather, yourself!"

"How about that!"

Despite Cy's reaction, Deborah was sure that he knew the child was not Tommy's. She tried to think of a new subject to fill the awkward silence that followed, and was thankful when the telephone rang. Hurrying to the parlor to pick up the receiver, she returned a moment later with a question.

"Mr. Sheldon is on the line. He wants to know if we'd like to go ice skating at the Palestra. I told him we haven't any skates, but he said he'd bring some from the store. Penelope is to meet her friends at the arena at four, and Mrs. Sheldon is going, too. May I tell him we'll go?"

Tommy turned to his father. "You've got to skate at the Palestra!"

Cy nodded. "Only if it doesn't interfere with Mrs. Dunston's plans."

Luella waved off his concern. "It will do you all good to get out after this big meal, and I'm sure we'll be finished opening our gifts by four."

Deborah accepted Mr. Sheldon's invitation, returning to the table for a second helping of turkey. When most of the bird and its trimmings had been polished off, and ginger-bread men had become scarce, Luella led the adjournment to the parlor. There, she imposed upon Tommy to act as Santa Clause for the gift exchange. He gladly passed around the presents that had accumulated under the tree, including several from the Caledonia relatives that had arrived with his father.

Among the gifts for the men were fur-lined leather gloves, embroidered handkerchiefs, cashmere mufflers, and fancy suspenders. Luella received a woolen shawl and lap robe, a fancy silver thimble engraved with her initials, writing paper, and a new gold pen. And Deborah was thrilled with the length of fine white linen and skeins of silk embroidery floss from Ottilia, the newest sheet music from Caroline and Joshua, and a book of devotions that Luella had written in her own hand.

Tommy saved his gift from Deborah for last—a medium-sized box, oval in shape, done up in gold paper and red satin ribbon. From the frequent arguments she'd given him the last couple of weeks about dressing more warmly to walk to work, he had a fairly good idea what was inside, and he was not disappointed to discover a fur hat made of Persian lamb. But what pleased him most was the embroidery his precious wife had sewn inside. In precise stitches were several words followed by a tiny little butterfly. He read the message aloud. "This hat belongs to T. Rockwell." Pulling it onto his head, he reached for Deborah. "And this wife belongs to T. Rockwell." He pulled her close and kissed her briefly. "Thank you, Butterfly."

She smiled up at him. "You look mighty fine in your new fur hat, T. Rockwell. Now hang it on the hall tree and put away the golf yacht cap until spring."

Luella reached for one of the pieces of discarded wrapping paper that were strewn across the floor. "That's not all that needs putting away. We'd better tidy up before Mr. Sheldon arrives."

With help from the others, the room was soon put in order. Deborah took the last of the gifts—sweaters and leather chews for Spotsy and Topsy—to them in the kitchen where they were confined until Topsy was completely housebroken. On her return to the front parlor, she noticed a buggy, too small to be the Sheldons, pulling to a stop out front.

"Aunt Luella, someone's come calling. Shall I answer the door for you?"

Luella gazed out the front window. When an imposing figure stepped out carrying a large basket, she said, "You stay put, I'll let him in." A moment later, she led the wide-shouldered, bespectacled gentleman into the parlor and made introductions. "Mr. MacNaughton, this is Mr. Rockwell from Marshall, and his son, Tommy, and daughter-in-law, Deborah, who live with me. Cy, Tommy, Deborah, may I present Mr. James MacNaughton, Superintendent of the Calumet and Hecla Mine."

MacNaughton shifted the large fruit basket to one side to extend his broad hand to Cy. "We've met a few times before, in Boston each spring at the annual meeting of the shareholders—"

Cy cut in. "Good to see you again. Merry Christmas!"

Turning to Tommy, he said, "So this is your son. I had no idea he was married to the canary of Calumet." To Deborah, he said, "I heard you sing at the Palestra in October. Professor Broadman should feature you more often. In fact, I think I'll have a word with him about it!"

Deborah beamed. "Thank you for the generous compliment!"

With a nod, he turned his attention to Luella. "I don't intend to stay. I just wanted to bring you a basket of fruit and wish you a Merry Christmas."

"Thank you kindly, Jim. You know how I enjoy fresh fruit this time of year." To Tommy, she said, "Would you please take Mr. MacNaughton's basket to the dining table while I see him out?"

When Tommy reached for the basket, MacNaughton said, "You aren't employed at the C&H, are you?"

He shook his head. "I'm in sales at Sheldon's Furniture and General Merchandise."

Cy said, "And an excellent salesman, he is! Made a mighty fine commission this past month."

MacNaughton said, "With the holidays over, I won't be at all surprised if Sheldon lays you off for a spell. When he does, come see me. I've got a nice position for a young up-and-comer. The pay is good, and the work is steady year-round."

"I'll keep that in mind," Tommy promised. When he returned from the dining room, he saw that Mr. MacNaughton was pulling away, and Mr. Sheldon was driving up. Suddenly, he felt uncomfortable about his boss, wondering if indeed he planned to do as Mr. MacNaughton had implied and lay him off after the holidays. He pressed the concern aside, determined not to let it dampen his holiday spirit. Helping Deborah into her heavy cloak and boots, he donned his own woolen coat and pulled on his new Persian lamb hat, determined to enjoy what remained of Christmas Day with his wife and father.

At the Palestra, Deborah was slightly annoyed that Tommy would not allow her to skate alone, but insisted that he and his father skate on either side of her at all times to avoid any possibility of her falling. They made for an awkward threesome in the crowded rink that included four hundred fifty other skaters out to enjoy the holiday. But she accepted the constraint, the first of many she knew were to come in the months ahead.

When they returned her to the sidelines, Cy sat with her. He seemed overly fatigued and out of breath as they watched Tommy skate alone, but when Deborah asked Cy about it, he simply passed it off as old age. Then he told tales of his youth, when he was able to beat all his peers in footraces. Deborah enjoyed listening to him, but she couldn't help wondering if all his braggadocio was only a way to hide from the truth.

Chapter
23

February 14, 1906

Deborah watched from the front parlor, eager for Tommy to arrive home from the mine office. The day had been cold and bleak, with snow flying horizontally and drifts filling in the walkways almost as quickly as Oskari cleared them. But the parlor was warm and inviting, with pretty candles emitting a soft glow, fresh potpourri lending the sweet essence of roses, and the ever-dependable steam heat sending out waves of warmth along with the pings and pangs of pipes. At her feet lay Spotsy, and snuggled in beside her, Topsy, each with a wide red satin bow about the neck. These were the last and the least of the Valentine's preparations Deborah had completed today.

She had been planning for Valentine's Day for a month, since the second week of January, shortly after Tommy had lost his position with Mr. Sheldon. Even though he had immediately gained new employment, starting in the accounting department at the Calumet and Hecla Mine the very next day, she could see that Tommy had taken his dismissal from Mr. Sheldon's employ hard.

For the first time since their wedding, he had grown quiet and somber. Deborah could hardly get over the abrupt change. He had been so lighthearted and happy throughout the holidays, especially with his father visiting. On the second day of the New Year—the day his father went home, the day Mr. Sheldon let him go—he turned into a different man.

Although he never spoke of his feelings and never criticized his former boss, neither had he spoken the name of Sheldon in all the weeks since. In fact, on the first Sunday in the New Year, the first time Deborah stayed home from church due to the advancing stage of her delicate condition, Tommy refused to go to services with Aunt Luella, and had continued to avoid church services every Sunday since.

He insisted that he wasn't trying to snub Mr. Sheldon, but Deborah and the old woman had concluded otherwise. When they tried to get him to talk about his glum mood, he grew irritated, then went silent. How Deborah missed Tommy's former bright spirit! How she missed the way he used to sing and joke and make fun with her at the piano in the back parlor! Now, his evenings consisted of quiet hours reading first the newspaper, then the books in Captain Dunston's collection, then turning in early.

Determined to get her old Tommy back, Deborah had begun planning a very special Valentine's celebration. With the help and cooperation of Aunt Luella and Lempi, she would make this Valentine's Day one to remember without ever having to leave the house. And perhaps by the time the evening was over, she would see Tommy smile and hear him laugh again!

These were her hopes and prayers when she saw Tommy's tall figure moving in the shadows of dusk up the front walk. She hurried to the door to let him in, pleased to see that he had brought a parcel with him. He handed her the oddly shaped box wrapped in brown paper, brushed his lips against hers in a perfunctory "hello" kiss, and bent to fuss over Spotsy and Topsy who all but turned back flips in competition for his affection. When the dogs had calmed down, he began shedding his heavy coat and unbuckling his goulashes, all without comment to Deborah.

She knew better than to ask him how his day had gone. She'd learned after his first week in the accounting department that his only comment would be a dry, "It was a balancing act." Instead, she greeted him in song, an idea that had come to her a few hours ago. To the melody of *We Wish You a Merry Christmas* she sang instead these words.

"I wish you a Happy Valentine's Day, I wish you a Happy Valentine's Day, I wish you a Happy Valentine's Day and a year full of love!"

Tommy almost smiled. "Thanks, Butterfly." He pulled her close, bestowing a kiss that lasted a few seconds longer than the first one, then released her saying, "Open your present."

She sat on the sofa, hoping Tommy would join her there, but he went instead to the chair opposite her while Spotsy and Topsy crowded in to thoroughly sniff out her package. A stern command sent them on retreat to the kitchen.

Slipping the string off her present, Deborah folded back the plain paper to discover a butterfly-shaped valentine atop a fabric-covered box. She stared at the young maid in the center of the two butterfly wings—a near perfect reflection of herself with fair face and blond hair. She wore a diaphanous multi-colored gown to match the wings behind her. The sight of it made Deborah gasp!

Suddenly, she was no longer in Calumet, but back in Caledonia at her wedding ceremony where she had imagined herself sprouting butterfly wings and flying away while Tommy faded from the picture. The parallel was too real! She *had* flown from Caledonia in a sense, and although Tommy had remained in the picture, he was now emotionally withdrawn, a faded version of his former self.

255

She closed her eyes and shook her head, determined to shake the disturbing images from her mind. Focusing on the card in front of her again, she realized that a message had been inscribed in gold on the wings. She read it aloud.

"'To my sweet Valentine.' It's a lovely sentiment!"

Again, Tommy's mouth only hinted at a smile. "Thought you'd like it. Now look at your gift."

She put the card aside. Beneath it lay a padded pink satin box made in the form of two irregularly shaped hearts. Their points joined in the center to give the impression of butterfly wings, and the edges were trimmed with white ruffled lace.

"Oh, Tommy! This is beautiful! Thank you!"

"Open it," he said, a trifle impatient.

She carefully lifted the lid. Inside the box were nestled several miniature chocolate butterflies in both milk and dark chocolate, each attractively decorated—some with silver balls, some with red-hots, and others with tinted sugar. "These look too good to eat! You had them custom made especially for me, didn't you?"

He nodded.

"And the box. It must have cost a small fortune."

He shrugged. "It's only money."

Deborah rose from the sofa, holding the candy in front of him. "Try one?"

He shook his head. "You try one."

She pondered the prospect, the aroma of fine dark chocolate tempting her mightily. Then she replaced the cover. "After dinner we'll both try one. I'd hate to spoil my appetite. Now come to the table." She led him to the dining room that lay in darkness except for the light spilling from the open kitchen door. When he reached for the wall switch, she pulled his hand away. "Would you please light the candles while I fetch our dinners from the warming oven? The match safe is on the buffet."

"Where's Lempi?"

"She's out with Matti tonight." She named a young Finnish miner who had been sweet on Lempi since their meeting at the Palestra a few weeks ago.

When Tommy stared curiously at the two places set at the table, Deborah could see the next question forming in his mind and answered it before he asked. "Aunt Luella ate earlier. She's adjourned to her room so we can enjoy an evening alone together." Retrieving the match safe from the buffet for him, she said again, "I'll fetch our dinners."

She returned a moment later carrying a tray laden with two covered dinner plates. When she had set one at each of their places, Tommy held her chair for her, tenderly caressing her shoulders for one brief moment before he took his place kitty-corner from her.

Reaching for her hand, he said, "Why don't you ask the blessing tonight?"

Deborah bowed her head. "Thank you, Lord, for the beautiful Valentine and the box of chocolate butterflies Tommy brought home for me, for the food we are about to eat, and especially for the opportunity to celebrate Your greatest gift of all, love. In Jesus' name, Amen."

"Amen."

Deborah watched Tommy closely as she lifted the cover from his plate.

He inhaled the aroma of the rising steam. "It looks good, it smells good. What is it, Butterfly?"

"Blanquette of chicken with potato balls and squash patties. I made everything myself," she said proudly, removing the cover from her own plate and lifting her fork to try one of the chicken strips that had been steeped in cream sauce and bound by a border of rice.

"You made it?" he asked, tucking into the chicken and rice.

She nodded, swallowing the first bite that proved even more tender and tasty than she'd anticipated. "I did have some help from Lempi and Aunt Luella," she admitted. "A lot of help, actually."

Tommy swallowed his first bite and went for more. "I've heard that too many cooks spoil the stew. Evidently, that's not true of chicken. This is excellent."

His compliment pleased Deborah greatly. She had never cooked for Tommy before, and she wanted desperately for this first attempt to be successful. Still, he didn't smile, nor did he continue the conversation, instead remaining quiet and introspective, as had been his habit at meals during these last several weeks.

Deborah took it upon herself to fill the silence with an account of the developing romance between Lempi and Matti. She described in detail the three-layer die-cut Valentine he had given the young maiden, reciting the message that had read, "Thou art my joy, my life, my light, and all my hopes are thine. So trust me near and out of sight, my fond, fair Valentine." She described, too, the perfect red rose he had brought her, wrapped in layer upon layer of tissue and encased in a chipboard box to prevent damage from the extreme cold. And she told of the plans the young couple had made to dine at Curto's, and how Matti had escorted Lempi down the walk, arm in arm, to a buggy hired especially for the occasion.

Sensing that Tommy was barely listening to her lengthy monologue, she turned the topic in his direction, saying, "I suppose the fellows in the accounting department all had plans to please their wives and sweethearts today."

He looked up, his eyes unfocused, as if seeing beyond her into a different world before his gaze came to settle on her. "I'm sorry, did you ask me something?" He rested his fork and knife on his empty plate.

Deborah swallowed the last of her chicken, and the miff that threatened to spoil the evening. "I'm wondering if you are ready for dessert?"

"I'm always ready for dessert, Butterfly."

"Then I'll fetch it." She loaded up the tray with the dinner plates and silver and retreated to the kitchen, emerging again with the little heart-shaped citron cakes she'd baked and decorated. She placed Tommy's before him, its white butter cream frosting setting off the red icing script that declared "I love you!"

He didn't wait for her to taste the cake first, but plunged in, putting a substantial forkful into his mouth and savoring it before offering his opinion. "Excellent, Butterfly, excellent!" He even smiled before digging in again to polish off the confection in a total of four bites.

Deborah made haste to finish her own dessert, saying, "Shall we adjourn to the back parlor? I have something for you there."

Tommy settled in Captain Dunston's chair while she retrieved her gift for Tommy from the piano bench. She handed him the slim, tissue-wrapped volume and sat in Luella's chair to watch him open it.

He untied the red satin bow and peeled back the white tissue, revealing a red leather-bound book with white pages upon which she had transcribed her favorite passages about love from the Bible, and from poems and romantic scenes in plays.

He began reading the snippets, flipping randomly from page to page. "'As the Sun is in the Firmament, so is Love in the world.' 'Love like virtue is its own reward.' 'Love is not love which alters when it alteration finds.' 'Better is a dinner of herbs where love is, than a stalled ox and hatred therewith.'" He snapped the book shut. Out flew the bookmark she had tucked between the center pages. He retrieved it from the floor and stared at it for a few seconds, finally reading aloud the words she had embroidered into the perforated paper. "My love I give to thee, now and forever. D.D.R. February 14, 1906." He ran his thumb over the butterfly below the date then placed the bookmark inside the front cover and set the book on the table between them. "Excuse me, Butterfly," he said in a quiet, shaky voice she'd never heard from him before, "It's time to take the dogs outside."

"Tommy, are you all right?" she asked, rising to follow him, but she heard the back door slam shut before she even reached the kitchen.

While waiting for him to come inside, she opened the box of candy he'd given her and sampled a piece of the dark, creamy chocolate. As it melted slowly on her tongue, she realized how its flavor seemed to parallel the experiences of the evening—both bitter and sweet. She set the box on the buffet and cleared away the dessert plates while waiting for Tommy to come back inside. When several minutes had passed and he still hadn't returned, she went to the back door to look for him. To her dismay, there were no signs of Tommy or the dogs in the backyard, excepting their tracks leading away from the house. She noticed, too, that the dog coats and leashes were gone from the entryway, and so were the old winter coat, goulashes, and gloves of Captain Dunston's that Tommy kept there for dog-walking.

She opened the door a crack. Frigid air wafted in, but the strong winds had died down. She was of half a mind to pull on her cloak and go looking for them. Dr. MacQueen had encouraged her to continue walking Spotsy and Topsy daily to maintain good health, and she had done so, confident that her cloak sufficiently concealed her bulging figure and the fact of her delicate condition from casual observers. But she ruled out the thought of venturing outdoors tonight. Intuition told her that Tommy needed some time alone, and that he would not welcome her trailing after him.

Tending to her kitchen chores, she began washing up the dinner dishes, and was putting the last of them away when Tommy and the dogs returned. When he had scrounged a scrap of chicken for each of them and settled them on their rug beside the stove for the night, he came to her. Taking the plate from her hand and stowing it in the cupboard, he turned her toward him, his arms gently cradled about her.

"Thank you for the fine book of love sentiments, and for the bookmark, Butterfly." He kissed her forehead, her nose, and each cheek. "I'm sorry I was in such a dismal mood." Pulling her close, he hugged her tightly for a moment. Then he released her and turned to go.

"Tommy, what's bothering you?"

He paused. "Nothing, Butterfly. I'll be in the back parlor. Come sing for me when you're finished?"

She nodded. Hanging up towels and dishrag, she headed for the back parlor, taking the box of chocolates with her. Tommy chose a milk chocolate butterfly, making sounds of approval as he polished off that piece, and one of the dark chocolates, besides.

When he had finished, he asked, "What are you going to sing for me, Butterfly?"

"Nothing."

"But—"

"I'll sing for you when you tell me what's been bothering you."

Jaw clamped tight, he reached for the newspaper, but Deborah snatched it from his grasp.

"It's Mr. Sheldon, isn't it? Tommy, I'm sorry you're still angry with him, but—"

"I'm not angry with Mr. Sheldon."

"Yes, you are!"

"No, I'm not!" Tommy insisted. "Never was! Well, maybe just a little when he first let me go, but it only lasted till I started at the C&H."

"I don't believe you," Deborah replied. "You refuse to ride with Mr. Sheldon to church. Since he let you go, you never once spoke his name until just now. Admit it. He hurt your pride and you're angry with him."

Tommy sighed. "If you insist." He took up the volume of love verses and began paging through the book.

Deborah softened her approach. "Tommy, if you aren't angry with Mr. Sheldon, then what is bothering you so? Is it your job at the C&H?"

"My job at the C&H is fine," he claimed testily.

"If you don't like your job, maybe you could ask Mr. MacNaughton to transfer you to another department. There's no point in spending every day at a task that makes you miserable."

Tommy peered over the top of the book, jaw tense. "I said my job at the C&H is fine. Now, instead of going on about it, why don't you put your voice to much better purposes and sing for me?"

"Why don't *you* put your voice to much better purposes and just tell me what's been making you so sullen and grumpy and out of sorts for the last six weeks? If it's not Mr. Sheldon, and it's not the new job, then what? Has your best friend died, and you just forgot to tell me about it?"

Tommy sprang to his feet "Now you've done it. I'm not going to listen to this anymore." Tossing the book down on the chair, he stomped out of the room.

Deborah hurried after him, progress hampered by her bulging form. "Tommy, wait! *Please* tell me what's wrong!"

Before she caught up with him, the front door had closed behind him with a firm thud. His Persian lamb hat and winter coat were missing from the entryway, but his goulashes remained. She wondered how far could he go in the heavy snow without them.

Worried, and bitterly disappointed, she returned to the back parlor, popped a chocolate butterfly into her mouth, and began pacing from room to room, checking the front parlor window several times for signs of his return. She dipped into the box of chocolates again and again before finally turning off all but the front entry light and heading upstairs. Donning her nightgown but too overwrought to sleep, she propped her pillows against the headboard and climbed beneath the covers, taking her scrapbook from the bedside table. She immediately turned to the back where she had tucked the unmounted articles Tommy had continued to clip for her from the paper. Even though she could no longer attend performances, she still loved reading about the productions and gazing at the newspaper photographs of the stars. She sorted through the loose pieces until she found the one from the current week. When she had read a description of the romantic comedy playing this very night at the Calumet Theatre, she lay it face down. Immediately, the headline of an article on the backside caught her eye. "Lured Her Away." She read the subheadings that followed. "Young woman of Laurium tells her story in court. With her eyes filled with tears, she took witness stand.

Expected to receive position with good wages. Brought to immoral resort."

Before she could read farther, she heard the front door open, then Tommy's footsteps on the stairs. Setting the scrapbook on the bedside table, she waited for him to come through the bedroom door.

Chapter
24

Tommy paused at the bedroom door before entering, his cheeks and nose bright red from the frigid wind. Shoulders drooping, head low, he came to sit on Deborah's bed. When his blue eyes met hers, she could see that they too were red, as if he'd been crying.

He took her hands in his cold ones, wishing that the warmth she shared could magically sweep through him, purging the cold wretchedness from his heart. How he hated the way he had felt these last six weeks, silently trapped in a private world of grief and pain. He hated more that he had hurt his beloved Butterfly. And he hated most of all that in the midst of his personal darkness and despair, God had abandoned him to bear his cross alone. But he couldn't worry about God right now. He must make amends with his wife.

When he spoke to her, he hardly recognized his own voice, faint and halting as he choked back a persistent knot of emotion. "I'm sorry, Butterfly . . . Sorry I've been so out of sorts . . . Can you . . .forgive me?"

She could see moisture welling in his eyes. She'd never seen him cry before, but he was weeping now, albeit silently. Her heart ached for him. "Of course I can forgive you, but I'd like to know what's bothering you so. Tell me, Tommy, what is it?"

He released her hands and stood, turning his back to her

as he fished his handkerchief from his pocket and blew his nose. Organizing the words he must share, he put away his handkerchief and sat again. "Papa gave me strict orders not to tell you this until well after the baby was born. He said you have enough on your mind, but you deserve to know why I haven't been myself." He paused, drawing a tight breath. "The fact is, on the night before my father went home, we had a long talk. He told me that my mother had passed away the week before he came to see us."

"Oh, no! I'm so sorry, Tommy!" She remembered the death of her own mother, the deep sense of loss, and the pain that had lingered as a dull ache in the pit of her stomach for weeks afterward. Reaching for his hand, she said, "And here I thought it was just the loss of your job with Mr. Sheldon that was making you unhappy."

One side of his mustache rose. "If I hadn't been feeling so badly already, I'd have probably been upset about losing that job. The fact is, I really hate my post in the accounting department, but it doesn't seem all that important compared to losing . . . "

Deborah squeezed his hand. "I just can't help wondering . . . "

Tommy squeezed her hand in return. "What, Butterfly?"

"Why your father didn't notify you of your mother's death the day she died."

Tommy shook his head in frustration. "It's just like him, to keep sad news under his hat. His plans were already in place for the trip up here, and he didn't want to spoil our holidays. Then, he learned that you were in the family way, and it just confirmed a notion he'd had all along to put off a memorial service until next summer so more of the out-of-town relatives could attend."

Deborah tried to fully comprehend all that Tommy had revealed these past few moments. "Your mother is gone, your position at the C&H is a daily dread, your father has set the example of not troubling others with bad news . . . no wonder you've been quiet about all this, and so dreadfully glum." After a moment's silence, she said, "But things are sure to get better, with God's help. Would you like me to pray?"

Tommy withdrew his hand from hers, rising again to pace the floor. "There's more."

Silently, Deborah waited until Tommy was ready to continue. Moments later, he sat again, tears staining his cheeks. "It's my father. Do you remember how thin he was?"

Deborah nodded. She remembered, too, that he had seemed more winded than normal after skating around the rink at the Palestra on Christmas Day.

Tommy continued. "Papa's seriously ill. He hasn't long to . . . " His voice choked with emotion and he turned away.

"Don't tell me he's going to die, too!" Reaching out, she pulled him close, cradling his head against her shoulder. His silent sobs pulsated against her, making her cry, too. She remembered how Cy had blamed his fatigue on old age. Now, she knew different.

A few moments later, when Tommy had regained control of his emotions, he released himself from Deborah. "I feel so torn. I know Papa will be bedridden soon, if he isn't already. I wasn't there when Mother died. I don't want the same thing to happen with Papa, but—"

"Then you must go to him."

Tommy shook his head.

"You must!" Deborah insisted.

"You don't understand," Tommy said irritably. "Among

the other things Papa told me before he left was that he did not want me coming to Marshall to watch him die. He said my place was here with you. He has a doctor and a nurse to see him out of this world and a lawyer to contact me when he's gone. And just to make sure he gets his way, he's written in his will that I'm to be disinherited if I come back before he dies."

"How cruel!" Deborah exclaimed. "Doesn't he understand how miserable he's making you? Doesn't he realize that I've got Aunt Luella, and Dr. MacQueen to take care of me?"

Tommy remained silent, lines sinking deeper than ever in his forehead.

Deborah continued. "There's no question, but you must go to your father. Show him that your love and concern for him are far more important than any doggoned inheritance. If you stay away, you'll regret it the rest of your life."

Tommy paced the floor again, torn within by his choices. A minute later, he returned to Deborah's bedside to say reluctantly, "You're right. I'll give notice at work first thing tomorrow. I'll pack tonight, and after I've spoken with Mr. MacNaughton, I'll take the first train south. We've got money in our savings account to see you through until I return."

"Let's pray." Deborah reached for his hand.

He pulled away, claiming bitterly, "I have nothing to say to God."

"Tommy!"

"Since Papa left, I've written him every week, telling him how badly I want to be with him, pleading with him to let me come. With every letter I mailed, I begged God to soften Papa's heart. And what have I gotten in return? Silence! From Papa and from God!"

"I'm sure God hears," Deborah said confidently.

Anger surged anew. "Then why hasn't He answered? Why hasn't Papa written?"

"I don't know," Deborah replied softly, "but maybe you'll find out when you get to Marshall. Pray with me that it will be so."

Tommy stood. "You pray. I'm going to the attic to fetch my valise."

When Tommy had gone, Deborah bowed her head. "Heavenly Father, please comfort Tommy in this time of trial. Let him be reunited with his earthly father in love, and his Heavenly Father in faith. Protect him in his travels. Go before him, beside him, above him, beneath him, and behind him until we are reunited again. Thank you, Father. In Jesus' name, Amen." Immediately, she went to Luella's room to explain the unhappy circumstances. When the old woman had listened to everything Deborah told her, the two of them together petitioned the Lord, asking Him to uphold His promise to make all things work together for good at this time of crisis.

Returning to her room, she helped Tommy pack. When he had finished, he set his valise by the door then came to Deborah, taking her in his arms and speaking softly in her ear. "Thank you for understanding, Butterfly. I hate to leave you. You know that, don't you?"

"I know, Tommy. I love you. I'll miss you terribly. Will you write?"

He kissed her ear, her cheek, then closed his mouth over hers. When their lips parted, he said, "Of course, I'll write, and I'll be expecting a letter from you every day. Promise?"

"Promise," she replied, knowing letters would be poor substitutes for time together, but trusting the Lord to fill the gap until the crisis had passed.

The following morning after breakfast, Deborah tearfully saw Tommy out the door. When she had finished her Bible lesson with Aunt Luella, she tried to practice her singing, but her heart wasn't in it. Every song, no matter how peppy, sounded dull, devoid of her usual joy. All she could think of was that Tommy had left Calumet and she didn't know when she would see him again.

Cutting the practice session short, she retrieved her scrapbook and the loose newspaper clippings from the bedside table and brought them downstairs. Settling at the dining table, Topsy at her feet, she spread the articles out before her. In the turmoil of last night, she had forgotten about the story, "Lured Her Away," that she had discovered on the backside of one of Tommy's clippings. She read it now with renewed interest.

From Laurium to Superior

With her eyes filled with tears
She took witness stand
Expected to receive position with good wages
Brought to immoral resort

With tears in her eyes and in scarcely audible tones, says the Duluth News-Tribune, pretty seventeen-year-old Molly Mulligan related the story to a jury in superior court at Superior yesterday of how she had been lured from her home in Laurium, Mich., to Superior on representations by Minerva Johnson that she was to receive a position at good wages and instead was about to be dragged to a life of shame. She proved a fair witness with the exception that she seemed to forget many of the details of what occurred and was said to her at the Johnson residence and failed to remember the answers that she made to a number of questions during the course of the trial in the municipal court.

On being questioned by District Attorney Foley, Miss Mulligan said that she came to Superior in October and went to the residence of Mrs. Johnson on Third street. She had known Mrs. Johnson several years ago, when both had resided in Calumet and said that some months previous to Molly's coming to Superior, the defendant had written to the girl's mother that she would give her a good position with good wages and on such representations she came to Superior. When she arrived at the Johnson residence improper proposals were made to her and during the same day of her arrival Mrs. Johnson took her to Duluth where they went into a saloon and then upstairs to a lodging house over the saloon. At the lodging house Molly was introduced to a young man that called at the Johnson residence in Superior the following day.

Continuing, Molly told of having been offered money and being told of how much she could make by carrying out Mrs. Johnson's wishes. The girl stated that she wanted nothing to do with such circumstances and only wanted to return to Laurium. Mrs. Johnson promised to put her on the next train home, then served her a cup of tea. Molly related how she fell into a deep sleep and woke up at the lodging house where she was forced to cooperate with Mrs. Johnson's scheme.

Molly remained there with two other girls for several weeks, often drugged into submission, until a police raid closed down the business. She has since returned to Michigan and is again residing with her mother in Laurium.

Deborah stared at the article, numbed by the story. Her heart went out to Molly. How devastating to endure such circumstances, and as if that weren't enough, to have it published in the paper for all to read! She knew full well the shame Molly was feeling, and the darkness that was closing in around her. She knew of the nightmares and the shunning, the helplessness and hopelessness.

She knew, too, that she must go to Molly and share her own story. She must let Molly know that she was not alone, and that anytime she needed someone to talk to, someone who would understand completely, she could count on Deborah. She waited until Luella had finished with Lempi's English lesson, then joined her on the sofa in the front parlor, Topsy settling at her feet.

"Aunt Luella, I'd like you to read this article I found on the back of one of the theater stories Tommy saved for me."

Luella adjusted her spectacles. "'Lured Her Away. From Laurium to Superior . . . Brought to immoral resort.'" Reading silently, she finished the article and handed it back to Deborah. "Lord have mercy. This Mulligan girl is surely in need of it."

"I know Molly Mulligan," Deborah stated. Noting the rise in Luella's brow, she explained. "I met her on the train when I came up here in September, then I saw her twice at the Palestra last October. I want to go and see her, Aunt Luella."

"But the weather—it's frightfully cold and windy, and it wouldn't be good to take a chill in your condition."

"I'll be plenty warm in my cloak," Deborah assured her.

Luella shook her head. "I don't think it's wise."

"Didn't you just ask the Lord to have mercy on Molly?"

"I did."

"What could be more merciful than for someone who's been through the same thing to go to her and assure her that no matter how badly she's feeling right now, God is there to help her, and so am I?"

Topsy responded to the earnest tone of her mistress's voice, putting her front paw on Deborah's lap and demanding attention. Deborah ruffled her ear, a wonderful idea coming to her. "Aunt Luella, I know you've been trying hard to find a home for Topsy."

Luella sighed. "No one at the church wants to take her, and the neighbors have turned me down, too."

"I think we should take her with us and give her to Molly. I know how much comfort Spotsy was to me in those first days after Tommy rescued me from the 'resort.' Topsy would help take Molly's mind off her problems."

"Maybe the girl won't want Topsy," Luella cautioned.

"Then we'll bring her home again, but it wouldn't hurt to try. What do you say?"

"Do you know where in Laurium this Mulligan girl lives?"

Deborah shook her head. "I was hoping you could help me find out."

Luella went to the telephone beside her chair and placed a call. After a brief conversation with the editor of the *Copper Country Evening News,* with whom she was obviously well acquainted, she told Deborah, "The Mulligans are living in the upstairs rooms in a home on Tamarack Street. They have no telephone, so we'll just have to take our chances and hope that the girl is in when we come calling. I'll arrange for Oskari to drive us there at two."

Oskari pulled around front promptly at two o'clock. Down Depot Street he drove, continuing past Hecla Street and Laurium Street to Tamarack, coming to a halt at the designated address. Deborah went inside and upstairs to the second floor.

The Molly that opened the apartment door to speak through a narrow gap was not the Molly she remembered. Her dancing blue eyes had grown lifeless and rimmed with circles, aging her five years in appearance. Her red hair hung in dull, tangled tresses. And when she spoke, her words were utterly devoid of inflection.

"Please go away, Mrs. Rockwell. I don't want to see anybody today."

When she started to close the door, Deborah pressed her hand against it, thrusting her foot across the threshold. "Molly, wait! We need to talk!"

"Not today," the girl insisted, pressing the door firmly against Deborah's toe.

Deborah remained steadfast. "Listen to me, Molly! I was lured away, too. I know what you've been through!"

Molly opened the door, her eyes wide with disbelief.

Deborah spoke rapidly. "I spent ten weeks last summer in a white slave house. I know how awful you feel. I want to help you!"

A tear trickled down Molly's cheek. Deborah embraced her.

When Deborah's large belly pressed against Molly, the girl drew back. "You're with child?"

Deborah nodded, opening her cape for Molly to see. "It happened after I was lured away. I'd like to tell you more, if you'll let me in."

Molly nodded and stepped aside.

Deborah hesitated. "My great aunt, Luella Dunston, is with me. She helped me through the bad times, and wants to help you, too. She's brought you a present. May I bring her up?

"Mrs. Dunston is calling on the likes of me?" she asked

in disbelief.

"I'll be right back." Deborah returned to the buggy for Luella and Topsy, asking Oskari to return in an hour. When they reached the second floor, Deborah assured Molly that her puppy was completely housebroken, and the girl led them into a small parlor. Though sparsely furnished, its delicate Irish lace curtains softened the effects of the dark wood floor and molding, brightening the room. On the wall, a print of a Madonna and a cross carved of walnut attested to the Mulligans' Irish Catholic heritage.

Topsy, extremely curious, sniffed everything she encountered, and strained to explore farther than her leash would allow from the radius of Deborah's chair.

Molly took an immediate interest. "What's your pup's name?"

"Topsy," Deborah replied. "She's the only one to survive from the litter my dog, Spotsy, had in October. Would you like to meet her?"

Molly nodded, calling Topsy by name. The pup immediately strained in her direction, and Deborah unclasped the leash.

Molly knelt down to play with the pup, receiving a thorough face washing that made her smile. When she sat in her chair again, Topsy begged to come up on her lap, and Molly obliged, petting her and scratching her ears.

While Molly and Topsy made friends, Deborah explained how she and Tommy had acquired her. "Topsy's mother, Spotsy, was a stray down in Caledonia, where we were living before we moved up here. She came to us on Labor Day, soon after Tommy rescued me from the house of shame. A few days later, Spotsy and I came to Calumet, and she's been a real comfort."

Aunt Luella said, "Of course, at the time, we didn't

know she was going to bless us with Topsy. She's yours to keep, if you'd like. Lord knows, she's in need of a good home. We've been looking for someone to take her for weeks."

Molly hugged the puppy. "She surely is a beauty, but I'd have to ask my Ma." Smile fading, she carried Topsy back to Deborah who put hands up.

"You keep her for now. Introduce her to your mother, and if she's opposed, we'll take Topsy back." She handed Molly the pup's leash and the girl sat again.

Deborah continued. "You'll need to take her out whenever she goes to the door and whines. And be sure to walk her a couple of times a day. She loves to get out and explore the neighborhood."

Molly hung her head. "I couldn't do that, now that my story's out. Folks 'll stare."

"I can understand how you feel," Deborah said sympathetically, "but you can't hide in this apartment all your life."

When Molly's gaze met Deborah's, she could see the hurt and anger in the young girl's eyes. Jaw tight, she told Deborah, "It's all that Johnson woman's fault. I hate her! I hope she burns in—"

Deborah cut her off. "I'm sure God will see to her punishment, Molly. But don't punish yourself by choosing the life of a recluse."

Abruptly, Molly stood, dumping Topsy on the floor to confront Deborah. "My life's over! Don't you understand that? No fellow will ever want me now! I'll never marry, never have children or a home of my own!"

Luella spoke up. "You don't know what the Lord has in mind for your future."

Molly turned to her, eyes ablaze. "Nor do I want to!

276

He let me down!"

Luella countered. "It's *people* who let you down, Molly, not God. He only wants the best for you."

Deborah spoke up. "Look at me, Molly. I have a loving husband, and soon, a baby, too."

"A bastard!" Molly accused.

Deborah bowed her head, cut to the core. With a silent plea for God's help, she placed her hand on her belly, looked Molly straight in the eye, and quietly made her reply. "Molly, I may not know who fathered this child, but I know who the child's father is. It's my husband, Tommy Rockwell, and God is its creator. You have your whole life ahead of you, Molly. Don't let hatred and shame steal it from you."

The girl turned away. Obviously deep in thought, she sat again. Topsy begged for a place on her lap, and she lifted the dog up, cuddling her and stroking her head.

Luella opened her Bible. "Molly, God says 'Many sorrows shall be to the wicked: but he that trusteth in the lord, mercy shall compass him about.' This is His promise in Psalm 32, verse ten. Claim it for your own, Molly. Don't cut yourself off from God, not now, when you need Him most."

Molly spoke hesitantly. "I . . . I don't know if I can believe in God again. I don't know if I want to. Where was He all the time I was in that house of shame, begging Him to set me free?"

Deborah was quick to reply. "I asked that same question, Molly. But with Aunt Luella's help, I finally realized it was the *wrong* question. The right question is, what does God want you to do now?"

Molly simply stared at her and shrugged.

"I can help you find the answer, if you'll let me. I can

277

help you find God again, the way I did. There's hope for your future, Molly."

The girl sighed. "My life is naught but a nightmare."

"And so was mine, for a time," Deborah explained, "but with God's help, nightmares can be transformed into sweet dreams."

Luella spoke up. "Listen to Deborah. She knows what she's talking about. Let her help you." After a moment's silence, she continued. "When Deborah came to stay with me, we established a routine to study the Bible every day. After breakfast, we go to the back parlor and open God's word. Why don't you join us? I'll send my driver around to fetch you at a quarter to nine tomorrow morning."

Thoughtfully, Molly stroked Topsy's head. "And leave the pup here? I couldn't."

"Bring her along," Luella suggested. "Goodness knows we're accustomed to her at my place."

Deborah rose and went to Molly, placing a comforting hand on her shoulder. "Say you'll come. You've got nothing to lose but nightmares, and everything to gain."

With obvious reluctance, Molly admitted, "Putting it that way, a lass 'd be a blame fool to turn ya down."

Luella stood. "Then we'll see you tomorrow. Remember, my driver will be here at a quarter to nine."

Molly stood to see her guests out, Topsy at her heels. "Yes, ma'am. Thank you, ma'am."

At the door, Luella turned to look straight into Molly's eyes. "Young lady, I just don't feel right leaving you without a word of prayer. Would you allow me?"

Molly nodded, bowing her head.

"Heavenly Father, thank you that Molly was willing to invite us in today. Please comfort her and keep her until we meet again, in Jesus' name. Amen."

"Amen," Deborah echoed. "See you in the morning, Molly." Pointing to Topsy, who was eagerly waiting for the door to open, she added, "And you'd better hold onto this little one, or you'll be out chasing after her."

"Yes, ma'am," Molly replied, picking up the pup. "Good day, Mrs. Rockwell, Mrs. Dunston. And thanks."

In the carriage on the way home, Luella said, "I could be wrong, but I think Molly's going to send Oskari away and stay home tomorrow morning."

"Do you really think she would? She said she'd come," Deborah insisted.

"I know, but she's got all night to talk herself out of it, and I have no doubt the devil will be right there putting shame in her heart and reminding her she isn't worthy to venture out of her mother's apartment."

"Then there's only one thing to do," Deborah replied.

Luella gazed at her, brow raised expectantly.

"I'll come with Oskari."

"A noble offer, but in your condition—"

"My condition didn't stop me this afternoon," Deborah reminded the old woman.

Luella sighed. "I suppose you have a point. I'll pray that all goes well, and Molly's ready to get into the carriage when you arrive."

Chapter

25

Fatigued from the long trip downstate, and worried about the reception he would receive, Tommy paused at the front door of his childhood home. How he wished his Butterfly were here beside him. Surely his father wouldn't dare to cause a scene in her presence. But she was hundreds of miles away.

The very thought of the distance between them made his heart ache. He'd missed her from the moment he'd walked out of Aunt Luella's door early yesterday morning. Not a minute had gone by that he hadn't thought of her. She'd haunted his days and possessed the one night they'd been apart. He tried to put thoughts of her aside and focus on what he would say to his father.

He would be angry—probably angrier than when Tommy was fifteen and had gotten into a collision with his father's brand new horse and buggy. His father might even throw him out. But he wasn't about to turn around and head back to Calumet now, not after all his father had put him through these last six weeks.

Words coming to him, he firmly grasped the handle and pressed on the latch, prepared for the verbal explosion that would soon follow. Instead, silence greeted him. He set his valise beside the table in the front hall and shucked off his coat, hanging it on the hall tree along with the Persian lamb hat that his Butterfly had given him for Christmas.

Except for the entryway light, the rest of the downstairs was dark. But a faint light shone on the landing, spilling down from the second floor hall. He reached for his valise, ready to carry it up with him when suddenly he froze, astonished at what he saw in the mail basket on the hall table. There, plain as day lay a letter he had written to his father. He picked it up, only to discover beneath it another letter and another. Swiftly he searched the contents of the entire basket finding all six of the letters he had written since his father's return from Calumet, every one of them unopened.

He bounded up the steps, pausing outside the open door to his father's room. Cy lay in bed, propped up on a pile of pillows, his face thinner and paler than ever. On the far side of him, spoon in one hand, uncapped bottle of patent medicine in the other, sat slim Mrs. Pritkin, the widowed housekeeper of many years.

"It's time for your evening dose," she said in her bristly manner. "Before I pour it out, Mr. R, I want you to promise to swallow it down like a good fellow. It does you no good, spilt all over your bed covers."

"That stuff tastes worse than hair tonic," Cy grumbled weakly.

"Now, how would you know, Mr. R?"

"Go away and let me sleep," he replied, his eyes closing.

Tommy stepped into the center of the room. "Hello, Papa."

Cy gazed up at him, his expression one of surprise and confusion. "Tommy? Is that you, son, or am I a dreaming fool?"

Tommy couldn't help smiling. "I don't know about the

281

fool part, Papa, but you're not dreaming."

Eyes glistening, Cy beckoned, his quiet voice full of emotion. "I'm so glad you're here, son. I never thought I'd see you again."

Swiftly, Tommy closed the gap between them, hugging his father, dismayed by the frailness of his slender form and the strange smell emanating from him.

Mrs. Pritkin rose. "Welcome home, Tommy. I'm mighty thankful you're here. Maybe you can talk your father into taking his medicine." She passed him the spoon and bottle.

A stronger version of the off-putting odor emanated from its narrow opening. Tommy read the label. "Dr. Johnson's Curative. Promotes appetite. Restores energy."

"Tastes like hair tonic," Cy repeated.

Mrs. Pritkin wagged her finger. "If you'd complain less and cooperate more, maybe you could stand to get out of bed for longer than the ten minutes it takes me to change your sheets." To Tommy, she explained, "Your father took quite a bad turn after his trip up north. Nearly lost him. I've been tending him night and day, but he barely eats, and fusses like a babe when it comes time for his medicine."

Tommy could tell from the wide circles beneath her eyes that she had lost many a night's sleep. "I'll see that he gets what he needs, Mrs. Pritkin. Why don't you take the rest of the night off while I sit with Papa?"

"You needn't say it twice!"

When the woman had left, Cy said again, "I'm so glad you're here, son. You're not going to make me swallow that hair tonic, are you?"

Tommy read the fine print on the label. "'Contains Pepsoids. If you don't kill the disease germs in your stomach, they will kill you. Pepsoids are guaranteed to clear germs out of the stomach and rebuild it.'" Finding the bottle cap on the bedside table, he capped off the foul-smelling tonic and set it on the dresser along with the spoon. Then he put the straight back chair Mrs. Pritkin had been using in the corner and pulled his father's thickly padded platform rocker to his bedside. "Maybe what you need is some good chicken soup instead of tonic."

Cy nodded. "You're all the tonic I need right now, son." With an effort, he reached for Tommy's hand.

Tommy clasped his father's thin, bony fingers in his strong, padded ones, unable to speak past the knot in his throat.

Cy spoke in a quiet, breathy voice. "I never should have said what I did that night before I left Calumet." He paused, and Tommy could tell that even the effort to talk was taking quite a toll on him.

"Rest now, Papa."

Cy shook his head. "I'll rest when I've said my piece." Pausing to catch his breath, he continued. "I didn't want to disrupt your new life with Deborah. But when I lay at death's door, my only prayer was for one more chance to see you again."

Tommy squeezed his father's hand. "Your prayer has been answered."

Cy started to close his eyes then opened them again. "How is Deborah?"

"She's in good health, growing larger. Now get some sleep."

A smile slanted Cy's mouth. Then his eyes closed, and he faded into dreamland.

Laying his father's hand at his side, Tommy switched off the bedroom light and leaned back against the rocker, worn out from his two days of travel. Visions of his

Butterfly filled his mind the moment he closed his eyes. With a prayer for her protection and continued good health, he fell into a light sleep, frequently awakened by his father's troubled breathing and quiet mumbling.

Calumet

In the darkness of the lonely bedroom, Deborah lay her head on her pillow, wishing fervently that life could go back to the way it was before Tommy's father had left Calumet. How she longed for Tommy to be with her now, and for the restoration of his happy disposition. How she longed, too, for the old Molly to be restored. But longing would do her no good. She must face life's challenges believing that God would answer her prayers for restoration and that He was in control even when His enemies seemed to be winning.

Hearing Spotsy's toenails clicking against the wood floor, she patted the bed cover, inviting the dog up. She too was in a state of longing now that Topsy had found a new home. Quickly, she snuggled into the crook of Deborah's knees, letting out a deep sigh.

Deborah tried to relax, but the events of the day haunted her. When she had arrived at Molly's apartment at quarter to nine that morning, it was like Aunt Luella had predicted. The girl waved Oskari off. With instructions for him to return in an hour, Deborah stepped out into a bitter cold wind thick with snow and climbed the stairs to knock on Molly's door. Inside, Topsy barked excitedly.

"Topsy, it's me, girl. Go get Molly."

When Topsy recognized her voice, she began to whine with longing.

"Topsy, get Molly!" Deborah commanded again.

Topsy only whined louder, releasing a soulful, heartrending howl.

Deborah pounded on the door. "Molly Mulligan, open up and let me in!"

The apartment door on the floor below opened. An infant's cry and a woman's voice pierced the stairwell air. "Pipe down! My baby's trying to sleep!" The door closed with a thud before Deborah could apologize.

From the opposite side of Molly's thick, oak door, Deborah heard the girl's faint voice. "Please go away, Mrs. Rockwell."

"I'm not going away, Molly. Now let me in! It's not polite to lock out a woman heavy with child!"

After a moment's silence, the door opened slowly. Catching Topsy by her collar to keep her from running out, Deborah stepped inside and quickly closed the door behind her. To her dismay, Molly looked as careworn and disheveled as she had the day before. Her dark skirt and white blouse were so wrinkled Deborah was certain they'd been slept in.

But if Molly was not pleased to see Deborah again, at least Topsy was. She barked excitedly, jumping up at Deborah, then scratching at the door where her leash dangled from a hook.

"Sit, Topsy!" Deborah commanded, and the puppy obeyed. Noticing an unpleasant odor, Deborah asked Molly, "Have you taken Topsy outside this morning?"

Molly hung her head. "I guess I forgot."

Deborah took Topsy's leash from the hook where it hung on the door and clasped it to her collar. Then she removed her cloak and draped it on Molly's shoulders. "While you two are out, I'll set some water to boiling. I could use a hot cup of tea right now. How about you?"

285

Molly nodded, reluctantly following Topsy as the dog pulled her out the door.

In the kitchen, Deborah found the source of the unpleasant odor, evidence that Topsy hadn't been taken outside when necessary. She cleaned up the mess, then filled the teakettle and set it on the burner. Over a nice cup of tea, she would have to gently remind Molly to take Topsy out more often.

As Deborah drifted off to sleep, the remainder of the day played itself out again. Over tea, Molly began to talk and weep, unburdening the horrors of the house of shame. Deborah listened and consoled, thankful that she could be Molly's special friend at this time of crisis. And when Oskari pulled up an hour later, she told him to return for her at four that afternoon, asking him to relay her plan to Luella.

So her day had been long and heart wrenching. Molly's descriptions had rekindled memories of Deborah's own nightmarish experiences, her questions about God, and why He allows such horrible things to happen. Especially disturbing was the fact that Molly had done nothing to deserve her trouble. She hadn't been disobedient, as Deborah had been, when lured away. Rather, Molly had been duped by people she had known and had no reason to distrust.

In seeking to comfort Molly, Deborah had reminded her that according to Psalm 32:10, "Many sorrows shall be to the wicked, but he that trusteth in the Lord, mercy shall compass him about." Even so, Molly would remain troubled for some time, Deborah knew.

She tossed and turned, struggling to clear the day's events from her mind and to focus on the good that had come out of it. Inside her, the unborn child kicked again and again. Getting out of bed, Deborah pulled on her robe

286

and sat in her rocker, covering herself with two thick afghans. Spotsy settled at her feet and while Deborah gently rocked back and forth, her thoughts centered on the more pleasant part of her day.

By mid-afternoon, she had convinced Molly to press her wrinkled outfit and wash her bedraggled hair. When it had dried, she even let Deborah fashion it in a pouf. Molly's thick, red hair behaved beautifully. Deborah fussed and fussed, and when she had finished the style to perfection, she handed the girl a mirror.

For the first time all day, Molly smiled. She stared at herself for several minutes, amazed at the improvement in her appearance. When she put the mirror down, she announced that she was hungrier than she had been in weeks, and went to the kitchen to reheat the soup she had barely tasted during lunch. And before Oskari appeared to fetch her at four, Molly had agreed to come to Luella's in the morning for Bible study.

Deborah yawned. Laying afghans and robe aside, she returned to bed, falling fast asleep with Spotsy snuggled in against her back. Too soon, morning dawned. Though tempted to remain between the cozy covers, Deborah rose and dressed. After all she had been through with Molly, she wasn't about to take the chance that the girl would wave Oskari off again. Today, with God's help, Molly would be sitting in the back parlor with Deborah, taking comfort in the Bible study Aunt Luella had prepared especially for her.

Chapter 26

Marshall
Wednesday, April 18

Warm breezes tilted at hyacinth blossoms, sending their distinctive, sweet essence to Tommy as he sat out on the front porch with his father on a sunny afternoon. An arm's length away, Cy moved back and forth in his wicker rocker, a smile slanting his mouth as he drew in a deep breath.

"Ahhh. There's nothing like the perfume of hyacinths on an April breeze. Your mother planted the very first ones the year we were married—added more over the years when the blossoms got old and tired. Did you know that, son?"

Tommy shook his head. There were many things about his mother that he hadn't known, but had learned in these last two months while his father regained his strength. Today, for the first time, the weather had been warm enough and his father, strong enough to venture outside. Tommy silently thanked God for the improvement his father had made. He thanked God, too, that Cy had made it through the rough nights when it was almost certain he'd expire before morning. But those seemed to be over, and Mrs. Pritkin's chicken soup had proved a very effective tonic— far more helpful than that foul-smelling patent medicine the woman had been trying to force down his father's throat.

Tommy liked to think that the doctor had been wrong. His father wasn't going to die. Yes, he was far from being the healthy man he was at the wedding last September, but whatever was ailing him—and the doctor never had said exactly what it was—the ailment seemed to be on the way out. Just maybe Papa could beat it if he kept going the way he had been the last couple of weeks.

But his father never seemed convinced. One day he'd invited over Gideon Courtade, his longtime friend and lawyer to assure Tommy that all the necessary papers were in order for settling of the estate. Tommy had listened reluctantly, still unable to accept the possibility that his father's days were near an end.

On his mind daily were thoughts of his Butterfly and the coming child. Even during his early morning runs around the sleepy village, he couldn't escape doubts over his ability to be a good father. When he was with her it was easy to put on the face of confidence. Hundreds of miles away, he wondered whether he would be able to accept Deborah's child as his own, even though he had already promised that he would. Sometimes he wondered who was better at play-acting, him or his Butterfly?

When his father spoke again, he realized how far his own thoughts had strayed from the subject at hand.

"I wish your mother were here now to smell her hyacinths. They were her favorite blossoms of spring, hardy and strong and demanding to be noticed . . . just the opposite of her."

"Maybe that's why she liked them," Tommy conjectured.

"Maybe so." Still smiling, Cy continued. "I remember the first time I really took notice of your mother. It was May Day back in . . . I don't recall the year. She was dancing around a Maypole that the Sunday school had put up, her skirt flowing in the breeze." He paused, thinking. "A few years later, we married and moved in here with my folks. Then you were born." He chuckled. "It wasn't easy for her, bringing you into this world, but once you got here, you were a happy little fellow, the light of our life," he admitted fondly.

Talk of his birth only heightened Tommy's painful longing to return to his Butterfly. Soon, now, their baby would enter the world, and despite his doubts, the desire of his heart was to be in Calumet. He pulled her latest letter from his pocket, the one that had arrived in this morning's mail, and opened it again.

"How's Deborah doing? The baby hasn't come yet, has it?"

Tommy shook his head. "Any day now." He read from her letter. "'Molly Mulligan'—that's a friend of hers—'and Lempi and Aunt Luella have been making certain that one of them is with me at all times, and Spotsy is a great comfort, night and day. The piles of snow have not yet disappeared completely from Calumet, but today I saw the first crocus blossom. Topsy is quite something. Molly got her to "shake" for the first time today.'" He skipped past her professions of love to the last line on the page. "'Give our love to your father. He is daily in our prayers.'"

"They're working," Cy said.

"I'll be sure and tell her in my next letter," Tommy promised.

Cy shook his head. "No, son. No more letters. Go home and tell her in person."

"But—"

"Pack your bags and get on up to Calumet. Mrs. Pritkin can take care of me."

Tommy was torn. He'd do anything to be with his Butterfly again—anything but leave Marshall when his father needed him.

Cy spoke again. "Remember last January when I said you wouldn't inherit a penny if you came here to watch me die?"

Tommy nodded.

"I lied. I never put that in my will. But I'm going to disinherit you if you don't go upstairs and start packing your bag right now."

Tommy didn't budge. He didn't know what to think.

"Don't sit there staring at me. Go on! I'll just stay here for a while longer, taking in the hyacinths." He drew a deep breath, leaned back, and closed his eyes, gently rocking back and forth.

Calumet
9 P.M. Friday, April 20

Deborah sat in the back parlor at Captain Dunston's desk, staring down at the blank sheet of stationery. What could she possibly say to Tommy about a day when she'd done nothing but wait for the baby to come? She was pondering the dilemma when she heard Spotsy get up from her place by the piano and let out a low growl.

"It's okay, girl," Deborah said idly, knowing that the dog's acute hearing often prompted her to react to noises on the street that were inaudible to humans.

The dog ran from the room, letting out a gleeful squeal from the front parlor followed by joyful barks and more wildly happy squeals. Deborah hadn't heard Spotsy sound this enthusiastic since Tommy had left. Suddenly, she knew he was back.

"Tommy?" She rose from the corner desk, turning her broad form around to discover him standing in the parlor doorway, his mouth drawn into a wide, slanted smile. Beneath his arm, were two wrapped and beribboned boxes, and in his hand, a butcher bone that had Spotsy jumping and yipping with excitement.

He commanded her to sit before rewarding her with the bone and sending her off to the kitchen. Then he simply stood there, beholding the woman he adored. The fact that she was now ponderously heavy with child detracted not one whit from her loveliness, rather adding to it. Above the broad expanse of her midriff, her face had lost none of its stunning beauty, but glowed with clear evidence of her inner peace, and shined with tears of happiness that now trickled down her cheeks. He closed the distance between them, depositing parcels on the piano bench, then wrapping his arms about his wife and the child that would soon enter the world as their own.

Deborah hugged Tommy's neck, overcome with joy at his return, basking in the security of his embrace. Even before he spoke, she could smell clove on his breath, the essence that had been absent from her life for too long.

"I've missed you, Butterfly."

"I've missed *you*, Tommy."

"I've brought you a present—both of you!" he joked affectionately, feeling the unborn child kick in protest against the pressure of his embrace. But when he would have released his Butterfly, she clung to him.

"Don't let go—not yet. For two months, I've been longing for your hug."

Tommy squeezed her tight, then covered her mouth with his own, eager to make up for the kisses they'd been denied. When he finally let her go, he simply held her hands in his and gazed at the woman he loved.

"You truly are a sight for sore eyes, Butterfly."

Deborah laughed with a girlish giggle. "I surely don't *feel* like a butterfly. I feel like an elephant—and look like one, too!"

"Then you're the most beautiful, elephant-sized butterfly God ever made!"

She kissed his cheek. "And you're the most gracious and complimentary husband God ever made." With a nod at the presents he'd brought, she added, "And did I forget to say thoughtful, too?"

Indicating Luella's chair, he said, "Sit and give your feet a rest while you open your surprises." Placing the packages on her lap, he asked, "Where's Aunt Luella?"

"At the theater," Deborah replied, not quite successful in hiding the longing in her voice.

"And Lempi?"

From behind him came the Finnish maid's voice. "Velcome home! Vould you care for some tea?"

"Hello, Lempi! Your English has improved so much, you've almost lost your accent!"

Her eyes twinkling with mischief, she replied with an outpouring of Finnglish—a combination of English and Finnish commonly spoken by her countrymen in the Keweenaw.

Tommy laughed. "Maybe I spoke too soon."

The maid shook her head. "I only make fun. You vant tea?"

When Tommy and Deborah had both expressed their desire for some of the Earl Gray tea that Aunt Luella always kept on hand, the maid left them alone again.

"Now open your presents," Tommy said, eager to see her reaction to the gifts he had brought.

She opened the larger box first, folding back tissue paper to find a delicate infant's dress of white nainsook.

293

Tiny tucks ran down the bodice, alternating with Valenciennes lace insertion. Torchon lace edged the ruffled neck, and the narrow cuffs of the bishop sleeves. "This is absolutely lovely," Deborah said, "and so finely made."

"My mother sewed it for my Christening," Tommy told her.

"That makes it the first of our Rockwell family heirlooms," Deborah said, "a true keepsake. Thank you." She leaned over and kissed his cheek, more pleased than words could say by his thoughtful, unexpected gift.

"Now open the other present," he said eagerly.

Laying baby gown aside, she untied the ribbon on the smaller box, peeled back the wrapping paper, and lifted the hinged lid with a gasp. Inside, against a lining of dark blue velvet, rested a gold butterfly pendant, its design a larger version of the exact same butterfly on her wedding band.

"It's stunning!" Deborah exclaimed, awed by the large diamonds that sparkled from each wing.

"Let me put it on you," Tommy said, removing it from the box and fastening it around her neck. Sitting back to admire it, he said, "It *is* stunning, but nothing compared to the woman who wears it."

"You're too kind," Deborah replied.

Tommy would have disagreed, but Lempi entered with the tea tray, and discussion turned to the events of the past two months. Although Deborah had shared nearly every detail in her daily letters, she amplified her descriptions now of Molly's ongoing recovery from her shameful experience, the progress in Topsy's obedience training, and the developments in Lempi's romance with Matti.

At half-past ten, Luella returned from the theater and joined them in the back parlor, welcoming Tommy home and bringing him news she had learned during intermission at the performance. "Mr. Sheldon is looking to hire. I'm sure he'd welcome you back. No sense in returning to the C & H when you were so unhappy there."

Tommy shook his head. "At Sheldon's, I'd just be setting myself up for another let-down, come January."

"No, you wouldn't," Luella argued, a smile wrinkling her mouth. "George is expanding his business—setting up another shop in Laurium. He can't be in two places at the same time, and he's desperate for a fellow who's reliable and experienced to handle the Calumet store while he gets the new one on its feet."

Deborah reached for Tommy's hand, giving it a squeeze. "Sounds perfect!"

Tommy squeezed her hand in return. "I'll go see him tomorrow."

With a yawn, Deborah said, "If you'll excuse me, I'll turn in, now. I can't seem to keep awake any longer."

Tommy was instantly on his feet, helping her from the chair, then gathering gift boxes, wrappers, and christening gown. "I'll turn in, too. See you in the morning, Aunt Luella."

"Good night."

Eight days later.

Tommy lay in bed late at night, not quite asleep as he silently thanked God for the new job he had taken at Mr. Sheldon's store. He was still amazed at how quickly his old boss had hired him. The moment he walked through the door, he'd been offered the position of manager of the Calumet store, taking over all the duties his boss had been performing, and at a handsome weekly salary, to boot. He'd started work immediately, and had already deposited a healthy sum into his bank account.

The week had been a busy one, too. With mild breezes in the air melting the Keweenaw from winter's grasp, shoppers were looking for spring merchandise. George had warned him that new goods would be arriving daily, and that a large share of Tommy's time would be required to unpack and display the latest fashions, gadgets, and household products to assist women customers with their spring cleaning. Barrel after barrel, crate after crate of new yard goods and sewing notions, garden tools and seed packets had come in, sometimes selling within minutes of making it to the shelves.

Silently, Tommy thanked God that the week had been full of blessings. He had even received a letter from his father. It was only two sentences, but long enough to reassure Tommy that he was still improving little by little.

In the bed opposite his, he heard Deborah stir. The doctor had expected her to deliver by now, but as yet the child within had been reluctant to make its appearance, a source of frustration and impatience for his Butterfly, who was growing more uncomfortable every day. She shifted her position with a moan.

"Butterfly, are you all right?"

"I think it's the sausage I ate at dinner. It didn't set well." She pushed herself up into a sitting position. "I'm going to the bathroom. I'll be back in a minute." She swung her feet over the side of the bed, but the moment she stood, a painful cramp seared through her abdomen.

She sat quickly, and would have doubled over in agony were it not for the bulge at her midriff. Instead, she simply groaned.

"I'll get Aunt Luella," Tommy told her, hastily donning slippers and robe.

"Maybe you'd better. I don't think it's indigestion after all," Deborah admitted, both elated and scared.

The elderly woman moved quickly, but by the time she reached Deborah's bedside, the expectant mother was lying comfortably beneath her covers.

"I'm sorry we woke you, Aunt Luella. I'm all right, at least for now," Deborah said apologetically.

"No bother, dear. I wouldn't want to miss a moment of this blessed event. Tommy will you please bring me a chair, and your timepiece?" When she had settled into the rocker, Tommy's watch in hand, she told Deborah, "You let me know when the next pain starts."

Feeling helpless, Tommy asked, "Is there anything I can do?"

"Yes. Go downstairs and set some water to boiling. When I know how far apart Deborah's pains are, I'll have you ring up Dr. MacQueen. In the meanwhile, I could use a cup of hot tea."

Chapter
27

In the front parlor, Tommy lay his head against the chair back, events of the last twelve hours replaying in his mind. Dr. MacQueen had arrived in the wee morning hours, then sent Lempi downstairs to tell him that progress was slow. Spotsy demanded her morning walk at eight, then plopped beside his chair where she was content to sleep. Tommy rang up Mr. Sheldon to tell him that Aunt Luella wouldn't need a ride to church, then he sat down to read the newspaper. But concern for Deborah took over.

Would she and the new baby make it through the delivery in good condition? Would he be everything this child needed in a father? Would he and his Butterfly come to agreement on a name for the child? For weeks, they had favored different choices.

Suddenly, their difference of opinion seemed silly. The wellbeing of mother and child was of greatest concern. Putting newspaper aside, he bowed his head, closed his eyes, and clasped his hands, praying silently but fervently that the Lord would bless mother and child with good health. He'd been in communion with God for some time when his prayer was interrupted.

"Mr. Rockwell, Mr. Rockwell!"

He opened his eyes to find Dr. MacQueen staring down at him, smiling.

"You may go up and see your wife now."

Tommy's heart skipped a beat. "How is she? How is the baby?"

"Your wife is tired, but otherwise doing fine."

"And the baby?" He imagined a sweet, infant girl asleep in his Butterfly's arms.

"Congratulations! You have a son! And a fine, healthy fellow he is!"

Tommy grabbed the doctor's hand and pumped it vigorously. "Thank you, Dr. MacQueen!" He bolted for the stairs, taking them two at a time, Spotsy at his heels. When he reached the bedroom, he paused at the threshold, telling Spotsy to lie down in the hall. Inside, his Butterfly lay against a stack of pillows, her silky, blond tresses cascading over one shoulder. Against the other lay the new baby, all wrapped in white flannel so that only his face showed. She was gazing down into his blotchy complexion with such tenderness and love it was obvious that this newborn was the most precious thing to ever come into her life.

Aunt Luella vacated the bedside chair and beckoned Tommy to sit. "It's been a long night. I'm turning in. Lempi is just down the hall if you need anything."

Tommy thanked her and sat down. His first close-up view of the baby inspired half a dozen thoughts at once.

He was homely, but he was beautiful! He was conceived in sin, but he was innocent of sin! He would never know his father, but he would know who his father was!

The last thought was a sobering one. Suddenly, fatherhood weighed heavily on Tommy's shoulders. For some reason, he had always imagined that this first child would be a girl—someone for his Butterfly to train and nurture in the ways of a woman. But God had other plans. It would be up to Tommy to teach his son the ways of a man. To mold him and shape him and direct his path. Could he live up to such an awesome task? Silently, he prayed.

Almighty God, please help me to be the best father I can be to the son you have given me. Thank you! In Jesus name, Amen.

No sooner had he finished the prayer, than the most remarkable thought came to mind. God surely must believe that Tommy was equal to the task, otherwise, He wouldn't have entrusted him with this little boy! The reassuring knowledge made him smile.

When Deborah looked up, the smile that slanted Tommy's mouth was all she needed to cast away any doubts that he could raise this child as his own. He leaned down and kissed her, then brushed his finger against their new-born son's chubby cheek, saying, "He's a miracle!"

"He truly is!" Deborah agreed, having already forgotten the pains of delivery. "Wait until you see his hair."

"I thought babies were born bald."

"Not this one," Deborah replied, pulling back the white flannel that was covering their son's head.

Beneath it was the reddest hair Tommy had ever seen! "Does this color hair run in your family?"

Deborah shook her head. "I was hoping it ran in yours."

Tommy laughed. "It does, now!" He stroked the fuzz, so soft against his hand. The baby yawned, and Tommy marveled at the tiny little "o" formed by his toothless mouth. Without a sound, the infant drifted off to sleep again.

In that quiet moment, Tommy heard Spotsy's toenails clicking against the hardwood floor and turned to find her sneaking toward the bed. He was about to send her out again when his Butterfly spoke to her quietly.

"Come meet your new playmate, Spotsy."

She eased up to the side of the bed, sniffing at the blan-

300

ket that covered the child. Tommy held her back by the collar to keep her from breathing in the baby's face, then commanded her to lie down. When the dog had settled between her mistress's bed and the bassinet to the left of it, Tommy told Deborah, "Spotsy could get quite jealous over the baby, but it looks like she's just curious."

"I don't think she'll cause any trouble," Deborah said, knowing how heartbreaking it would be to have to give up the dog that had comforted her so for these past several months.

A silent moment passed while she and Tommy simply admired their sleeping son, then a new thought came to her. "I've chosen a name for him."

"What is it?" Tommy asked eagerly, remembering the lists of names they'd made for boys and girls.

"Cyrus Thomas," she replied.

"Cyrus Thomas," he repeated thoughtfully. "I like it."

"You should wire your father with the news."

Tommy nodded. "He'll be honored."

Deborah smiled, then yawned.

"You're tired. Should I get Lempi to put the baby in his bassinet?"

"Would you like to do it?"

He shook his head. "I don't know anything about babies."

"It's not hard," Deborah insisted. "Just keep your hand behind his head and neck, like so, whenever you lift him."

Tommy followed her instructions, amazed that little Cy was barely bigger than the two man-sized hands that held him. Laying him gently into the bassinet, Tommy draped the netting over the top, pleased that the tiny baby never woke up. "I'll go ring up Western Union and send Papa our good news."

Deborah nodded, another yawn taking over.

Tommy bent to kiss her. She smiled, then closed her eyes and drifted off to sleep. He was about to walk away when he noticed the Family Bible on the table beside her. He reached for it, opening to the first page where Aunt Luella had penned the date he and his Butterfly had been married. Sitting down again, he pulled his pen from his pocket and began to write.

When Deborah heard the quiet scratching of a pen nib against paper, her eyes opened. "What are you doing?"

Tommy finished making his entry, blew it dry, and handed the Good Book to his Butterfly.

Silently, she read what he had written on the line below the date of their marriage. *Born April 29, 1906, at half-past ten in the morning, our first precious child—a gift from God—Cyrus Thomas Rockwell.* Beside the entry, he had drawn a small butterfly.

Tears welled up as she recalled the vision of two divergent paths she'd seen the night Aunt Luella had given her the Bible: one of a butterfly-filled lane leading to children and grandchildren; the other dark and foreboding, ending abruptly on the edge of a bottomless black pit. Unable to speak past the knot in her throat, she reached up, caressing Tommy's cheek as she silently thanked God that she was indeed on the butterfly-filled lane.

That evening, Tommy was sitting in the back parlor taking tea with Luella and finishing the Sunday paper when the doorbell rang. Spotsy raced down from upstairs where she'd been keeping vigil all day long, barking frantically. Upstairs, little Cyrus came awake with a cry demanding equal attention, quickly cut short by the assuring murmur of a new mother's voice.

Tommy hurried to the door, finding a Western Union agent with an envelope in his hand. "Mr. Thomas Rockwell?"

"Yes?"

"I've been asked to deliver this message to you, personally."

Despite the solemn look on the agent's face, Tommy smiled, certain that the envelope contained a congratulatory reply from his father. Waiting until he had returned to Captain Dunston's chair to open it, he read the message to Luella.

"'Congratulations on the birth of your son. Regret to inform you that soon after your father heard the news, he passed away peacefully in his sleep. Mrs. Pritkin.'"

Luella set down her teacup. "I'm so sorry, Tommy."

He simply sat there reading the message over and over again, unable to accept it.

Quietly, Luella said, "You'd better go and pack. I'll ring up Mr. Sheldon and tell him what's happened. The first train going downstate leaves at half-past eight tomorrow morning."

"I can't go now!" Tommy exclaimed. "Little Cy isn't even a day old!"

"He's in good hands," Luella assured him.

His mind still spinning, he said, "I don't understand! Papa was doing well, getting stronger all the time when I left him ten days ago!"

"God knows best," Luella said comfortingly.

But the words were no consolation to Tommy. He wanted to rail against God, demand to know why He had taken his father now! Wadding the telegram into a tiny ball, he tossed it angrily across the room, watching it bounce off the bookcase and roll beneath the piano bench. Then he headed for the stairs, the weight on his shoulders almost too heavy to carry.

Six days later, after a late evening run through the quiet streets of Marshall, Tommy sat at the desk in his old room, took pen in hand, and began to write.

Saturday, May 5, 11 P.M.
Dear Butterfly,

Papa is gone. I still can't believe it. When I tossed the first handful of dirt over him, it was as if I was watching someone else go through the motions. I am numb, unable to grasp the finality of it. I walk past his room and expect to see him there. His presence is still so strong in this house that I can hear his voice in the hallway and his footsteps on the stairs.

I have not yet told your Uncle Charles and Aunt Ottilia that he is gone. Had they come here for the service today, I would have had too many explanations to make for your absence. When the time is right, we will tell them of Papa's passing and of his name living on in our son.

I miss you and Little Cy desperately. I promise I will return to you as quickly as possible. Write to me!

All my love, Tommy

Wednesday, May 9
Dear Tommy,

I wish you were here to see little Cyrus. He is gaining weight every day now, and his lungs are very healthy. I'm convinced that even the deaf could not

304

sleep through his crying!

I have no lack of help in caring for him. Either Aunt Luella or Lempi is available day or night. And Spotsy is always with me, my ever-faithful, four-footed companion.

Then there is Molly. She comes each morning for Bible study at nine. Afterward, she stays to dote over Little Cy and me while Aunt Luella gives Lempi her English lesson. When they are finished, she helps Lempi prepare luncheon, and often remains until four or five in the afternoon. That way, Lempi can return to her household chores and Luella can see to her charitable duties, or call on her friends without the added burden of concern for Little Cy and me.

I am so grateful for Molly's help and her company. She has lots of experience with newborn babies, having cared for her sister's two little ones. I've offered to pay her for her time, but she says she's only returning the favor I did for her when she first came out of the "resort."

Still, I wish I could hire her as Little Cy's nanny. She loves the child dearly and would be perfect for the job. Perhaps in time she will accept my offer.

I will close. Little Cy is demanding his next meal. I pray that you will be able to wrap up your father's affairs in Marshall with great expediency and return to your loving wife and son before another letter need be written.

Affectionately,
Your Butterfly and Little Cy (Spotsy, too)

Saturday, May 12, 9 P.M.

Dear Butterfly,

I am angry. Not at you, but at Papa. Why did he have to die so soon? He never even got to see little Cyrus. Worst of all, he has forced me to be away from the two of you to deal with all he left behind. Every nook and cranny is filled with treasures and keepsakes from the past, going back to Papa's folks who built this place before he was born.

Today, in the basement, I found the cradle in which my grandfather, my father, and I all have been rocked to sleep. I found my baseball, glove, and bat, too. I thought of little Cyrus, and how I would love to see him rocked in the cradle. And when he is old enough, I would like to teach him to play catch and to hit the ball in the back yard the way my father and grandfather taught me.

Later, I came across a quilting frame and an old sewing box that were once used by my grandmother. I asked myself, "Would my Butterfly ever use these?" And I was answered by silence. What to keep? What to sell? What to toss out? I can't decide without your help.

Then, there is the house itself, my family home. I've never considered myself to be foolishly sentimental, but I am discovering an attachment to this place that I didn't know I had. I wonder whether I really have the heart to sell it.

My darling Butterfly, I never imagined that my life would take so many twists and turns, or that some would cause such anguish. When I was in Calumet working for Mr. Sheldon last fall, I dreamed of building our home there. So much has changed since then. I now feel the weight of the family legacy on my shoulders.

Even though Papa appointed his lawyer as the executor of the estate to deal with legal matters, I am the only heir. As such, I am determined to see to it that the family home is not neglected. The lawyer says it could take several months to sell this place, and there is no shortage of funds to cover the expense of living here. But I can't stand to live here without you and Little Cy. I have thought, I have prayed, and now I leave you with a request.

Butterfly come home.

I know how dearly you love the theater and how happy you have been in Calumet. I promise that once things are settled, we will return if that is your desire. But for now, I have of necessity resigned my position with Mr. Sheldon in order to remain here, and I need you with me. As soon as little Cyrus can safely make the trip, pack your essentials into a bag and get on the train. You needn't go to the trouble of bringing everything now. This house contains all you could ever need. If not, I will get it for you in an instant. Just come. I can't close the door on my past without your help!

All my love, Tommy

Ten days later, in the basement with Mrs. Pritkin, Tommy tried to concentrate on cleaning out the contents of an old chest of drawers, but his thoughts kept straying to his Butterfly, and the fact that he hadn't heard from her since his letter asking her to come. Surely sufficient time had lapsed for her reply to arrive. She could have at least written to say that Little Cy wouldn't be ready to travel for awhile. But again today, the mail delivery had failed to bring any word from her. He worried that her silence was another way of saying that she simply wouldn't come at all.

Mrs. Pritkin interrupted his pondering. "I thought I tossed this out a long time ago. It's moldy and stinky." She dropped his old baseball glove into the trashcan—the same glove she had discarded ten days earlier. But he had retrieved it and put it in a trunk—a trunk she was now attempting to empty of needless clutter.

"Don't you dare throw my glove away!" Tommy warned, retrieving it for the second time.

"You'll never get it clean again."

"Yes, I will, with saddle soap and a brush," he argued, setting it on a shelf she had recently cleared of old chipped and cracked flower pots.

"What about this moth-eaten old thing? Seems to me we could put it in the trash." She held up a Civil War uniform.

"We can't get rid of that! Grandpa wore it when he served in the Michigan artillery!" Tommy pointed to the darkly tarnished pin of crossed cannons.

She grew testy. "Keep the pin and get rid of the uniform. The wool is only food for moths and mold down here!"

Tommy set his jaw. "Just put it back for now."

She tossed the outfit back into the trunk and closed the lid with a bang. "I give up! For two and a half weeks, I've been trying to put this house in order, but it's impossible to make any progress with you so attached to every little thing. From now on, it's up to you!" She stomped up the stairs in quick time, slamming the creaky door behind her.

Tommy slumped onto the lid of the trunk, gazing at the piles of clutter that still remained and muttering to himself. "Butterfly come home! I sure do need you right now!"

He hung his head, overwhelmed and defeated by the task that still lay ahead. His heart ached so for his Butterfly that he could hear her voice, and the cry of little Cyrus. So real was the sound that he could have sworn it was coming from just above him in the kitchen.

Chapter

28

Tommy heard the basement door creak on its hinge. A dog barked with enthusiasm. Little Cy's cry and the voice of his beloved Butterfly floated down the stairs to him.

"Tommy? Are you there?"

His heart raced. "Butterfly?"

"I'm home!"

He scrambled to the bottom of the stairs and looked up. In the cellar doorway he recognized the silhouette of his wife, their baby in her arms, their dog at her side. The brightness of the sunny kitchen lit her from behind, forming a halo about her blond head that gave the impression of an angel. Taking the steps two at a time, he caught her and little Cyrus in his arms. Beside him, Spotsy pawed his leg for attention.

Near exhaustion from the long train ride with her tiny babe, Deborah cherished the security of Tommy's warm embrace. With his strong arms wrapped about her and Little Cy, the familiar scent of clove on his breath, and Spotsy snuggled against them, she knew she was home at last, no matter where they were.

Tommy covered her mouth with his in a lingering kiss, brought to a premature end by the fussing of Little Cy and the insistent nudges of Spotsy. Releasing his embrace, he stroked the cheek of his unhappy son. "Sorry, little fellow.

I suppose I hugged you both a bit too tight."

Deborah laughed. "I don't think it was the hug so much as his wet diaper."

Spotsy barked, demanding her share of attention, and Tommy bent down to ruffle her ears and hug her neck. "Good to see you, girl!"

A young woman stepped into the kitchen, Topsy at her heels. The girl's face seemed vaguely familiar to Tommy, as did her voice when she spoke.

"I'll take Little Cy, Mrs. Rockwell." Smiling at Tommy, she said, "Good to see ya again, Mr. Rockwell. Ya probably don't remember me. I'm Molly Mulligan. Y're wife asked me to come with her to help with little Cyrus." She took the whimpering boy from Deborah's arms.

Tommy remembered Molly from their brief meeting months ago at the Palestra, and from Deborah's letters. "Welcome to Marshall, Molly!" When Topsy pawed at his leg, he stooped to scratch her ears. "You too, Topsy!"

She barked playfully.

Just then, Mrs. Pritkin entered the kitchen. "I was upstairs, cleaning up, and I thought I heard a dog."

Tommy hastened to make introductions, saying, "Molly needs to change little Cyrus. Would you please show her to my bedroom? My wife and I will take my folks' room."

With a nod, the housekeeper led Molly and Little Cy upstairs, a curious Spotsy and Topsy following close behind.

Alone with Tommy, Deborah wrapped her arms around his neck and placed her lips to his for another clove-spiced kiss. Again, he held her close, cloaking her in the security of his embrace. When the affectionate moment finally ended he said, "You should have wired ahead. I would have met you at the station."

She shook her head. "I wanted to surprise you." Just then, her stomach made hungry noises. She laughed with that lilting giggle that Tommy had missed so desperately, making his heart soar for the first time in two months. Her blue eyes twinkling, she said, "My stomach is telling me it's almost time for dinner but I'd like to freshen up first. I'll get my bag from the front hall."

"I'll carry it upstairs for you," Tommy said as he followed her through the dining room. He stopped short when he reached the hallway. There stood not one bag, but several, along with trunks and crates that took up all but a narrow passageway to the front door.

"What's all this?" he asked in bewilderment.

She turned to him, a beautiful smile gracing her mouth as she said simply, "Your Butterfly is home to stay."

The next day, after Little Cy had been put down for his morning nap, Deborah found Tommy in the parlor where he was fully absorbed in rummaging through a stack of newspapers. Spotsy snoozed beside his chair. The room was nearly unchanged since she'd last seen it as a small child. The same flower-and-lace wallpaper covered the walls. The leather gentleman's chair where Tommy was sitting and its smaller companion still stood on either side of the lamp table at the far end of the room. The piano occupied its customary place on the interior wall. Only the sofa had taken on an updated appearance in the form of a relatively new tapestry slipcover.

Deborah wandered over to the piano, opened the keyboard cover, and quietly tinkled out the first few bars of *Polly, Wolly, Doodle*, recalling the times when she had come with her cousin, Caroline, from the house next door just so Caroline could play the Rockwells' piano.

Tommy smiled up at her. "Butterfly, I didn't hear you come in. I'm looking for an article I saw in the *Marshall Expounder* last week—one I meant to save for you." He shuffled through more papers, finally holding one up. "Here it is. Take a look!"

She perched on the chair closest to his and read the headlines out loud. "'An Opera House at last. S.F. Dobbins and E.H. Grand will remodel Academy of Music into fine playhouse. It will be opened September the first. Work has already been commenced cleaning the place for the painters.'"

"You remember the Academy of Music Hall, don't you?" Tommy asked. "It was condemned back in January of '04, after the Iroquois Theater fire in Chicago." He referred to the fire that had prompted the closing of several upstairs opera houses across the country as fire hazards.

Deborah said, "I remember Aunt Ottilia being very picky about which performances she would attend there with Uncle Charles."

Tommy went on. "Well, it looks like you've come to town just in time for the reopening. Not that Marshall's opera house can compare with the one in Calumet, but at least we'll have a theater again."

Deborah read in the article about plans to get on the circuit of performances scheduled by B.C. Whitney of Detroit's Whitney Theater fame. The timing seemed too good to be true. Even before she had left Calumet and the theater she had loved so dearly, Marshall had been planning to reopen its own theater. Surely the Lord was showing her that she needn't give up attending her beloved theater performances now that she and Tommy had settled in Marshall.

But the last several months of confinement and having little Cyrus had taught her much about what is truly important in this world, and never again would the theater be as important to her as it had been prior to those life-changing experiences. Thoughts of little Cyrus reminded her of the reason she had come downstairs to find Tommy in the first place. Folding the newspaper, she lay it aside.

"Maybe we could take a walk over to State Street and see how the work is coming on the music hall. Molly tells me little Cyrus could use some more diapers. I'd like to buy some diaper flannel, and see how this town has changed since I was here all those years ago."

Tommy rose, quickly pulling her from her chair. "I'm sure Spotsy would like to go for a walk, too."

In no time, the dog was on her feet, bouncing with anticipation and letting out little barks of joy which drew Topsy from upstairs.

Tommy chuckled. "Okay, you may go too, Topsy!"

Deborah said, "I'll go up and tell Molly we're all going for a walk."

By the time she had returned, Tommy had put leashes on both dogs and was waiting for her on the front porch. They stepped off in the direction of West End Park, a small section of land bound by a traffic circle a couple of blocks from the Rockwell home. When they reached the park, Deborah noticed again something that she had seen yesterday on her ride from the Michigan Central Depot on Kalamazoo Avenue to the Rockwell home on Mansion Street. An electric car cable had been strung over the street on the south side of the park.

"When did Marshall get electric car service?" she asked.

"Three years ago," Tommy replied. "They started laying track four years ago. It was quite something, watching the huge steam engine put down the rails. They wanted to go straight through the park, but the city wouldn't let them."

"I'm glad," Deborah replied. "It would have been a shame to give up the park."

"I agree," Tommy said, his mouth slanting in a grin that led to a chuckle. A quizzical look from Deborah prompted an explanation. "I was just recalling the time one of the cars went too fast around the park and jumped the tracks. I imagine the engineer was cursing the curve that saved the park about then."

"He probably didn't make that mistake twice," Deborah conjectured, pausing beside the fence that surrounded the fish pool in the center of the park.

Walking on, they approached the Honolulu House, a unique mansion that had been built in a tropical design decades ago. It, too, had changed.

"Has the Honolulu House lost a couple of towers, or am I imagining things?" she asked.

"You're not imagining things," Tommy assured her. "Mr. Wagner sold the place to Mr. Bullard four years ago and he took down the two rear towers."

Moving on, they continued west on Mansion Street for a couple of blocks, then returned home to leave the dogs with Molly while they shopped for diaper flannel. Taking Grand to State Street where the business district was located, Deborah immediately recognized big changes in its appearance.

"When did they pave the street?" she asked excitedly. "What happened to the telephone poles and hitching posts? And are those new street lights I see?"

"The lights were replaced two years ago. They laid bricks and removed the telephone poles and hitching posts when the interurban came to town three years back," Tommy replied.

"Here comes an electric car, now!" Deborah exclaimed,

315

still amazed by the fact that old-fashioned Marshall had become so modern.

"It's bound for Battle Creek," Tommy explained. "We could get there and back in no time, if you like!"

The thought was tempting, but Deborah shook her head. "Some other time, when our son is a little older. Right now, we need to buy diaper flannel." As they continued down State Street, Tommy pointed out that many of the businesses Deborah had known as a child had changed ownership. The three-story shop on the northeast corner of Grand and State was still a grocery store, but the name had changed from Watson to Williams since she'd last seen it. The squat building alongside it was no longer a memorial works, but a harness shop. Beside that, the fruit store from her childhood days had become a drug store, and the next shop had changed from selling shoes to selling feed.

They encountered two new buildings next. Arndt's Cigar Store boasted the distinction of a barber pole on the sidewalk out front. Across the alley beside Arndt's stood the interurban depot. The one-story building had a steep roof that slanted down on all four sides to offer a protective overhang for waiting passengers and the drays that pulled into the alley to pick up freight. Deborah was particularly fond of the eyebrow window at the peak of the roof that seemed to be watching for the arrival of the next electric car on the street below.

Continuing down the block, Tommy made note of other changes since Deborah's last visit to Marshall. The Spanola Fruit Market was now Trupiano's fruit store; Boughton's Paint and Wallpaper, had become a café; an agriculture implement store now sold hardware; and Prior's fruit shop was now Elk's Cigar Store. Doan's laundry had given way to Keinath and Bradburn Dry Goods. Hertkorn Meats was still selling meats, but ownership had changed to Ford and Frietag. In the last shop on the block, E.G. Brewer Dry Goods was still under the same ownership. Crossing Eagle Street, Tommy pointed out that Green Drug Store was just as it had been years ago with the exception that a doctor by the name of Starr Church had hung a shingle on the second floor. The Shepherd Meat Market hadn't changed, nor had J.F. Kaumeyer Restaurant and Candy Shop, where Tommy insisted on purchasing a pound of chocolate drops. The enticing aroma of melted chocolate and the sweet blend of vanilla and cream brought back fond memories as Deborah allowed one of the candies to melt in her mouth.

They continued on, past Miss Kate Billings Dry Goods & Notions. It had been a shoe store when Deborah had seen it last, but the store next to it hadn't changed at all. It still belonged to Mr. and Mrs. Stevenson and had been her Aunt Ottilia's favorite dry goods before she had moved away.

"We simply have to shop at Stevensons' for the flannel," Deborah told Tommy. "Do you think they'll recognize me?"

He squeezed her waist. "Only because you're with me, Butterfly. I explained to them awhile back that you and I were wed last September. They remember you as the little girl they caught pilfering gum drops from their candy jar!"

Deborah's face grew hot. "I'd forgotten all about that. Aunt Ottilia was furious. She gave me some money and made me come back to pay for the candy and apologize. Then I had to help her can tomatoes until I had worked off my debt. The worst part was, you and Caroline and Parker were off playing in the park while I was suffering in the hot kitchen."

"Was that the last of your pilfering days?" Tommy asked.

Deborah laughed, giving no answer as she stepped through the door that Tommy held for her. Inside, she was reminded of the reasons why Aunt Ottilia had favored Stevensons' Dry Goods over other stores in town. The pleasant scent of rose potpourri greeted them when they stepped through the door, and the displays of hats, furnishings, and household goods were orderly and attractive. The quality of their merchandise was certainly a cut above, and the owners were both courteous and efficient. While Mr. Stevenson made change for the previous customer, Mrs. Stevenson came from behind the counter, the picture of current fashion in her white blouse and mannish tie. Although the woman's brunette hair was now showing a substantial infusion of gray, and her brown eyes had taken on a few wrinkles at the corners, her voice remained cheerful and her manner energetic.

"Good morning, Mr. Rockwell! I see you've brought someone with you today!"

"This is my wife. You remember Deborah, don't you?"

Mrs. Stevenson's hand flew to the side of her face. "Good glory, you've grown into such a beautiful young lady, I never would have recognized you!"

Deborah extended her hand. "It's been at least ten years since I've seen you, but I would have known you anywhere. You've hardly changed, Mrs. Stevenson. You're looking wonderful, as usual!"

When they had spoken briefly about Deborah's arrival in Marshall with little Cyrus, Mrs. Stevenson asked, "What can I do for you today?"

Deborah replied, "I need five yards of diaper flannel. Have you any?"

"Right this way." Mrs. Stevenson led her to the yard goods display. While she measured out the flannel, Mr.

Stevenson calculated the total, making small talk as he completed the transaction. "I'm glad to know you've decided to make Marshall your home. You be sure and bring that little fellow by soon, so we can get a look at him!"

"We will," Deborah promised. On her way out of the store, she paused by the millinery display. One particular hat laden with several pink roses, a matching satin bow, and more flowers and bows tucked beneath the flare of the brim in back, caught her fancy. She removed her plain straw boater and tried it on, peering in the mirror to admire the effect.

Tommy looked on approvingly. "That hat is perfect on you, Butterfly! Let me get it for you!"

She removed the hat and read the price tag, shaking her head. "It's awfully expensive. Besides, it doesn't even have a silk butterfly on it."

"Are you sure you don't want that hat? I'll be glad to buy it for you right now, if you'll wear it."

The offer was tempting. Deborah knew that she could easily purchase a silk butterfly and add it to the hat, but she dismissed the notion and headed for the door. "There's plenty of time for fancy hats later," she told Tommy, ever mindful of the additional expense of caring for Little Cy.

Mindful, too, that she needed to head back soon for Little Cy's next feeding, she nevertheless asked Tommy to walk her as far as the Academy of Music Hall. A small vestibule was under construction at the sidewalk entrance, and inside, they could see several changes underway. A new incline floor was being laid; suite boxes were being installed on both sides of the stage; and four fire escapes were being built. Deborah stood at the rear of the theater, imagining the way it would look when the painters had finished their decorative motifs, and three hundred electric

319

lights had been installed as described in the newspaper article. Though smaller than the Calumet Theatre, this new hall would serve a town of Marshall's size very nicely, indeed, and she was already dreaming of the opening scheduled for the first of September.

Returning home via the south side of State Street, Deborah noticed that changes there followed a similar pattern to those on the north side. The Grace Brothers Grocery store was the same, but the small grocery beside it was now Mrs. Wagner's Café. The Waidelich Meat Market had become the Jennings Barber Shop, and farther on, a restaurant had become a billiard hall; a harness shop had been turned into a plumber's store; and a blacksmith shop had become a meat market. Seeing all the changes that had taken place in only a couple of blocks of the business district made her realize that she would need to reacquaint herself with Marshall all over again in the days to come.

One morning several days later, while Deborah was working with Tommy in the basement, her hair piled beneath a kerchief, an apron covering her blouse and skirt, she couldn't help thinking how quickly everyone had adjusted to the new arrangements. Upon checking with the lawyer concerning finances, Tommy had learned that the estate could support the expense of additional domestic help, and had given her permission to offer Molly a permanent position as Little Cy's nanny. Molly had been ecstatic—more than willing to make Marshall her new home.

Additionally, Mrs. Pritkin had agreed to stay on as cook and housekeeper. She had taken a shine to Little Cy and developed an excellent rapport with Molly. Even Spotsy and Topsy had settled in, each finding a favorite napping place—Spotsy in the front parlor and Topsy in the upstairs hall outside Little Cy's room. All that remained was to finish cleaning and organizing the place from bottom to top.

Deborah continued rummaging through the musty old trunk, finding stacks of papers tied in bundles—school records from when the elder Cyrus had been a boy, and correspondence between Tommy's grandparents dating from the War Between the States. She paused, sitting on the trunk lid to read a letter sent from Maryland carrying news that Tommy's grandfather would be home soon, the war having ended. Her reading was interrupted by Tommy's quiet voice.

"I've been thinking, Butterfly."

She looked up to find the contemplative look that so often ruled his features now that his father had died. She missed the slanted smile that had once dominated, and prayed that the happiness of those days would return in time.

He pulled up an old kitchen chair that had been relegated to the basement because of a broken rung, and straddled it, facing her. "We really ought to pay a visit to your aunt and uncle in Caledonia soon. I should have told them a long time ago that my folks are gone. I'd hate for them to hear it from someone else."

"Who are they going to hear it from?" Deborah asked, unwilling to return to a town filled with so many bad memories. "I made Aunt Luella promise not to mention it until we'd had a chance to break the news ourselves. She hasn't told them about little Cyrus, or even that I was in the family way." With a sigh, she added, "I'm not looking forward to hearing what Aunt Ottilia will have to say when she sees the red hair on Little Cy's head."

Tommy covered Deborah's hand with his own. "Don't fret, Butterfly. It was just a thought. I'll go up to Grand

Rapids and talk to Charles alone, if you'd rather. It's just that . . . " His chin sank.

"What, Tommy?" she gently prodded.

He kissed her fingertips. "You know how I hate to be away from you. And we hardly have any family left—you and me. There's your aunt and uncle and Caroline and Parker. Your mother didn't have any other relatives, and on my side—"

"Tommy, I've got a great idea!" Deborah said excitedly. "Let's go to Caledonia for the Fourth of July!"

"That's more than a month off," Tommy calculated. "Today's only the first of June."

"I know, but Caroline's baby is due at the end of this month, and I'd like to wait until she's had her child before we go to see her. Parker and Roxana's baby is probably a few days old by now, if it came on time. And if I know Aunt Ottilia, she'll do her best to have the whole family in town for the holiday." Kissing him briefly, she asked, "Can you wait until then?"

He squeezed her hand. "If it will please you, Butterfly."

She smiled. "I'll write to Aunt Ottilia in a couple of weeks and tell her we're coming. I'll ask if she can put us up in our old room for a couple of nights, and if Molly can use Aunt Luella's room."

A smile slanted Tommy's mouth. "Good idea, Butterfly. I'll ask Mrs. Pritkin if she'll feed the dogs while we're gone. I know she's not crazy about them, but—"

Deborah drew a sharp breath, covering her mouth with her hands.

"What's wrong?" Tommy asked, his smile vanishing.

"It won't work," Deborah replied. "Mrs. Pritkin already has her heart set on spending the month of July with her sister in Charlotte."

322

"The entire month?" Tommy asked in disbelief.

"She's no spring chicken, and after all she's been through since the first of the year, she deserves a long vacation," Deborah explained.

"Then we'll have to go to Caledonia some other time," Tommy concluded. "Still, I hate to put it off until August. Are you sure you don't want to go this month? We'll wait until the last week. Maybe Caroline's baby will come early."

"Maybe it will come late," Deborah pointed out. After a moment's thought, an idea came to her. "I know what we'll do. We'll take the dogs with us!"

"On the train?" Tommy asked skeptically.

"We already have their crates. It would be easy, just going the short distance from here to Caledonia."

"But you know how your Aunt Ottilia feels about dogs," Tommy countered.

"I'm not going without them," Deborah stated. "I'll warn Aunt Ottilia to expect them."

"Whatever suits you," Tommy concluded, thankful that his Butterfly was willing to go at all.

He returned to the chore of organizing the basement, opening up a leather salesman's case that had belonged to his father. Inside were copper fittings and hardware of the finest quality. Upon close inspection, he discovered a note in his father's handwriting that said they were products made of copper from the Calumet and Hecla Mine. At first he was surprised to learn that his father had been a salesman for products made with C&H copper. He'd never mentioned it, even when he'd been in Calumet. Then he remembered Christmas Day when Mr. MacNaughton had recognized his father from earlier meetings and the connection made sense.

In other compartments of the case he found samples of fine screwdrivers from a company in Utica, New York, and hammers, planes, and other items from other companies his father had represented as a salesman. Tommy removed a ratcheting screwdriver from the strap that kept it in place. It was a North Brothers ratcheting screwdriver with forward and reverse and interchangeable bits, model number 30-A with a patent date of 1895. As he gripped its fine wooden handle, he wondered how many times his father's palm had grasped the very same screwdriver when showing it to a client. The thought put a lump in his throat. He returned the tool to its place and snapped the case shut, sorry that he hadn't learned more about his father while he was still alive. Setting the case aside with other belongings to keep, he went on to a shelf cluttered with old toys, carefully sorting out those which could be repaired and handed down to Little Cy from those which must be discarded. Time passed quickly as he reminisced over each one, telling his Butterfly when and how he had acquired them. In no time at all, the morning had vanished and Mrs. Pritkin called down the stairs to say that the midday meal would soon be served.

Before cleaning up and sitting down to the dining table, Tommy checked for mail in the front hall. On the table was a letter from Aunt Luella, which he gave to Deborah, and beneath it, an envelope addressed to his father from a bank in Boston. While Deborah was reading Luella's letter aloud, he slit open the envelope from Boston wondering what business a bank there could possibly have with his father. When he saw the contents, his heart skipped a beat. Surely, there was some mistake. His pulse racing, he read again the address on the envelope and the name on the document inside. Both of them were no doubt meant for his father. He tucked them into his shirt pocket, eager to consult his father's lawyer for an explanation as soon as the midday meal was over.

His Butterfly's voice cut into his thoughts. "Isn't it wonderful, Tommy?"

"I . . . I'm sorry, Butterfly. What were you saying?"

"I was saying that Lempi and Matti are to be wed this fall. Isn't it wonderful?"

"Of course," he said, still puzzled by the item from Boston. "Listen, Butterfly, I have to take some papers to Papa's lawyer after we've finished eating. Let's leave the rest of the basement clean-up until another day."

"Is anything wrong?" Deborah asked, sensing Tommy's distraction.

"I don't think so," he said uncertainly. "I'll know more after I see Mr. Courtade."

Chapter

29

Dressed in shirt, bow tie, and vested suit, Tommy walked the short distance to Gideon Courtade's law office in balmy June weather that made him wish he were on the ball diamond ready to swing his bat. Vivid memories of his father pitching to him in the back yard on Saturday afternoons, reminding him again and again to keep his eye on the ball until he became the best hitter in all of Marshall, made his heart ache with missing him. To chase away the sadness, he set his thoughts on the future, looking forward to doing for Little Cy what his father had done for him—enjoying the days of his son's youth and teaching him how to become the best he could be in each of his pursuits. But one thing would be different. Tommy was determined not to spend the better part of each week away from home on business. If he could have changed anything about his father when he was a lad, he would have changed the fact that his father was away from home Monday through Friday every week. But the choice had not been Tommy's to make. His father had been a very successful salesman who loved his job and his family, and Tommy couldn't fault him for the path he had followed.

At the law firm, he saw that Mr. Courtade's office door was closed, and sat down to wait for him to finish with the previous client. When the door opened, old Mr. Stevenson, the balding owner of one of the town's most successful dry goods stores, emerged with a greeting as hearty as his broad form.

"Well, hello there, Tommy! How's it going with that baby boy of yours?" Before Tommy could answer, Stevenson laughed, adding, "I don't suppose I need ask, seeing as how you brought that pretty little wife of yours into the store a week or so ago to buy a considerable length of diaper flannel."

Tommy chuckled. "Little Cy is just fine. How are you? I assume business is brisk as usual."

He smiled. "Too brisk for an old man like me. I'm looking to sell the place and retire. In fact that's why I came to see Gideon. To get some ideas on the best way to go about it, seeing as how I haven't any sons to take over."

"This town won't be the same without you behind the counter at Stevenson's Dry Goods," Tommy said. "You've been there since I can remember."

"Twenty-eight years—since before your folks were even wed." He paused, adding thoughtfully, "I sure do miss them. Your ma, when she was well, and your pa right up until the last few months, they were regulars at my place." His countenance brightening, he continued. "But now you're here with your wife and son to carry on." With a glance at his timepiece, he said, "I'd best get back to the store. My wife's there alone. You take care of that new family of yours, now, you hear?"

"You can count on it," Tommy replied.

When the shopkeeper had left, Gideon Courtade ran his hand casually through the shock of white hair gracing his forehead. "What brings you by, Tommy?"

He pulled the envelope from his vest pocket. "This came in the mail today. It was quite a shock."

"Come into my office," Gideon suggested, taking envelope in hand. When Tommy had been seated opposite him at the broad desk, the lawyer slipped the contents out of the envelope, nodding as if he'd seen similar documents in the past. "This is a quarterly report and dividend check from the Bank of Boston for the Calumet and Hecla stock held in your father's name."

"I didn't know he owned any stock," Tommy admitted. "He never spoke of it, but when I saw the check and the memo that came with it, I was forced to conclude that either Papa owned a considerable number of shares, or the bank had made a mistake."

"There's no mistake," Gideon was quick to assure him. "This is one of four payments each year. They pay out on the first of March, June, September, and December."

"March?" Tommy asked, thinking he'd been with his father then, taking care of the mail, and would have noticed such a check. Then he recalled that his father had been feeling quite well at that time and had insisted on opening his own mail, sending Tommy on an errand to his banker with a sealed envelope one day.

Gideon's voice interrupted his thoughts. "March, June, September, and December," he repeated. "You'll receive checks four times a year as long as the mine is profitable and the board of directors votes to issue dividends to the shareholders."

Tommy could scarcely believe it, even though Gideon had said it two times. One such check a year was a handsome sum, but with four times the amount that had arrived in today's mail, a man could support an entire household in true prosperity without ever lifting a finger. Suddenly, questions flooded his mind, pouring off his tongue before he could stop them. "How did Papa get this stock? And why didn't he tell me about it?"

"It passed on to him from his father."

Before Gideon could say more, Tommy sprang from his chair, pacing the floor agitatedly. "Grandpa died when I was just a kid. If Papa was so rich, why did he spend all those years traveling the country as a salesman? He left on Monday morning every week, and didn't return until Friday night. Why didn't he just stay home?"

When Tommy had calmed down and was ready to listen, Gideon began to talk. "Your father loved selling on the road. He was blame good at it, too. It gave him true joy to go out and represent the best products available, and to convince others to believe in them the way he did. True, he didn't need the commissions he made, but I think the fact that he earned a sizable income all his own gave him great satisfaction." Gideon smiled as he relaxed against the back in his chair, evidently reminiscing about his former client. Then he leaned forward, his expression sober. "There was another reason your father went out and worked hard—a reason even more important than the love of being on the road as a good salesman."

After a moment's silence, Tommy asked, "What was that?"

Gideon stared him square in the eye. "It was his love of *you*, Tommy. He wanted to set a good example for you. He never wanted you to think that you had the world on a platter. He wanted you to understand that it's a man's duty to go out and work hard every day, to make a positive contribution to this world, and to do it in an occupation that you truly enjoy."

Tommy thought about his father and knew that Gideon was right. He never could have been happy living a life of leisure, but he had found true happiness in his family and his work.

Gideon spoke again. "Tommy, do you remember when you were fifteen and you borrowed your father's new horse and buggy?"

"How could I forget?" he asked. "It took me two whole years working on the Franklin farm to pay Papa back for the damages after I got into an accident. The worst part was, I missed two seasons of baseball." Suddenly, the irony of the situation hit him full force. "Papa said he was counting on me to earn the money to pay off the loan he took out to fix the rig, but he didn't need that money at all!" Instantly, Tommy was angry again. "He let me miss out on two years of baseball, and for what? For nothing!"

Gideon shook his head. "You're wrong, Tommy. It wasn't all for naught. It was to teach you a lesson. Tell me what kind of a fellow you'd have turned out to be if your papa had bought your way out of every problem?"

Tommy didn't have to think long to know the answer. "I'd have gotten into a lot more trouble."

"Exactly. He wanted to teach you to take responsibility for your actions. Now do you understand better why he never let on that he was a man of means?"

Tommy nodded, still struggling to absorb the full meaning of his situation.

Gideon sat back, hands folded on his ample belly. "He was mighty proud of you, Tommy. When his health started to go and we were getting his papers in order, he'd tell me how much he admired you. He bragged about how smart you were, finishing college in three years instead of the usual four. He credited your mother for your high degree of intelligence. Said he wasn't much of a student, himself, leaving college after one year to go out and sell.

"We reminisced, too, about the days when the Chappells lived next door to you, and Charles was a clerk here in my office before setting up his own practice in Grand Rapids and moving to Caledonia. Do you remember that time one summer when your folks invited me and my wife and the Chappells over for dinner? You were just a kid."

Tommy smiled. "I do. I remember, too, that my wife was staying with Ottilia and Charles at the time. After we kids were excused from the table, she insisted we all go into the parlor where she began directing Caroline and Parker and me in a play she had seen her mother perform at the theater in Detroit. She was quite a little actress, even then, insisting that I pretend to propose marriage to Caroline, then bursting onto the scene to spoil the moment."

Gideon chuckled. "A while back, your father confided to me that after he sent you up to work for Charles, you took him quite by surprise when you said you wanted to wed his niece. But when he saw the two of you together, he knew you were head over heels for her. His biggest regret was that he wouldn't get to enjoy his grandchildren."

Tommy was sorry, too, remembering fond times with his own grandfather. Thoughts of the kindly gentleman who had died when Tommy was a child brought to mind another unanswered question. "Mr. Courtade, you said my father inherited the mining stock from his father, but how did Grandpa get it in the first place?"

"That's a very interesting story, Tommy. My understanding is . . . "

Tommy listened with rapt attention, learning that his grandfather's connections in Boston had proved crucial to his decision to purchase the stock. At a time in the mid-1860s when Edwin Hulbert ran mining operations in the Keweenaw, a group of Bostonians provided financial backing for the Hulbert Mining Company. Then the backers spun off two more new companies to raise capital: the

Calumet Mining Company and the Hecla Mining Company. When discouraging letters arrived in Boston regarding the prospects for the future of these mines, investors in the Calumet Mining Company sold their stock. It was then that Quincy A. Shaw and his friends and relatives, including Tommy's grandfather, bought up much of the stock and began to direct operations. In March 1867, Alexander Agassiz was appointed superintendent and turned the company around. In the spring of 1871, the companies consolidated into the highly profitable Calumet and Hecla Mining Company, and on August 1 of that year, Agassiz became president.

" . . . So there you have the story of your mining stock, and now, it's up to you what to do with it," Gideon concluded.

Tommy could scarcely grasp the enormity of his inheritance. God had blessed him beyond his wildest imaginings. He was still coming to grips with the good news when Gideon spoke again.

"Tommy, your papa told me a while back that you were quite the salesman at a dry goods store up in Calumet. He said you really took to that line of work, seemed to be made for it."

"I loved my job there almost as much as I loved playing baseball when I was in school," Tommy replied.

Gideon scratched his chin. "I don't want to speak out of turn, but as Mr. Stevenson said, his place is up for sale, and I wouldn't doubt for a minute that you could be mighty successful if you took it to mind to become the next proprietor. You've got some experience. I'm sure Mr. Stevenson would stay on for a few months till you got acquainted with all aspects of his store's operation. Most important, with the C & H shares, you've got the means—"

"I'd never sell my family's shares of the mining stock to buy a store," Tommy stated adamantly.

"I don't mean to suggest that you sell. But with the stock as collateral, the bank would certainly grant you a loan if you put down, say, the sum of one of these dividend checks." He lay the draft from Boston in front of Tommy.

Suddenly, the idea held possibilities. Tommy began to dream out loud. "I could make a down payment and take out a loan. Then, if I work hard, I'll be able to make the loan payment each month . . ." He envisioned the new sign above the store, *Dry Goods—Thos. Rockwell, Prop.*

Engrossed in thought, he barely noticed when Gideon took a fat folder from the small safe in the corner of his office, then removed a bank book and plunked it down alongside the dividend check. "I don't mean to rush you, son, but it's nearly time for the bank to close. Here's the bankbook for your father's savings account. As you can see, he added your name to it some months ago. Why don't you deposit that check, then go and have a talk with Mr. Stevenson."

Tommy picked up the bankbook, opening to the latest account balance. He had to swallow hard to keep from choking when he saw the huge sum entered on the bottom line. He slipped the check into the book then slid them both into his jacket pocket and rose. "Thanks for everything, Mr. Courtade."

The elderly man stood, accepting the hand Tommy offered. Picking up the thick folder that he'd taken from the safe, he casually thumbed through the contents, saying, "We'll go over the rest of your father's papers some other time. You come see me when you're ready. You'll be surprised to learn how generous your papa was with the money from the C & H!"

"I'll be back to see you real soon," Tommy promised, torn between his curiosity, and his need to get to the bank.

When he reached the office door, Gideon said, "One last piece of advice, son."

Tommy paused, wondering what word of wisdom could have been left unsaid.

Grin in place, finger wagging, Gideon ordered, "Enjoy!"

With the lawyer's last word in mind, Tommy headed directly to the bank to deposit the check and acquire an ample sum of spending money. On his way to Stevenson's Dry Goods, he stopped by the Shepherd's Meat Market to order a custom-cut steak, promising to return for it later. In Stevenson's Dry Goods, he saw that Mr. Stevenson was busy with a customer at the counter so he paused by the display of ladies' hats near the front of the store. Looking them over, Tommy recalled how his Butterfly had taken a fancy to one particular design laden with several pink silk roses, a matching satin bow, and more flowers and bows tucked beneath the flare of the brim in the back.

Mrs. Stevenson came toward him. "Can I help you, Tommy?"

Without hesitation, he replied, "I'll take this hat for my wife if you'd be willing to make one minor change." When he described his request, Mrs. Stevenson swiftly complied, modeling the custom-decorated hat for him.

"Perfect!" Tommy exclaimed. "Would you be so kind as to put the hat in a box and tie it with a pretty pink ribbon, please?"

"I'd be more than happy to!" Mrs. Stevenson swiftly complied, tying the box with a wide, lace-edged satin ribbon of dusty rose. When she had finished, he quickly picked out appropriate gifts for the other members of the household, adding, "Before I go, I'd like to speak with Mr. Stevenson, if I may."

"Certainly!" the woman replied, hurrying to tell her husband of Tommy's request.

While she wrapped his purchases and tied them with string and Mr. Stevenson finished business with his customer, Tommy took a few moments to look around. He had noticed on previous visits how well kept the store was. Now he took more careful notice. The display of tin ware was neat and orderly, with pails hanging from hooks and wash boilers up against the wall rather than cluttering the aisle. Household utensils—funnels, graters, dippers, and pans—so often overstocked and disorganized, were lined up on shelves where customers could easily find what they needed. And signs touting the latest bargains were professionally hand-lettered and strategically placed for the best effect.

Mr. Stevenson's customer left the store and the old gentleman approached him with a smile. "My wife said you'd like a word with me."

"Yes, sir, in private if possible," Tommy replied.

"Come into the back room. No one will disturb us there," Mr. Stevenson said, leading the way.

Even the storage area, so often cluttered with empty crates and spilt excelsior, was neat and tidy, Tommy noticed, as Mr. Stevenson pulled up a couple of stools. When they sat facing one another, Tommy spoke forthrightly. "If we can work out a suitable agreement, I'd like to be the next owner of Stevenson's Dry Goods."

"That's wonderful news!" Mr. Stevenson exclaimed. "Your papa said you'd got some good experience up north at this sort of business—took to it like a polar bear to an iceberg, as he put it."

Tommy chuckled. "I did, but I have plenty more to learn. I need a few weeks to wrap up my father's affairs. That will give us time to come to an agreement and work out an arrangement with the bank. With any success, we'll be able to sign the papers by the second week of July. Then, I'll be ready to take over here."

"Sounds like a good plan," Mr. Stevenson agreed. "I'm already looking forward to retirement."

"Not too fast," Tommy cautioned. "I'd like you to stay on here part time as my advisor for the next year."

Mr. Stevenson nodded. "I'll help you get acquainted with the vendors and customers. Everyone will feel more comfortable about the change in ownership if they see the two of us working together for a spell."

Tommy stood and extended his hand. "Thanks, Mr. Stevenson. I look forward to working with you."

"Thank *you*," he replied with a hearty handshake.

In the front of the store, Mrs. Stevenson had stacked his parcels neatly on the counter. "Would you like Mr. Stevenson to deliver these after we close?"

Tommy scratched his chin. The goods would be hard to carry, considering that he still needed to stop by the butcher shop to pick up his order. Still, he didn't want to go home empty-handed. Glancing around, he spied the perfect solution to his problem. Wheeling a perambulator up to the counter, he set the hat box and packages into the buggy, paid Mrs. Stevenson for his purchases, and wheeled the baby carriage out the door. Parking between the candy shop and the butcher shop, he ordered up a selection of sweets, then collected his custom-cut steak and two shinbones for the dogs and headed for home.

Chapter 30

Deborah stood in the back yard, bucket of soapy water at her feet and scrub brush in her hand, wondering if she would ever be able to make the old perambulator usable again. She had found it in the basement laden with nick-knacks soon after Tommy had left and had emptied it of its eclectic contents before hauling it up the stairs and into the back yard for thorough washing. But in the bright June sun, she was having doubts as to whether the baby carriage could ever be restored to a usable condition.

Years of neglect had turned the white wicker to a dull gray, laden with dust, dirt, and mold as it was. Try as she may, some of it simply wouldn't yield to her scrubbing. In addition, two holes required repair, and the entire carriage needed a coat of fresh paint. Afterward, a new cushion would have to be made to line the interior, the old one being fit only for the trash. She stepped back assessing the results of an hour of hard scrubbing, disheartened by what she saw.

"At least the wrought iron wheels will never give out," she mumbled to herself. Suddenly, movement on the side-walk out front caught her eye. She had to blink twice and look again to make sure she wasn't dreaming.

Sure as the sun, Tommy was coming up the street pushing a brand new baby buggy in front of him. He was whistling *Hello, Ma Baby* as he went, a happy sound she hadn't heard from him in six months or more.

Quickly, she dragged the old carriage back down the cellar steps and pushed it into the corner where she'd found it. She was draping it with a moth-eaten blanket when she heard Tommy's voice calling to her from the top of the stairs.

"Butterfly, are you down there?"

"I'm coming, Tommy." She hurried to the bottom of the steps, looking up to see the big slanted smile on his face begin to fade.

"I told you we could leave the basement clean-up until another day, Butterfly. I didn't want you to go at it alone."

"I just wanted to make good use of my time while you were gone," she explained, smiling as she climbed the steps to join him at the top.

"What have you gotten into down there? Your face is all smudged." He took his handkerchief from his pocket and wiped her forehead and cheek clean, regretting keenly that she hadn't waited for him to help her with the dirty chore.

"I was just trying to clean up the family keepsakes," she replied casually, eager to change the subject. "How did your meeting go with the lawyer?"

Tommy's broad smile returned. "Better than expected. Come with me. I have something I want you to see." Wrapping his arm around her waist, he escorted her to the front parlor where Spotsy and Topsy were circling the perambulator, sniffing intensely.

When Deborah approached the baby carriage, she gasped with delight as if seeing it for the first time. "This is simply beautiful, Tommy, exactly what I need! It will be absolutely perfect for Little Cy! And what are all these packages inside? Is this Christmas in June?"

"You could call it that!" he replied with a chuckle.

Pulling out the parcel containing the shinbones, he said, "While I'm tying the dogs outside to enjoy their treats from the butcher shop, would you please call Mrs. Pritkin in here for me? And ask Molly to bring Little Cy. And don't you dare peek at the presents until I return!"

"Yes, sir!" Deborah replied, hurrying to do as he asked.

When everyone had assembled in the front parlor, Tommy handed a parcel to the housekeeper. "Mrs. Pritkin, this is for you."

"Whatever for?" she asked skeptically.

"Because it's Christmas in June! Now go on and open it."

She did as he requested, revealing a bright white apron edged with ruffles. "My, my. This cost you a pretty penny down at the store."

"I expect to see you wearing it tonight when you're working on this." Tommy handed her another package.

She slipped off the string and folded back the butcher paper. "Sirloin steak, two inches thick! It really *must* be Christmas in June. I haven't fried up a steak like this in . . . I can't remember when!"

"I want my portion medium rare, please," Tommy said. When Molly and Deborah had seconded his request, Mrs. Pritkin headed off to the kitchen to start dinner preparations, humming a tuneless melody as she went.

Next, Tommy pulled a beribboned parcel from the baby buggy, untied the bow, and opened it for Molly. Her face lit with a smile. "Licorice ropes and peppermint sticks, lollipops and fireballs. Thank ya kindly, Mr. Rockwell! Ya sure know the way to a girl's stomach!" She popped a fireball into her mouth.

"Don't eat too much candy before dinner, Molly. Mrs. Pritkin will be serving that steak soon," Tommy cautioned.

From the buggy, he took another parcel tied with string and offered it to Deborah. "Since our son is too small to open this for himself, I'll let you do the honors."

She slid off the string and folded back the paper, holding up a sailor suit that was meant for a toddler-aged child. "Little Cy will look very handsome in this, Tommy, but you'll have to wait a couple of years to see him in it."

"I know it's big for him right now, but he'll grow into it in no time," Tommy said confidently.

Little Cy woke up and began to fuss, so Tommy removed the last item, the hatbox from the carriage, set it aside, and parked the buggy in front of Molly. "Here's something that Little Cy can fit into right now. Give it a try, Molly. Maybe he'll stop crying."

Deborah said, "I think he's hungry. I should probably go upstairs and feed him." Molly lay the infant in the buggy and pushed it back and forth. Much to Deborah's surprise, he quieted down. "He's taking to his new buggy much quicker than I thought," she admitted.

No sooner were the words out of her mouth than the baby wrinkled up his face and began crying even louder than before. Taking him in her arms, she headed for the stairs.

Molly closed the box of candy. "Thanks, again, Mr. Rockwell. I'd better put these treats away in a candy tin." She disappeared into the kitchen.

Hatbox in hand, he headed upstairs to the master bedroom, finding his Butterfly in the nursing rocker, their son suckling contentedly. He set the hatbox on his wife's vanity and sat in his winged chair, silently thanking God for the blessings of the day, then reading the newspaper.

When Little Cy had finished his feeding, Deborah burped him and rocked him to sleep, then lay him in his bassinet. Curiosity high over the contents of the hatbox, she sat at her vanity to untie the fancy ribbon and remove the lid, catching her breath at the sight of the hat inside.

"Oh, Tommy!" she exclaimed, her cry of delight disrupting Little Cy's sleep. "Sugar! Now I've woken him," she fretted, heading for the bassinet.

Tommy swiftly intercepted, turning her back toward the vanity. "You try on your new hat. I'll hold our son." Lifting the crying baby into his arms, he rocked him back and forth, quickly quieting him while his wife donned her new hat. He watched his Butterfly as she posed in front of her vanity mirror, then in front of his mother's cheval glass for a better view.

Deborah turned this way and that, pleased with her new look. Careful to keep her voice low, she told Tommy, "I loved this hat the moment I saw it, but it's even more attractive now than when I noticed it in the store." She pointed to the silk butterfly nestled among the cluster of roses on the brim.

"I asked Mrs. Stevenson to add that just for you," Tommy explained, his voice just above a whisper. Laying a sleepy Cy in his bassinet, he approached his beautiful wife, ducking beneath the flared brim of the hat to kiss her cheek.

Deborah removed the hat, laying it aside to wrap her arms around Tommy's neck and kiss him soundly on the mouth. "Thank you for my beautiful new hat, Tommy! Now tell me what prompted this unexpected shower of gifts? Did you find a pot of gold somewhere between here and the lawyer's office?"

"Not quite," Tommy replied, "but when I got there, I *did* find some copper—a whole mine full of it!"

"What are you talking about?"

"Sit down. I'll explain." He pulled her nursing rocker beside his winged chair and talked in hushed tones, unfolding the story about the Calumet and Hecla stock that had passed from his grandfather to his father to him. Then he told her of his desire to buy Mr. Stevenson's store, and asked her opinion.

Deborah tried to comprehend all that he was telling her. "Who ever would have imagined that your father would leave behind such a fortune in stock that you could become the owner of your own store? I think if you want to buy Mr. Stevenson's place, you should do it!" As she pondered the news, a dark thought struck her. Suddenly, she cried out, her hand flying to her mouth to stifle the sound.

"What is it, Butterfly?"

She shook her head, murmuring, "Oh no! Oh no!" Deeply troubled by the memory that was coming to her, she began to pace the room, her heart racing.

Tommy went to her, taking her gently by the shoulders and turning her toward him. "What's wrong, Butterfly? Please tell me!"

Her voice trembled. "Oh, Tommy, this is the worst possible thing that could have happened!"

Tommy took her hands in his, leading her back to her rocker. "How could you possibly think that, Butterfly?"

Reluctantly, she sat on the edge of the chair. "Do you remember when I went to that clairvoyant at the Central Hotel last fall?"

Tommy laughed quietly. "I remember you didn't want to admit that you'd spent your hat money on a fortuneteller."

"That's not the worst of it," Deborah said gravely. "He told me that he saw a vision of a loved one in a casket, and hovering above it was a cloud with a silver lining contain-

342

ing an object that started with the letters s-t. I thought he meant 'stage' but I can see now that he meant 'stock.'" Rising to pace again, she said, "Oh, Tommy! If I hadn't gone to that fellow, your father would still be alive. Now, he's dead, and it's all my fault!" She began to sob, trying desperately not to wake Little Cy who began stirring in his bassinet.

Tommy went to her again, pulling her close. Cupping her face with his hands, he forced her to look straight into his eyes. "There's nothing at all to what that fellow told you, Butterfly. Fortunetellers say those things all the time. Death is an everyday occurrence. How could they be wrong in predicting it? And who doesn't want to hear that they're going to come into a fortune?"

"But those things came *true!*" Deborah insisted.

"It was God's plan, not some fortuneteller's vision," Tommy insisted. "God has appointed a time for everything!" Swiftly, he retrieved the Bible from the bedside table and opened it to the Old Testament. "'To every thing there is a season, and a time to every purpose under heaven: A time to be born, and a time to die . . . ' It says so right here in Ecclesiastes, Chapter Three." He pointed to the first two verses.

"But does it say anything about a time for a fortune?"

Tommy smiled. "It sure does. It says there is 'a time to get, and a time to lose.' Read it for yourself!"

Deborah read the words of verse six, but her guilt persisted. "I don't know what to think," she admitted, pacing again.

Tommy put the Bible down. "Whenever I feel confused, I take the advice of King Solomon, the wisest man who ever lived. 'Trust in the Lord with all thine heart and lean not unto thine own understanding.'"

Deborah went to Tommy, wrapping her arms about his neck. "Thanks for your wisdom. I needed to hear those words." Putting dark thoughts of the past aside, she smiled. "Do you know what I think?"

His arms about her waist, he chuckled quietly. "You're so full of surprises, Butterfly, I never know which direction your thoughts are fluttering in."

"Then listen carefully. I think you're going to be the best dry goods businessman in all of Lower Michigan, and I'm looking forward to helping you run the store—picking out ladies' furnishings, and such!"

Tommy kissed her briefly. "I'm glad, Butterfly. I'm sure that between the two of us, we can make the business prosper!"

Chapter

31

Deborah's hand grew moist, clasped tightly within Tommy's in the summer heat. As the train rumbled along the last few miles to Caledonia, her thoughts turned again and again to the note she had written Ottilia two weeks ago and her aunt's reply. Thankfully, Ottilia had issued a most cordial invitation to Deborah and Tommy to return to their old room and to bring Molly, who was welcome to occupy the guestroom where Luella had slept. She had written enthusiastically about Parker and Roxana and their baby daughter, who would be occupying their usual room at the end of the hall, and about Caroline, healthy and waiting for her baby to come at any time. Ottilia had even said that Spotsy and Topsy would be no trouble. But despite her warm response, and her telegram five days ago announcing that Caroline had given birth to a son, Charles Joshua, and was looking forward to seeing her and Tommy, Deborah dreaded returning to the town. She had been dreading it for days, and her reluctance increased with every clack of the train against the track.

She glanced across the aisle. Little Cy lay asleep in Molly's arms while she gazed out the window at fields of wheat and corn passing in rapid succession. How Deborah longed for the peace and contentment they shared.

Releasing her hand from Tommy's, she told him, "I wish we hadn't come."

"Don't say that, Butterfly." He offered a slanted smile. "I know you had a hard time of it in Caledonia last September, but things are different now. No one's going to insult you as long as I'm by your side!"

"Maybe not, but—"

"But, nothing!" Tommy asserted. "Everything's going to be fine."

After a silent moment, Deborah said, "God knows how badly I wish that were true."

"It *is* true," Tommy quickly insisted.

Deborah shook her head. "Listen to me, Tommy." Words tumbling out, she continued. "I know I said I'd tell Aunt Ottilia about Little Cy, but I just couldn't do it. She doesn't know we have a baby!"

Knowing Ottilia, he couldn't completely blame his Butterfly for not wanting to tell her everything. He drew a deep breath and enfolded his wife's hand in his own once again. "Don't worry, Butterfly. In a few minutes, Ottilia will know all about Little Cy, and I can guarantee you, everything will work out fine."

Silently, Deborah prayed for God's help when she stepped off the train. She had anticipated the scene in her mind dozens of times. Now, with the train rolling up to the Caledonia Station, her heartbeat quickened. From her window, she could see Ottilia and Charles waiting alongside the track among a dozen others, her aunt's expression full of anticipation, while her uncle appeared interested, but at ease.

Across the aisle, Little Cy was still sleeping in Molly's arms. When the train had stopped completely, Molly was the first to rise, quietly asking Deborah, "Do you want to take your babe now?"

She shook her head. "I might wake him."

Tommy reached for the small bag containing Little Cy's essentials, then helped Deborah and Molly down the steps. Seconds later, Charles and Ottilia approached them, exchanging warm embraces with Deborah and Tommy.

Then Ottilia turned to Molly with a smile. "And you must be Molly. Deborah didn't tell me you had a baby. What's his name?"

Before Deborah could correct her aunt's mistaken impression, Molly answered, "Cyrus Thomas Rockwell, ma'am."

Ottilia looked aghast at Tommy.

He suddenly found himself tongue-tied. "I . . . you . . . it's . . ."

Ottilia's face faded to lily white. She swayed.

Tommy dropped Little Cy's bag and scrambled to help Charles catch her as she swooned, letting her come to rest gently on the ground.

The commotion woke Little Cy, who began to cry.

Deborah took her son from Molly who removed her straw boater and began waving it back and forth in front of Ottilia's face. "Wake up, Mrs. Chappell! I didn't mean to upset ya! The babe doesn't belong to me!"

Ottilia's eyes blinked open.

Charles was kneeling beside her. "Ottilia, are you all right?"

She moaned, hand resting over her stomach. "I feel queasy."

Charles dabbed her moist forehead with his handker-chief. "Stay still, dear. The feeling will pass."

Little Cy's crying grew louder. Deborah knew he was hungry and wouldn't stop fussing until she nursed him.

Making the most of the opportunity, she said, "Aunt Ottilia, if you don't mind, I'm going straight to the house. It's time for my son's feeding, and he won't quiet down until he gets it."

"*Your* son?" Ottilia asked. "You mean Molly isn't his mother?"

Molly was quick to reply. "I'm just his nanny, ma'am. Mr. and Mrs. Rockwell are the babe's parents."

"But Molly's red hair and the baby's red hair—"

Deborah cut in. "Are pure coincidence."

Ottilia sat up, regarding Tommy and Deborah suspiciously. "Why didn't you tell me about this child?"

Tommy said, "We were saving the news as a surprise. We didn't mean to upset you so."

Little Cy continued to cry and fuss, drawing unwanted attention from passers-by.

Charles lay his hand sympathetically on Deborah's shoulder. "Go on to the house and feed the little fellow. And tell your cousins we'll be along shortly. They're all there, eager to see you."

Deborah hurried down the street to the big white house. A sick feeling stirred in the pit of her stomach reminding her of the reason she had left so abruptly ten months earlier. Thankfully, Little Cy's urgent need overrode her own bad memories, sending her swiftly up the front steps. Before she even reached the door, it swung open.

Her older cousin, Parker, greeted her with a kiss on the cheek. "Good to see you again, Deborah! Who's the little one?"

"Meet your second cousin, Cyrus Thomas Rockwell— Little Cy, we call him. He's past due for his feeding and making sure everyone knows."

"A second cousin! How about that! Bring him straight

348

into the music room. Caroline and Roxana will be delighted to see you."

Deborah stepped past the front parlor, taking scant notice of Joshua as she hurried toward the music room. There sat Caroline and Roxana in rocking chairs, quietly nursing their own babies. Caroline's face lit with a bright smile the moment she saw her cousin.

"Deborah! I'm so glad you could come! But who—?"

"Meet Cyrus Thomas Rockwell!"

Her mouth opened wide with surprise.

Before she could inquire further, Deborah said, "I didn't want to say anything until you could see him for yourself."

"But when—?"

"Little Cy was born on the twenty-ninth of April. That makes him two months and three days old today, and very hungry at the moment."

Roxana shifted her infant to her shoulder and rose from her chair. "Sit here, beside Caroline. Anne Marie's finished nursing and likes to be walked while I burp her." She patted the baby as she strolled back and forth.

When Little Cy was nursing contentedly, Caroline asked, "Where's Mother? I'm surprised she didn't come back to the house with you. She must be beside herself with the news of Little Cy."

"That's putting it mildly." Deborah explained about Ottilia's fainting spell.

Caroline smiled. "That sounds just like mother. Now catch me up on your news. The letters haven't exactly been flying between the two of us over the last ten months."

Deborah told the sad news of Tommy's parents, cautioning Caroline to keep mum until Tommy could break the news to her parents. She explained, too, Tommy's plans to take over the dry goods store that belonged to Mr.

Stevenson.

Caroline extended condolences, recalling the Rockwells fondly, and asking to be remembered to the Stevensons, a couple she had known well from her early childhood years in Marshall. Then she spoke of her music academy with fifteen students enrolled, and her work as substitute organist at the church. She was taking the summer off from both, she explained, and would resume in September when Ottilia and her mother-in-law would take turns looking after baby Charles while she taught music lessons.

Deborah spoke briefly of her musical experiences in Calumet: attending the theater; singing with the Calumet and Hecla orchestra in rehearsals; and her solos at the Palestra and at church.

Roxana, who had walked her daughter until she had fallen asleep, gently laid her on a blanket on the floor and pulled up a chair beside Deborah. "I can understand why you wanted to live in Calumet, but Parker and I were sorry you didn't move into our old apartment in Grand Rapids last September. Tommy was really something, the way he convinced the landlord to let you have a dog there!"

"Tommy planned for us to live in your old apartment?" Deborah asked in surprise.

Roxana nodded. "He never mentioned it?"

"Not a word," Deborah replied. She was on the verge of inquiring further, but the conversation came to an end when Tommy and the others arrived from the station with their belongings, including both dogs and the cradle they had brought for Little Cy to sleep in. Taking her contented, tired son upstairs to put him down, Deborah returned to the room she and Tommy had shared before their move north. Ottilia's sign still hung on the door, proclaiming it "Tommy and Deborah's Place," only now, it needed amending to include Little Cy. Inside, it looked almost the same as the morning she'd left so abruptly all those months ago, with dressing screen, easy chair, rocker, and now, the cradle Tommy had placed near her side of the double bed. There, too, were the items she and Ottilia had bought last September when they'd gone shopping—the owl night-light and the chocolate brown dolphin dish.

She carefully lay Little Cy in the cradle so as not to wake him. Alone in the room with her son while Tommy took the dogs for a walk, she sat in her rocker, remembering the days when she had last stayed here. Immediately, the pain she had felt all those months ago came back to her: the humiliation she had suffered because of that Nixon woman; the need she had felt to escape Ottilia's domineering ways. She remembered, too, her deep longing for Tommy to be here with her while at the same time doubting that their marriage could last. Roxana's talk about Tommy renting an apartment in Grand Rapids had her curious. She wondered why Tommy had never mentioned it. She would ask him about it later, when they were alone.

Her gaze settling on the dolphin dish, she retrieved it from the dresser and sat again to admire it. As she lifted the fish-shaped lid to peer inside the empty chocolate glass vessel, she remembered the story about the silver sardine server that Uncle Charles had presented to Aunt Ottilia on their wedding day. Ottilia's words came back to her almost as if she were there in the room telling the story a second time.

"I had my heart set on a different gift entirely . . . I was so let down that I never so much as lifted the lid on the thing. I simply packed it away. It's sitting in the attic of this house somewhere . . . Every year I ask Charles what he wants for his anniversary, and he replies, 'a tin of sardines served in that silver sardine server I gave you on our wed-

*ding day.' Then he asks me what I want, and I tell him a
cameo like his mother used to wear. Every year on the fifteenth of July, I give him a tin of sardines, but I make him
go out on the porch and eat them from the tin so I won't
have to smell them . . . Maybe next year he'll give me a
cameo. We'll celebrate our twenty-fifth anniversary next
July."*

Thoughts rushing into Deborah's mind, she quietly rose
from the rocker, set the dolphin dish on the dresser to be
packed later for the trip home, and headed for the stairs that
would take her to the attic.

After dinner that evening, while the three babies napped
on blankets spread on the music room floor and the men
congregated on the porch for conversation and lemonade,
Deborah discreetly invited Caroline and Roxana to her
room, leaving the infants under the watchful eyes of Ottilia
and Molly.

Focusing on Caroline, Deborah said, "Your folks will
have their twenty-fifth wedding anniversary this month.
Has there been any talk of a celebration?"

Caroline lapsed briefly into her woodpecker-like laughter, explaining, "Mother has insisted again and again that
we children are far too busy with our new babies to go to
any fuss. She has arranged for Papa to take her on a little
anniversary trip to Traverse City. All she expects from us
is a simple gift."

Roxana added, "And she has even picked it out—a silver lamp at Hale's. Caroline has made the purchase and is
keeping it under wraps at her apartment until the night
before they leave. We're all coming here for a family dinner then. Vida is planning to cook something special, and
to bake a fancy cake."

Deborah thought a moment. "I'm wondering if you all would be willing to have a little dinner celebration before Tommy and I return to Marshall." She recalled the story of the sardine tin and rose bush tradition Ottilia had told her all those months ago.

Caroline chuckled. "How familiar I am with the anniversary tradition. The rose bushes Papa plants always flourish. He claims it's because he saves the last sardine in the tin for fertilizer. I can still see him dropping it in the hole just before he sets the bush. But why celebrate early?"

Opening the bottom drawer of the dresser, Deborah showed Caroline and Roxana what she had found in the attic, sharing her idea for a most memorable anniversary dinner. With enthusiastic support from them both, and a brief consultation with Vida regarding an earlier date for the special meal, the anniversary celebration was set to be held in three days, and to be kept a secret from Ottilia and Charles.

Chapter

32

Late that evening, when Deborah and Tommy were in their room alone, she spoke quietly to him so as not to wake Little Cy. "I learned something new about you today from Roxana, something that really surprised me."

He took her in his arms, gazing down at her with a slanting smile. "I can't imagine what that might be. I hardly know Parker's wife, but I hope she said something good."

Deborah explained. "She told me that last September you made arrangements to rent their apartment in Grand Rapids—the small one they had before they moved."

Tommy recalled the incident vividly, and his sharp disappointment when he arrived in Caledonia only to discover that his Butterfly had flown away. He pressed her more tightly to him. "It's true. I was heartsick for wanting you that first week after our wedding. I needed you in Grand Rapids so I could spend every night with you. Roxana and Parker's place was about to be vacated and it seemed like God had planned it just for us."

Deborah drew back, gazing into Tommy's eyes with her deep blue ones. "And when I went to Calumet, I thought I was doing what God wanted me to do! I even remember the verse in the Bible that seemed to speak clearly to me about my plan. 'I will instruct thee and teach thee in the way which thou shalt go: I will guide thee with mine eye.' I know now that I never should have left without talking to you first. It's just that—back then, I was scared to death that our marriage wouldn't work!"

Tommy covered her mouth with his clove-flavored one for a long, deep kiss. When their lips parted, he said, "God has a way of turning our mistakes into something good, if we let Him. I should have asked you first before I rented Parker and Roxana's apartment. In Calumet, living with Aunt Luella, we were able to make a good start together. Now, with God at the head of our marriage, we're ready for whatever comes."

Deborah ran her finger lightly over the slant of his mouth. "You're the best husband a woman could ever hope for, Tommy. The best!" She kissed him on the cheek, then released herself from his arms. Opening the bottom drawer of her dresser, she said, "Now, I simply have to show you what I found in the attic today. It concerns the anniversary ritual between Aunt Ottilia and Uncle Charles regarding a rose bush and a tin of sardines . . . "

The following morning—Independence Day—dawned clear with the promise of dry weather for the parade down Center Street and the contests that would follow. After putting Little Cy down for his morning nap, Deborah joined Molly, her relatives, and the two dogs on the porch, taking a seat beside Tommy to enjoy the shade on a day that was already turning hot. Ottilia was sitting near one of her hanging baskets waving a fan, sending the pleasant scent of heliotrope in Deborah's direction as she spoke.

"You young people should take Charles over to the parade and games now, while I stay with Little Cy and Anne Marie. Caroline and Joshua will be looking for you."

Deborah said, "I'll stay here with you, Aunt Ottilia. I'd rather not risk any unpleasant encounters like I had last September."

355

"If you're referring to Grace Nixon, there's no chance you'll run into her," Ottilia said with assurance. "She hasn't been seen on the streets of this village in weeks—ever since her darling Julianna and her beau ran off and eloped. Some say they're soon to be parents—too soon. I suppose it's all too much for Grace. She stays to herself the whole day long, a broken-hearted woman from what I hear. I went over to her place a while back, but she absolutely refused to answer my knock."

Tommy reached for Deborah's hand. "See, Butterfly? There's nothing to worry about. We'll have a grand time. And who knows? Maybe I'll win you another fifteen dollars in the footrace! I should have a pretty good chance at it. Spotsy and Topsy and I have done a lot of walking and running these past several weeks."

When Deborah remained silent, Molly spoke up. "You've got to come, Mrs. Rockwell. Remember what you told me not long ago. You can't hide all your life. Besides, it wouldn't look right—me there with Mr. Rockwell instead of you."

Molly's words put Deborah into motion. Rising from her chair, she pulled Tommy to his feet. "Come on! What are we waiting for?"

On Center Street, the parade and games went much like the Labor Day celebration had the September before. Tommy even managed to repeat his victory in the final heat of the footrace, presenting her with his winnings. But Deborah couldn't help thinking of the Nixon woman and her reversal. An idea came to her—one concerning her Aunt Ottilia. The following morning, when the babies were napping and Ottilia was taking coffee on the porch, Deborah took a seat in the wicker chair beside her aunt's and began to speak of her plan.

"I'm considering paying a call on Mrs. Nixon today."

Ottilia looked incredulous. "*You* want to call on *her* after the way she treated you last September?"

Deborah nodded. "I was wondering if you'd like to come? Perhaps we could take her a few blossoms from your garden. A bouquet of fresh flowers might brighten her spirits."

Ottilia remained puzzled. "I'm still surprised that you would go out of your way to be kind when she's been so mean to you."

Deborah shrugged. "After what you told me about Mrs. Nixon yesterday, I no longer think of her as my enemy. I think of her as a downhearted woman in need of a friend."

Ottilia turned abruptly away, as if pierced by some troubling thought. When she spoke again, her tone was genuinely contrite. "There's more truth to your words than you know, Deborah, and I am truly ashamed that I haven't been a better friend to Grace Nixon than I have."

She continued, explaining how Grace Nixon had grown more and more uppity over the last several years and how her friends had been willing to tolerate it. But the night she walked out of Deborah's performance had been a turning point. Grace's friends were no longer willing to put up with her high and mighty attitude. They began to distance themselves from her and sided instead with Ottilia. By the time Julianna had run off with her beau—a perfectly fine fellow her mother disapproved of just because he was a farmer—there was not a one among Grace's former friends that the woman could turn to. "I've known for a long time that Grace really needed a friend—someone who could be kind but honest in pointing out her fault. I should have done more," Ottilia lamented.

"But yesterday, you said you had tried to call on her,"

Deborah countered.

"I did, but when she didn't answer in a minute or two, I was quick to turn away, relieved even."

Deborah grew resolute. "Today, Aunt Ottilia, we're going to Grace Nixon's together, and this time, we won't leave until we've had a visit with her."

Rising to her feet, Ottilia said, "That's exactly what we'll do! I'm going to the garden this very minute to cut some blossoms, then we'll be on our way."

Deborah silently prayed the entire ten-minute walk to the Nixon place for God's guidance in word and deed, and for Him to calm her racing heart. She hadn't expected to feel anxious, but by the time they arrived at the Nixons' front door, she was suffering from the equivalent of stage fright.

Climbing the steps to the front door, Ottilia placed the bouquet of flowers into Deborah's hands. "You're the one who should give these to Grace. They were your idea, after all."

Deborah held the flowers while Ottilia commenced knocking. When Grace didn't answer, she tried the door. It was unlocked. Gesturing for Deborah to follow, she stepped into the front entry where a doorway stood open to a parlor on the left, a staircase rose to the upper floor, and a hallway led to the back of the house.

Ottilia spoke loudly, her voice resonating off the oak-paneled walls of the entry and hall. "Grace? Are you here? It's your old friend, Ottilia!"

Footsteps sounded on the upper floor, then a timid voice. "Ottilia? Is that you?"

"Yes! It's been a long time since I've seen you, Grace! Come downstairs! Let's have a chat!"

A moment later, Grace replied, "Wait for me in the parlor. I'll be down in a minute."

Deborah followed Ottilia into a dark, stuffy, front parlor, crossing a green flowered carpet and taking a seat on a brocade lady's chair while Ottilia raised shades and opened windows to let in the morning sunlight and fresh air. Footsteps sounded on the staircase. Suddenly, Deborah's heart was pounding in her ears like a regiment of bass drums. Ottilia went to greet Grace in the hall outside the parlor door. She heard her aunt saying, "I've brought someone with me," then Grace entered the room.

She paused just inside the doorway, staring silently at Deborah with a look that could have sliced steel.

Deborah reached deep within. Gathering all the stage presence she could muster, she smiled, rising on weak knees to approach the woman. "Good morning, Mrs. Nixon!"

Grace's face blanched. She pointed an accusing finger at Deborah. "You! *You! YOU!*"

Deborah wished desperately that she could turn into a butterfly, rise up on wings, and flutter past the woman and out the door. Instead, she boldly spoke words that came to her from a prompter within. "Mrs. Nixon, I've brought you some flowers," she held out the bouquet, "and I just want you to know that I forgive you for walking out on me when I sang at the church last September."

The woman's eyes widened, color returning to her cheeks. "You *do?*" She asked in disbelief.

"I do," Deborah replied.

Tears filled Grace's eyes. Her chin quivered. She took shaky steps toward the nearest chair. Collapsing onto it, she buried her face in her hands, blubbering through her sobs. "I've made such a mess of my life . . . lost all my friends, my daughter too . . . all because I've been a haughty, arrogant woman. I don't deserve for—give—ness," she wailed.

Ottilia patted Grace's shoulder. "There, there, now, Grace. You haven't lost all your friends. I'm still your friend. Deborah wants to be your friend, too. Isn't that right, Deborah?"

"Yes, I do," she replied.

Grace blubbered some more. "I don't deserve it . . . I don't deserve it . . . but I'm glad you're my friends!"

Ottilia pulled a handkerchief from her pocket and offered it to Grace. "Dry your eyes, old friend. I'll go to the kitchen and set the water to boiling for tea. And I'll put these posies in a vase for you, too." She took the flowers, leaving Deborah alone with the Nixon woman.

Grace dabbed her eyes, blew her nose, and stared at Deborah. "I still can't believe it. You forgive me. You forgive me!"

"'Blessed is he whose transgression is forgiven, whose sin is covered.' Psalm 32:1. Isn't that a wonderful promise from our Lord?"

Grace nodded. "Now, if only my daughter would forgive me."

"Have you asked her to?"

Grace sighed. "She won't listen long enough to hear me out. I'm sure she doesn't think I've really changed."

"Maybe Aunt Ottilia has some ideas," Deborah suggested.

A few minutes later, over tea, Ottilia offered to act as mediator between Grace and Julianna, planning to invite them both to her home to work out their differences. That night, when Deborah said her prayers, she thanked God for the changes in Grace Nixon, and asked His help in reconciling her to her daughter.

Early the following evening, Deborah sat with Caroline,

Joshua, and Roxana on the porch, each rocking their babies while they awaited the arrival of the 7:25 train. It would bring Charles, Parker, and Tommy—who had decided to spend the day in the city helping out his former boss—from Grand Rapids for the anniversary dinner celebration. As Deborah rocked back and forth, she realized how swiftly her days in Caledonia had passed, and how important this trip had been in improving her relationship with her family and their community. She chuckled to herself at the way Ottilia had insisted that Mr. Kinsey, the village photographer, stop by the house to take pictures of the three infants. Earlier in the afternoon he had posed them propped up against pillows on a fluffy blanket spread on the front lawn. Deborah looked forward to seeing the portrait on her next visit with her relatives.

Silently, she thanked God for the opportunity for renewed friendship with her cousin, Caroline, a new, affectionate relationship with Ottilia, and an unexpected alliance with Grace Nixon. She thanked God, too, that in three short days, little Cyrus had completely captured his great-aunt's heart and become totally accepted as a member of the family, red hair and all. Even Spotsy and Topsy had gained approval during their stay, content to remain tied outside in the yard or to snooze on the porch when the warmth of the July sun grew too hot.

Molly, bless her heart, had made a highly favorable impression, helping Vida in the kitchen and Ottilia in her garden when not needed for Little Cy's care. She had been essential in obtaining a rose bush and a tin of sardines without raising suspicion, and in keeping Ottilia out of the kitchen while Vida created the anniversary cake. She was in the kitchen at this very minute assisting Vida with the dinner preparations while Ottilia, oblivious to the surprise that would soon be revealed, was bathing and dressing after a hot day of gardening.

The scent of Ottilia's carefully cultivated heliotrope came to Deborah now, wafting down from hanging baskets with a sweetness that characterized the very essence of her stay in Caledonia, and the events of this evening that were yet to come. In the distance, she heard the faint sound of a train approaching from the west, growing gradually louder until a whistle announced its arrival. Within minutes, Tommy and Parker were coming up the walk. Deborah's heart raced. Her Uncle Charles was nowhere in sight. One look at Caroline and Roxana confirmed their own concerns for the missing family member. Deborah was the first to voice her worry, followed by Caroline and Roxana the minute the fellows stepped on the porch.

"Where's Uncle Charles?"

"You two were supposed to make sure Papa was on that train!"

"Surely you didn't let him stay in the city to work the whole weekend through?"

Tommy and Parker remained stone-faced and silent, their chins low.

Chapter

33

In that silent moment, Deborah's thoughts raced. Vida's hard work in the kitchen, and all of the other carefully laid plans to make the evening special—were for naught!

Then, Tommy lifted his gaze to meet Deborah's, a wide smile slanting his mouth. "No need to fret! Charles will be along."

Parker grinned. "Papa just stopped to talk with the railroad agent for a minute. He wanted to make sure he and Mother will have seats on the train north on the fifteenth."

Breathing a sigh of relief, Deborah welcomed Tommy's hello kiss and his gentle caress of Little Cy who continued sleeping peacefully in her arms.

As predicted, Charles soon appeared. Ottilia came down from her bath, and when the adults had enjoyed glasses of mint lemonade on the porch, they went into the dining room, leaving the infants in Molly's care in the music room. Vida served the prime rib she had roasted to perfection, greens fresh from the garden, and her fluffy dinner rolls. When plates had been cleared in preparation for dessert, Caroline and Deborah excused themselves on the pretense of checking on the babies, only to return with a gift done up in fancy silver paper, a smaller item wrapped in tissue, and an even smaller box camouflaged by brown paper. Deborah set the two smaller items on the sideboard for later while Caroline placed the largest gift in front of her mother.

"I know we had agreed to hold your anniversary dinner later this month, but with Deborah and Tommy in town, we decided tonight would be a better time. Happy Anniversary, Mother, Papa."

Ottilia smiled. "How thoughtful! I wonder what this could be?" she said in a tone that bespoke of foreknowledge. Pealing away the fancy paper, she revealed the silver lamp with the pierced, lace-trimmed shade. "This is just the perfect lamp for our bedroom! And it's even engraved! 'To Ottilia and Charles, 25 years, July 15, 1906, from your children and grandchildren.' Thank you, all!"

Charles offered his thanks, adding, "Wish I'd known. I'd have bought your mother a rose bush."

Ottilia replied, "It's just as well. I haven't bought you any sardines."

Caroline said, "There's still plenty of time before you go north for the annual exchange of sardines and roses."

Her comment was followed by Vida's arrival with the anniversary cake. Its unique decoration—frosting replicas of rosebuds and fish in an alternating pattern all around the rim—caused much laughter, but the message in the center followed tradition. Ottilia read it out loud. "'Happy 25th Anniversary Ottilia and Charles.'" Turning to the hired woman, she said with a smile, "Vida, you have truly outdone yourself with the cake this year. Thank you!"

"You're velcome, Mrs. Chappell." Vida cut and served pieces of cake all around before returning to the kitchen.

As Deborah savored the sweet lemon flavor of the cake in combination with the creamy vanilla frosting, she hoped Vida would be willing to reveal the recipe for Mrs. Pritkin's use. When the last of the crumbs had disappeared from everyone's dessert plate, Parker skillfully steered the conversation back to a former topic.

"Mother, Papa, remember what you said earlier about not having a rose bush or sardines to exchange tonight? Well, that's not exactly true. There's a rosebush on the side porch just waiting to be planted, and Deborah just happens to have a tin of sardines."

Deborah retrieved the tissue-wrapped item and the brown paper-clad box from the sideboard and approached Ottilia. "I remembered the story you and Aunt Luella told me last September about the sardine server Uncle Charles presented to you on your wedding day and how you had hoped to receive a cameo, and I decided to rummage around the attic to see what I could find." Removing the tissue paper, she placed the silver server in front of her aunt.

Ottilia drew a sharp breath. "I'm surprised you found that old thing!"

Removing the brown paper from the tin of sardines, Deborah set them beside the server and silently returned to her place.

Ottilia wrinkled her nose and pushed the tin of sardines aside.

Charles spoke up. "Dearest, I've been waiting twenty-five years for you to put my sardines in that server. Don't you think it's time?"

Ottilia replied, "And I've been waiting twenty-five years for a cameo like your mother used to wear."

Caroline reached for the tin, removed the key, and began opening the sardines.

Ottilia protested. "Don't open those smelly things here in the house, Caroline! Give them to your father to take out on the porch!"

Ignoring her mother, Caroline continued to open the sardines, saying, "I'll be glad to put the sardines in the server for you, Mother, if you'll just remove the silver lid."

When Ottilia hesitated, Parker said, "Go on, Mother. Take the lid off the server. Caroline will do the rest."

Obviously frustrated, she finally lifted the silver lid. Instantly, her face went pale. With trembling hands, she removed a stunning cameo from its cushion of blue velvet. Eyes shining, she spoke in a voice that barely exceeded a whisper. "Oh, Charles . . . your mother's cameo was right there all these years, wasn't it?"

He rose from his place at the opposite end of the table and came to her. Pulling her to her feet, he took the cameo from his wife's shaky hands, pinned it to the center front of her high, lacy collar, and enfolded her in his arms. Though his words were spoken quietly into his wife's ear, Deborah was sure she heard her uncle say, "Sometimes, it just doesn't pay to be so stubborn. I love you, Ottilia."

"And I love you, Charles. Who else would put up with my headstrong ways?"

Wisely refraining from a reply, Charles kissed her on the cheek, reached for the tin of sardines that had not yet been transferred to the silver server, and headed for the front porch saying, "I'll plant that rose bush for you as soon as I've finished my treat."

Deborah was still pondering the happy outcome of the anniversary dinner on the way home from a picnic at Campau Lake the following day. Aunt Ottilia had already been in rare good humor with two grandchildren and little Cyrus to fuss over, but she had been happier than a lark since Uncle Charles had pinned the cameo on her collar.

Deborah thought, too, how this day had brought a fitting end to a delightful stay in Caledonia. The sun had shone the whole day through while the country breeze blowing across the lake had kept them comfortably cool. A picnic in the shade of an old maple tree and a row around the lake had made for a carefree afternoon. As little Cyrus lay asleep in her lap, she glanced back over her shoulder, finding Molly half-asleep in the rear seat, Topsy dozing beside her, and Spotsy napping comfortably at her feet—all victims of a day in the fresh air.

Tommy spoke quietly as he drove her uncle's rig back into town. "Butterfly, would you mind if I make one stop before we go home? I'd like to pick up a couple of catalogs Joshua wanted me to see."

"I don't mind," Deborah assured him. "We're all so tuckered out from the fresh air, we'll be sound asleep by the time you come out."

Moments later, Tommy pulled onto Center Street, parking beside a swayback nag tied up at the hitching post in front of Bolden & Sons Furniture and Hardware. "I'll only be a few minutes," he promised as he set the brake and stepped down from the buggy.

When he had disappeared inside, Deborah couldn't help noticing a ragged old rig parked nearby. The horse hitched to it was the same chestnut color as the gelding hitched to the rig Tommy had borrowed from her uncle, but there the similarities ended. The other horse appeared underfed and neglected to the point that its ribs were showing through a dusty hide that hadn't been groomed in weeks. Deborah felt sorry for the animal as she began to nod off, unable to keep awake in the warmth of the late afternoon sun. Visions of Campau Lake floated into her mind, and she was back in the rowboat with Tommy once again. Voices of picnickers in another boat grew louder as they approached, slapping their oars against the surface of the water to make splashes that sent spray in all directions.

Tommy rowed away from them, skimming smoothly

across the lake and out of range of their intended shower. Suddenly, for seemingly no reason, the boat rocked. Then a booming voice shocked her awake, along with Topsy's barking.

"What 're you doin' in my buggy?"

Deborah's eyes flew open to discover a foul smelling, disheveled fellow on the seat next to her, his beard unkempt, his breath reeking of beer. Instantly, she recognized him as Spotsy's former owner, the belligerent fellow who had picked a fight with Tommy last September. Fear gripped her. Little Cy began to cry and she clutched him to her.

"Get out of here! Now!" she sternly ordered.

"Whadda ya mean? This here's my buggy," he brazenly insisted, his foul body odor permeating the air.

In the back, Topsy began to growl.

The man's glassy gaze shifted to Topsy and Molly. "This here's my buggy, and that there's my dog!" He pointed to Topsy.

"Is *not!*" Molly countered. "Now go away!"

Spotsy whined and cowered beneath her skirt, drawing the drunk's attention.

"By gol', you're right! That ain't my dog. *That's* my dog!" He pointed to Spotsy instead.

Deborah argued. "That's not your dog any more than this is your buggy! Yours is over there!" She pointed to the weatherworn rig parked a few yards away. "Now, get out!"

Paying no heed to the other rig, he turned again to Deborah. A hank of greasy hair fell over his narrow forehead as he spoke again in his drunken drawl. "Hey, I know you. Y're the slut that done stole my dog last year!"

"Did not!"

"Ya stole my dog, now y're tryin' to steal my rig!"

"You're all wrong! It was a rescue from cruel abuse, plain and simple." Deborah insisted.

"Well, if ya won't get out, y'll just have to ride along!" Kicking off the brake, he slapped the reins hard against the horse's back. "Git on home, Gracie!"

The gelding lunged ahead, pressing Deborah hard against the back of the seat.

"Tommy! Help!" she screamed at the top of her lungs, but the sound seemed to get lost in the rattle of the rig and the pounding of hooves as the gelding charged across the railroad track and up Center Street.

Chapter

34

From the back room of Boldens' store, Tommy thought he heard loud voices outside, then a dog barking.

"That sounds like Topsy," he told Joshua. "I'd better check." Leaving catalogs behind, he headed for the front door, reaching the sidewalk in time to see Charles's buggy headed on an erratic path up Center Street.

His heart pounded. Without aforethought, he unhitched the nag tied out front, climbed into the saddle, and dug his heels hard into her sides.

To his surprise, the old girl took off at a gallop. His golf yacht cap flew off his head as over the tracks she went, giving chase up Center Street past West Street.

Ahead of them, the rig charged on at much too great a speed to make the turn at the end of Center. Tommy had to catch up and slow it down or it would crash for sure! He spurred the nag again.

With a new burst of energy, she pulled even with the rig. Almost as if she could read Tommy's mind, the old nag eased next to Charles's gelding. He grabbed hold of the halter, bringing the rig to a stop just short of the schoolyard.

Immediately, he confronted the fellow, instantly recognizing his nemesis from last year's Labor Day celebration.

"You! Get out!" Grabbing a fistful of shirt collar, he yanked him out of the rig.

The drunk landed in the dust with a thud. Pushing himself up from the ground, he came at Tommy. "Wait'll I git my hands on you, ya dirty dog thief!"

Tommy ducked, easily missing the slow right fist thrown by the drunk. "Back off, or you'll be sorry!" he warned, but the fellow came at him with a left.

Again evading the blow, Tommy grabbed the fellow's arm and twisted it behind his back until he crumpled to the ground. As he lay at the side of the street, moaning, Tommy tied the nag to the back of Charles's rig and climbed in, pulling a safe distance from the troublemaker, then turning to his wife.

"Are you all right, Butterfly?"

She nodded. Too numb to speak, she smiled through the tears dampening her cheeks as she clutched Little Cy, whose crying quieted.

Tommy turned to Molly in the back. "Everything okay back there?"

Her arm was wrapped about Topsy, who barked as if in reply. At her feet, Spotsy whined. Molly let out a sigh of relief. "I'm still a bit rattled, but otherwise fine."

With a gentle slap of the reins, he headed back down Center Street, pausing at the railroad crossing to retrieve his golf yacht cap. Slapping it against his thigh, he pulled it on his head and returned to Boldens', finding a small gathering of townsfolk to greet him as he tied Charles' rig to the post.

An old farmer stepped forward, unhitching the nag. "I seen ya take off on old Ethel. That's the fastest this old hay burner has moved in many a year!"

Tommy laughed. "Thanks for the loan." Pulling a five dollar gold piece from his pocket, he pressed it into the fellow's hand. "Treat her to an extra ration of apples and carrots. And if you ever decide to part with her let me know.

She saved my family today!"

A dark-bearded fellow wearing a star-shaped badge stepped forward. "I'm Abram Konkle, village constable. Heard some shouting going on. Next thing I knew, Charles Chappell's rig was headed up the street on a wild path and you were giving chase."

"Some fellow with too much liquor under his belt got a mind to drive off with it," Tommy told him.

Deborah stepped down from the rig, Little Cy in her arms, eager to explain further. "The brute insisted my uncle's rig was his own, and told us to get out. We tried to reason with him, but he wouldn't pay any heed. The next thing we knew, he was driving up the street like a madman."

Tommy said, "I caught up with them at the end of Center Street."

The old farmer tapped Konkle on the shoulder and pointed. "Here he comes now—Buster Dudley—the village drunk." Sure enough, the fellow was staggering down the street, cussing and grumbling in his drunken drawl. The farmer spoke again. "That's his rig, over there." He indicated the ragtop buggy that Deborah had noticed earlier.

Konkle grumbled. "That's just like Dudley, to get so blind drunk he can't tell Charles Chappell's fine polished rig from his old rattle trap. He's due for some time in the clink."

The old farmer said, "If I know Dudley, he won't go willingly."

Konkle unclasped the handcuffs hanging from his belt. "Then I'll give him a little encouragement." He started toward the belligerent outlaw, a knot of villagers with him.

Joshua stepped beside Tommy, catalogs under his arm. "After all that, you probably don't even want to look at these, anymore."

Tommy reached for the catalogs. "Far from it. After all this trouble, I plan to read every word!"

Marshall
Sunday, July 8, very late in the evening

Deborah stood at her dresser removing the rose-laden hat Tommy had given her a little more than a month ago. Setting it carefully aside, she contemplated the image in the mirror. A weary, but contented woman stared back at her.

The trip from Caledonia had been tiring for everyone and she was pleased to finally be in her own home. But she was glad, too, that she had made the trip. Finally, her conscience was at peace knowing that Aunt Ottilia had met her grandnephew and accepted him as part of the family.

Her focus shifted from her satisfied smile to the butterfly pin on her bodice. If brooches could talk, this one would have tales to tell. She had worn it from the day they had put her mother into the ground in Detroit. It had traveled with her to Caledonia where she wore it every day during the last few months of her senior year in high school, and it had made the trip to the white slave house where she had been held against her will.

She ran her finger over its enamel surface, remembering the encouragement she had taken from it, believing that somehow she would escape to fly free like a beautiful butterfly again. And when Tommy had arrived to rescue her, the pin had accompanied her to freedom, the cherished symbol of dreams fulfilled.

Little did she know then that she was not really free at all, but imprisoned by her dark past. The pin went with her to Calumet, where she had run from her bad reputation, yet could not escape the memories of her horrid experience. But every night of dark visions and frightening memories ended in a new day of hope. She had worn the enamel butterfly during Aunt Luella's Bible lessons and had learned how to fly free of spiritual darkness and into the light of her Savior.

She had learned many Bible truths in her hours with Aunt Luella, and she had learned about her namesake in the Good Book as well. Deborah of the Old Testament had inspired soldiers in combat and had judged a great nation. She was industrious, eloquent, and wise. And the Hebrew name had an interesting English translation according to Aunt Luella. Deborah was contemplating the true meaning of her name when Tommy came into the room, evidently finished with taking the dogs out back for the last time before turning in.

Tommy sensed something different about his Butterfly the moment he stepped near. Rarely did he catch her contemplating her image in the mirror. With a wide yawn, he pulled the golf yacht cap from his head and laid it beside Deborah's rose-laden one. "I'm so doggoned tired, I forgot to leave my cap on the hall tree before I came up." When she made no reply, he moved closer, caressing her shoulder and gazing into the mirror at the reflection of the two of them. "You're mighty quiet, Butterfly. Something on your mind?" He expected to hear her say how pleased she was to be back. She had told him more than once on the train that she could hardly wait to get home.

Deborah briefly brushed her cheek against the large, strong hand on her shoulder. Fingering the brim of his golf yacht cap, she recalled the trips it had taken since the first week of their marriage. From Caledonia, he had worn it to

Calumet where he donned it daily until hard winter set in. She had sent it to him when he was visiting his father, and he had worn it back to Calumet for the birth of their son. It had seen the burial of his father and had hit the dusty street when he had rescued her from Buster Dudley. Now, by God's mercy and the lapse of his tired mind, it lay beside the silk roses of her own hat on the dresser.

Her fingers moved from the brim of the cap to her brooch as she recalled her earlier thoughts of the true meaning of her name. "I've decided that I'm not a butterfly anymore, Tommy."

"You're not?" he asked curiously, sensing that her conclusion was no casual statement.

She shook her head. "I've decided that I'm a bee. Aunt Luella taught me the origin of my name. 'Deborah' in Hebrew means bee, the symbol of eloquence, industriousness, and wisdom." Removing the brooch from her bodice, she contemplated it briefly, then pushed its pin through the wool fabric of his golf yacht cap and slid shut the clasp. "No, Tommy, I'm not a butterfly anymore, I'm a bee. But best of all, we're together forever, and we're home to stay."

Turning her toward him, Tommy pulled her close, his mouth covering hers for a long, deep kiss. When it ended, he nibbled her ear, whispering, "No matter what, you'll always be my Butterfly!"

Five Years Later

Deborah sat in a white wicker rocker in the back yard watching little Cyrus play catch with his father as she nursed baby Luella. At her feet lay Spotsy, too tired to chase the ball when Little Cy failed to catch it. In the garden to her left, a bee hummed, collecting nectar from the geraniums she had planted. Above the phlox on her right floated a butterfly. For years, now, she had given up the notion that she was a butterfly, even though it was still Tommy's pet name for her. He had always kept the golf yacht cap with her butterfly pinned to it, and though it was growing threadbare he wore it still, and had it on this very minute!

Looking back, she realized that the parallels between her own life and that of a butterfly were undeniable, for God transforms the caterpillar over and over again, taking it from an egg, to a worm-like insect, to a chrysalis, before allowing a beautiful new winged creature to emerge. God had altered her in a similar way until He had made her completely new in Christ. Equally amazing were His blessings for Molly, giving her a husband and a child and a home of their own.

Silently, she thanked God for Molly's transformation and her own. She thanked Him, too, for Tommy's faithful, abiding love, and for their children. Wholeheartedly, Tommy had accepted Little Cy with his flaming red hair and his willful ways, as his very own son. Now, they had a daughter too, a perfect little girl. Deborah marveled at how God could transform darkness and shame into life's greatest blessings.

Watching little Cyrus play, she realized that she wouldn't be calling him "little" for long. He was big for his age, and destined to grow strong and tall like his father. But when Tommy was at work and Cyrus was listening to her read a Bible story, his dramatic side came out. He would remember the lines of the story and act them out with great conviction. And he would sing his Sunday school songs without any prompting. He was a natural born performer, and she could see that the day wasn't far off when he would be taking music lessons and performing on stage in recitals at the Empire Theatre.

As for her long-ago dream of performing before an audience in the Calumet Theatre, she had never quite forgotten it, but she had decided that it couldn't possibly be more satisfying than her daily performances as wife and mother.

ABOUT
DONNA
WINTERS

Photo by Don Olson

Donna adopted Michigan as her home state in 1971 when she moved from a small town in upstate, New York. She began penning novels in 1982 while working full time for an electronics firm in Grand Rapids.

She resigned from her job in 1984 following a contract offer for her first book. Since then, Thomas Nelson Publishers, Zondervan Publishing House, Guideposts, and Bigwater Publishing have published her novels. Her husband, Fred, a former American History teacher, shares her enthusiasm for history. Together, they visit historical sites, restored villages, museums, and lake ports purchasing books and reference materials for use in Donna's research.

When researching Calumet, she traveled with her husband and two dogs to the Copper Country of Michigan's Keweenaw Peninsula to tour the theater, a museum, and a nearby mine. The photographs, notes, and books she brought home expanded her knowledge of the area's history. But most valuable was the guidance and historical knowledge contributed by her reader-turned-friend, Joanne Olson, who continued to research details of Calumet's history until the book's completion.

Donna has lived all of her life in states bordering on the Great Lakes. Her familiarity and fascination with these remarkable inland waters and her residence in the heart of Great Lakes Country make her the perfect candidate for writing *Great Lakes Romances*®.

More *Great Lakes Romances*®
For prices and availability, contact:
Bigwater Publishing
P.O. Box 177
Caledonia, MI 49316

Mackinac, First in the series of *Great Lakes Romances*® (Set at Grand Hotel, Mackinac Island, 1895.) Victoria Whitmore is no shy, retiring miss. When her father runs into money trouble, she heads to Mackinac Island to collect payment due from Grand Hotel for the furniture he's made. But dealing with Rand Bartlett, the hotel's manager, poses an unexpected challenge. Can Victoria succeed in finances without losing her heart?

The Captain and the Widow, Second in the series of *Great Lakes Romances*® (Set in South Haven, Michigan, 1897.) Lily Atwood Haynes is beautiful, intelligent, and alone at the helm of a shipping company at the tender age of twenty. Then Captain Hoyt Curtiss offers to help her navigate the choppy waters of widowhood. Together, can they keep a new shipping line—and romance—afloat?

Sweethearts of Sleeping Bear Bay, Third in the series of *Great Lakes Romances*® (Set in the Sleeping Bear Dune region of north-ern Michigan, 1898.) Mary Ellen Jenkins has successfully mastered the ever-changing shoals and swift currents of the Mississippi, but Lake Michigan poses a new set of challenges. Can she round the ever-dangerous Sleeping Bear Point in safety, or will the steamer—and her heart—run aground under the influence of Thad Grant?

Charlotte of South Manitou Island, Fourth in the series of Great Lakes Romances ® (Set on South Manitou Island, Michigan, 1891-1898) Charlotte Richards, fatherless at age eleven, thought she'd never smile again. But Seth Trevelyn, son of South Manitou Island's lightkeeper, makes it his mission to show her that life goes on, and so does true friendship. Together, they explore the World's Columbian Exposition in far-away Chicago where he saves her from a near-fatal fire. When he leaves the island to create a life of his own in Detroit, he realizes Charlotte is his one true love. Will his feelings be returned when she grows to womanhood?

Aurora of North Manitou Island, Fifth in the series of *Great Lakes Romances*® (Set on North Manitou Island, Michigan, 1898-1899.) With her new husband, Harrison, lying helpless after an accident on stormy Lake Michigan, Aurora finds marriage far from the glorious romantic adventure she had anticipated. And when Serilda Anders appears out of his past to tend the light and nurse him to health, Aurora is certain her marriage is doomed. Maybe Cad Blackburn, with the ready wit and silver tongue, is the answer. But it isn't right to accept the safe harbor *he's* offering. Where is the light that will guide her through troubled waters?

Bridget of Cat's Head Point, Sixth in the series of *Great Lakes Romances*® (Set in Traverse City and the Leelanau Peninsula of Michigan, 1899-1900.) When Bridget Richards leaves South Manitou Island to take up residence on Michigan's mainland, she suffers no lack of ardent suitors. Nat Trevelyn wants desperately to make her his bride and the mother of his two-year-old son. Attorney Kenton McCune showers her with gifts and rapt attention. And Erik Olson shows her the incomparable beauty and romance of a Leelanau summer. Who will finally win her heart?

Rosalie of Grand Traverse Bay, Seventh in the series of *Great Lakes Romances*® (Set in Traverse City, Michigan, and Winston-Salem, North Carolina, 1900.) Soon after Rosalie Foxe arrives in Traverse City for the summer of 1900, she stands at the center of controversy. Her aunt and uncle are about to lose their confectionery shop, and Rosalie is being blamed. Can Kenton McCune, a handsome, Harvard-trained lawyer, prove her innocence and win her heart?

Isabelle's Inning, Encore Edition #1 in the series of *Great Lakes Romances*® (Set in the heart of Great Lakes Country, 1903.) Born and raised in the heart of the Great Lakes, Isabelle Dorlon pays little attention to the baseball players patronizing her mother's rooming house—until Jack Weatherby moves in. He's determined to earn a position with the Erskine College Purple Stockings, and a place in her heart as well, but will his affections fade once he learns the truth about her humiliating flaw?

Jenny of L'Anse Bay, Special Edition in the series of *Great Lakes Romances®* (Set in the Keweenaw Peninsula of Upper Michigan in 1867.) Eager to escape the fiery disaster that leaves her home in ashes, Jennifer Crawford sets out on an adventure to an Ojibway Mission on L'Anse Bay. In the wilderness, her affections grow for a native people very different from herself—especially for the chief's son, Hawk. Together, can they overcome the differences of their diverse cultures, and the harsh, deadly weather of the North Country?

Elizabeth of Saginaw Bay, Pioneer Edition in the series of *Great Lakes Romances®* (Set in the Saginaw Valley of Michigan, 1837.) The taste of wedding cake is still sweet in Elizabeth Morgan's mouth when she sets out with her bridegroom, Jacob, from York State for the new State of Michigan. But she isn't prepared for the untamed forest, crude lodgings, and dangerous diseases that await her there. Desperately, she seeks her way out of the forest that holds her captive, but God seems to have another plan for her future.

Sweet Clover—A Romance of the White City, Centennial Edition in the series of *Great Lakes Romances®* (Set in Chicago at the World's Columbian Exposition of 1893.) The Fair brought unmatched excitement and wonder to Chicago, inspiring this innocent romance by Clara Louise Burnham first published in 1894. In it, Clover strives to rebuild a lifelong friendship with Jack Van Tassel, a childhood playmate who's spent several years away from the home of his youth. But The Fair lures him back, and their long-lost friendship rekindles. Can true love conquer the years that have come between, or will betrayals of the past pose impenetrable barriers?

Unlikely Duet—Caledonia Chronicles—Part 1 in the series of *Great Lakes Romances®* (Set in Caledonia, Michigan, 1905.) Caroline Chappell practiced long and hard for her recital on the piano and organ in Caledonia's Methodist Episcopal Church. She even took up the trumpet and composed a duet to perform with Joshua Bolden, an ace trumpet player whom she'd long admired. Now, two days before the performance, it looks as if her recital plans, and her relationship with Joshua are hitting sour notes. Will she be able to restore harmony in time to save her musical reputation?

Amelia, Encore Edition #2 in the series of *Great Lakes Romances®* (Set in Chicago and Springfield, Illinois, 1903.) Amelia Ansley's anticipation of marriage to Morley Vernon was spoiled by only one small matter—his involvement in politics. The office of State Senator seemed unimportant and bothersome. Why couldn't he get elected to the Senate in Washington? Morley Vernon's loyalty to party politics was equaled only by his loyalty to Amelia Ansley— until Maria Burley Greene stepped into his life. This woman attorney who was also a suffragette was the embodiment of exquisite daintiness, wholly feminine and alluring. Impulsively he offered to promote her cause, only later realizing that this decision could either make or break both his political career and his relationship with Amelia.

Bigwater Classics™ **Series**
Great Lakes Christmas Classics, **A Collection of Short Stories, Poems, Illustrations, and Humor from Olden Days**—From the pages of the *Detroit Free Press* of 1903, the Traverse City *Morning Record* of 1900, and other turn-of-the-century sources come heart-warming, rib-tickling, eye-catching gems of Great Lakes Christmases past. So sit back, put your feet up, and prepare for a thoroughly entertaining escape to holidays of old!

READER SURVEY—*Butterfly Come Home*

Your opinion counts! Please fill out and mail this form to:
Reader Survey
Bigwater Publishing
P.O. Box 177
Caledonia, MI 49316

Your
Name:_____

Street:_____

City,State,Zip:_____

In return for your completed survey, we will send you a bookmark and
the latest issue of our Great Lakes Romances® Newsletter. If your
name is not currently on our mailing list, we will also include four
note papers and envelopes of an historic Great Lakes scene (while
supplies last).

1. Please rate the following elements from A (excellent) to E (poor).

_____Heroine   _____Hero   _____Setting   _____Plot

Comments:_____

_____

2. What setting (time and place) would you like to see in a future
book?

_____

(Survey questions continue on next page.)

3. Where did you purchase this book? (If you borrowed it from the library, please give the name/location of the library.)

4. What influenced your decision to read this book?

_____Front Cover _____First Page _____Back Cover Copy

_____Author _____Title _____Friends

_____Publicity (Please describe)_____

5. Please indicate your age range:

_____Under 18 _____25-34 _____46-55

_____18-24 _____35-45 _____Over55

If desired, include additional comments below.